WATERBORNE

KATHERINE IRONS

BRAVA

KENSINGTON PUBLISHING CORP.
www.kensingtonbooks.com

CHAPTER 1

Ranirao Atoll, Tahiti, the present . . .

It was a night made for an assassin.

At three a.m., a thick layer of clouds hung low over the tropical island, swathing the thin crescent moon in ghostly shadows and wrapping the *Anastasiya* and her companion yacht, the *Tsarina,* in warm, hazy blackness. The heavy fog that rose from the surface of the ocean muffled the slap of waves against the vessels' hulls, dimmed the rotating searchlight from the *Tsarina,* and distorted the vision of the four guards stationed bow and stern on the *Anastasiya*. The all-encompassing mist provided a perfect cover for the figure that slipped soundlessly from the water and made his way onto the deck of the *Anastasiya*. Gregori Varenkov's luxury yacht showed not a single light burning, which suited the intruder perfectly. The Russian target had evaded retribution in Crete and barely escaped with his life in Rangoon. Grigori Varenkov had been judged and found guilty by a high court, from which there was no appeal. Tonight, the appointed executioner would carry out the death sentence.

Alex flattened himself against a lifeboat and assumed the color and pattern of the canvas covering as the thin beam from the *Tsarina*'s searchlight scanned the deck, revealing lounge chairs and a table, a marble-lined hot tub, and an equally extravagant outdoor shower area. All was as it had been when Alex last scouted the yacht, except for one notable exception.

The shower was occupied.

Alex's gut tightened. He'd not expected anyone to be on deck but the two armed guards. Varenkov was fanatical about his routine and his security. Six nights a week, the Russian ate his evening meal in his stateroom, where he remained until twelve sharp, at which time a Zodiac arrived from the *Tsarina* with four guards to replace the ones on duty. Men stood six hour shifts around the clock, and walked the perimeter of the deck every two hours.

At twelve-fifteen, Varenkov showered for twenty minutes and retired, wearing only a towel around his thick waist, to his library where he conducted business by computer for three hours. At precisely three-thirty, regardless of the weather conditions, the Russian came up on deck to savor a large glass of Stolichnaya, his favorite brand of vodka. Varenkov remained for thirty minutes before returning to take phone calls from various associates around the world. This half hour on deck was when the target was most vulnerable.

Alex stared at the woman. In the six months that he'd stalked Varenkov, he never saw the Russian bring a visitor or an associate aboard the *Anastasiya*. And the crew and captain never came on deck after ten p.m. unless the vessel was underway or encountering bad weather.

This redhead, with her high, perfect breasts, neat waist, and long shapely legs that seemed to go on forever, shouldn't have been here on deck in the middle of the night. She wasn't the captain of the *Anastasiya* or one of the dozen or more regular crew members, and she wasn't one of the guards. That left only the chef who'd boarded the vessel in San Diego three months ago to replace the

Ukrainian torturer who'd cooked for Varenkov for the past two and a half years.

Whoever she was, she was here, naked as the day she was born, and—to borrow a distinctly American expression— *throwing a wrench* into Alex's perfectly choreographed plan to assassinate Varenkov. Alex should have been angry. By Zeus's stones, he had every right to be. But the sight of such a delightfully formed female in a complete state of innocent seduction was almost more than he could be expected to endure.

Alex took advantage of the permeating darkness to move closer to the woman, and then held his breath as the searchlight illuminated her alluring figure once again. Had she been a figment of his over-active imagination? Or, had his imagination lent her attributes she didn't possess? He wasn't disappointed. She was real enough, he concluded as beads of excitement prickled the nape of his neck and trickled down his spine. Magnificent. She stood there as motionless as a Greek statue, back arched, head tilted back, letting the warm spray darken her red-gold hair and run in rivulets over her soapy body.

Though he usually had rigid self-control when conducting a mission, Alex's body responded. Heat welled in his loins, his pulse quickened, and his throat tightened. Human or not, she was a rare vision. And the males of his kind were not known for their disdain of sexual pleasures.

The woman's skin was unusually fair, almost alabaster in tone, and so silken in appearance that Alex could imagine what it would feel like to stroke and caress the curves of her ripe body. But regardless of the delight he might take in admiring such lush perfection on an ordinary evening, her presence tonight might ruin the best opportunity he'd had in months to take out the Russian.

The safest thing to do would be to eliminate her before Varenkov appeared on deck for his nightly vodka. In seconds, Alex could subdue her and dump her body over the side, where the sharks would quickly dispose of it. Predators prowled beneath Varenkov's vessels wherever they were anchored because Varenkov insisted that his employees chum the waters with bloody meat to attract them. Tonight, Alex had seen more than a dozen large tiger sharks feeding not only on the scraps from Varenkov's galleys, but on each other.

The sharks served a well-thought-out purpose. An Israeli swat team had nearly succeeded in ending Varenkov's career two years ago off Hong Kong. Three divers, who'd trained with America's Navy Seals, had actually made it on deck before the Russian's private army cut them down with a rain of armor-piercing bullets. Soon after, Alex noticed that Varenkov had added sharks to his yachts' safety net.

It was a clever scheme and worked well against human adversaries, but Atlanteans were not human. Alex had been trained to defend himself against sharks since he was a young child. While he had a healthy respect for the big ones, and for the danger of being present during any feeding frenzy, he didn't consider individual tiger sharks to be much of a threat to him. They could be merciless eating machines, but they were highly intelligent, and rarely took on an adult Atlantean who wasn't sick, feeble, or wounded. And he was none of those things; he was a warrior in his prime, with a lethal instinct every bit as developed as that of a tiger shark.

This unexpected civilian presented a huge problem in the middle of his killing zone. For more than a moment, Alex hesitated as duty warred with conscience. She was so close . . . only a knife's throw away. He could be on her and do what had to be done before she could even cry out.

If only she weren't so beautiful . . .

Humans and Atlanteans were natural enemies, and if Varenkov survived, many more lives would be lost. Yet, this female was a noncombatant. He could kill Varenkov or any of his guards without hesitation, and he'd never lose sleep over his actions, but murdering an innocent woman was different. Why hadn't she simply remained below deck where she would have been safe?

He cursed himself for his own weakness. An assassin had no room in his heart for pity, and less for allowing lust to interfere with his intent. Not to mention that he had out-distanced his team. Bleddyn and Dewi would be here before dawn. Attempting the kill without their backup went against his own code. Yet . . . Varenkov had slipped through their net so many times before. Waiting for backup might mean that Alex would lose the best chance he'd had of ending the Russian's long reign of terror.

Abruptly, a movement to the woman's left caught Alex's attention. As he watched, one of Varenkov's camouflage-clad guards lunged out of the shadows and grabbed the female's arm. She cried out and tried to pull free, but he yanked her against him, pinning her with one hand and running his other over her naked breasts and down between her legs.

Instinct won over reason. Alex dove at the struggling pair, locked an arm around the guard's throat and dragged him toward the railing. The man fought back with all of his strength, but Alex easily overpowered him. He went over the side with only a single strangled groan. And when the searchlight again scanned across the deck, the woman had retreated to the shadows.

Alex's element of surprise was lost. The only sensible action would be for him to follow the would-be-rapist over the gunnel before he was seen by the woman or illuminated in the searchlight. But, by now the tiger sharks would be making the area beneath the boat a bloody mess, and he didn't need to compound a series of errors with a bigger one. Instead, he cast an illusion, assuming the likeness of Varenkov, complete with an oversized bath towel—which would have been a brilliant disguise if the real Varenkov hadn't chosen that moment to come through the hatchway.

For a heartbeat, the Russian froze and stared, his eyes bulging with shock. And then the towel dropped, and Varenkov raised his right hand, revealing a Makarov PMM semi-automatic pistol. Dropping to a kneeling position, Varenkov sprayed the deck with a hail of nine-millimeter bullets. Shouts came from the *Tsarina,* followed by the pounding of boots as the reinforcements came from the bow at a dead run.

A bullet tore into Alex's thigh, and a second one plowed a furrow along his neck. He dashed into the shadows and changed his appearance from a balding Russian gangster to a buff oriental soldier-of-fortune, complete with an automatic rifle and full gear. When the next rotating beam lit up the deck, Varenkov stopped shooting at him and turned his firepower on the woman. The bullet hit her midsection, knocking her backward, and Varenkov followed with a killing shot to her heart.

Alex had counted nine shots. The regulation Makarov PMM fired eight shots, but special models were often refitted for ten or twelve, meaning that Varenkov had either one or three bullets left. Alex decided he didn't like the odds. It was time to leave.

His mistake was to cast one final glance at the dying female. She lay stretched on the deck, eyes open, hand outstretched in a plea for mercy. Blood seeped from under her body and ran in rivulets into the hot tub, turning the salt water an ominous scarlet.

"Mother of Ares!" Alex swore. He couldn't leave her.

He scooped up the woman in his arms and leaped over the side as the Russian emptied the chamber of his pistol in their direction.

Out of fire and into the caldron! Now, men were shooting at him from the deck of the *Tsarina* as well. Hungry sharks and armor-piercing bullets. Perfect. Alex hated guns. The use of guns proved just how depraved humans were—they weren't content to destroy each other with natural means; they had to resort to all sorts of flesh-destroying inventions.

A ten-foot tiger shark came at him, and Alex used a burst of imagination to conceal both himself and the female with the illusion of a thirty-eight-foot squid. As an additional incentive for the shark to turn its attentions elsewhere, Alex included a good measure of ink and one spiked tentacle. The tiger shark backed water, rolled his eyes until the whites showed, and turned his attack on two of his comrades who were fighting over a tattered fragment of what had been the unlucky guard's right leg.

Alex couldn't hold the disguise for more than a few seconds. Sharks weren't nearly as easy to fool as humans. He used the respite to dive deep and put distance between him and the two yachts. Two sharks followed, and he had to dispatch one and wound the other before it broke off the encounter.

Watercraft erupted from the *Tsarina* overhead. Any moment, Alexander expected Varenkov's private army to begin strafing the water and dropping depth charges that would shred him, the human female, and the sharks indiscriminately. Dismissing the finned predators as the lesser of evils, Alex swam for his life. He would have made an easy target if the sharks pursued him, but when the first explosions sent shocks through the water, the sea wolves scattered as well.

By the time Alex reached the underwater cave at the edge of the atoll, the woman had been deprived of air for a lethal amount of time. *Noble try,* he told himself. She's gone, drowned, shot to death, or both. She was human, after all. Not his worry, not his fault.

Except it *was* his fault. He'd screwed up. If he'd abandoned the mission when he'd first caught sight of the female, she'd be alive. He'd been too cocksure, impatient, and certain that he could improvise and still take out Varenkov. He should have waited for Bleddyn and Dewi. He could just picture himself attempting to explain how things had gone so wrong so quickly.

Poseidon and the high court would have none of it. Alex's mission. His responsibility. He was supposed to be a professional. How many kills? He'd lost count of the enemies he'd eliminated in the past several hundred years. All clean hits with no loose ends. And now this . . .

Already the damage done by the bullets to his flesh was healing. The sea had marvelous healing powers—if you were an Atlantean. Humans were much frailer creatures. Their bodies tended to break easily, and they had only elementary regeneration powers. Their life spans were minute, barely a hundred years, and they died of diseases that Atlanteans had conquered eons ago. The kindest thing he could do would be to let the woman's body drift away on the tide, to give her to the sea. Her body was only a physical shell, and it was not as if her spirit would be lost for eternity. Even humans were reborn in new bodies.

But he kept remembering how vulnerable she'd been—first to the guard who'd tried to assault her and then to Varenkov, who had ruthlessly turned on her. She'd been unarmed and helpless, and the Russian had shot her down without hesitation.

Still, it had been Varenkov who'd killed her, not him. His responsibility was to his own people and finishing the job he'd been given. *Let her go and forget she ever existed,* Alex told himself. *Make at least one logical decision today.*

Instead, cursing himself for being all kinds of a fool, he bent over her and covered her mouth with his. He summoned the blue force and breathed healing energy into the woman's lungs. *Live!,* he commanded her silently. *Live!*

Nothing. Her head hung back, her red-gold hair streamed out behind her in the rushing surf, and her limbs and torso dangled limply in his arms. Her blue eyes were lifeless, as flat as glass, without a spark of illumination.

"Damn you!" he cursed. "Obstinate woman." He cradled her against his chest, pressed his lips to the hollow of her throat, and willed her to fight. The effort was tremendously draining. He could feel his own strength ebbing.

Stubbornly, he refused to surrender her. He forced himself to swim deeper into the cave, threading through narrow passageways until, at last, he surfaced on a starlit strip of sand. They were deep beneath the landmass. The light here came from the shells of a giant clam, the *urrou,* that had become extinct in his grandfather's time. Long ago, the warlike inhabitants of this part of the world, distant relations of the Atlanteans, had used the shells as sources of light.

Arching cave walls and ceiling rimmed the narrow beach, but the sand was soft and dry. Alex carried the woman out of the water and laid her on the warm shoal. Was it his imagination, or had her color improved? He pressed his fingertips against her lips, but he could feel no breath of life. With a sigh, he gathered her in his arms once more and again breathed into her mouth.

She stirred and gave a weak moan.

Alex ground his teeth together. "I'll be sorry I did this. I'm sorry already." The sound of running water caught his attention, and he glanced toward the source. A spring bubbled from one wall of the cavern. *Humans need fresh water,* he reminded himself. When they'd left the sea, salt water had become poisonous to them. How crazy was that?

He put the woman down again, carried a broken conch shell to the spring, and filled it with fresh water. Returning to her side, he cradled her head and began to drip the liquid between her lips, one drop at a time.

She choked, and he had to pound her on the back to keep her from drowning a second time. Her color was no longer fish-belly white; it was more of a rotting oyster yellow. The fingers on her left hand fluttered. It was a slender hand, almost delicate. Her nails were delicately shaped and freshly adorned in a soft peach coloring.

Something shifted in the pit of his stomach, and a warm protective feeling washed through his veins. He wished he knew her name. If he couldn't save her, would she haunt his dreams, this frail human beauty?

She wasn't Atlantean, but he found her very alluring, or she would have been if Varenkov hadn't extinguished her life force. *What would it be like to have those hands stroke my face?* he wondered. *Or to have those sweet lips seek mine in an act of passion?*

"Who are you?" he asked. "Why did you have to come above deck tonight? Why didn't you just stay in your galley where you belonged?"

She coughed again and a gush of seawater spilled from her mouth.

There was nothing to do but try again. He concentrated all his will on reviving her, on finding the spark of life that he imagined still clung to her fading body and fanning it to a flame. He did it, knowing the consequences it would have, knowing full well what price there would be to pay for such a transgression . . .

Because regardless of who pulled the trigger, she was an

innocent and his mistake had caused her death. The truth was, he wasn't nearly as heartless as he tried to pretend. He couldn't live with himself if he didn't try to right the wrong that he'd done.

She would hate him for it, but he would do what he had to. . . . As he always had.

The battle to save the woman was not easily won. Hours became days, and three times she sank into that abyss that could only be death. But each interlude became shorter, and gradually Alex felt the life force begin to course through her body. And as she grew stronger, he grew weaker, until finally, he had to risk leaving her alone to return to the depths off the atoll and let the clean seawater heal his own body and soul.

She still could be lost, perhaps more so than if he'd allowed nature to take its course. Now, she could never return to an entirely human existence, but neither was she Atlantean. Her suffering at the loss of what she had been might be worse than death. And if she slipped away, where would her spirit go? Would she be trapped forever in a void, caught between one world and another?

Again, he wrestled with his own conscience, wondering why he'd been tempted to break his own code for an alien . . . wondering if he'd lost his edge. Had his failure to kill Varenkov been bad luck and an error in judgment, or had he burned out? Hunting down and eliminating enemies of Atlantis was all he'd been trained to do. If he no longer possessed that ability, would he be relegated to some bureaucratic office job reserved for royal losers or would he end up in charge of iceberg security beyond the boundaries of civilization?

When he surfaced near the spot where the yachts had been anchored, Varenkov was gone. In one direction,

Alex could clearly make out the beach and swaying palm trees of the atoll. But, if he turned his back to the land, the open sea stretched as far as the eye could see.

Alex had expected no less. Undoubtedly, the Russian had given the orders to sail within minutes after the last shot was fired, and had left the area by helicopter. By now he could be leagues away, anchored off a thousand nameless islands or on route to another ocean.

All Alex's careful plans had come to nothing, and he would have to return home and explain why he'd failed. Again. He'd also have to explain the woman and why he'd felt compelled to break laws that had stood for thousands of years, putting not only himself but the kingdom in danger.

He returned to the cave, afraid but also half-hoping that he would find the woman dead. She wasn't, but her wounds had begun to seep blood again and her vital signs were weaker. If he'd been anywhere in the Atlantic, he could have defied the authorities and carried her to the temple where trained healers might have saved her. But here, Lemorians commanded the oceans, and relations between Atlanteans and Lemorians were dicey at best. More so since he and his twin brother Orion had surprised a raiding party and held Prince Kaleo for ransom, before sending him home in disgrace.

Lemorian healers were not as skilled as their Atlantean counterparts, but they possessed more knowledge than he did. For better or worse, he couldn't wait for Bleddyn and Dewi to find him. He had to take the human to Lemoria or admit that he'd taken on a task he hadn't had the ability to complete. And considering what Lemorians thought of humans, there was a good chance that neither he nor the human female would survive the encounter.

CHAPTER 2

When she was eleven years old and well into her training, Ree had accompanied one of her master instructors and two other students to the American History Museum in Washington, D.C., where they had watched a black and white movie starring Charlie Chaplin. The film had been jerky, the images marred with inky imperfections, and the only sound had been a jarring and tinny rendition of a player-piano.

The images flashing across the screen of her fog-enveloped mind reminded Ree of that experience, except that the accompanying music wasn't that of a piano, but the rhythmic crash of surf. And, she could not only see it, but she could feel the sensations against her skin, smell the salt water, and taste the sweet-acrid flavor of blood in her mouth.

The pictures clicked one after another, each photo remaining only for a fraction of a second before being replaced by another. Flash! The glistening spray of water falling from the showerhead onto her naked body. Flash! A wide beam of light spilling across the deck of the *Anastasiya*. Flash! A figure watching her from the shadows—an apparition so alarming as to raise the fine hair on the nape of her neck. Flash! A burst of gunfire. Flash! Blue water, ivory teeth looming over her, and then blackness sucking her down into a bottomless vortex.

Flash! A blue man with beautiful green eyes. Flash! The shower. Slow motion . . . each drop of warm liquid caressing her skin. The water was everywhere, flowing over the deck, drowning the *Anastasiya,* buoying her up, lifting her in powerful arms, washing through her.

After a long time, the photos dimmed to black, the images replaced with the presence of someone . . . of *something* strong and benevolent hovering around her. Normally, Ree would have had no trouble identifying her surroundings, but she seemed encased in warm sand or perhaps trapped in a glass chrysalis like some jungle moth in a fantasy novel. She could feel him, and it was definitely a *him,* but beyond that, she was clueless.

Other sounds filtered into her sealed coffin: the trickle of water, a woman's moans, and a man's deep voice. She couldn't understand his words . . . couldn't identify the language although she spoke seven fluently. She thought she remembered pain, but she was in none now. Drifting on the waves . . .

Thirst clawed at her throat, swelling her tongue, heating her skin. Drops of molten gold seared her nerve endings and sent waves of pain shimmering through her tortured flesh. Thoughts of water tortured her. Glasses of ice water dripping beads of condensation . . . bottled spring water . . . bubbling fountains. She willed her eyes to open, strained until sweat broke out on her body. For an instant, she saw scattered stars, and then the shadowy fog closed in again. With it came the terrible thirst and a deep and grinding agony, a pain that threatened to rip her apart. She fled from it, retreating deep inside . . . sliding back and back.

Huge soft flakes thudded against the car windows, muffling the sound of the tires against the dirt lane. A man's gloved hands on the steering wheel and Nick's warm laughter as he turned into a hidden drive hemmed in by Canadian hemlocks . . . She was laughing with him as the Volvo's wheels slipped on the icy incline and the car slid sideways.

"I guess we're stuck here," he said.

"I guess we are," she'd answered.

Nick . . . Nick . . . She reached out for him, needing his arms around her, knowing that the cabin waited for them with its blazing fireplace, stocked refrigerator, and soft feather bed. They'd struggled against this for so long, and now she knew what was inevitable. She could imagine the feel of his lean body against her own, and her throat and face flushed hot with desire.

"Oh, Nick."

But even as she said his name, his image faded, and the snow was gone, replaced by a sandy beach and a black night sky studded with glowing stars. Salt tears clouded her eyes and she felt the pain radiate out from the place where her heart should have been. Nick . . .

The pain tore at her, ripped and chewed with savage ferocity. Ree opened her mouth to scream but nothing came out. Her skin was on fire . . . her tongue swollen and dry. If she believed in hell, she could have believed that she'd died and ended up there. But she didn't . . . she'd given up believing in anything when she was six years old.

Flash! The pictures were back, jerking across a tattered gray screen. A ship's galley. Flash! Nick's head on the pillow next to hers. Flash! A cavalcade of black limousines and the cloying scent of lilies.

"No!"

Nick's arms were around her, lifting her, carrying her. His mouth covered hers in a searing kiss of passion as a wall of water engulfed them. She wasn't afraid. The water felt good on her hot skin; it soothed the raw ache that gnawed at her stomach and sent shards of glass through her head. She felt the water on her parched lips, tasted the salt, and inhaled the cool moisture deep into her lungs.

The blackness came and went, came and went. In between, she thought she saw impossible scenes around her . . . walls of ancient cities, fallen columns, and a road of giant blocks of stone that stretched out to the curve of the earth. Swaying forests of green kelp rose around them. Red and yellow, blue, and purple fish darted and floated between the leafy fronds of foliage. Massive creatures slid past amid the haunting songs of ghostly leviathans.

She had so many questions she wanted to ask Nick. Why was his hair so light and how had his beautiful brown eyes turned to green? How had he found her on the deck of the *Anastasiya* and why was she so thirsty? But, try as she might, no sounds would pass her lips.

She wanted to wrap her arms around his neck and feel his mouth on hers, but she found it impossible to break free from her crystalline prison. And this time, when the dark tide threatened to sweep over her, she didn't fight it. Nick was here, and he would take care of her. If Nick had found her, everything would be all right.

She opened her eyes to see a wall of molten lava erupting from the forest around them. Heat flashed against her skin, and she clamped her eyes shut against the glare. But not before she'd seen the impossible, seen the tattooed men with their flashing spears and heard their hideous war cries.

"Don't be afraid," Nick said, and this time, it seemed that she heard his voice in her head. "I won't let them hurt you."

Why would they hurt me? she wondered. *They aren't real. Any minute the piano will begin to play and the Little Tramp will throw his hat and knock them all down. They will fall like dominoes. Flash. Flash. Flash.*

★   ★   ★

"How dare you show your face here?" 'Enakai demanded. She rose from her massive jade throne and glared down at him from the height of the marble dais.

Alex ignored the theatrics and held out the woman in his arms. It wouldn't do to make 'Enakai any angrier than she was, but neither was he willing to bend his knee and beg for mercy. Instead, he simply stated his purpose. "I have need of your healers."

"For a human?" Her upper lip curled as she stared with contempt at the woman's unconscious form. "Why would we use our sacred arts on a human?"

"Because you're the supreme ruler of Lemoria."

"And high priestess," she reminded him.

"And high priestess," he conceded. "I appeal to you because whatever you order will be done." He flashed her the hint of an arrogant smile. "And because you always pay your debts."

A ripple of disbelief rose from the onlookers. This was not the great court reception hall of Lemoria, but only a smaller one. Still the space was packed with the members of the royal household, minor and high nobility, and bureaucrats, palace guards, servants. Not to mention the soldiers—some of whom had made a good stab at killing him only a short time ago.

'Enakai's eyes narrowed. She was very beautiful, Alex conceded, her appearance young and lithe, as slim as a snake with great black eyes and hair that fell unbound to her hips. "What debt do I owe you, prince of Atlantis?"

He shrugged. "I sent your brother back to you, didn't I?"

"After we paid a fortune in pearls and jade for his release."

"Prince Kaleo took part in an unprovoked attack on an unarmed trading outpost in the south Atlantic. If he were human, he'd be no better than a pirate. You're fortunate I didn't return his head to you in a fishnet."

"You lie! My brother was on a diplomatic mission."

"If you believe that"—Alex said—"you're either a fool or you've been sadly misinformed."

The women around her glared and whispered among themselves. "Kill him," one murmured. "Kill him and throw his body into the flow."

"Silence!" 'Enakai's captain of the guards commanded, driving the butt of a trident into Alex's ribs.

He gritted his teeth and held back the gasp of pain that resulted. The blow had knocked him off balance, and he took a step back, but managed to regain his composure without dropping his human burden.

The captain was female as well, or what passed for female among these outlandish Lemorians. Here, in this rival kingdom in the Pacific, no king ruled. Instead, a woman sat on their highest throne. Warrior women filled the ranks of their armies and guarded the palace, and held the important offices of state, while males of noble blood were more often artists, musicians, poets, and sexual playmates kept and provided for by their mistresses.

Among the Atlanteans, there were women who sat on the high court and served in the armies. Every position but that of Poseidon was open to them, but these Lemorian warrior-maids were a race apart. The elite palace guards shaved their heads except for a single, braided scalp-lock at the back of their skulls, and each bore a row of intricate tattoos across their upper face, making it appear that they wore patterned masks, black against their pale green skin. Additional designs were tattooed across their back and down their arms. Those were considered badges of honor representing bold deeds or battles they had survived.

Some of these elite female soldiers had one breast surgically removed to more easily shoot a bow or cast a trident, and they were tall and stocky, muscled beyond what most Atlantean men would find attractive in a sexual partner.

Many Lemorians of the lower classes had only a thumb and three fingers on each hand and thick webbing between their toes, making them powerful swimmers. These, unlike the nobility, were of another species, an elusive blend of fish and mammal. All were workers, fishermen, soldiers, or servants, and they were neither male nor female, but both in the same body. They were fearless fighters, but none of their class could rise above the lowest ranks, and it was said that they were of limited intelligence.

The supreme ruler 'Enakai was petite and feminine enough in appearance, but as cruel and calculating as a moray eel. Her skin was a shimmering indigo in hue, and her heavy-lidded eyes were black as ink, large, and almond-shaped. Ropes of pearls dangled from her elongated earlobes, and a golden disk bearing the likeness of an octopus was pinned through the cartilage of her nose.

Alex had heard it said that 'Enakai took beautiful young men to her bed, and when she tired of them, she had her guards strangle them so that they could not carry tales of her bedchamber. But so alluring was she, that it was also said that there were no lack of lovers willing to risk all for the chance to find paradise between her thighs.

Anger radiated from her as she fought to maintain control of the audience. Alex was walking a thin strand of kelp and well he knew it. One mistake and she'd order her guards to slice him into small slivers and feed him to the royal jellyfish.

"I ask you again, prince of Atlantis"—'Enakai demanded—"why should we waste our magic on a human?"

"Because she is no longer human, but something more," Alex replied, with more certainty than he felt. "She possesses great powers of her own. Among her own kind, she is considered a powerful magician." It was as good a lie as he could come up with on the spot. He wished Orion were here. His twin was positively diabolical when dreaming up mad plots to get them out of jams like this.

'Enakai studied the human woman. "She doesn't look like a witch. What's wrong with her?"

"Another human, jealous of her powers, shot her with his gun," Alex lied smoothly. "I was in the process of transforming her, to restore her life force, when I realized that she needed the art of your healers."

"So you admit to inadequacy?" 'Enakai said. Her women twittered like Balinese oysters.

"In some areas, your highness." He flashed her a smile. "But not in others."

"If we save your little pet, there will be a price to pay."

"Restore her to health, and then we will talk of payment."

'Enakai motioned to an older woman with purple skin and an elaborate turban covering every strand of her hair. "Take the creature to the temple, but keep close watch over her. If she is a witch, see that she casts no spells."

"I hear and obey, light of the sea." The woman placed her palms together, bowed low, and then summoned two of the female guards to take the human from Alex's arms.

"Treat her with kindness," Alex said to the turbaned matron.

"And you?" 'Enakai demanded. "How should we treat you?"

"As a royal ambassador from Poseidon's court to yours, your highness. As you would wish to be welcomed, if you were a guest in my father's house."

"I will consider your request," 'Enakai said coldly. "Until then, you may consider what other pleasures we might have in store for you." She clapped her hands. "Take him away. I've wasted enough time on him and his pet. There are other matters which demand my attention."

"Take him where?" The heavily tattooed captain of the guard stepped forward and slammed a fist against her right shoulder-shield in salute. She was a striking specimen, even among the ranks of her Amazon comrades. Her scales were gilt rather than green in hue, and the luxurious weight of her lavender scalp-lock hung behind her to mid-thigh, proof that she had never been bested in battle.

"To the dungeons. Where else would we house an enemy intruder? But leave him a single light-fish. We would not cast him into total darkness like barbarians." She smiled with her mouth, but her eyes remained crystalline chips of ice. "I trust you are in no hurry to return to your own kingdom, Prince Alexandros," she said.

Alex inclined his head slightly. "No hurry at all." His weapons had been confiscated at the wall of fire, after he'd been overwhelmed by Lemorians and before he was escorted into the city proper. He was no coward, but neither was he a fool. Now, he assumed a stoic expression as his wrists and ankles were bound in lengths of silver chain, and he was surrounded by a platoon of female soldiers.

Lemorians stared and pointed as the guard hustled him down the columned hallway with its rows of giant oysters and outcrops of living coral. The palace was unlike that of Atlantis, despite the widespread use of marble floors and walls, as much of it was roofed over in woven kelp as the humans of the Polynesian cultures used thatch on their dwellings. Here, the pink coral columns were carved into the shape of giant palm trees, and great stone heads with jade eyes reared from the ocean floor at every turn. The dungeons lay deep below the seafloor beneath a massive complex of windowless pyramids.

Nothing could prevent a feeling of unease as the guards led him deeper and deeper into the prison. Here, the passageways were narrow and low, the cells small and dark.

Alex could hear the cries of prisoners as they strode past. Some extended hands or tentacles as they pleaded for food; others proclaimed their innocence and begged for justice. Others merely howled for a merciful death.

As if reading Alex's mind, the captain of the guard stopped and stared at him with obvious contempt. She was a formidable warrior with wide shoulders and muscular thighs. Her arms and legs bore the scars of many battles, as well as the elaborate tattoos proclaiming her prowess in battle. She retained both breasts, which were high and shapely, but somewhere in the past, she had lost an eye. A patch covered the missing orbit but did not completely hide a healed scar.

"It may be that you too will be forgotten here, Atlantean scum," she said. Her voice was husky, as if she were more accustomed to giving orders than offering sarcasm. "Many prisoners are. It might have been kinder had the supreme one ordered you thrown into the flow."

He looked into her eyes. "My name is Alexandros."

"I am Anuata of the Hundred Battles." Her features hardened. "Don't think to use your courtly wiles on me," she warned. "I've killed more of your kind than I have scales on this hand."

"Anuata. It means woman of the shadows, if I remember my Lemorian," he said. "I will remember you."

"As I you, prince of Atlantis." Her tone grew deeper. "Look well on my face. It might be the last you ever look upon." She pointed to a low door in the wall, and another soldier flung it open. "Inside," Anuata ordered.

Darkness loomed within. "'Enakai commanded that you leave me a light-fish," Alex reminded her.

She smiled. "Don't tell me that you fear the dark, warrior-prince?"

One of her companions chuckled, and Anuata stiffened and rested a hand on the curved knife at her waist. Instantly, the soldier dropped her gaze and mumbled in submission. Anuata shrugged and pulled a small light-fish from the pouch at her waist. "Enjoy it," she said to Alex. "For when that goes out, you will learn what darkness truly is."

CHAPTER 3

"**K**ill him. He's too dangerous to keep alive." Caddoc rose up on one elbow and gazed at 'Enakai with heavy-lidded eyes. She'd pleased him well this night, and he was certain that she was equally impressed with his prowess. Any male Atlantean worth his salt was better in bed than a dozen pampered Lemorian men, and Caddoc had long prided himself on his sexual vigor and creativity in matters of physical pleasure.

"Your own brother?" 'Enakai brushed aside a length of midnight-black hair and stared back at him. Her lips were bruised and slightly swollen and her bare breasts bore the imprint of his teeth.

Yes, Caddoc thought. *She has the look of a woman well serviced.* He smiled at her. In the throne room, 'Enakai might command the respect of all Lemoria, but here, in her bed, she was just a woman, hungry and grateful for what he could give her. "Come here," he commanded.

She laughed and tossed her head.

He could still taste her sweet juices on his tongue, and as she crawled across the bed toward him, he felt his groin tightening with desire. This time, he would throw her down and ride her like a dolphin until she screamed. He grabbed hold of a section of her hair and wound it around his fist. "On your knees, woman," he ordered.

"Ohh . . ."

She squealed as he flipped her face down so that her naked buttocks lay nestled like pearls on the bed of seaweed. He was rock-hard as he covered her with his body and plunged deep inside her.

"Ah . . . ah."

The sensation of her ridged passage excited him even more. Groaning, he yanked the rope of her hair across her mouth to silence her as he drove into her again and again. She bucked and twisted, intensifying his pleasure, and he used his free hand to grasp one of her breasts, squeezing and kneading her soft flesh until spasms of excitement rocked her body. He could feel his own climax gathering, rising to a crescendo of need. The scent of her was maddening, whipping and magnifying his urge to possess her fully. Again and again he pounded his engorged phallus into her.

"You're mine, 'Enakai!" he screamed. "Mine! Do you understand! I am king here!" And finally, with those words, he slipped over the edge of the chasm and he found the sweet release that so often eluded him.

Satiated and panting, he fell back against the cushions. Dimly, he heard her sobbing beside him, whether from pain or pleasure, he didn't know or care. He seized a handful of her thick hair and pulled her to him, using that dark, silken mass to wipe himself clean. He wondered whether his seed would take root in her belly. Perhaps. Atlantean-Lemorian hybrids were possible, and he imagined he was as virile as his father. And if she did quicken with his offspring it might strengthen his position here in 'Enakai's kingdom.

"Do as I say," he murmured, stroking her back, marveling at the erotic texture of her indigo scales and the tiny stub of a ridged tail that so intrigued him. "Kill Alexandros at once."

She lifted her head. "And what of the human female?"

Caddoc shrugged. "Kill her as well. Or throw her into the flow. It will please your priestesses, won't it? They're always pestering you for fresh sacrifices."

"And if I do dispose of Prince Alexandros, does that put you one step closer to Poseidon's throne?"

"I am the eldest. The crown should have been mine when our father died. If you would lend your support, I could still be high king."

"My support or my armies?" She chuckled. "You're ambitious, Caddoc. I like that in a man. It's refreshing."

His hand tightened around her wrist. "Then you'll help me? When I'm Poseidon—"

"Not when, but if," she said. "I'll think about it. I'd have to be convinced that it would be in Lemoria's favor to make war on Atlantis. My first duty is to my own kingdom. Wars are costly in many ways. My people would be hard to persuade."

He lifted her hand and pressed kisses against her knuckles. "Your word is law. No one would dare to oppose your decision."

She nibbled her bottom lip thoughtfully. "You don't understand, my darling. It's easy to command people to do what they want to do, not so much if they disagree. I am the supreme ruler because I give the Lemorians what they desire—peace, plenty, freedom."

"You're too soft, 'Enakai. A queen should not concern herself with the opinions of lesser mortals. When I am Poseidon, I'll rule with an iron hand. You'll see then what—"

"Enough of such serious talk," she purred. "The night grows short, and I have an early council meeting in the morning. We should make the most of the time we have left . . . " She smiled at him suggestively. "Unless you're already weary?"

"Never."

She shrieked with laughter as he seized her shoulders and pressed her back against the cushions. He ground his mouth against hers and wrapped his legs around hers. He wasn't sure if she would heed his advice or not, but he wasn't without resources. Alex needed to be eliminated, and if she couldn't see that, he'd have to take matters into his own hands. Warrior or not, a man in prison was vulnerable. Anything could happen to him. And if he suffered a fatal accident, doubtless 'Enakai would be pleased that her problem had been solved for her, without her having to give the order.

Ree opened her eyes and stifled a scream. What appeared to be a giant, eight-armed, lime-green octopus with bulging red eyes hovered inches from her face. She threw up her arms to protect herself just as the cephalopod mollusk recoiled and backed water, apparently equally shocked to find Ree staring at it.

For an instant, a spattering of loud static blasted inside her head. The noise was so painful that Ree clamped both hands over her ears. Almost at once, the sound altered, becoming first a series of clicking and then something that resembled a blue whale's song. Ree blinked, trying to orient herself. Where was she? She didn't think she was dreaming, yet . . . she seemed to be floating in a pale blue liquid in some enormous fish tank.

Is this reality or a drugged state? Years of training had taught her to trust her own senses, but never to discount the possibility of illusion—either chemical or psychic.

"Mean . . . you . . . we not hurt."

Ree caught her breath and looked at the green octopus. Was it smiling? Could an octopus smile or was that the look it gave you before you became its dinner? If the thing wanted to eat her, she doubted that she could stop it. Still . . . Had it just spoken to her? In Pidgin English? If this was an illusion, it was an odd one. And if it was real-ity . . . Simply considering the possibility made her dizzy.

"Not . . . hurt. Healing . . . we mean you good . . . hu-man female."

The message was definitely coming from inside her head, rather than from outside. The meaning was plain, and the language was a form of English, even if the pro-nunciation was somewhere between that spoken in Glas-gow and Australia. If this wasn't a dream, someone had slipped her some powerful drugs. But she didn't feel drugged. In fact, she felt great, strong, healthy, and hun-gry. When had she eaten last?

As if reading her mind, the octopus spoke again. "Have you . . . wanting the need to feed?"

"Where am I?" Following her host's pattern, Ree didn't speak the question but thought it.

"Healing . . . place . . . temple place."

Ree fought to regain her balance. She was obviously submerged, but she wasn't having any problem breathing. She took a better look at the octopus as it swam closer to her. It was bigger, larger even than she'd first calculated, and definitely different in appearance from the ones that had appeared on her dinner plate. She considered the pos-sibility that this *thing,* whatever it was, had only *assumed* the form of an octopus. She'd come in contact with beings not generally included in the population counts of first world countries, but never a talking octopus. She decided to reserve judgment.

"Be not fear," the creature said in a gentle voice. The pronunciation was becoming clearer, or at least easier for Ree to understand.

She'd lost track of time, but she didn't think she was delusional. She distinctly remembered being in the outside shower on the deck of the *Anastasiya.* She had perfect re-call of Varenkov shooting her with a Makarov PMM semi-automatic, 9 mm. She'd taken more than one direct hit to the midsection, another to her arm, and her hip. She remembered the shock of the bullets striking her hard, like blows from a hammer. There must have been pain, but that blurred into blackness. Things got hazy after that.

The blue man . . . Just before Varenkov appeared on deck, one of the guards had assaulted her and . . . *Shit!* There had definitely been a blue man. What had happened to the blue man?

She'd been born with extraordinary mental gifts and had spent years improving her abilities. But now, she was totally at a loss. If she'd taken that many bullets to her belly, she should be dead or mortally wounded. Taking a deep breath, she looked down at her midsection, expecting to see a gaping wound, but there was nothing but pink scar tissue. Likewise, her arm, chest, hip, and thigh seemed to bear faint scars but no shattered bone and flesh. The fact that she was stark naked registered, but didn't seem important at the moment.

"Am I dead?" she asked. There was the distinct titter of laughter from her fishy companion.

"Not. Living, you are. Feel you dead?"

Ree shook her head again. "This is a little overwhelming. You say I'm in a temple of healing . . . a hospital of sorts. Where exactly?"

"In the sea, of course."

"Of course." She looked around again. The room seemed immense with rows of clear bubbles. Things were floating in the bubbles, but she wasn't ready to consider what kinds of things they might be.

The walls and ceiling, if they were walls, were luminous, shimmering with a rainbow of colors. The light was soft, rather than glaring. "This doesn't look much like Tahiti, which is where I was the last time I checked."

"Lemoria, the mother of all cities."

Her host's speech flowed more smoothly now, or perhaps Ree had simply tuned her reception to a more powerful frequency. "In the Pacific Ocean?"

"The Lemorian Sea, yes. Some species call it the Pacific."

"Was I . . . was there someone with me? A man?"

"Rest now. All your questions must be satisfied when you meet with the great one. If you have need of sustenance, I can be arranging that."

Ree made a stab at the obvious. After all, if you hear hoofbeats on the bridge, look for a horse, not a zebra. "You say I'm alive and not dead. Is this a drug induced dream?"

Again, the gentle laughter. "Awake and lucid you be. Strange it must seem for you, but all you see is real. You humans are not alone on this Earth, you know. Older races share this planet."

That much, at least, Ree knew to be true. Still, she wasn't one for trusting, least of all a talking octopus that she'd just met under dubious circumstances. "Am I in danger?"

"Not. Not. Suspicious you have, but be at peace. Consider. Easy to let you die. Not so easy to work the healing. Taken an oath, have I. No harm do I. Be welcome here. I will send food." An arm extended. At the end of the tentacle was a bundle. "I have belief that your kind garbs themselves in lengths of material." With that, her host swam away, disappearing through a small opening that appeared along one wall.

Ree looked around. The other bubbles gave off a low hum, and somewhere, she had the distinct feeling that she could hear water flowing, but she didn't sense any immediate danger. Cautiously, she examined the garment the octopus had given her. Ree wasn't familiar with the material, but it consisted of rows of tiny scales, was silver col-

ored, and soft to the touch. Not knowing how it was supposed to be worn, she wrapped it sari-style around her
hips and draped the remaining length over one shoulder
and tucked it in. The cloth molded to her body, almost as
if it were alive. A strip of similar material, sewn with
pearls, floated to the floor. Ree retrieved it and used it to
secure her hair into a single braid.

She rubbed her eyes and massaged her forehead. *Under
the sea? Was it possible?* Somehow, it didn't seem any
stranger than being alive after being nearly murdered by
Varenkov or coming in contact with a mysterious blue
man. This situation had definitely never been covered by
any of her textbooks or instructors. High rises, jungles,
desert terrain, urban nightspots and alleys, but never the
floor of the Pacific Ocean.

It was possible that she hadn't died, that the Russian had
taken her somewhere for medical treatment and then had
her shot full of drugs, the better to soften her up for inter-
rogation. But that seemed out of character for Varenkov.
If he'd suspected that she was there to kill him and he
wanted to take her prisoner, a single bullet to the kneecap
would have been sufficient to put her out of action. No,
he'd definitely intended to eliminate her. And if she was
being held for ransom or whatever, there were a lot of
other scenarios more consistent with Varenkov's organization.

She had to consider that she really was somewhere beneath the surface of the Pacific in a city called Lemoria.
She'd heard the name before, but in the realm of myth,
filed in the same category as Atlantis and Shangri-La.
Lemoria was supposed to be an ancient civilization in the
Pacific, pre-dating the Old Kingdom in Egypt that had
been destroyed by earthquakes, erupting volcanoes, and
tidal waves. Nowhere had Ree ever read that Lemoria was
beneath the sea, or that it existed anywhere but in legend.

In any case, wherever she was, she had to get out and report back to her superiors. She had to explain what had happened and why she'd failed to complete her mission. How she was going to accomplish this, she wasn't sure, but it hadn't been the first time she'd found herself in deep water without a paddle.

She'd set about finding a way out of here just as soon as she felt stronger. She just needed to get a little sleep . . . make a plan. She yawned and blinked, trying to shake the heavy feeling of exhaustion that had settled over her. Soon, she decided, soon, but her eyes were already closing and her limbs were losing their strength. She slipped to the floor and fell into a deep, almost trance-like slumber.

"You're to make it appear that he's escaped," Caddoc said. "Tell him anything, but get him out of the cell and far enough away that you can dispose of the body without anyone being the wiser." He lowered his voice. "Have I made myself clear? No mistakes and no excuses. I want him dead before the tide turns."

The muscular figure in the shadows nodded.

"Cut off his right hand. Bring it to me, and you'll be suitably rewarded." Not that he didn't trust his liegemen, but it never paid to get sloppy.

Alexandros has a scar between his thumb and index finger. Caddoc had been teaching his younger brother the finer points of swordplay when Alex was ten or eleven, and the brat had been slow to get his guard up. A pity the blade hadn't cut deeper. A maimed prince could never mount the throne of Atlantis. It would have been the perfect solution then, but not now. Alexandros, minus a hand, would still be as dangerous as a moray eel. Dead, he would pose no more problems.

"And whatever you do, don't mention my name when you're moving him," Caddoc warned. "He doesn't know

I'm here. If he did, he might be suspicious. The two of us have never been what you'd call close."

The warrior grunted and nodded a second time.

"Don't fail me in this," Caddoc said, resting a hand lightly on the hilt of his ivory-handled scimitar. "Because if he doesn't die before the next tide, you will. And, I guarantee you won't care for the manner of your passing."

CHApter 4

Morgan, Poseidon, high king of Atlantis, stood with his beloved wife Rhiannon and their children on the great balcony of the royal palace overlooking the city. Both king and queen were splendid in full court regalia and wore the priceless jeweled crowns that had been crafted in the mists of time. Their young daughter, the Princess Danu, was garbed in a simple lavender tunic; her delicate coronet a circle of golden dolphins. The baby prince wore no crown, but his golden cuirass, kilt, and royal purple cloak were an exact duplicate of Poseidon's, in miniature.

Below, thousands of cheering Atlanteans—soldiers, nobility, members of the priesthood, and common folk alike—had gathered for this moment, the presentation of the new crown prince. Scattered among the crowds were dolphins, clusters of tiny fairies, naiads, merfolk, and nymphs. From every ocean, well-wishers had gathered to welcome Poseidon's firstborn son and heir.

Shouts of congratulations and approval rose like crashing surf around Poseidon as he lifted his year-old son from his mother's arms. Gently, Poseidon raised the chubby toddler high over his head, and the massed throngs went wild with joy. Their high king and queen had produced a healthy male heir, another Poseidon-In-Waiting, securing the long line of Atlantean kings.

For a full year, from the time of his birth until today, the precious baby prince had been sheltered in his mother's quarters, kept from the public eye, and had not been named. This would be his official recognition when his royal uncles, his grandparents, aunts and uncles, and the full force of the military and the courts would swear their fealty to him. Likewise, allies, such as the fairy nation, would recognize Poseidon's heir and pledge again their support for the treaty that bound their kingdoms in friendship.

The naming of a new crown prince might come only once in centuries and the kingdom-wide celebration would go on for weeks. During that time, Poseidon would provide free food, drink, new clothing, and vouchers for the coming year's taxes to every citizen. Students would be on holiday from their classes, convicted prisoners pardoned, and debts forgiven.

Contests, games of athletic prowess, musical and academic competitions would be held in the temples of learning and sports arenas, offering opportunities for young men and women to prove themselves worthy of recognition. Those who excelled might be awarded citizenship or even raised to the rank of nobility. Priests and priestesses would hold prayer services of thanksgiving daily, and gifts would be exchanged between families and friends.

In honor of the young prince, every child in the kingdom would receive special presents, and every home would echo with laughter and the sound of feasting. But most of all, the ties of kinship and loyalty to Atlantis would tighten, as every family considered the promise of new life and possibilities.

"I give you my beloved son, Prince Perseus!" Morgan shouted. "Long may he reign!"

"But not for eons!" came back the roar of hundreds of thousands.

The queen looked anxiously at her little one, fearful that the tumult would frighten him, but the little prince laughed, kicked his legs, and waved the small golden trident clutched tightly in his right hand.

"He likes it," his sister Princess Danu cried. "You're a brave boy, aren't you, Perseus?"

Again the king raised his son for all to admire and then, smiling, gave him over to the waiting arms of the queen. Then, Morgan took his small daughter's hand and led her to the edge of the balcony. "And to you I present our daughter, Princess Danu! It is our wish that you give her the same loyalty and support you offer our son!"

Again the cheers rose above the thud of soldiers' tridents striking the marble pavement and the clash of swords against breastplates. Princess Danu, once human but now Atlantean, had long won the hearts and minds of her people with her keen mind and courage. That she showed promise of becoming a powerful healer only endeared her to them more.

"Princess Danu!" the onlookers cried. "Long live our princess!"

Still others took up the queen's name, and the roar of "Queen Rhiannon!" echoed down the columned avenues and rose above the temples and palaces. Morgan looked back at his wife and encircled her shoulder with a strong arm. Blushing, she allowed him to lead her forward to stand beside him and their daughter to receive her due accolades.

"Poseidon! Poseidon! Poseidon!"

The king raised his golden trident in acknowledgment a final time, then turned and ushered his family back inside. A guard hurried to close the doors behind them, shutting out the tumult from the city.

Rhiannon gave a sigh of relief and passed the now fussing baby to Prince Orion, who dangled him upside down until Perseus began to giggle again. "I think someone's hungry," he ventured.

"And sleepy," the queen added. She removed her heavy gold crown set with pearls and sapphires and handed it to a waiting servant. "And he's not the only one."

Morgan slipped off his crown and tossed it to his younger brother Paris. "Try that on for size," he said.

"Not me," Paris replied. Instead, he balanced it on little Perseus' head. The crown promptly slipped forward and lodged on a dough blob of a nose. The prince crowed with laughter and tugged at the crown. Perseus tilted his head forward, the crown tumbled off, and a dolphin nursemaid caught it neatly before it hit the marble floor. "See"—Paris said—"already a king. What he doesn't like, he won't tolerate."

"I'm glad that's over," Rhiannon said, removing the baby's cuirass and kilt, leaving him in a simple soft loincloth. "Isn't that better?" she murmured to Perseus. He gurgled happily and patted her cheek. "You know how I dread these state occasions."

"You shouldn't," Morgan said, motioning for Perseus' nurse to take him. "Your subjects love you." He leaned down and brushed her lips with his. "Your king loves you even more."

Rhiannon's mouth curved in a smile as she rubbed the back of her neck. "And I love you. But . . ." She grimaced. "You and Danu are better prepared to cope with this formality than I am. If I had my way, I'd never attend another state occasion."

"Objection noted," Morgan said. "But . . ." He shrugged. "Some things we have to do. And today assures our children's future safety and the loyalty of their subjects."

"I suppose"—Rhiannon agreed as she unfastened her

bracelets and necklace of pearls and rubies and passed them to a lady-in-waiting—"but I've never been fond of crowds, and there are too many people out there to count. It's a little overwhelming."

"For one not born to royalty, you manage admirably," Lady Athena said. "Her highness, the dowager Queen Korinna, says that you have arranged a magnificent feast for this evening." She bent to tickle the baby and was rewarded with a giggle.

"With Queen Korinna's help," Rhiannon insisted. "I couldn't imagine trying to manage the palace staff without her." She smiled at the baby's nurse. "I think it's time for the prince's nap, don't you? He'll be a bear if he's over-tired."

"He will, your highness." The stout woman nodded, curtsied, and carried little Perseus off to his bed.

"We have a chamberlain, don't we?" Morgan said, continuing the conversation. "Can't you delegate some of these tasks for entertaining?"

"Nevertheless, I'm proud of you," Athena said, tactfully ignoring Morgan's remark.

Rhiannon smiled at her mother. "Now, if you'll excuse me, I'll just check with the chefs one last time. Lady Athena, Danu, would you two like to come with me?"

Orion waited until the queen, Lady Athena, and his niece left the chamber before gesturing to Morgan. "We need to speak."

With a last glance to make certain that his son was well cared for, the king followed his brother into a small antichamber. "Any news of Alex?"

Orion shook his head. "Nothing. I just received confirmation from Dewi that the target has been sighted in Fiji. He left the *Anastasiya* and flew into the capital by helicopter. Bleddyn was unable to locate Alex. He wasn't at the meeting place, and he hasn't made contact."

Morgan's jaw tightened. He'd had a bad feeling about this mission. "It doesn't mean Alex is in trouble," he said, more to convince himself than Orion. "It wouldn't be the first time he tried to go it alone."

"That's what worries me. I'd like to take a regiment out to the Pacific. See what's happening firsthand."

"You can't. I need you here. The kingdom is vulnerable during Perseus' celebration. You're the best I've got, and your place is with your troops here in the city."

"And Alex? How long do we wait before we start to worry?"

Morgan's gut knotted. Of his brothers, Alex was always the one he was most concerned about. He took too many risks, and Morgan was afraid he was beginning to believe the legend that had grown up around him. "It's a big ocean, Orion. There's no guarantee you could find him, even with a regiment. Dewi and Bleddyn know their stuff. They'll find him, or he'll find them."

"I hope you're right." Orion fixed him with a hard stare. "If anything bad happens to him, and I could have prevented it . . ."

It wasn't a scenario Morgan wanted to consider. There were a lot of reasons that might prevent Alex from rendezvousing with his team. "If the worst has happened—if Alex made a strike at Varenkov and failed—it's too late already," he said gruffly. "But if I were the gambler Alex is, I'd bet my crown on our brother turning up safe and sound."

Orion gripped Morgan's shoulder. "That's your final decision?"

"It is." And as Orion turned away, muscles rigid and green eyes as clear as polished emeralds, Morgan smothered the thought that rose in his mind. *Be glad you weren't firstborn and don't have to give these orders.*

*   *   *

Alex sensed, rather than heard, someone coming. The darkness was absolute. The light-fish's radiance had faded and gone out hours or days ago. It was impossible to see anything but stygian blackness around him in the tiny cell. Above him, he could feel the weight of the city pressing down on him, and below . . . And in the depths below were only the creaking and hissing of molten rock, rivers of lava, and the grinding of shifting earth plates.

He'd not wasted his strength on trying to break down the door. Instead, he'd folded himself into a compact form and tried to sleep. Hunger had plagued him, but it was a minor annoyance. It was fear that had worn away at him, fear that no one would come to open the cell, that he would remain here until he shriveled and died. Tight enclosed places were his bane. He hated them, and it took all of his willpower to hold back the terror that threatened to overcome his wits.

Now, someone was coming. For good or evil, the waiting was over. The presence halted in front of his cell.

"Prince Alexandros?"

He recognized the voice. It was that of 'Enakai's captain of the guard— Anuata. "Where else would I be?" he answered with more bravado than he felt. "Have you come to escort me to the high priestess's bedchamber?" Considering where he was, that might be a possibility he'd consider.

The bolts on the massive door groaned and scraped.

Alex steeled himself for the first blow. If Anuata had come to execute him, there wouldn't be a better opportunity. He could hardly move, let alone defend himself.

"I've come to get you out of here," Anuata said. "Be quick. A death bounty has already been placed on your head."

Alex's muscles were stiff as he climbed out of the hole, but he forced himself upright. "What of the human female? Is she alive?"

"Alive and well," the captain answered. "The palace is buzzing about her presence. Even 'Enakai is curious to inspect her." Anuata extended a hand and clasped Alex's right forearm. "Did you think I'd abandon you?"

He gripped her muscular arm tightly. "The thought crossed my mind."

"And mine, truth be told." She slipped into the common tongue. "You've put me in an uncomfortable place, Atlantean. Do I honor my post or turn traitor to my own kind and keep the promise I made to you years ago?"

"Saving your life was a gift. There's no need for you to feel beholden to me."

Anuata laughed wryly. "And if our roles were reversed? Would you betray Atlantis for me?"

"I can't answer that," he said. "What I can do is offer you a place fitting your rank among my troops. If you're willing?"

"Later. Let's see if we can get out of here with skin intact, shall we?"

"Why should I trust you?"

"You shouldn't." Anuata laughed again. "But what choice do you have?"

"Good. Sleep make healing."

Ree opened her eyes to see the now familiar octopus. She was reclining on a bed of thick moss beside one of the bubbles. Her first thought was that only a few moments had passed since she'd last seen the healer leave by the doorway, but when she glanced down, she found that she was wearing a different garment from the one she remembered putting on. Then, before she could pose a question, her stomach growled, and she realized that she was ravenous. "I must have dozed off," she said.

The octopus produced a sound that could only be an amused twitter. "Not to have alarm," the voice in Ree's head said. "Rest and nourishment aids recovery."

Suspicion curled in the far corners of her mind. "How long were you gone?" she asked.

Her physician waved a tentacle. "Our time has not yours. Worry not."

"How long did I sleep?"

The octopus shrugged. "Your injuries terrible. Your heart, especially, needed time to heal."

"My heart?"

"From missile? Shooting weapon?" The physician spread two tentacles in a human-like gesture. "Pee-stall?"

"Pistol?"

"Yes. Pistol missile." The octopus shook its round head. "Heart beyond saving. Time it takes to regrow from cells."

"You're telling me that my heart was destroyed and you replaced it?"

"Your own biology." Again the shake of the head. "Human heart have you still. A pity. Not so strong as Lemorian or even Atlantean. But adequate."

Ree stretched and stood up. "I feel fine. Wonderful."

"Have you hunger?"

She nodded. "I'm starving."

"Good. Nourishment you shall have. No more need you me. Time only. With time you stronger grow." The octopus patted her arm with a long tentacle. "Pleased am I to treat your kind. Never before a human. Other species, but not human. Much you add to my knowledge." The healer swam effortlessly toward the doorway. "Be of peace. Food I order for you."

"If it's more seafood, could I have it cooked?" Ree asked. "I love sushi, but a steady diet of raw fish . . ."

The physician chuckled. "Strange are ways of humans, but see I will what preparers can find."

"Thank you, and thank you for the . . . the new heart."

A final wave of a tentacle and the healer swam away.

Ree counted to two hundred before trying the opening that the octopus had exited. It was an arched doorway leading to a hall. It should have been no problem for her to pass through. Nothing barred the way but a spray of bubbles, but when she tried to go through, an invisible barrier sealed the space from floor to ceiling. The material was warmer than the surrounding water and smooth. It even gave a little under Ree's touch, but when she tried to force her way through, the substance was impenetrable.

Suddenly, she felt more prisoner than patient, and she didn't like the feeling at all. Deciding that there had to be multiple entrances, Ree began a quick examination of the walls. The possibility that this was a dream tugged at her, but she brushed it aside. She'd spent a lifetime trying to separate reality from the intangible, and she'd learned to take every situation deadly serious until it proved otherwise.

It bothered her that she couldn't remember what had happened just before she'd been shot. Normally, her memory was photographic. She should have sensed Varenkov before he reached the deck. Something had blocked her ability to pick up on his intent. It was unnerving. And everything that she'd experienced since waking up here in this room stretched the bounds of sanity. Not that she hadn't seen her share of craziness, but a *talking octopus*? A new heart? At what point did she assume she'd taken a bullet to the brain and was suffering from a loss of gray matter?

But despite whatever had happened during and after the fiasco on the deck of the *Anastasiya*, she seemed to be thinking clearly now. And every ounce of self-preservation told her that this wasn't someplace she wanted to be. Something was wrong here, and the sooner she got out, the better.

She'd passed by two bubbles, both empty, but the third was filled with a pink liquid. Suspended inside the eight-foot-high capsule was what appeared to be a large maroon and yellow jellyfish. It was football-shaped and definitely alive because she could see pulsating organs, rather she assumed they were organs, and she could see the multiple trailing tentacles writhing. Each tentacle seemed to bear rows of cactus-like mouths. The thing gave her the creeps, and although she couldn't see any eyes, she had the distinct impression the coelenterate was staring at her with malevolent intentions.

Still looking for other doors, Ree moved past another empty capsule and then one with an injured dolphin inside. The dolphin had evidently gotten the worse of some encounter because it had several jagged wounds around its head and midsection. The dolphin had eyes, but they were closed, and the animal appeared to be sleeping or in a state of unconsciousness. The liquid in that bubble was a pale green. Ree felt none of the apprehension concerning this patient that she had with the jellyfish.

Abruptly, an inner warning went off in Ree's head. She took shelter behind the dolphin's capsule and crouched down to conceal herself from whoever was coming. *What* rather than who was accurate. Ree's heart lodged in her throat. She hadn't expected *this,* but what this was, she wasn't prepared to make a guess.

Had the man been human, Ree would have classified him as a Pacific-Islander, probably Samoan or Maori. He was six and a half, maybe seven feet tall and wide as a tree trunk, spiky green hair cropped short, hands and feet like canoe paddles. His gorilla nose was cut in two by a grotesque scar; his teeth were filed into sharp points, and the coral war club in his hand could have battered down a house. But the thing that burst into the infirmary wasn't human. Ree was certain of that. Not only wasn't it human, but it definitely wasn't friendly.

"Shit," Ree muttered under her breath as she looked around for some kind of weapon. But the only thing she saw within reach was a tiny blue and silver sea horse bobbing up on the outside of the dolphin's capsule—hardly an equalizer.

Stand back. I've got a sea horse, and I'm not afraid to use it. "Double shit." *Whatever this thing is, it hasn't come to bring me candy and flowers.*

Ree rose to her feet, her gaze locked on the Samoan. He had stopped just inside the doorway and was scanning the room. He tilted his ruined head back and sniffed, as though trying to catch her scent. Then he lunged forward, coming at a full run, directly toward her hiding place.

Discretion was the better part of valor. Ree remembered that from her earliest lessons. She turned to run and slammed into the arms of her blue man.

CHAPTER 5

The woman's eyes widened when she caught sight of him, and she tried to duck away, but Alex caught her and pinned her against his chest. She was far stronger than he would have expected from one of her species. He grunted as she drove a hard knee into his groin and attempted a potentially fatal strike with the flat of her hand to his throat. He caught her wrist and pinned it behind her, which only made the physical contact between them more intense.

Her assault hadn't hurt him; Alex couldn't help admiring her pluck. Someone had taught this little human a thing or two about combat.

But more than her defiance, what surprised him was his own reaction to having her body pressed intimately against his. A red tide of lust flooded his veins and he forced himself to take a step back from the intensity of his desire. Fighting his thoughts and his male reaction to the intimacy, he yanked his attention back to the immediate danger—his brother Caddoc's man coming toward them swinging a war club over his head.

"Hold her!" Alex shouted to Anuata as he shoved the human out of the path of Tora's charge and into Anuata's arms. "Don't hurt her!"

"Let me take him!" Anuata countered, but she caught her as he moved to intercept the enraged Samoan.

"Stand off or die!" Alex warned his attacker.

Tora's answer was to swing the coral-headed club at Alex's head. Alex danced aside and the club crashed down, shattering the nearest bubble and spilling an acrid yellow fluid into the room. Tora twisted and drove the club at Alex's belly. For all his primitive appearance and limited intelligence, the Samoan moved surprisingly light on his feet. Tora was fast and powerful. His cold, expressionless eyes reminded Alex of those of a hammerhead shark that he'd once battled with off the coast of Fiji.

Alex had exchanged blows with Tora before, and he knew not to underestimate him. Given the slightest chance, the man would crush his skull with that club or disable him by smashing a leg bone before ripping out his throat with his pointed teeth. Caddoc had once boasted that Tora was a cannibal who preferred flesh raw. Alex could well believe it.

Growling deep in his throat, the Samoan charged again, and again Alex wove and dodged the attack. Alex kept his gaze locked with Tora's. His fighting master had taught him that a man's eyes always signaled his next move. But that might not be true of Tora. From what Alex had seen of him over the years, he might be more beast than humanoid. He made another rush, pivoted, and struck at the left side of Alex's head.

Close, Alex thought. *Too close.* He twisted out of reach of the murderous blow and kept distance between them, the better to tire Tora before he made his move. A year ago, this same brute had attempted to kidnap his sister just outside the great library of Alexandria. For that, if for no other reason, Alex had a good reason to kill him. But Alex hadn't survived as long as he had by acting first and thinking afterward.

If the Samoan was here, Caddoc must be as well, and Alex wondered if his half brother would suddenly appear eager to strike at his back while he was concentrating on Tora. No one had seen him or heard of Caddoc since he'd fled Atlantis soon after his attempt on their father's life. If Caddoc had taken refuge in Lemoria, it might mean that he hadn't abandoned his scheming to seize the crown of Atlantis. And if he was whispering treachery in 'Enakai's ear, it could well mean war between the two kingdoms.

"Watch out!" Anuata yelled.

Alex caught the gleam of a blade as Tora followed up his swing with the war club with a quick strike from a short-stabbing sword in his left hand. Alex blocked the blow with his own sword, and sidestepped the jab aimed at his knee. "Drop your weapon, and you'll swim out of here alive," Alex said. As much as he wanted to rid the seas of the Samoan, there were questions he wanted answered first.

Tora's small eyes narrowed and he snarled, revealing a jagged cavern of a mouth. Alex hadn't expected an answer. Someone had cut out the Samoan's tongue long ago.

Behind him, Alex heard Anuata cursing. He supposed the woman was giving Anuata grief, but he couldn't worry about that now. Tora hadn't known he was here, so he must have come for her. Was it possible that Caddoc had sent him to snatch her? Or had he been ordered to kill her? And if he had, why would his brother want her dead?

Tora came in hard and fast, dropping low at the last moment and swinging his club at Alex's knees. Alex leaped high enough for the blow to pass harmlessly beneath him and delivered a slash to the Samoan's left shoulder that laid it open to the bone.

"Mother of Vassu!" Anuata yelled.

Tora should have gone down, but the Samoan was too stupid to know how badly he was hurt. With a bellow of rage from his thick throat, he lowered his head and charged, bowling into Alex and knocking him backward into another capsule before he could free his blade from Tora's body.

The walls of the bubble collapsed under their weight and the hapless patient, a naked Lemorian courtier, thrashed wildly out of the chaos, gasped, and ended tangled in several lines of clear tubing, his life's blood pumping out into the water.

Locked in combat, Alex and Tora rolled free of the capsule. For a moment, Alex was on top, but then the Samoan wrapped his powerful legs around Alex's and flipped him over. Seemingly heedless of the pain and blood loss from his injury, the Samoan drove the club into Alex's chest and tried to gut him with his short-sword.

Alex struggled for leverage to bring his own weapon down as the Samoan's massive hands closed around his throat. Black spots floated before Alex's eyes as he fought to deliver the coup de grâce to the nape of Tora's neck. But an instant before his sword descended, Tora's body went rigid and thick fingers released their choking grip. Convulsing, he fell away, and an oily black substance obliterated Alex's vision.

Shoving Tora off him, Alex scrambled upright to find Anuata standing over Tora's twitching corpse, her curved sword dark with the Samoan's blood. A second mouth gaped below the Samoan's jagged one, and Alex realized that Anuata had cut Tora's throat from ear to ear.

"Why?" Rage washed over Alex.

Anuata shrugged. "You looked like you needed my help."

Alex gritted his teeth. Tora had committed enough foul acts to warrant the death penalty several times over, but his life ending in this manner left a bad taste in Alex's mouth. "I didn't. I had him."

"If you say so." Anuata didn't look convinced.

"I expect the members of my team to obey my orders."

She looked faintly amused. "I understand the chain of

command, my prince. I began my career as a common soldier-at-arms. But you gave no order. I assumed that allowing an enemy to kill my team leader on my first watch would be poor judgment on my part."

"I had questions to ask him."

She glanced at the dead man. "A little late, I'm afraid."

"Next time, when I want your help, I'll ask for it."

"Understood." She motioned toward the doorway. "But you might save your sympathy for him. That scum butchered a healer on his way in. No Lemorian would dare to commit such a crime. Our healers are defenseless, forbidden to take lives, even to defend their own."

Alex glanced into the passageway. The mutilated corpse of what appeared to be an octopus floated just outside the hatchway. Several tentacles had been hacked away, and its head was distorted. "That's the physician?"

She nodded. "You mean *healer.* It's a species you may not be familiar with in Atlantis. Highly intelligent, despite its primitive form. Not related to the common octopi at all. The *jysynarr* are descended from beings that traveled here with the starmen."

"I've heard of them, but I've never seen one."

"There are few left. This one was Grenjiy-Xtzn, a healer of the highest order. Very old and very wise. Her skill saved your human."

Alex slid his sword back into his belt. "Where is my human? I thought I told you to hold her."

Anuata folded her brawny arms over her bare breasts. The intricate tattoo pattern on her face made it appear that she was peering out at him through a mask. "She can't go far. Other than the way we came in, which she'd never find, this is the only entrance. This is a sealed unit, for disease control."

"And you just happened to know of a secret doorway."

"I should. The palace is full of hidden passageways, and I'm head of security." She grimaced. "Or I was, before you showed up and put an end to my promising career."

He rubbed at his shoulder. He'd taken a blow from Tora's club that had torn away some of his skin and flesh, but the wounds would heal soon enough. "You can still change your mind. Let them think someone else helped me escape."

Anuata shook her head. "If a prisoner escapes, the ultimate responsibility is the captain of the guard's. And the penalty for that is an unpleasant death. I'll take my chances with you, Atlantean—even if you are squeamish about dealing with your enemies."

Alex looked up at the dangling patient who'd been so abruptly knocked out of his healing capsule. "Is he . . ."

"Dead," Anuata said. "We won't have to worry about him telling anyone we were here." She glanced back at the entrance and brushed her lavender scalp-lock back over her shoulder. "We shouldn't remain here any longer. Another healer or one of the novices will come to check on the patients, and they'll raise the alarm."

"Let me get the woman, and we'll—"

"Leave her. She'll only slow us down." Anuata wiped the blade of her sword on a length of material before slipping it into a sheath at her belt.

"We came here for her. I'm not leaving without her."

"As you wish, but . . ."

"What?"

"I've not been trained as a sex provider, but if you have need, I can give you release."

Alex's gut clenched as he thought of sharing bed pleasures with Anuata. "Thanks for the offer," he said. "But if we were lovers, you couldn't serve under my command. It's against my—"

"Who said anything about lovers? I know enough about Atlanteans to realize that your species' weakness is an intense need for sexual—"

"As you said, it's time we made ourselves scarce. Unless you care to join me in that cell?"

"You don't need to worry about that. If they catch us, neither of us will live long enough to go back into the dungeon."

Alex moved down the rows of capsules. "Where are you, woman?" he called. "There's nowhere for you to hide so—"

She stepped out from behind a bubble containing a large orange and purple sunfish. "Stop calling me woman. My name is Ree. Ree O'Connor."

"Fair enough." Again, Alex felt a ripple of admiration for her bravery. Doubtless she'd seen the fight and Anuata's death stroke. She should have been cowering in a corner, but instead she faced him, as bold as a new tide. Heat coiled in his belly as he took in her restored body, no longer quite as human and vulnerable as it had been, but delicate as coral lace compared to Anuata.

"Who are you?" Ree asked. "What is this place, and how did I get here?"

"It's a long story—too long to go into now," Alex answered. "You'll just have to trust me. We mean you no harm."

"Right." Ree glanced at the Amazon who appeared to be trying to outflank her on the left. "I'm not going anywhere with either of you, until I get an explanation." So far as she could tell, the only exit was the one that the Samoan had come through, the one she'd tried to leave by without success.

"You'll come with us if he still wants you," the warrior-woman said.

Ree ignored her. She couldn't take her eyes off the blue

man. He was the same one she'd seen on the ship. And if he wasn't as solid as her own right hand, someone had given her some very good drugs—or bad ones.

As she studied him, he wasn't really blue. It might be her eyes playing tricks or the way the light filtered through the water. What she was certain of was that he was the most magnificent example of a male that she'd ever seen.

He was beautiful and terrible—big, tall and muscular, sinewy shoulders and a massive chest. His legs were long and equally muscular, almost too perfect to be real. The man staring at her possessed a haunting, almost classical allure to go with the to-die-for he-man physique, golden blond hair, and glittering green eyes that penetrated her to the core. He was the most handsome man Ree had ever laid eyes on, but there was nothing soft about his movie-star looks, his high, chiseled cheekbones, square chin, and strong nose. Instead, Ree felt almost a visceral attraction.

He was as delicious as a box of Godiva chocolates, and she wanted to savor every bite.

"You'll have to trust me," the blue man said.

"Trust you?" she countered. "How can I trust you? I don't even know your name."

"I saved your life back on the *Anastasiya*. Or don't you remember that?"

Had he? He'd been there, and someone had brought me away from that abattoir.

"My name is Alexandros."

"A mouthful."

The corner of his mouth twitched. "Alex will do."

"And you?" Ree glanced at the Amazon.

"Anuata."

"This is all very civilized," Alex said. "But if we continue to stand here chatting, some nasty palace guards are going to come with big knives and chop us to shark chum."

"I see." Ree swallowed, trying to dissolve the knot fist-ing in her throat. She couldn't tear her eyes off him. Handsome men had never particularly turned her on, but this one made her wet just thinking about what it would be like having his mouth on her . . . having him deep inside her. She liked sex as much as the next woman. Maybe more, because she'd never equated sex with codes of morality. But she'd rarely found herself this eager to share her body with a total stranger. Let alone one she wasn't even certain was human.

"We've got to get out of here," Anuata said. "Either grab her and take her or kill her. Better yet, I'll kill her for you."

"Back off, bitch," Ree warned. "You might get more than you bargained for."

Without another word, the blue man moved forward and held out his hand. Ree hesitated. "Come," he said. "If you stay here, they'll kill you."

Ree looked back to where the body of the Samoan floated. Death didn't frighten her, but she'd seen enough of the struggle between the two men to guess how dangerous this Alex was. "What were you doing on the *Anastasiya?*"

"I could ask you the same thing."

"I worked there. I was Varenkov's personal chef."

He arched a golden brow. "He must have hated your food."

"Stop talking!" The tattooed bodybuilder stared at Ree with eyes that were almost human. "She's going to get us all killed."

Ree tried to make sense of what was happening. This was too real to be a dream, and she felt too alert to be drugged. But why wasn't she able to pick up something from Alex's aura? She was highly gifted at reading people, but with him . . . it was as though there was a glass wall between them. And her utter lack of intuition was both terrifying and intriguing.

A cry of alarm sounded from the hallway.

"Didn't I warn you?" the tattooed Anuata said. "In two *dyaks,* we'll have a full platoon of armed guards here. I'm good, but I can't hold off nine of them while you two play the beast with two backs."

"Come with me," Alex said, still holding out his hand. The green eyes held her mesmerized.

Trembling, Ree reached out. Her fingers touched his, and a jolt of energy that nearly brought her to her knees surged between them. His big hand tightened around hers, and he pulled her hard against him. Before she could protest, Alexandros threw her over his shoulder. "It will be faster this way."

"Let me down!"

"*Vassu* protect us," the Amazon muttered. "I still say we should kill her."

"You don't get to decide that, Anuata."

"You'll regret it."

"Probably."

"You'll regret it if you don't put me down!" Ree protested.

"Quiet," Alexandros said. He launched himself through the water, swimming faster than Ree would have thought possible.

She heard a grinding sound, almost as if a stone had been slid aside, and he ducked his head and stepped into utter darkness. Ree heard Anuata right behind them. There was that scraping sound again, and then Anuata squeezed past them so close that her shoulders and side brushed against Ree.

"Put me down. Please," she said.

But almost at once he was off, swimming again. Twice

she felt the rough surface of stone rub against her shoulder, and once her heel was dragged over a jagged section. Ree squinted, trying to see light, but there was nothing but utter blackness.

They turned and twisted, sometimes swimming straight up and other times turning sharp corners or diving down. Once, Alexandros shifted her off his shoulder, and holding her by one wrist wiggled through a tight passageway, pulling her after him. She gave up trying to orient her sense of direction. They could have been swimming in circles for all she knew.

Abruptly, they slid down a fast-running channel of water into a cavern filled with blue, almost iridescent, light. There were waterfalls and pools, whirlpools, and glorious sculptures of pink and gold coral. Schools of fish, sea anemones, jellyfish of every size and color, and great oysters as large as hot tubs. The water here seemed warmer on Ree's skin, and she hoped that they would slow their pace so that she could take in the wonders of this place, but instead, Anuata plunged headfirst into the largest of the whirlpools, and Alex turned and looked at her.

"If I lose you, you'll never find your way out. Do you think you can put your arms around my neck and hold on?"

She nodded.

"I'm dead serious. If you aren't strong enough, I might be able to tie you to—"

"I won't let go," she promised.

"Good enough."

She locked her arms around him, and a heartbeat later, Alex dove into the maelstrom. They were instantly caught in the vortex and sucked down at an impossible speed. This water was icy cold and powerful, and the noise was deafening. It took every ounce of her willpower to hold on.

Again, Ree was swallowed by darkness, but this time,

there was the pressure and roar of crashing waves all around her. She was afraid that she wouldn't be able to breathe, but that fear was unfounded. The descent however was terrifying, and they seemed to be tumbling in space, even though she knew that they were surrounded by and constantly assaulted by salt water.

Time lost all meaning. She didn't know if she'd been spinning for minutes or hours, when gradually she became aware that the currents were growing weaker. She opened her eyes to find a faint green light. The spinning stopped and they continued to drift downward, but now, she could see green, verdant walls on either side. The walls grew farther apart; the light grew brighter, and they hit a final whirlpool before tumbling over a wide waterfall and landed on a sandy seafloor.

"Are you all right?" Alex asked, peering at her face.

Ree rubbed her hands over her arms and legs. "I think so. Yes, I'm in one piece." She looked around, but there was no sign of the tattooed Amazon woman.

"That was rough, but Anuata is certain we'll be pursued. I've got to get you to a place of safety before they catch up with us." He touched her cheek with the back of his hand. "You did well. You have courage."

She took a step and stumbled. She felt lightheaded and nauseous. "Maybe not so well," she admitted.

Alex slipped a strong arm around her and gathered her up in his arms. "It's all right. I can carry you these last few meters. We'll be going into darkness again, but only for a few minutes. When we reach the old city, you'll feel better."

Ree had always needed to be in control. Being carried like a child should have been shameful, but Alex was so strong. It was so easy to lie back against his broad chest and close her eyes . . . so easy to let him take care of her.

"Trust me," he murmured into her hair. "All we have to do is cross over the field of lava and we'll be fine."

CHAPTER 6

"Lava? As in volcano?" Ree stiffened, and her eyes snapped open. "Okay." She pushed against his chest. "Put me down. We're not going any further into this nightmare without an explanation."

"This isn't the place, believe me," Alex said as he lowered her feet to the sandy bottom.

She tried to gather her wits when all she wanted to do was to leap back into his arms. She must be on drugs. Sure, Alex was a hunk, but she'd never let personal feelings interfere with business. "That's what you told me before." She looked directly into his eyes. "Either tell me what's happening and why, or we're going to part company."

His expression became skeptical. "And you have an alternative?"

"Maybe. I'm pretty good at taking care of myself."

"But you aren't stupid." He waved a hand, encompassing the landscape, which had become increasingly desolate, almost like she imagined the surface of the moon. There were spiky outcrops of coral or rock that jutted up like chimneys and a bone white substance covering the seafloor that reminded her of snow. "This isn't your element. You are . . . or were human."

"Were? I can assure you I'm very human." Well, maybe

not exactly. She would never have been chosen for training as a young child if there hadn't been substantial differences in her makeup.

And then she honed in on the implication. "So you're telling me that you're something other than human?" Where the hell was she? And how could she get back to someplace she could understand—a place with sky and sea and land, all arranged in the right sequence? "No, you aren't human, are you?" She steeled herself. "Are you going to tell me you're some kind of space alien who just happened to land on Varenkov's yacht?"

"The truth is going to be difficult for you to accept."

"No kidding." She rested balled fists on her hips. "After talking octopi, your Martian sidekick who looks as though she escaped from a Japanese martial arts' flick, and discovering that I can breathe under water and swim like a fish? I can't wait to hear it."

"It would be better if you'd let me take you into sanctuary, and we had this conversation there."

He glanced to the left, and Ree turned to see what he was looking at. Several enormous orange, black-striped, bioluminescent jellyfish bobbed there, gray and black tentacles drifting behind them. She'd never seen jellies so large, but she had seen something in the news about giant jellyfish that weighed as much as six hundred pounds invading the Japanese fishing grounds. These weren't that big, but big enough. The umbrellas were at least five feet across and the dangling comet-like tail and tentacles three to four times as long.

Ree's insides clenched. She hated jellyfish. Once, when she was young, her instructors had taken her and several classmates swimming in the Chesapeake Bay in late August, and she'd been badly stung. Those jellyfish had been the size of a man's hand, and the poison had made her extremely sick for days.

"Are they dangerous?" she asked, trying to keep her tone light. The exercise had been a prelude to lessons on the *cnidarians'* biological makeup and life cycles, and since she had a photographic memory, pieces of her teacher's lesson came back to her. *Ancient denizens of the seas, mostly made up of water, but extremely efficient in survival. What appeared to be tentacles were lined with stinging, sticky structures, some of which would entangle prey, paralyze it with toxin, and hold it fast until the jelly could devour it.* Jellyfish, she remembered, had no hearts, and that had haunted her fever-racked nightmares. The idea still made her uneasy. Gooseflesh rose on the back of her neck as she stared at the beautiful creatures.

"Very dangerous." Alex gestured to the right, and Ree saw perhaps a dozen more. "Their stings are deadly to any other species but Lemorians," Alex said. "No antidote."

"Lemorians. And you and the Amazon woman aren't Lemorians?" Another jellyfish, more salmon-colored than orange, drifted into sight. This one, if possible, was ten feet from one end of the umbrella to the other, and its dangling tentacles were deep crimson while the center trailing comet flashed a sickly violet light.

"Actually, Anuata is a Lemorian. But, I'm not. And neither are you. Which means those things"—he nodded toward the nearest cluster of jellyfish— "could be unpleasant for us."

She held up her hand. "I thought we'd already established that I'm human."

"Do you want the truth, Ree?"

She wasn't sure she did, but she nodded. What was there about this man that radiated sensuality? Just being near him made her uncertain of everything she'd ever known and believed.

"All right." A jade flame flickered in the depths of those

beautiful eyes, and his voice deepened to a husky timbre. "The truth is that I'm an Atlantean."

"As in from Atlantis?" She shivered and forced a small sound of amusement. It wasn't possible—was it? And yet . . . "I suppose that isn't so strange," she admitted. "Since we're under water, and I haven't drowned yet."

A muscle twitched in the sinewy column of his throat, and she thought again how much she wanted to run her fingers over his neck and chest . . . to tangle her fingers in that golden hair and feel the controlled power beneath those faintly blue scales. Blue scales? Had she lost all reason? Where had she gotten that notion from? Alex wasn't blue. And his flawless skin was bronzed from the sun and wind. No, not totally flawless. A few scars marked his chest and magnificent thighs and legs, but they only added to his sense of virile mystique. He looked like some ancient Greek warrior come to life from a marble statue.

"I'd love to continue this conversation with you"— Alex said—"but our friends over there are hungry. I'd rather not end up paralyzed and eaten alive by anything. So, come with me willingly, or stay here and take your chances." Again, he offered her his hand. "Your choice, Ree."

"An Atlantean?" Her mind raced to keep up with the pounding of her heart against her ribs.

He nodded.

Stop it! Stop thinking of having sex with him and concentrate on finding out what's going on! "What were you doing on Varenkov's boat?" she demanded sharply.

"Your employer is a very nasty piece of work."

Alex wasn't telling her anything that she didn't already know.

"He's responsible for wholesale destruction of some of the most fertile sections of the oceans, and he profits from the slaughter of fur seals, dolphins, and endangered whales. I was sent there to put an end to his career."

Her eyes widened. "You went to the *Anastasiya* to kill Varenkov?" Of all the explanations he could have given her, this was the most far out—and made the most sense. *Alex, whatever else he is, is an assassin. How could I have missed it?*

"And I would have completed the mission if you hadn't been on deck. You weren't supposed to be there, Ree. I don't make war on civilians. I feel responsible for what happened to you. That's why I couldn't leave you there."

"Couldn't leave me to die?"

"Technically, you were already dead. Or, as good as. But I thought I could save you . . . at a price."

"And the price?"

"Complicated." He glanced over her shoulder. "Another score or so have joined the pack. Can we elaborate on this later?"

A look confirmed what Alex had just told her. "All right," she said. "I don't trust you, but . . . as you said, I don't really have a better option at the moment."

"Hold on to my back again. Your swimming is better than it was, but you haven't recovered your full strength."

"And you know this *how*?" She didn't trust herself to be that close to him. The thoughts that rose in her mind were all possibilities, but they really didn't seem appropriate when they were attempting to keep from being sucked up by monstrous jellyfish.

"Stop arguing, woman. I'm losing patience with you. Just do as I say."

She hated giving in, but on the other hand, he did swim like the devil. Reluctantly, she did as he asked, and he began to move through the water like some sort of jet-propelled watercraft. When she looked over her shoulder, she saw that the jellies were following.

But not for long. They hadn't gone more than a short

distance when Ree began to see columns of steam rising from the ocean floor and the water temperature grew noticeably warmer. What had Alex said about a lava field? This didn't look like lava, but . . .

"Stop," Alex said. "You're giving me a headache. Do you never stop talking?"

"I didn't say a word."

"You were thinking," he said.

"What? You read minds, too?"

"Something like that."

"Fine. I won't think. I'll just cling to your back like a barnacle and not think a single thought." Immediately, she began to wonder if he'd also picked up on the other thoughts she'd been having . . . the ones that had to do with—

"Ordinarily, I'd be only too happy to take you up on that offer," he said. "But just now, I've got more important things on my plate."

Ree felt her cheeks and throat grow hot. "You have a wonderful imagination."

He laughed. "You're an extraordinary woman, Ree O' Connor. Don't betray your own nature to play games."

"I don't know what you're insinuating," she lied.

"I think we're two of a kind."

"And that means?"

"What we want, we're not afraid to reach for."

A geyser of molten lava shot up from the ocean floor only a few hundred feet away. Sparks and burning debris showered the water, sizzling and steaming. Ree buried her face in Alex's back as the wave of heat washed against her skin. "Does it get worse?" she ventured.

"Afraid so." He began to swim faster, and when Ree next ventured a look, she saw that vast sections of the seabed were running with rivers of fire. "It's best if you sleep now."

"Sleep? Are you crazy?" But she found her eyelids were heavy, and an unexplained drowsiness seeped over her. Suddenly, it seemed impossible to lift her head. Instead, she inhaled the clean-male scent of Alex's body and let the rhythmic movement of his muscles lull her into a twilight state of nothingness. She hardly noticed when she slipped from his back and he gathered her in his arms and began to swim with her cradled against his chest once more.

Even without the woman to worry about, crossing the lava field would have been a tricky maneuver. With her, it wasn't a feat Alexandros wanted to repeat anytime soon. It had taken all of his strength to keep up a barrier against the intense heat from the flow that would protect them both while maintaining the illusion that would keep Ree asleep. Had she seen what they had to pass through, he wasn't certain if she would have panicked. He didn't think so, but he couldn't take that chance. He had to reach sanctuary in the Old City, and he had to do it before 'Enakai's troops caught up with them.

The first shattered blocks of the sunken road beckoned to him like a fresh salt breeze. Here, he was able to put the mossy stones between him and the seafloor. The current brought cool water and the first glimpse of schools of fish and living sea grass and kelp.

He let Ree sleep. There was no guarantee that the Lemorians weren't here ahead of him. If they were, he might have to do the unthinkable—kill her quickly and painlessly while she was wrapped in deep slumber to prevent her from falling into their hands. It was a decision he hoped he wouldn't need to make. He'd already risked too much to save her life.

He wanted her. And he was used to having what he wanted.

As a human, she had been forbidden to him. As a human, she should have been repugnant to him. Humans were a lesser species, inferior in every way to Atlanteans . . . weak, stupid, and without an understanding of the things that were important in life.

It had been such a simple step. He'd seen her die, partially because of an error on his part, and he'd felt pity for her. Instead of letting his folly be, he'd abandoned the Russian and carried the woman into the sea, intending to save her life.

He hadn't realized how important she would become to him or how deeply he would desire her. And he hadn't intended to compound his mistake by becoming entangled with the Lemorians.

One misstep and Ree's life was changed forever. Not only her life but that of Anuata. Neither of them could ever go back to what they had known. The enormity of what he'd done weighed heavily on his soul. He'd been the first to warn his brothers against becoming involved with human females, and now he'd broken the same law.

And for the first time, he wondered if they'd all been wrong—if it wasn't their weaknesses at fault, but a bad law. What if everything he'd believed about the human race was wrong? What if Atlanteans and humans were far closer than anyone realized? Hadn't they once been one race?

But whatever his doubts, there would be a price to pay. He'd be neck-deep in trouble when he returned to Atlantis, and he'd be lucky if he didn't spend the next several hundred years entombed in a coral prison or buried beneath tons of pack ice in the Antarctic.

A sharp whistle pierced his thoughts, and he scanned the ruins of a partially fallen wall ahead. Almost at once, Anuata swam from a cluster of washa kelp and waved at him.

"You made it," she called, as he approached. "I've been

watching for you." She glanced at Ree. "She's still alive, I see."

"She is."

The Lemorian warrior-woman shrugged. "Men. She'll be a liability if we have to fight."

"Mine, not yours."

"It's your neck." She motioned toward a crack in the wall. "Take that way. There's an inner courtyard beyond and two doorways on the far side. Take the left passage. It will lead you to a section of the old palace that is reasonably secure. Then follow the music. It will lead you to sanctuary. I'll keep watch."

"You've seen no sign of any patrols?"

Anuata shook her head. "With me gone, they'll put Jar'tare in command of the guard, but this far away, we'll have scouts to contend with. There are wild dolphins here. Some may be willing to carry a message to your people for you."

"You think we're better hiding here than making a run for it?"

"Yes. No one will expect you to know of this place." She regarded him with interest. "When I went ahead across the flow, did you expect me to betray you?"

Alex shook his head. "I knew you wouldn't."

"Good." Anuata smiled. "The two of you will be safe here for a while. Few Lemorians are willing to enter the Old City. They say it's haunted by the ghosts of those humans who died when the earth opened and the sea swallowed the island."

"And you don't fear ghosts?"

She laughed. "Stories to frighten children."

He grinned at her. "A woman after my own heart."

"Have you ever been here to this place of sanctuary?"

"No, but I've heard tales."

"Haven't we all?" She laughed. "Walk softly and break no rule of sanctuary at your peril."

"And how will I know them?"

"Oh, they'll tell you. You'll find food here and welcome. Take your rest, while you may, prince. You'll need your wits and strength if any of us are going to get out of here alive."

CHAPTER 7

Ree opened her eyes to the sound of music. For an instant, she couldn't remember where she was or even who she was, but then the events of the last few hours and days came back to her. She supposed she should have grown used to expecting the unexpected, but once again, she was totally at a loss to comprehend this new situation.

She seemed to be standing in a forest glen, the grass and trees around her a hundred shades of green. Above, sunlight dappled through the leaves of massive oaks and she could glimpse the flicker of colors as songbirds fluttered through the branches. The rays of sun felt warm on her skin, and the music soothed and massaged her spirit.

She'd never heard music like this. At first, she thought the notes might be Indian or somewhere from the mists of the Himalayas. The air smelled of wildflowers and oddly . . . of rosemary and thyme. But it was the bright notes that brought a catch to her throat and a tear to her eyes. She had the strangest feeling that this was all familiar from long ago. Yet, she couldn't remember ever being in such a place or even seeing a movie with such a setting.

What was this and how had she gotten from the bottom of the ocean floor to a lush forest? Was this a dream, or had everything she'd thought she'd experienced since she'd been shot on Varenkov's yacht been a drug-induced illusion? She hoped not, because the man she'd believed had carried her off the boat and under the sea was too hot to be a figment of her imagination. Just thinking about him sent her imagination soaring.

Ree grimaced. Maybe it had been too long since she'd been on leave. Lovemaking was something she'd always taken for granted. Sexual pleasure was one of the joys of living, and her education hadn't included the artificial rules that bound most women's possibilities. Not that her upbringing had been permissive. It hadn't. Boys and girls in the program had always been kept apart after regular class hours, and none of her instructors had ever crossed the line with any of the students.

There had been rumors of one rogue teacher at the institute. As the story went, he'd used his position to manipulate and gain the affections of several of the boys in a class several years ahead of hers. When the sexual intimacies had been discovered, the instructor had been eliminated, and the entire class had vanished. Where the students had gone, whether they had returned to civilian life or something more sinister, remained a mystery. But after that time, all exercises off campus had been under the direction of a pair of instructors, one male and one female. The dormitories for novices over the age of ten had been replaced with private rooms, rooms that were locked at night with a high-tech security system that the state prison system might have envied.

Upon graduation from the third level at age eighteen, institution rules about social interaction between boys and girls were relaxed. Students were encouraged to act upon natural male-female urges and to experiment, so long as no one was harmed or forced into anything they didn't want to do. The unspoken command was that each novice was to keep in mind that sexual foreplay and intercourse was as normal as eating or sleeping; sentimental attachment to a temporary partner was a weakness not to be encouraged.

Ree smiled, remembering how well she'd embraced that belief, and how she'd followed it religiously until Nick had come into her life and changed everything. They'd served together for two years, four months, and twelve days before the inevitable happened. She'd fallen hard, head, heart, and mind, and for nine months she'd been the happiest she'd ever been in her life . . . until she had gotten him killed . . .

Ree swallowed against the constriction in her throat. Where had that come from? She hadn't thought about Nick for days . . . not for hours anyway. It had been a long time ago. Any normal person would have put that behind her. She'd learned her lesson well. Take what pleasure you can find, enjoy every experience, but don't drop your guard and don't become emotionally involved. Never again. Losing Nick had almost killed her. It had been her own weakness that had opened her to the pain, and she wouldn't make the same mistake again.

A shadow passed over her, and she studied the trees more closely. Were they too perfect to be real? Was this woodland Eden a figment of her own imagination? She could swear she heard the sound of a rocky stream—no, it was a waterfall, and when she took a few more hesitant steps, a break in the trees to her left showed just that, a misty cascade of tumbling water. Mossy green banks ran down to a pool so clear that she could see trout swimming in it. She brushed aside a leafy branch and ventured closer.

Chattering squirrels peered at her from the branches, and a yellow and brown bird chirped merrily. Blooms of every color and shape grew in clusters throughout the small clearing, hemmed in by lacy ferns and flowering vines. Ree couldn't shake the thought that the colors were too bright and the setting too beautiful, more like a movie set than real life. But as she watched, a deer pushed through the ferns followed by twin, spotted fawns. Ree stopped. Motionless, she watched, entranced, as the doe lowered her head into the crystal water and drank.

"Come closer."

The booming voice echoed in her head.

Ree looked around, but saw no one.

"Who comes seeking sanctuary?"

The woods shimmered, and the trees receded. Fog settled around her, so thick that she could no longer see the waterfall, although the sound of the water rushing over the rocks and falling remained. Ominous shadows drifted behind the curtain of mist, and the bright music took on a haunting air.

"Why do you come?" The tone became a whisper. "Why? Why? Why?"

"I can't play your childish game if I don't know the rules!" Ree cried.

What is real, and what is an illusion? "Show yourself!"

The ground shook beneath her feet. She nearly fell, took a stumbling step, and slid down the slippery grass bank into the water. The water was icy cold, but not as cold as the howls and shrieks that rose from the surface.

Fear lapped against her. Every instinct urged her to flee. The water rose to her hips, and bony fingers scratched and tugged at her legs and clothing. "Damn it!" she snapped. "Show yourself!"

The voice came again, low and ghostly. "Why do you seek sanctuary here?"

"Who says I do?"

"Ree."

That voice she knew. It was faint, but compelling. "Alex? What's going on?"

"Run before it's too late!" came the specter's warning.

"It's a test to see if you can be frightened away," Alex said. "Demand sanctuary. Promise that you will honor their laws and ask to be admitted."

Rationality warred with emotion. Could she trust Alex? She certainly didn't trust whoever was behind the vanishing Robin Hood set and the picture-perfect deer. And where the hell had the ocean gone?

"Hurry!" Alex urged. "The window is closing. I'm already inside. Trust me. Ask for sanctuary before it's too late."

"Oh, hell," she muttered. And taking a deep breath, she shouted, "I demand sanctuary!"

The water began to swirl around her, and a strong undertow swept her off her feet. Before she could utter another word, she was dragged under, and then pulled up and into the darkness behind the waterfall. There was a loud bong, as if someone had struck a great metal bell, and then she sprawled facedown on a thick carpet.

Strong arms went around her and lifted her up. "It's all right," Alex said. "Our hosts are into theatrics. You're safe here."

Dizzy, she looked around. She was in a round room with a domed ceiling, a room that was draped in gauzy draperies. "Are we under the ocean again?" she asked.

"In a manner of speaking," Alex said. "But there's no water here. We're breathing air again."

"A submarine?"

"More of a terrarium, not strictly speaking, of course. This is a reinforced sphere with an artificial atmosphere. Physically, we're beneath an ancient city that sunk in an earthquake before the first Egyptian pyramids were dreams in an architect's imagination."

Ree glanced around the large chamber. The room was dominated by a great bed, curtained, like the walls in filmy draperies. In one section of the room, more curtains only partially concealed a bubbling hot spring and crystal bath with marble steps leading down into it. There was a marble fireplace against one curved wall, and in it, logs burned merrily. An animal-skin rug lay on the floor in front of the hearth, but she could only guess what the origin was. The fur was thick and white, soft under her bare feet.

"Polar bear," Alex said with a twinkle in his eye. "You would have known what it was if they'd left the head attached."

"*They*. Who, exactly, are *they*? More giant jellyfish, or talking octopi?"

"Our hosts. The *keepers* of sanctuary. This sanctuary, at least." He waved toward a large crystal-framed window. "That scenery should make you feel more comfortable, although it's a bit strange to me."

Outside, Ree could see rolling wooded hills and a wide river. The trees were clothed in red and gold autumn foliage, and the river twisted and rolled over rocks and through deep canyon walls. There was no sign of human habitation, but deer grazed in the fields and birds flew through the blue sky. White billowing clouds arched overhead. "It isn't real, is it?" she asked. "It's all an illusion."

He shrugged. "Perhaps. Sometimes, it's difficult to tell what's real and what's not. It depends on your perception of reality." He spread his hands. "But sanctuary is real. We can only stay a short time, a few of your days, at most. But while we're here, we're safe from predators, including Lemorians, sharks, jellyfish, and wandering mercenaries."

"Are we?" The strains of music drifted down from the dome, seeping into her bones and easing her fears. Ree knew she was being manipulated, but it was such a delightful manipulation that she couldn't resist. Each note rang clear and sweet, and again she had the oddest feeling that she'd heard this melody long ago.

He nodded. "You've had a rough time of it, haven't you, Ree?"

It was her turn to shrug. When had things ever gone easily for her? And why would she expect differently? "We're still at the bottom of the Pacific Ocean?"

"Yes."

"And you aren't going to turn into a two-headed troll in the next five minutes?"

"Cross my heart." He chuckled. "Hungry?" He waved toward a low table. Covered dishes emitted delicious odors. "I'd venture that the food is wonderful, and I can promise you'll find some of it to your liking."

"It isn't drugged, is it?"

"Nope. The hosts are quite peaceful, and they don't care a dried flounder for our quarrels. They don't take sides, and so long as we don't break their rules of hospitality, we're as safe here as we'd be in the high temple of Atlantis."

"Why doesn't that give me much comfort?" Her eyes narrowed. "What are the rules?"

"Nothing too difficult. I had to leave my weapons at the door, so to speak. We can't murder each other or our hosts, and we're to refrain from slaughtering the wildlife or causing destruction to the sphere or our chamber." He uncorked an onion-shaped bottle that might have been fashioned centuries ago and began to pour wine into a silver goblet. "Wine?"

She nodded. She needed a drink. Maybe two drinks. Maybe the whole damned bottle.

The food, as Alex had promised, was to Ree's liking. There were whole grilled lobsters, shrimp bisque, warm loaves of whole grain bread, bowls of fresh fruit, and tempting dishes of peas and onions, nuts, berries, stewed apples, cooked seaweed, roast beef, fried flounder, and more pies and sweet muffins and cakes than she wanted to count. They ate and drank, and with each goblet of wine, Ree found the flavor more delicious.

"If this is an illusion, it's a good one," she admitted after they'd finished the first bottle and gone on to a second. She wasn't intoxicated, but she was feeling much more relaxed. Learning to consume alcoholic beverages had been an important part of her education. A woman or a man who couldn't hold their liquor was in the wrong line of work. All things in moderation, she'd been taught . . .

When it came to sex with the right partner however, she had her own ideas . . .

He smiled at her, and her heartbeat quickened. It was impossible to be so close to this magnificent man and not feel the attraction between them. Alex radiated virile male power, and try as she might, she couldn't stop thinking about what it would be like to make love to him. Would he be a generous lover, or like so many handsome men, was he all about his own rewards? Somehow, she thought he would be better than that. Something told her that Alexandros, whoever he was, would be an accomplished and generous lay.

She liked her men big, and Alex filled the bill. She looked into his sea green eyes, trying to decide if he could read what she was thinking. It really didn't matter. She was past the point of being hampered by her few inhibitions. And when his gaze dropped to take in the curve of her breasts and the narrowness of her waist, she felt liquid heat slide under her skin.

"Are you built like other men?" she asked, her glance dipping to skim over his short gold tunic and metallic armor.

He should have looked silly. What was he doing costumed like some actor in an Italian *sword and sandals* flick? But his garments, what there were of them, weren't a cheap imitation. And he wore them without a hint of awkwardness. Not every man had legs like that. She couldn't ever remember seeing a male with such a beautiful physique. Alex was muscular without being bulky, tall and impossibly broad-shouldered with a chest that any bodybuilder would have envied.

"I'm glad you approve." His smile became a wicked grin. "Would the lady care for a closer inspection of what's under my cuirass and armor?"

She laughed to cover her chagrin. She'd thought she didn't care if he read her mind or not, but it was unnerving to think that he could hear her thoughts even as they blossomed in her mind. "How would I know? I've never taken an Atlantean to my bed before. You might have scales and a tail."

Dark jade swirled with emerald flames in his large, haunting eyes, and her stomach knotted as he caught her hand and brought it to his lips. She wondered if he was going to kiss it or sink fangs into it like some underwater vampire, and she had to force herself not to tremble as moisture flooded her woman's cleft. Instantly, an intense desire to have him inside her, here and now, seized her.

Alex brushed his lower lip with the tip of his tongue, turned her hand and pressed his warm mouth against the hollow of her wrist. Pleasure shot through her, making her heart pound and her breathing quicken. He pulled her into his arms and their lips met. She slipped her arms around his neck and pulled him closer as his hard body stiffened against hers.

His mouth scorched hers in a searing kiss of intensity that sent her thoughts reeling. Every cell in her body responded to his touch. Strong fingers tangled in her hair and pulled her head back as their tongues met and entwined, and sweet sensations swept to the tips of her toes. "Come," he whispered hoarsely. "Bathe with me."

The sound of his voice echoed in her head, making her tingle and turning her bones to water. His fingers traced the line of her neck, sliding down to caress her buttocks and clasp her ever closer. She could feel the molten heat of his swollen sex. He was larger than she had suspected, and the knowledge that he wanted her badly added to her desire.

"Maybe we should skip the foreplay and get right to the main course," she suggested as Alex lowered his head to nibble at her throat and press warm kisses in the hollow between her breasts.

He laughed as his big hand spanned her hip and stroked the curls at the apex of her thighs. Ree shuddered and pressed against his hand, sighing as he slipped a finger into her damp cleft.

"Yes," she urged him. She wanted more . . . needed more.

"Not yet," he said as he slipped an arm beneath her legs and gathered her in his arms to carry her to the pool. "Every meal is better for a little spice." Controlling his own need was difficult, but it was important to him that he give as good as he got. Alex could felt the gathering storm of sexual need overwhelm him. He knew he had to rein in the urges that set his blood to boiling and his soul aflame.

She was warm and pliant in his arms, and her skin tasted of the salt sea. No longer human and not quite Atlantean, Ree was a rare and delicate flower, exotic and mysterious, and eminently intriguing. He'd lost count of the number of women he'd made love to, but this one promised to be unique. He kissed her naked shoulder and nipped at her ear, savoring the silken texture of her skin and inhaling her delicious scent as he waded into the enchanted pool.

"Wait," she said, and untied her garment so that it fell around her waist, leaving her beautiful breasts bare. They were round and full with shell-pink nipples, and the sight of her made him half mad with wanting her—wanting to fill her with his hot flesh and possess her. But still he held back the rising tide of passion.

The water rose around them to his waist and shoulders. Still holding her tightly against him, he ducked under the surface, letting her clothing fall away and the bubbling foam anoint every inch of their skin. He lifted her up above him and she wrapped her shapely legs around his waist.

"Make love to me," she said. "Now!"

CHAPTER 8

A lex laughed and brought his mouth down to hers. He wanted her with every fiber of his body. His heart thudded against his ribs. Human or not, his blood burned for her. Being with her like this went against everything he'd ever been taught or believed, but at this moment, it didn't matter.

He wanted to savor every moment of their lovemaking. He wanted to taste every inch of her skin and discover the curves of her woman's body. He wanted to hear the cadence of her heartbeat and quickening of her breathing. Every instinct told Alex that she was wet and ready for him, but no matter the physical pain he experienced in waiting, he wouldn't trade immediate gratification for the greater pleasure he expected to give them both.

Instead, he found her mouth and kissed her, tenderly at first as they fitted lips to lips, and then with greater intensity. He trailed kisses over her face and down to her throat. "Ree," he rasped. "Beautiful Ree."

Matings between adult Atlanteans were so intense they sometimes bordered on violent, but when both parties were willing and eager, the lines between pleasure and pain were faint and often disregarded. Holding back the red tide of passion would be a challenge for him, one Ree made even more difficult by her quick shuddering breaths and the heat radiating from her body.

Her hands were on him, moving over his neck and shoulder, massaging and stroking. "Alex," she murmured. "Alex." She cupped a full breast and lifted it in invitation. "Kiss me," she said.

Her nipple was a swollen bud, sweet as honey between his lips. He teased the hard nub with his tongue, then drew it between his lips and suckled until she squirmed and gasped with pleasure. "Do you like that?" he asked her as he moved to caress and kiss her other breast.

"Yes . . . yes." Her nails dug furrows across his back and she arched against him, rubbing her warm flesh against him until he thought he would go mad with wanting her.

His groin ached, his swollen phallus so rock-hard and sensitive that he could feel the blood pounding through it. Need crashed over him, dragging him into the undertow and threatening to rip away every scrap of his control. He wanted her . . . had to possess her . . . make her his in every way.

Ree gasped as he laved her nipple with his tongue, and then suckled again until sweet ribbons of bright pleasure coiled through her body. The water lapped against their naked bodies, soft and warm, and pulsing with sensuality, driving her need for fulfillment and stripping away the last vestiges of caution.

She had to be closer to him, had to fill the aching emptiness that throbbed in her core. Vaguely, she was aware that she was crying out, but she didn't care. Nothing mattered but this moment and the feel of his hands and mouth and the promise of his hard member bringing them both the climax they sought.

Whatever water bubbled in the pool and tumbled from the rocks seemed intoxicating, adding to her physical gratification, lubricating, and tingling, making every inch of her skin more sensitive than she'd ever felt before.

Alex caught her around the waist, lifting her high over his head, and when he lowered her and they tumbled over and over in the water, Ree gave as good as she received, nipping him with her teeth and molding her body to his. With every heartbeat and every caress, her arousal grew, until raw hunger possessed her and she knew she had to take every inch of him or die of frustration.

"Now! Now!" she screamed. But he captured her in his arms and carried her up and out of the pool, laying her down upon the bearskin rug, pushing her knees apart and burying his face in her wet, aching cleft. She felt the thrust of his hot tongue and exploded into a thousand shards of colored light. Waves of pleasure surged through her, and tears blinded her eyes.

"I want . . . I want . . ." she sobbed as she pulled him against her. Shuddering tremors shook her body and the sweet joy spread like sunshine from the crown of her head to the soles of her feet.

"I know what you want," Alex said huskily. "You want what I want." And with tantalizing slowness, he began to nuzzle her throat, kissing and nipping, sucking gently, and murmuring sweet words against her skin. At a torturous pace, he moved his fingers and lips and tongue over her body, caressing and stroking, slowly bringing her back to a state of arousal.

She closed her eyes as he rose over her and she felt the first nudging of his tumescent flesh against hers. She opened for him, eagerly clasping him to her, feeling the thick fur beneath her and the weight of the man above. He was even larger than she'd imagined and she struggled to take all of him, before crying out with joy as he thrust deep inside her.

He found her breast with his mouth and suckled as he drove hard and fast, withdrawing and plunging again to fill her with his presence. She rose to meet him and they fit together as one whole, rising together on the crest and plunging into the cataract of rapture.

Later when they had dozed and woke to kiss and laugh and eat, they made love to each other again. This time, they managed to reach the foot of the great bed before he claimed her on the floor. But she rolled beneath him and mounted to ride him long and hard, so that when she climaxed once more, she was utterly satiated and ready to curl up beside him on the crisp white sheets.

They woke sometime later, and this time their lovemaking was tender and sweet, but every bit as satisfying to Ree. She was content to lie for a long time with her head on his chest while he stroked her hair and they listened to the sound of the water falling over the rocks into the pool. She couldn't tell if it was night or day. The light outside the window hadn't altered; white clouds still rode against a blue sky, framing green hills and verdant meadows.

"Tell me again who you are," she whispered. She'd found that after sex was the best time to get the truth from men. Alex had been fantastic, over-the-top, the best lover she'd ever had intercourse with, but that didn't mean she trusted him. Trusting could get you killed in a hurry.

"Alexandros of Atlantis."

She concentrated, trying to pick up any hints that he was lying. She had good instincts, and she'd been trained to read men and women. Usually liars gave off clues such as averting their eyes or touching their nose, but sociopaths were a breed apart. If Alex was outside the normal range of behavior, none of the old rules worked. And he was certainly different enough and charming enough to arouse suspicion.

"And you claim to have gone to Varenkov's boat to kill

him?" She gave him her most adoring gaze. With men, it paid to use honey instead of vinegar. And if he was feeling as good as she was about the past six to eight hours, she thought Alex should be pretty mellow.

"I've already told you that I did. And I would have succeeded, if you had stayed below deck where you belonged. I had it timed perfectly. Varenkov would have come up for his nightly stroll and . . ."

He left the rest unspoken, and she punched him playfully in the ribs. "Isn't that just like a man," she teased. "Lord, the woman you gave me made me eat the apple."

Alex draped a big hand possessively over her hipbone and slowly traced a circle on her bare buttock. "You don't have a clue as to the trouble you've caused me. Atlanteans are forbidden to become involved with human women."

"That's right," she said. "I forgot. You aren't human, are you?"

"No." He shook his head. "I'm not."

"So, what just happened between us, all that great sex, wasn't supposed to happen."

"Was it great?" Alex pushed himself up on one elbow.

She shrugged. "You probably don't get a lot of complaints."

Alex chuckled. "None so far."

"None you'd admit to, you mean?"

"And neither do you, I'd venture."

She felt her cheeks flush. It was a redhead's curse. She could control a lot of things, but not her reaction to a compliment.

"Where I went wrong was when I interfered with the guard's attack on you, and then compounding that by removing you from the boat. Legally speaking."

His amused gaze made her pulse quicken. "And the sex? I suppose that's a hanging offense?"

He grimaced. "That's a gray area. You aren't really human anymore."

"I'm not?" She glanced down at her breasts. "You don't think so?"

"I'm telling you the truth." He took a lock of her hair between his fingers and brushed it against his lips. "You're free to believe whatever you please."

"You're an Atlantean."

"I am, and as hard as it may be for you to accept, my kind are as real as yours."

"You're right," she admitted. "It's a difficult concept."

He stared at her for a moment, and then his sensual lips curled into a smile. "You seem to be an intelligent woman, Ree. I could ask why you'd put yourself in harm's way by working for an international criminal. You couldn't have been so innocent that you didn't know what sort of man Varenkov was."

"Maybe I needed the job."

His smile faded. "Not good enough."

"Since you have the ability to read my mind, you shouldn't have to ask."

The smile returned, but this time the humor only glinted in his eyes. "It's not that simple. Some things I pick up from you because you're shouting in your head. Here, in this sphere, we're talking as you might be on land, but in the ocean, it's easier to send and receive thoughts mentally."

"So everyone's private thoughts are open to general—"

"No, it doesn't work that way." He shook his head. "With practice, you'll get better at hiding what you don't want common knowledge. Probing private thoughts is considered extremely bad manners. But I shouldn't have to tell you any of this. You're very perceptive."

"For a human?"

"I didn't say that." He leaned close and brushed a kiss over her lips. "I'm starving," he said, sitting up, and sliding his long legs over the edge of the bed. "Sleep a little longer, if you like."

She watched as he pulled a short white tunic with gold trim over his head. "Wait, that isn't what you were wearing before," she said.

Alex indicated a bench where a woman's tunic, jewelry, and sandals lay. "Our hosts provided suitable fresh clothing and breakfast."

Ree hadn't been aware that anyone had entered the room. The fact that they hadn't been alone while she slept was unnerving. Was she losing her edge?

"Who exactly are they? I believe I asked you before."

Alex belted on his sword. "And you didn't like the answer?"

"I have the feeling you're humoring me."

He nodded. "Maybe."

She rose from the bed and faced him, clad only in her tangled hair. "I told you, I want the truth."

"Actually, I'm not certain who our hosts are," he answered. "I've heard rumors that this is all the work of spirits . . . ghosts, if you will."

"You don't believe that."

He chuckled. "No. I don't. But I doubt that they're Lemorians. My guess is that our hosts are another kind of being altogether."

Her eyes widened, and she settled both fists on her hips. "Don't stop now. I can't wait to hear this."

"You have to stop thinking that only one species inhabits this planet."

Ree exhaled softly and reached for her own clothing. How could she explain to him that she already knew that, that she'd seen and experienced so many strange things in her life that she could almost accept that he might be an Atlantean? But invisible beings that ran an underwater B & B? That was a little much to swallow.

"You may as well hear it all at once," he said. "When I carried you off that yacht, you were dying, maybe already dead. I couldn't give you back the life you lost. All I could offer was something more. Maybe less from your point of view."

She belted her tunic with a silver chain. It was soft against her skin, woven of white fabric so fine that it seemed like silk and stitched so cleverly that she couldn't find a single seam. It fit perfectly, molding to her skin, and falling gracefully from the hip to mid-thigh. "Go on," she urged. "You have my full attention."

"The only way to save you was to alter your genes, to make you an Atlantean so that you could survive beneath the sea." He folded his arms across his chest. "But I was only partially successful. I had to take you to the Lemorian healers. I'm not certain, but I suspect you're now a combination of human, Atlantean, and Lemorian."

"A hybrid." She considered the possibility. "You aren't joking, are you?"

Alex shook his head. "What remains of your human body is anyone's guess, but you certainly adapted to breathing underwater, and I can see certain physical changes that are definitely Atlantean characteristics."

She dropped onto the bench. "Are these changes permanent?"

He nodded again. "I'm afraid so."

"You're telling me I've become some sort of mermaid, that I'll never be able to return to life as a human?"

"I don't know. I doubt if anyone could answer that question. All Atlanteans can breathe air for hours, even days, but we have to return to the sea, or we die. We can't survive on land."

"But I'm not Atlantean or human. I'm some sort of freak."

"I prefer hybrid. And being part Atlantean isn't all bad. We don't get sick, not as humans do. We aren't prone to cancer or heart disease, diabetes, or any of the sexually transmitted diseases. And we live a long time."

"How long is a long time?"

"Hundreds, sometimes thousands, of human years. We aren't immortal. We can be killed, but we have tremendous healing properties. And we're much stronger than your kind."

She wasn't sure how much of what he was telling her that she believed, but some of it made a perverted sort of reason. She'd learned that her own senses were the only things in the world she could trust, and she'd spent the last few days under water without drowning. So, if she wasn't locked up in a mental ward in some sanitarium and she wasn't in a coma and delusional, maybe . . . just maybe there was truth to it.

"All right, while we're playing twenty questions. Why are you—why am I dressed like someone out of a Hollywood version of ancient Greece?"

"When I take you to Atlantis—and sooner or later I'll have to—there are historians that can explain our similarities more fully, but the simple answer is that Atlantis existed first. Egypt, Greece, and, to some extent, the Mayan and Roman civilizations copy from our culture. We certainly taught them architecture, medicine, and science. Ours were the first roads, as you know them, the first coined money, and the first writing. The Phoenician alphabet is very close to Atlantean."

"Sorry, sandals under the water seem silly."

"They are more formal wear than for open ocean, or . . ." He spread his hands, indicating the space around them. "Or as we are now, in a land situation. Certainly humans have their own curious customs. Men's suits and ties? The necktie, I've read, was once necessary when your people traveled by horseback and needed a length of material to bandage a mount's injured leg. I've never observed that men like wearing them, but they seem to buy them in great quantities."

"All right." She chuckled. "I'll give you that point. Neckties on men are ridiculous. But the notion that all the great civilizations in the world came from Atlantis is stretching it."

"Not at all. Do you think it's a coincidence that there are similar pyramids in Asia, Africa, and Central and South America? Or that there are symbols carved into the walls of Peruvian cities that are identical to some I could show you in Ireland or the oldest section of Atlantis? And I never said that all civilizations developed from ours, only some of the greatest. And we can't take all the credit. Much of our ancient knowledge came from outsiders, travelers from the stars who visited Earth long ago."

She blinked, suddenly feeling a little dizzy. "You're serious, aren't you?"

"You asked for the truth."

"But how is it possible? If you . . . if your civilization exists beneath the ocean . . . why haven't we had contact before? Humans and Atlanteans?"

"We have." His gaze met hers and she read not only sorrow but anger. "Many times. But your kind dismisses ours as myth. Children's tales. Northmen, Britons, Koreans, and South Sea Islanders all have tales of mermaids and seal people. Sailors of every nation tell of strange beings they've sighted at sea, and all are laughed at. Your kind recognize the intelligence of whales and dolphins, yet you continue to hunt them for food and destroy them for sport."

"Not all humans."

His mouth tightened into a hard line. "Most."

"You sound as if you don't think much of the human race."

"I don't," Alex said. "And with good reason. Humans murdered my mother."

CHAPTER 9

"I'm sorry," Ree said. She believed him. He wasn't lying about this. She'd been taught to withhold the truth and give false information, and she'd learned how to distinguish the two in an opponent. Human or not, Alex's mind worked the same as hers, and on a gut level she knew that he was being absolutely honest with her.

"I wasn't looking for sympathy."

"I didn't think you were."

His pupils darkened. A muscle twitched along his cheek, and she noticed the faint shadow of fine gold hairs on his jawline. Alex barely had any body hair, other than that on his head and his groin area, making him a rarity in the men she'd known intimately. She'd always been attracted to dark-haired men, and hairy chests and legs were part of the package. But she had to admit that Alex's smooth body with its corded muscle and hard planes was sexy as hell.

She couldn't help thinking how different he was from Nick, both physically and in personality. Nick had been the only man that she'd ever loved and trusted. How was it possible that she could compare Nick and Alex? She barely knew Alex, and most of what he told her was impossible to believe. Added to that—by his own admission—this green-eyed Adonis wasn't even human.

And why had Nick come to mind? She made it a rule never to compare the men she'd shared sex with . . . but then, she supposed, rules were made to be broken.

"How old were you when you lost her?"

"I didn't lose her," Alex said. "She was murdered. And I was still a boy, young enough that it took me a long time to believe that she was really gone. I never saw her body, and I used to imagine that it was all a mistake, that I'd look up and see her coming . . . that I'd feel her arms around me again." He shook his head.

Ree's chest tightened as a rush of emotion caught her off guard. She'd been the one to ask, but she wished she hadn't. It was a bad subject, a door that was better left closed. Her own mother had died when Ree was six.

And not just her mother, but her father as well. In one awful night she'd gone from an adored only child to an orphan. No one had told her the truth for years, but she'd always known they had ceased to exist. She'd sensed the emptiness in her world, and she'd known the housemothers were lying when they said her parents were coming to visit in a few months. The visit never came. There was always a new excuse, until finally, she and the other students, who'd also been lied to, had stopped asking.

"They're young," Ree had heard a supervisor whisper to one of the instructors. *"Children forget."* But that was a lie, too. They didn't forget. At least she didn't forget. She still remembered the scent of her mother's perfume and the way her nose had wrinkled when she laughed. She'd had freckles on her nose, and Ree had teased her by drawing imaginary lines connecting the small imperfections on her skin.

The knot in her chest tightened. She remembered her father, too, a big dark-haired Irishman with a gift for music. How many times had she drifted off to sleep at night to the sound of the hammered dulcimer, the pennywhistle, or his flute? He'd been more distant than her mother, almost brooding at times, but when he drank too much, he would sing Irish rebel ballads, dandle her on his knee and call her his darlin' girl. Most of the time, he was a quiet man, cautious and watchful. Ree thought she inherited her skepticism from him, that and her gift of pyrokinetics.

"My mother was murdered, too," she said, surprising herself. She never talked about her parents, not even to Nick . . . not to anyone. He'd never mentioned his family either.

Alex regarded her closely. She could see the doubt in his eyes.

"Both my mother and father died in a fire." Her voice echoed in her head. *Fire . . . fire . . . fire.* "It wasn't an accident. Apparently my father had made political enemies, people who wanted him dead badly enough to burn the house down around them."

She hadn't been able to bring their murderers to justice, but over the years, she'd done her best to rid the world of other evil. The organization had trained her for that reason. Human garbage like Grigori Varenkov, dictators, drug lords, war criminals, gangsters, serial killers, those too wealthy or too powerful to pay for their sins, were judged by an impartial jury of nine. She and others like her used their special gifts to carry out the executions.

"Do you know who was responsible for your parents' deaths?" Alex asked.

"Not really. Either agents of a radical Protestant Irish party or the British government. *The Irish troubles.* My father was considered an undesirable."

"And your mother?"

"At the wrong place at the wrong time, I suppose. I

don't believe she was political, but I was young. I can't say for certain. I know she never went with him at night to his meetings. She always stayed with me."

"I'm luckier than you. I had my father . . . and my brothers."

"How many brothers do you have?"

Alex chuckled. "Many. My father was fond of marriage. But three that I'm close to." He waved toward the table. "Come, eat. Enough of this gloomy talk." He smiled at her. "I like you, Ree." His smile widened into a boyish grin. "You're a special woman."

And how many women has he delivered that line to? she wondered. But she couldn't blame him. There were courtesies that one offered to a partner the morning after. If it was a night . . . Here, beneath the sea, there seemed to be no division between day and night.

Ouch! When had the possibility that all this was real become solid? When had she come to believe that she was at the bottom of the Pacific Ocean sharing a morning *after* brunch with a hot Atlantean in a short skirt?

Alex looked thoughtful as he plucked fried shrimp from a golden bowl and heaped them in a large scallop shell before offering them to her.

"Thanks." She took one and tasted it. The shrimp was golden brown, cooked in a thin batter, and seasoned perfectly. It was delicious, and she reached for another with her fingers. "How did your mother die?"

"It doesn't matter. It was a long time ago."

"Not that long ago. You can't be more than what? Thirty? Thirty-five?"

"I'm older than you think. We don't count years as humans do." He poured a crystal goblet of white wine for her and offered her a napkin.

Ree looked at the linen. The stitching was exquisite,

but the material didn't seem to be one that she was familiar with. "What is this made of?" she asked.

"Fish skin, the same as your tunic. If you examine it closely, you'll see the minute scales. It's fairy work, very time consuming, but almost indestructible."

Ree glanced down at the soft folds of her garment and grimaced. "Fish skin? I'm wearing fish skin?"

He smiled. "What did you expect? Lamb's wool?" He broke off a section of bread and divided it, giving her half.

"More fish?" she asked. When she took a bite, it tasted of fruit and honey and walnuts. "I don't care. It's wonderful."

"Fairy bread," he said. "Any who eat of it are promised sweet dreams."

Abruptly, he rose and went to the window. Nothing had changed. The clouds were still as white, the sky as blue, and the hills and forests as green. Using an eating knife he'd removed from the table, Alex began to pry at the corner of the woodwork.

"Don't do that!" boomed a thunderous voice in Ree's ear.

"Show yourself," Alex said.

"Is this the way you repay our hospitality?" came a shrieking demand.

"What are you doing?" Ree asked. "Didn't you tell me—"

"Quiet!" Alex turned to the fireplace, kicked aside the burning logs, and thrust his hand up the chimney.

Ree jumped aside as the flaming embers vanished. Where the fire had been was nothing but a black hole.

"How dare—" The imposing timbre changed to the high-pitched tone of a small, frightened boy. "Let me go!" he squeaked.

Alex dragged something kicking and squealing into the room. Ree stared at the shrieking child in the green moleskin jacket and trousers, and then realized that it was an adult, a little person, either a dwarf or something else entirely. "I thought this had the odor of fairy dust," Alex proclaimed. "Ree, meet . . . Excuse me, but neither the lady nor I know your name." He stood the little man on the bench and stepped back. "Pardon my manners, but you have been deceiving us."

The tiny man glared back at them. He stood no more than two feet tall. His eyes were brown, his skin the color of clover honey, and his hair as black as a crow's wing. He wore a pointed Robin Hood hat with a red feather and red leather boots. At his waist hung a golden sword and a hunter's horn banded in copper. "Sorley," he said. "I am Sorley of the Well."

"And I am Prince Alexandros of Atlantis," Alex replied. "This is the lady Ree O'Connor."

The little man turned his black gaze on her. "An Irishwoman? You should know better than to allow this wicked giant to behave so badly in sanctuary."

"And you? Do you believe your behavior to be without blame? To hide yourself and pretend to be a ghost?"

The little man folded his arms over his chest. "Give me one reason I shouldn't turn you both out into the sea."

"Because the Atlanteans did your race a service, and you are in our debt."

Sorley scowled. "I'm not alone here, you know. One word from me and you'll be surrounded by armed soldiers and thrown to the mercy of those who hunt you."

Alex nodded. "If I've offended you, I offer apology. You have offered us sanctuary, and we appreciate it. But you were spying on us, and that is forbidden, isn't it?"

"I wasn't spying," Sorley said. "Observing. Making certain you weren't breaking rules, and I caught you attempting to destroy property."

"Observing when we sat down to eat, or observing

when we were otherwise engaged?" Ree asked. Sometime in the midst of their last lovemaking session, she'd had the suspicion that they were being watched. "What are you? Some sort of pervert?"

The little man's face turned a deep puce and his features twisted. "For an Irishwoman, you have no more manners than this underwater oaf."

"And for a gentleman, you play hard and fast with the truth," she replied.

"Shall we call a truce?" Alex asked. "We shall both forget the breeches we have committed. We shall take advantage of your hospitality for a few more hours, and you shall promise to refrain from spying on us."

"How do I know you won't do more damage?" Sorley demanded.

"Your earth-scape is a fanciful creation, but I'd prefer to see what's really outside this sphere," Alex said, motioning to the windows.

"I only thought to make the lady's visit more pleasant. She is a human, isn't she?"

"That's a good question," Ree said. "But I agree with Alex. I'd like to see truth beyond this room."

"As you please." The little man removed his hat, smoothed out his feather, and replaced the hat on his head. He turned around three times, spoke softly in a language that Ree couldn't understand, and waved his hand. Instantly, the hills and forests shimmered, the meadows dissolved, and the blue sky and white clouds swirled to a blend of blue-green watercolors. Grass became rock-strewn desert, and grazing deer and winged birds became fish and other sea creatures.

In the distance, Ree could see the shadowy outlines of an underwater volcano with fiery rivers spilling down its sides. Lightning-like flashes of light swept through the depths, illuminating hundreds, perhaps thousands, of jellyfish, and darker silhouettes of ominous shapes moving silently through their midst. To the right, Ree could see a raised ribbon of rock or coral and swimming over it were almost human figures.

She pointed.

"Lemorians," Alex said. "A scouting party."

"Do they know we're here?" she asked.

"Of course not," Sorley scoffed. "This is sanctuary! So long as you remain within, they can't harm you."

"My companion, the warrior that came before us. Do you know if the Lemorians caught her?"

"That one was Lemorian, was she not?" the fairy asked.

"Her name is Anuata," Alex said. "She said you have dolphins that could act as messengers. Could we—"

"The one you speak of left sanctuary. What happened to her later I know not. What do you think I am? Clairvoyant? I'm fairy, not druid. And I have no dolphins to lend you. Your friend sent out two. They haven't come back, and I don't know if they're safe or not. The jellyfish are very thick, and our dolphins are defenseless against their poison."

Alex glanced at Ree. "I'll have to leave you here for a while. It's important that I get word to my friends. We'll need help getting out of here, and the longer we stay, the farther away the Russian is getting."

Ree shook her head. "If you go, I go. You aren't leaving me here."

"I'm afraid I am," Alex said. "Sorley will look after you." He looked at the fairy. "You will protect the lady, won't you?"

"Time in sanctuary is limited."

"But you'll make an exception in this case. Keep her from harm until I return or . . ."

"Or what?" Sorley asked. "Is that a threat?"

"You should be warned," Alex said. "Ree O'Connor is

not what she seems. Look into her eyes and tell me that
you can't see the mark."

Sorley took a step back and studied Ree. "She's not
fairy."

"Not fairy, but she carries the blood of an older race,"
Alex said.

Ree opened her mouth to protest, but then restrained
herself. She'd often wondered what had set her and Nick
and the others who'd been trained with her apart. Why was
she born with abilities that others appeared not to possess?

"I'm serious, Alex," she said. "I'm coming with you. If
you're going after Varenkov, I want to be part of it."

"This isn't your war," Alex said. "You're a civilian."

"That's where you're wrong," she said. "After what
we've been through, you can tell me that? You've just admitted that I have certain talents, talents that might come
in handy."

"Varenkov nearly killed you," Alex said. "You got off
with your life. I won't place you in danger again."

Ree stared at him in astonishment. "You won't put me
in danger? Have you lost your mind? You started this. You
could have left things as they were, but no, you had to interfere. You brought me along. Now, you aren't going to
swim off and leave me here."

"Why shouldn't I?"

"How long have you been after him?"

"What difference does that make?"

She rested her hands on her hips. "Not been too successful so far, have you? Maybe you could use some help."

"And what could you do that could possibly help me in
killing a man like Varenkov?"

Ree turned toward the bed. She steeled herself, concentrated her energy, and stared at the corner of draperies.
In seconds a wisp of smoke began to curl up from the
hem, and an instant later, the curtain burst into flames.

"Whoa!" cried the fairy. "You can't—"

Ree exhaled and curled her fist, willing the flames to contract into a single dancing flame. The fire leapt from the bed curtains, bounced across the floor to land in the bowl of fried shrimp. The stench of burning seafood filled the room. "Can't I?" she said. She clapped her hands and the last vestige of fire extinguished.

Alex clapped his hands together, once, twice, three times, in slow motion. "Admirable," he said mockingly. "Good trick."

"Not a trick," she said.

"Isn't it?" His eyes narrowed. "I know a thing or two about illusion myself," he said. "It takes more than that to hunt down and eliminate a monster." He looked at Sorley. "Keep her here. Keep her safe."

"No!" Ree said.

"I'll come back for you as soon as I find reinforcements. You have my word on it."

"I won't stay here and—" But as she watched, Alex turned and vanished before her eyes.

"Where is he?" she asked. She ran to the spot where he'd disappeared. "How could he . . ."

Sorley doffed his hat and bowed. "As Prince Alexandros said, I will keep you safe until he returns. You need have no fears for your safety."

"Prince? He's no more prince than you are a fairy!" She turned on the little man, but found herself completely alone. "What am I?" she asked. "A prisoner here?"

"No prisoner, but an honored guest," came the booming voice in her head. "And as a guest, you're free to leave at any time. Provided, of course, that you have a plan for avoiding the jellyfish, the Lemorians, and the lava flow. Otherwise, Irishwoman, I'd suggest you cause no more mischief and pray to whatever gods you worship that the Atlantean does keep his word and come back for you."

CHAPTER 10

In the great throne room of Atlantis, many leagues beneath the surface of the North Atlantic, Prince Orion, brother to Poseidon, made his way through the throng of ambassadors and supplicants to the foot of the dais. The queen was the first of the royal party to notice him, and she leaned close to her husband and whispered in his ear.

Poseidon rose and raised a hand for silence. "A matter of state importance demands my attention. Queen Rhiannon will act in my name." Motioning to Orion to follow him, the king left the dais and led the way into a small antechamber. "Have you heard from Alex?" Poseidon asked.

"From Bleddyn. He and Dewi have had contact from an unknown informant, Anuata, a Lemorian who claims that Alex escaped from 'Enakai's prison and is safe in sanctuary under the Old City."

"But our brother is unhurt?"

"So they believe. Dewi and Bleddyn are on their way to meet this Anuata in the caves beneath Ranirao Atoll. That's where Varenkov's yachts last dropped anchor."

"But the Russian isn't there now?" Poseidon asked.

Orion shook his head. "My guess is that Alex either decided not to attempt to take him out there or tried and failed. The boats were gone before Bleddyn and Dewi reached Tahiti."

"Do we know where Varenkov is now?"

"I have reports of a sighting of the yachts several hundred leagues west of Ranirao, but it isn't confirmed. There's a good possibility that Varenkov was taken off by helicopter. In that case, he could be anywhere."

Poseidon ran his fingers through his blond hair. "This isn't the best time for our brother to start making mistakes. We've an oil spill in the North Sea, major cruise ship pollution in the Caribbean, and the slaughter of dolphins by the Danes. Not to mention the ongoing overfishing near the Georgian Banks. Varenkov's factory ships and wholesale netting must be stopped if we have any chance of stopping the decimation of the pilot whale population in the North Atlantic."

"I know we're stretched thin, but—"

His older brother grimaced. "I should be out there helping instead of dealing with bureaucrats and delegations from the Silkie Nation and the Mayan royal family. I'm not cut out to be king, Orion."

"Don't look at me. If you're thinking of abdicating, Alex is your best bet." Orion went to a table and poured himself a measure of wine. "Have you discussed this with Rhiannon? As it stands, Perseus is your heir. Would your wife want to see her son passed over?"

"The crown is heavier than you think. And our son may be as ill-fitted for the throne as I am. Rhiannon never wanted to be queen. We both expected father to live a long time."

"Didn't we all?"

"At least until our children were grown."

"So what do we do about Alex?"

"We wait to hear from Dewi or Bleddyn. Unless you want me to go—"

Poseidon shook his head. "Good try. I can't spare you from the city. I'm sending Paris and twenty men to the

Faroes to try and save as many pilot whales as he can. You'll remain here in charge of the city's security, and Alex will have to finish what we sent him to do."

"Where does that leave the oil spill and the Caribbean mess?"

"Another day, brother. We do what we can. I do what I can. We aren't gods. We're only Atlanteans."

In sanctuary, Ree practiced her martial arts discipline, stared out at the ever-changing ocean beyond the crystal windows, and waited for Alex to return. She wouldn't allow herself to think of what she would do if he didn't come back. That was beyond her control.

She saw no more of her fairy host, but food and drink continued to magically appear, and when she demanded reading material, that too was provided. Unfortunately, the scrolls and tablets were all written in languages that she couldn't understand. As for the maps, or what she supposed passed as maps, they were drawn of the seafloors, and she was unable to find any point of reference. Volcanoes, mountain ranges, deep canyons, and coral reefs had been sketched onto paper-like material. The drawings were beautifully done, but gave her no indication of the area, or how large an area the maps covered.

Never had Ree been out of contact with her handlers for so long a period since she'd been sent on her first assignment. She had no way to communicate with her superiors, and if she did, what would she say? They would be more than likely to think that she'd had a mental breakdown than to accept what she'd come to accept as reality.

She had died or experienced a near-death situation. She'd been rescued or kidnapped—depending on your point of view—by an Atlantean who claimed to be a prince. And now, she was being held against her will in an underwater sphere by a fairy with a bad attitude.

None of the above sounded plausible, yet it was all true. Had she made contact with her handlers, she would have refrained from mentioning the fantastic sex she'd shared with the said alien prince. Her personal recreation was nobody else's business. That said, she'd enjoyed every moment of the encounter and hoped to repeat the process as soon as possible. That was, if she didn't kill him first for abandoning her, leaving her—so to speak—like a bird in a gilded cage.

Varenkov could be in Moscow by now. Or Paris or New York, even Singapore. Wherever he was, he was up to no good, and had she completed her mission, his criminal career would have been over and drugs flooding Ireland and Scotland from the former Eastern Block countries would be reduced by thirty percent. But, despite months of preparation, she'd failed thus far to eliminate Varenkov. Headquarters would not be pleased with her. She'd worked too long to reach the top of her field to allow another agent to take down her target. The alternative was unacceptable.

Assassins who lost their edge were pulled out of the field, supposedly reassigned to teaching positions or desk jobs. Oddly, she'd met few of them, and she suspected that a peaceful retirement wasn't in the works. At the top of her game, she could pretty much live as she pleased, enjoy the finest food and scenery she wished, take vacations anywhere in the world, and indulge herself in petty pleasures such as investigating the inner workings of the British Secret Services and their actions in Northern Ireland during a particular ten-year period.

She hadn't committed herself to a plan of personal vengeance where her parents' deaths were concerned, but the idea had crossed her mind. Meanwhile, her search was an excellent mental exercise, much as playing competitive chess might be. She'd found and followed dozens of leads, including two solid possible hitters, both of whom had sadly already passed to a greater reward in whatever waited beyond the limits of this world.

She'd never considered herself a vigilante. The people she'd killed had been deserving of death, and she hadn't made the decision. She had faith in the organization's decisions. They were not made lightly. No innocent people were targeted, and none were selected who weren't personally responsible for the deaths of multiple victims. More than ten was the rule. Ree took no pleasure in eliminating these bad guys or in her own ability. It was what she did, what she was trained to do; it was her purpose for being. But if she ever learned who had ordered her father's death or who had lit the match that had ended her parents' lives, she was certain that she might take some satisfaction in righting a wrong long overdue.

One thing was blatantly obvious as Ree filled her hours with repeated physical exercise. Not only had she completely recovered from her injuries, but she was stronger, faster, and less fatigued than she'd ever been in her adult life. Alex had said that she was no longer entirely human, that she was now some sort of Atlantean hybrid. It seemed that there might be some truth in that, and if he'd been right about that . . .

She wiped the sweat off her forehead with the back of her hand. She'd spent a lifetime perfecting her body and mind to be the perfect weapon. And if she was some sort of bionic woman now, Varenkov didn't stand a chance.

Caddoc cringed as his mother threw him a withering stare. He should have known better than to answer her summons. When had catering to her whims ever been to his advantage? Even looking at her as she was now sickened him. Better she had died than have her beauty turned to that of a wizened crone.

Why hadn't he had the nerve to advise 'Enakai to refuse her admittance to Lemoria? It would have been kinder to give her a merciful death after she'd fled from Melqart's ruin. No, he'd had to admit that she was his mother and beg for 'Enakai to provide for her in the manner to which she was accustomed.

When his father had been alive, Halimeda had been a queen and a favorite of Poseidon, wealthy and powerful, widely acknowledged as the fairest woman in Atlantis. Now, her body bent and twisted and her once beautiful face a macabre mask, she was nothing but a thorn in his side. Yet, he could not free himself of her, and her words still had the power to wound him.

"What do you mean that your brother murdered your bodyguard and escaped?" she demanded. "Your Samoan was supposed to kill him, not the other way around. Are you so dim-witted that you can't carry out a simple order?"

"Have you forgotten, old woman? You no longer give orders to me or to anyone but three-fingered servants."

"No? You think not, you cowardly half-wit? It wasn't I who allowed Alexandros to escape. And it's hardly my fault that he killed your pitiful excuse for a bodyguard."

"Tora was a mighty warrior. If Alexandros bested him, it must have been through trickery."

"By Zeus's balls, have I taught you nothing? Trickery is the name of the game. Your brother was unarmed, locked in a tiny cell of rock. All you had to do was open the door and cut off his head. Would that have been so difficult?"

"I sent Tora because I was otherwise occupied," Caddoc retorted.

"Swiving 'Enakai. And not well, or you would be richer than you were when last I saw you. If you possessed the talented prick of your late father, 'Enakai would have given you an army by now and you might have reclaimed your throne from your bastard brother."

"Morgan is no bastard. Well"—Caddoc admitted— "he may be a bastard, but he's my father's lawful son."

"He's the son of that bitch Korinna, not my son. And he's younger than you. You should have been crowned the next Poseidon."

"Perhaps I would have been, had you succeeded in poisoning my father. But you couldn't get that right, could you, mother?"

With a shriek, she threw back the sheets and rose from the bed, leaving a naked guardsman cringing and trying to cover his private parts. Caddoc turned away in disgust. His mother's body was not one that a man could look upon without heaving. Her flesh had peeled away in strips, and her once shapely breasts and hips were little more than sacks and bony sticks. Open sores ran and dripped yellow mucus, and raw red eruptions threatened to burst and spray the room with noxious odors.

Not that he had ever particularly enjoyed viewing her naked body, regardless of the pleasure she might have taken in being viewed. He suffered the curse of being her only son, taking suck longer than was decent, and having far too much of her attention in the years since his birth. He had long come to accept that she was utterly without morals, but just once he would like to come into her presence without being belittled and made to feel inadequate.

"Get out!" Halimeda ordered her bedmate. "And next time I come for you, bring two companions. You aren't man enough for me."

The poor fool bowed low, snatched up his garment from the floor and fled the room.

"Well?" Halimeda hissed. "What are you staring at? Did you want to use him yourself before I sent him on his way?" She moved to a table and draped herself in a length

of cloth. "Surely you aren't such an innocent that you believe your mother past the age of passion?"

"No," he answered curtly. Strips of seaweed framed the
bed . . . strong, pale green lengths of foliage. Caddoc could
feel the texture of it between his fingers, imagine what it
would feel like to loop a section of it around his mother's
throat and pull it tight. He could almost see her eyes bulge
and her tongue protrude as the noose severed her throat.

He could do it. Once she had held the power of the
black arts, but with Melqart's diminished strength, his
mother's had become puny. Once, she could freeze him
with a glance, cause him to choke on unclean objects,
drive his mind to the point of madness.

"How weak are you, Mother?" he asked softly.

"Try me and see, my darling."

She smiled at him, and the hideous gap in her lips, the
shattered teeth, and her blackened tongue brought a clot
of thick bile rising in his throat. He was afraid of her. He'd
always been afraid of her. Yet, in some perverted way, he
loved her. And in some small, almost invisible part of his
mind, he admired her. Men scoffed at him. No matter
what his mother said, he was no fool. Not a great warrior
or legendary prince, but no fool either. He knew that he
was the butt of jokes. And no one suffered more from his
failures than he did. But for all his weaknesses, he was persistent. Sometimes, the ability to carry through without
giving up was enough. Sooner or later, his luck would
change.

"I will be high king of Atlantis, Mother," he said. "With
your help or without it, I will be anointed Poseidon. If I
have to kill one brother or dozens, it doesn't matter. I will
succeed. The question is, do you want to rule at my side
or not?"

"What a foolish question. Why would you ask such a
thing of me? Haven't I always had your best interests at

heart? Haven't I sacrificed everything for you, my only son?"

"And do you love me, Mother, truly?" He moved closer to the bed-hangings. How long, he wondered, would it take to strangle her? Would anyone hear her screams and come? And if they did, would anyone care?

"Of course, I do, my precious. Who else would I love?"

"Yourself. You've always come first."

Halimeda shook her head. "What a thing to say. You have the oddest way of putting things, Caddoc." She tottered forward and kissed his cheek. Her caress was cold and slimy; it made his skin crawl. "You always were somewhat . . . peculiar," she continued. "But I loved you all the same, my beautiful boy. You are my hope for the future."

"For me or for you?"

"For us both," she pronounced. "You need me. Never forget that. I have the brains you lack, and without me, what would you be? One more prince in a household of Poseidon's offspring. People would hardly remember your name."

He shoved her away, and then wiped his hands on his tunic. She felt sticky, and her odor . . . Really, there must be something the healers could do about the stench of rotting eels that lingered around her.

"So what will you do now?" she urged. "Find Alexandros and kill him."

"Good." She smiled that memorable grin. "And what will you do with Morgan and Orion?"

"Kill them. Kill them all."

"So you shall, my precious. And 'Enakai will help you. Her armies will give you the power you need to accomplish your destiny."

"To become Poseidon." The thought eased the tension in his shoulders and arms. He could no longer feel the seaweed between his fingers or imagine how black her face would become in the seconds before her death. "And if I do, will I be good enough then, Mother? Will you be proud of me?"

"And why wouldn't I?" she agreed. "Who wouldn't be proud of the greatest king to ever sit the throne of Atlantis? When you come to your own, when you are Poseidon, I will love you as no son has ever been loved by his mother."

"Promise?"

"I swear it to you, my darling. On my life."

CHAPTER 11

In the cave labyrinth that snaked beneath the Ranirao Atoll and the island of Tahiti, Alexandros' men, Dewi and Bleddyn, faced the gold-skinned Lemorian warrior-woman with drawn weapons. "Give me one reason why we should trust a member of 'Enakai's royal guard," Dewi said. "If you helped Prince Alexandros to escape as you claim, why isn't he with you?"

This purple-scalp-locked shrew had been waiting for them in a dark passage and now confronted them with a naked sword in one hand and killing spear in another, eyes glittering shark-like through a black tattooed mask. "If I intended to do you harm, I could have killed you when you entered the cave," she replied in only slightly accented Atlantean. "For a small man, you move clumsily."

Dewi's upper lip drew taut. "Small? You call me small?" His hackles rose and his knuckles whitened as he tightened his grip on his trident and glared into her eyes. How dare she insult him? Dewi of the Red Hands? Hero of the Wall where Prince Alexandros' father fell to Melqart's hordes? Winner of the coveted Silver Trident for bravery?

He looked at Bleddyn for support, but his partner only grimaced. "She does top you by two inches, maybe three."

"And you're both blind," Dewi flung back. "It's you, not I who is misshapen, woman! I am exactly the right height and breadth for a warrior." He glared at her. Whoever saw a female with tattooed breasts and as many battle scars as he had?

She shrugged in disdain. "You are not only lacking in height, but somewhat narrow in the shoulders. Atlantean or not, I doubt you could lift a half-grown sea lion in a stiff wind."

Dewi choked back the curse that rose in his throat. He'd not give this Lemorian slut the satisfaction of trading insults. He was within a hand's height of his prince and powerful enough to carry a wounded comrade to safety in a tidal wave. How dare she question his physique or his strength?

This battle-scarred harpy wasn't what he'd expected when they'd received a message concerning Alex's whereabouts. Dewi had served his prince long enough to know Alexandros' effect on females, and he'd assumed that this Anuata was another of his sexual conquests. It wasn't difficult to believe that another lovesick wench was willing to commit treason to save the life of her golden-haired lover. He hadn't been expecting to face naked blades in the darkness or a tattooed Amazon who appeared as formidable as her well-honed weapons.

Anuata tugged a gold arm ring from her bulging upper bicep and tossed it to Bleddyn with haughty nonchalance. "There is your master's token, Atlantean, to prove I come in his name."

"It's Alex's," his partner confirmed.

"I don't lie," Anuata said. "I have no need to."

Dewi's hand ached to plunge his trident through the arrogant barbarian's heart. "It proves nothing," he said, meeting her stare eye to eye. "How do we know you didn't ambush our prince, murder him, and strip his band from his dead body?"

"Enough," Bleddyn lowered his weapon. "She's right. She could have taken your head off as we rounded that corner. And the two of us are hardly worth the bother of the Lemorians setting up a trap to catch. It's not as if we're wealthy noblemen or generals."

"So where is he?" Dewi asked, reluctantly lowering his guard.

"Still in sanctuary. Safe enough for the moment, but time there is limited. He cannot remain there, and when he leaves, the high priestess' forces will do their best to take him."

"But you could pass through their lines?" Dewi was dubious. This Anuata still had to earn his trust. "It seems far-fetched."

She sighed. "Your head is as full of coral as your stance is weak, it seems. Prince Alexandros isn't alone. There's a female in his company."

"There's always a woman." Bleddyn chuckled. "So, it's the woman he can't get out. Is she Lemorian as well?"

"Not exactly. More human."

"Human?" Bleddyn grinned like a tiger shark. "By Apollo's golden crotch, that I'd live to see the day! Not normally a fan of humans, our prince."

"Well, he is now," Anuata said. "This one, at least. He believes himself in some sort of debt to her." She rested the butt of her throwing spear on the cave floor but kept her sword unsheathed. "I tried to talk sense into him, but he'd have none of it. We could both have been safe away if he hadn't insisted on going back after her."

"Going back where?" Dewi asked. This woman's tale was stranger and stranger. So far as he knew, Alex had taken his pleasure with every species from fairy to mermaid, but he never so much as looked at a human female. His hatred of their kind ran too deep.

"It's a long story," the Lemorian said. "Best told by your prince. And mine," she added. "He's taken me into his service."

Dewi swore an imaginative oath. "I'll not credit that until I hear it from Alex's own lips."

The woman glanced at Bleddyn. "Not too bright, is he? I wonder that Alexandros would have such as him as bodyguard. I know you lost many soldiers in the war against Melqart's horde, but your ranks must be thinner than we'd heard."

"I have been with Alex longer than you've been alive!" Dewi protested. "And I'll be with him when you're only a bad memory."

Anuata drew herself to her full height and confronted him, eye to eye. "Talk is cheap, little man. I've yet to see the strength in your sword arm or your courage in battle." She rolled her eyes and let her gaze travel down his body to linger on his groin. "Not to mention that I doubt you've much to boast of where it counts."

"Enough, you two!" Bleddyn swam between them and raised his hands. "I don't doubt we'll have more than enough to face out there without fighting between ourselves." He turned his attention to Anuata. "Lead us to this sanctuary the quickest way, but I warn you, if you betray us by word or deed, I'll part your head from your body and use that scalp-lock as a belt."

Alex crept soundlessly to the bed and looked down at Ree. She seemed to be sound asleep, her red-gold hair spread across the pillow, one arm thrown carelessly over her head, and the coverlet drawn to her waist. Again, he felt that same unfamiliar sensation as he took in her exotic beauty and her fragile vulnerability.

He'd supposed that once he'd bedded her, the powerful attraction that she held over him would fade. Instead, he found he wanted her more than ever, and not just for the pleasure he knew he'd find between those sweet, soft thighs, but something more . . . something elusive that troubled him. His throat tightened. How was it that he found her so enticing? She was built much as any other woman: breasts, waist, hips, and legs that seemed to go on and on. What made her so different, and why was she the spark to his flame?

He'd always been a man for women exclusively. Not all men were. Bleddyn, as staunch a fighter and as good a friend as any could ask for, found his sexual satisfaction in other males. Once, when they drank more than was good for him, Alex had asked if he'd ever taken his ease with a woman, and Bleddyn admitted that he had. But he'd found the experience less than he'd hoped for. Alex's half brother Caddoc, in contrast, boasted of happily futtering either sex, alone or in group situations. To each his own, Alex supposed. So long as no one was hurt, who was he to judge another man's intimate pleasures?

But never had he thought that he would be stirred to passion by a human female. There were rumors, of course. Legend said that Atlantean men were drawn to the intense sensuality of such women. But such unions were forbidden by law and custom, and any who failed to heed those admonishments were severely punished.

His own brother Morgan, now Poseidon, high king of Atlantis, had taken a bride that had been born only half-Atlantean. Alex's twin, Orion, had so forgotten himself that he'd wooed and won a human woman who was now his wife. But both these women had gone through the transformation that made them true Atlanteans. And as much as Alex cared for them as sisters and as family, he'd never understood how such a thing was possible. Until now . . .

Ree's breathing was even, and she hadn't stirred since he'd entered the chamber. Her lips were slightly parted, and her naked breasts rose and fell with each breath. His gaze was drawn to those pink and shapely mounds and to the shell-like buds. His groin tightened, and desire swept over him as he imagined drawing those hard nipples between his lips and suckling until she cried out with desire. He wanted to throw himself on her, to pin her hands against the mattress, to part her thighs and bury his throbbing erection deep in her moist folds.

Standing here, drinking in her beauty, filled him with exquisite torture. He could smell her skin, imagine the slightly salty taste of her mouth, and feel the heat rising from her unclad body. When he'd entered the chamber, he'd been hungry and weary. He'd wanted nothing more than to fill his stomach and rest his aching muscles with a few hours sleep . . . but not now . . . Now, a different kind of hunger seized him.

His gaze moved up over the rise of her breasts to the delicate throat with its soft and sweet-smelling hollows. One pink ear was exposed, the other hidden by a cascade of curls. A golden starfish earring dangled from a creamy earlobe. He wanted to lick that ear, to nibble it, to whisper suggestions that would surely turn her rosy cheeks a deeper hue of pink.

Carefully, he studied her face, taking in the high cheekbones, the fair and flawless complexion, and the thick, dark lashes that framed her large, oval eyes. Her nose was small, perfectly shaped, with a hint of a saucy tilt, and a dusting of gold freckles across the surface.

As hauntingly beautiful as a mermaid, he thought. Human, yes, but not quite human. He tried to remember her as she was when he first laid eyes on her, but the moments on the deck of the *Anastasiya* had been confused and fleeting—not to mention the darkness. When he'd carried Ree away under the sea, she'd been dying, blood-soaked and struggling for breath. And in the caves . . . No, he'd not remember her as she was then. That was the past. This

Ree, the one he admired now, was a different woman, not human, not Atlantean or Lemorian, but a fascinating combination of the three.

He wanted her. He wanted her now. He wanted to clasp his hands around her waist, to run his fingers over her hips and lift her hard against him. He wanted to feel her body arch to fit his own and to hear her sobs of ecstasy as he drove his length deep inside her.

Overwhelming heat swept over him, and he bent and clasped a hand over her mouth. "Ree," he whispered.

One second, he was leaning over her, his lips only inches from her own, and the next, she had seized his hand, twisted out from under him and sat astride him. Her forearm came down across his throat, and a knee threatened to turn his rich baritone to a permanent tenor.

"Ree! It's Alex!" he managed just before she whipped a sharply-honed eating knife from under the pillow and threatened to sever his carotid artery. "Have you lost your mind?" he shouted as he delivered a blow to her wrist hard enough to numb muscle and nerves and send the knife spinning across the room. He wrapped his legs around hers and flipped her onto her back, then pinned her right hand over her head.

As he attempted to capture the left, she drove the flat of her hand into his neck just below his ear. The blow nearly knocked him senseless, but he recovered enough to block a second attack and lock his fingers around her wrist. Breaking bones would have been simpler, but he held back, not wanting to injure her.

"Ree!" he cried. "Stop! It's me!" Somehow in the encounter, she'd sunk her teeth into his hand so that beads of blood welled up, crimson against his bluish scales. Vaguely, he was aware of a stinging pain, but the sensation only fueled his fervor.

Panting, she stared up at him, and gradually, the fierce light in her eyes banked to smoldering embers. "Never, never do that again!"

"No? And what if I do this?" He lowered his head and ground his mouth savagely against hers. Her body was soft and open beneath his. His sex swelled and throbbed with the ache of needing her, but she wasn't ready. He had to wait . . . had to have her willing.

She turned her face away. "Where the hell have you been?"

"Trying to get us out of here." He nuzzled the warm hollow beneath her ear. "Trying to save your neck." The scent of her was maddening. She parted her thighs but when he tried to settle his body between them, she slammed a knee up again to block his entry.

"You took your sweet time about it, you bastard!"

"Such sweet words for a lover."

"You blue son-of-a-bitch! I'll give you sweet words!"

Shuddering with controlled desire, he kissed his way back across her cheek to her mouth, pressed his lips against hers, and didn't flinch when she caught his lip between her teeth and bit him. Hard. He tasted the salt-sweet flavor of his own blood, and felt the tide of lust catch him in its undertow and drag him down.

Seizing her shoulders, he twisted her and pressed her facedown against the mattress. She struggled, kicking and elbowing him, but his greater weight made the difference, and he held her captive as he stripped away his armor and tunic, tossing them aside.

"I'll kill you," she threatened. "You'll not rape—"

"Never." Not rape. No force beneath the sea or sky could turn him to such villainy. He had other methods of persuasion. Before he was done making love to her, she'd beg him for intercourse.

She wouldn't lay still, and the feel of her body against

his drove him to the edge, so it was all he could do to keep a check on his own carnal desire. She cursed and thrashed, but he persevered until he was as naked as she was. "Shh, shh," he rasped, using the same tone he'd once used to gentle a giant unbroken sea horse. "Let me love you, Ree."

He pushed the weight of her hair off the nape of her neck and pressed damp kisses against her hot skin. He settled his groin over her sweet buttocks and took pleasure in the gasp that escaped her lips. He was rock hard and full to bursting. He released her wrist and ran his fingers down her back, skimming her small waist and lingering on the taut curves of her bottom. "Shh, shh," he crooned, and he stroked and caressed her body, and all the while, he kept kissing and licking her neck and back and shoulders, caressing the length of her spine and the first swelling of her buttocks.

"Sweet Ree," he murmured as he released her other wrist. She twisted under him as he knew she would, and he lifted his weight onto one elbow to let her. Which brought his seeking mouth level with a heaving breast and a hard, sweet nipple . . .

She cursed him again, but when he used his tongue to moisten that swollen bud, her breathing quickened, and he felt her tremble. And when he pinched her nipple between his lips and then suckled it, she cried out.

"Damn you, Alex! Damn you!"

Her fists, which had been pounding his head and shoulders unclenched, and she fell back, groaning as he licked and nibbled and teased first one nipple and then the other. His fingers slid lower, claiming her belly and the nest of red curls that guarded his greatest desire.

"You want me," he said. "Admit it. Tell me what you want."

She moaned and tilted her hips to meet his hands, gasping as he slipped two fingers into her wet folds, touching the silken softness, feeling the clench of her inner muscles against his probing. He let his mouth follow the path his hands had taken, kissing the hollow between her breasts, her stomach, and burying his face in those sweet nether locks.

But when he would have kissed and suckled her cleft, she wiggled out of his grasp. No longer cursing him, she rose onto her knees and pushed him back against the heaped cushions. Their gazes met; he saw that she no longer considered him her enemy, and he allowed her to do with him as she would.

Her revenge was bittersweet.

She began at his mouth, kissing him, nipping with tiny love bites, licking and kissing, moving slowly down his body as he had done hers. He felt her sharp, white teeth on his shoulders, felt them close on his nipples before she drew them between her lips and suckled until he thought that he would explode with need for her before she ever reached his phallus.

"Lie still!" she commanded. "It's my turn."

How strange and wonderful it was to feel Alex's barely controlled power beneath her, and how the anticipation of what was to come fired her own lust. Suckling at his nipples, laving the hard muscles of his chest, and caressing the silken sinews of his shoulders made her giddy with need. When she looked up and his gaze met hers, the intensity in his beautiful sea-green eyes shook her to her core. She knew she'd never known this degree of arousal. She wanted him now, wanted him hard and deep, wanted him plunging into her, filling her with his hot flesh and unleashed passion.

But, not yet . . . not yet. Not until Alex suffered as she had suffered from his torture. She would have her revenge . . . sweet revenge. She would make him pay for what she had endured, if it killed her.

She kissed her way down over his hard, muscle-ridged stomach and iron thighs until she was between his knees. He was shaking now, his fingers twisted in her hair.

"Ree . . . Ree . . ."

So big . . . he was so big. She took him between her hands, and he groaned with pleasure. Gently, she cupped the weight of his sacks and cradled his sex, stroking the length, caressing and teasing him.

"By Ares' seed, have you no pity?"

She pressed her lips against the silken column. Strange how a man could be so hard . . . as hard as ivory but the skin sheathing it soft and pliant as satin. Hot . . . he was as hot as fire.

She leaned close and tasted that satin skin.

Alex groaned and shuddered.

She drew her tongue around the base, and then slowly began to explore the length and breadth of this wonder.

"Woman! Am I made of stone?"

Laughing, she drew him into her mouth and suckled, gently at first and then with more strength. Strange how her mouth on his organ could make her own cleft contract and her nipples tingle. Strange how the flames leapt from his sex to her own.

She moistened her fingers with her tongue and continued to stroke and massage his tumescent phallus, kissing and licking, suckling until she tasted the first sweet milk of his ardor.

"Ree!" he cried out.

He tried to rise, but she placed her hands on his chest and pushed him back. "Wait," she said. "Wait just a—"

"I've had my fill of waiting!" he roared and seized her shoulders.

She laughed as he slammed her back against the cushions. "Are you truly a prince?" she dared. "If you are, show me."

CHAPTER 12

Alex sheathed himself in her soft, willing body, withdrew and plunged again. He reveled in the wet feel of her, felt himself whipped to a fiery heat by her urging cries. She locked her legs around him, clasping him to her, and welcomed his powerful thrusts. He could feel the thunder of her heart, the quick, hard gasps of her breathing. Most of all, he was aware of her sweet sex contracting around his shaft and the raw scent of aroused woman filling his nostrils.

How long they rode the crest of the rogue wave, he didn't know, but they were teeth and nail and raw primitive lust . . . sweat-soaked bodies clinging to each other, wild to find release, until at last Ree screamed with pleasure and he felt the racking shudders of her climax that sent him careening out of control and over the edge.

Somehow, when he regained his senses, Ree was still locked in his arms, and they found themselves laughing and kissing and whispering lovers' nonsense in a dozen languages..

"Am I still a bastard?" he asked as he kissed the tears from her cheeks.

"Yes. You are." She found his mouth and kissed him, savoring the salt-sweet taste of his mouth and the sensation of his tongue against hers. "You left me, and I didn't know if you were coming back."

"I told you I would."

"But I didn't know if I could believe you. What the hell would I have done here alone? I don't know how to get out—to get back to the surface . . . to get to land. Hell, I don't know if I can even exist on land anymore or if you've turned me into a guppy."

He kissed her again, long and hard, sending her thoughts spinning. "I don't know either," he admitted when the caress finally broke. "No one does, I suppose. You're one of a kind."

"A hybrid freak." She snuggled against him, unwilling to let the wave of pleasure go, stroking his wide chest and the swelling muscles of his massive upper arms.

"Or maybe a new species. Superior to all others."

He ran a broad palm possessively over her bare buttocks, and his touch brought instant response. Ree felt herself softening toward him. Bright wires of sensation tightened in the pit of her stomach and moist heat flowered between her thighs. If he didn't take his hands off her, they wouldn't be talking; they'd be into no-holds-barred sex again.

"Nothing you do could surprise me," Alex said. "Where did you learn those moves?"

She gave a small sound of amusement. "Are we discussing coitus or—"

"I was thinking of your combative skills. I outweigh you by half, yet you nearly made me a eunuch."

"Oh, that." She chuckled. "Never sneak up on me. And, besides . . . you deserved it. You shouldn't have left me." She rolled away from him and looked into his eyes.

Big mistake. Looking into Alex's eyes was like falling into a pool of hot chocolate. You knew you were drowning, but who the hell cared. She reached down and pinched a section of skin on her leg hard enough to clear her mind. "I take it you didn't find a way out."

"I did, but don't change the subject." A slow smile brought a dimple to his cheek.

Oh, shit, she thought. *He doesn't play fair.* He could turn the charm on like a floodlight whenever he pleased, and knowing that he was doing it deliberately didn't minimize the effect.

"Where did you learn to fight like that?" Alex persisted. "Not in cooking school."

He caught her chin between his fingers and tilted her face up. He leaned close and brushed her mouth with his, leaving her trembling and wanting more.

"Who and what are you, Ree O'Connor?"

"Just a woman who doesn't like to be bullied by a man." She seized a lock of his golden hair and gave it a sharp yank.

"Ouch," he protested.

"You deserved it."

Alex's voice deepened. "And have I been bullying you?"

"You have."

"Then I apologize. It isn't our way."

His eyes flooded with moisture, hypnotizing, making her think of swirling tides and deep currents, bringing her dangerously close to wanting to know more about him. And that would be breaking a rule that she'd vowed never to do again. Caring for a man or becoming personally attached to anyone opened the door to a personal hell. She wasn't in a line of work that encouraged bonds with other humans. People weren't reliable. They died or they left you. . . . And then there was nothing but lonely nights and tears.

Alex's voice dragged her back to the moment.

"Atlantean women have always been considered equal."

She gave him a dubious look. "In all things?"

"In everything but the throne. Poseidon, our high king, has always been male."

Her eyes narrowed. "So not quite equal."

"No male can give birth to a child. Does that seem equal? Both male and female are equally important."

"Are you really a prince?"

He sighed. "Guilty as charged." His mouth curved into the hint of a smile.

"Son of the king of Atlantis?"

Alex shook his head. "My brother is Poseidon."

"So I don't have to worry that you'll suddenly announce yourself Lord of the Sea?"

His beautiful eyes clouded. "I told you what I am, a soldier, an assassin. I've no wish to inherit my brother's crown."

"But you could?"

"Not unless Poseidon, his infant son, and my twin brother Orion should all die suddenly or abdicate."

She pushed up on one elbow. "You're serious, aren't you? You are a prince?" Maybe he was telling the truth. There was something regal about him, and she'd never met a man with more self-confidence.

"I told you I was, didn't I?" He sat up. "As pleasant as this is, and as much as I might want to share pleasures of the flesh with you again, I'm afraid our time here grows short." He rose and found his tunic where he'd tossed it.

"So you did find a way out?"

"After a fashion."

"With the help of your friends?"

He shook his head. "No. I've had no contact. I hope that Anuata wasn't waylaid by the Lemorian scouts."

"And that she didn't betray you?" Ree gathered her hair and began to braid it into a single thick plait, all the while watching him from the corner of her eye.

Just watching him dress was enough to make her remember the pleasure of Alex's touch. Hard muscle flexed and rippled gracefully beneath his skin. How could any man be so beautifully put together and still move with all the ease of a leopard? She'd always been fond of big cats: tigers, mountain lions, panthers, but she'd long given up going to zoos to see them. There was something so wrong about caging an animal that wild and magnificent.

They'd made quite a night of it, with both imagination and great vigor. What had they done? She couldn't resist a smile. What hadn't they done? And when could they repeat the experience? Whatever doubts she had about Alex and his background, she could honestly say that she'd never been so well laid.

"Anuata wouldn't betray me," Alex said. "She'd die first. Anuata lives by the warrior's code."

"But she isn't one of you. She's Lemorian."

"I had an occasion to do her a good turn. I saved her life, and by her code, that life belongs to me now. It's not a debt that can be released, and to refuse her service would be an insult that could be settled only by blood."

Ree slid her legs off the bed, found a ribbon, and secured her braid before reaching for her own garment. "Lovely. Sounds quite archaic to me."

"We are an ancient race, and we have our own customs—customs that have served us well through the eons." He strapped on his cuirass. "Wait, don't dress yet," he said, and then called out loudly. "Sorley? Sorley, my host, we have need of you!"

"What is it?" the fairy replied. Ree couldn't see him, but his voice sounded as if it were coming from beneath the stone tiles under her feet. "What more could you want? You haven't much longer, you know."

"We require boy's clothing and armor for the lady. And the return of my weapons. Give us what we need, and we'll trouble you no more." Alex winked at Ree and motioned toward the fireplace. She glanced down at the floor, but Alex shook his head. *Illusion,* he mouthed silently.

"Your weapons you may have," Sorley cried. "But where would I get Atlantean armor to fit a woman?"

"Bring us armor from the Old City, then," Alex said. "And a spear for the lady—a small one with a sharp point."

"And a knife," Ree suggested. "Or a sword."

Alex raised a brow quizzically.

"I took fencing lessons in college," she lied. "I know how to protect myself."

"Odder and odder," Alex remarked. "You heard Lady O'Connor," he said to the fairy. "A short sword and a dagger. One of your finest." He laced up his sandal and knotted it firmly at his calf. "One more thing."

"It's always one more thing with you," Sorley whined. "What else? An army at your beck and call? A gilded chariot pulled by dolphins?"

"A guide. We'll need a guide through the Old City catacombs."

The fairy retorted with a blast of harsh words, none of which Ree understood, but didn't think she needed them translated.

"Impossible!"

"If you want us gone from here, we'll need a guide."

"And where will I find one? Do you expect me to conjure one out of seawater? I should cast you out and let the Lemorians have you!" Sorley cried. "You've taken advantage of our hospitality."

"There is a debt," Alex reminded him.

"A debt, a debt! You abuse our rules. Never again will I open the portal for one of your kind."

"Oh, but you will," Alex replied smoothly. "And you will produce a guide."

"I'll put no fairy blood in danger for an Atlantean."

"I didn't ask for a guard, only someone who knows the secret passageways."

"A pox on you and all your house!" Sorley shouted.

"Careful," Alex warned with a grin at Ree. "The Lady Ree O'Connor is a powerful sorceress in her own right. She could well send your curse crashing back around your long ears."

An hour later, Ree found herself following Alex and a fairy named Hafoka through a series of tunnels and caves. Unlike Sorley, Hafoka seemed a pleasant enough fellow. He offered no insults and rarely spoke at all. She'd given up being surprised at the appearance of new beings in Alex's undersea world, but this sprite was clearly of a different species than the grumpy host of sanctuary.

Hafoka's skin was blue-black, his eyes a brilliant blue, and his short-cropped hair wiry and of reddish hue. He wore only a tapa-cloth wrap covering his loins and a band of sharkskin around his forehead. Hafoka carried no weapon other than a tiny knife at his waist and wore no decoration other than the chain of silver turtles tattooed on his chest and an ivory armband. His feet were bare, high arched, and dainty; his eyes were large and mischievous, and his lashes as long and thick as a girl's. As charming as Hafoka was, Ree would have had more faith in him if his smile didn't remind her of a used-car salesman's.

The fairy had led them into the catacombs through a hole beneath what appeared to be a tiered pyramid, after passing through a massive courtyard with fallen statuary and columns. Startlingly out of place in this ancient plaza was the hulk of a twentieth-century warship lying on its side, ghostly decks bare of whatever unlucky crew had followed it to the bottom. Strange fish and elongated squid swam in and out of the ragged hole in the ship's hull, and silt and volcanic ash had softened the sharp corners and draped the silent guns in gray shrouds.

"We must be deeper than light penetrates from the surface," Ree had observed. "How is it that I can still see clearly?" She would have liked to have had time to explore the ruins.

Obviously, a highly sophisticated society had laid out these wide avenues and constructed the enormous public buildings. Alex had explained that this city had been built thousands of years ago on a fertile island, an island that had been destroyed by earthquake and tidal wave long before the Egyptian pharaohs had raised the first pyramid.

The architecture was vaguely Asian, reminding Ree of an abandoned temple complex she'd once toured in the deepest jungles of Cambodia. Not even time could conceal the magnificent carvings and graceful arches . . . or the sense that ordinary men and women had once walked these streets, children had laughed and played here, and young lovers had sought each other in the crowds and shared dreams of a future together.

"An anomaly of the Old City," Alex had answered. "It's one of the reasons the Lemorians believe the ruins to be haunted. The stones produce their own light, as do the bones."

"Bones?"

"You'll see soon enough."

And she did. They'd not descended far into the first tunnel before she began to see chambers and passageways opening off on either side. Wedged into the walls were stacks of bones, skulls, and whole skeletons. And as Alex had warned her, the bones did glow, not with a white light, but an eerie blue. She wasn't easily frightened, but the caverns gave her the creeps. Swimming seemed to require more energy than normal, and she felt as though her legs and arms were made of lead.

At some point, the cheerful Hafoka had acquired a luminescent eel that he wrapped around his right wrist, up along his arm, across his shoulders, and down the other arm to his left wrist. The sinuous creature had an oversized head and prominent fangs, features that insured that Ree kept her distance. Yet, as they traveled deeper and deeper into the catacombs, the light source did make Hafoka easy to follow.

"Where do we go when we reach the other end?" Ree asked Alex. "Provided there is an end."

He glanced toward Hafoka and shook his head, clearly not willing to share his plans with the fairy. Obviously, Alex trusted the small man no more than she did.

The corridor grew narrower, and sometimes, where the roof had caved in or a flow of now-hardened lava had invaded the passageway, they had to crawl through low spaces between roof and fallen stone. Here, in these smaller places, bones were stacked from floor to ceiling. Strange outcrops of shellfish grew on the piles of human remains, and their twisted shells opened and closed, revealing whiskered orange and purple mollusks.

Jellyfish floated and drifted through the catacombs. Most were nearly transparent with black stripes, but some shimmered with all the colors of the rainbow. Thankfully, Ree noted that these were smaller than the tribe of jellies that had menaced them before they'd taken refuge in the sanctuary. None were larger than a dinner plate, and many were smaller than the palm of her hand.

"Take care that you don't brush against them," Alex cautioned. "These are poisonous as well. A sting might not kill you, but it will make you so sick that you might wish it had."

"Advice noted," she replied.

She found herself keeping close to him. She'd never liked caves or enclosed places, and this was one place she didn't want to find herself alone. The water was almost too warm for comfort and there didn't seem to be any tidal flow. Visibility was poor, and gas bubbles rose in lazy columns from the muddy floor making Ree think longingly of the lovely bath in the guest chamber they'd just left.

"How much farther?" she asked. The light was growing dimmer; the walls were nearly lost in shadow.

"Hafoka?" Alex asked. "Are we nearing the end of the tunnels?"

"Soon, soon," he chirped.

"Good. I'm beginning to think that this is worse than the lava flow," Ree grumbled.

Alex glanced back at her. "It isn't."

"Do you know the name of the island?" Ree asked him. "Were these people Polynesian?"

He glanced at their guide.

"Nobody remembers," the fairy chirped. "Too long ago. Forgotten they are. As long past as unicorns."

Loose debris began to drift down from the roof, and the sludge underfoot grew deeper. Now, they were not so much swimming as wading through a mixture of shell, mud and rock, and bones. Ree hoped that the fairy was telling the truth about them nearing the end of the catacombs. So long as there was a way out. She didn't want to think about retracing this route.

Abruptly, she began to feel nauseous. Momentarily, she felt a familiar sense of dizziness, and almost at once, images flashed behind her eyes. Etched across the screen of her mind, she saw an Atlantean warrior, crouched in hiding, a trident grasped in his hand.

"Alex! Look out!" she shouted. Not shouted, she realized. Sent the words as he did by thought. "Soldiers! Just ahead! Around that corner!" Instinctively, she gripped her spear and slid the dagger from her belt sheath.

"No! No!" Hafoka cried. "No soldiers! Safe here!"

Alex drew his sword, and the fairy fled, swimming straight up and squeezing through a narrow crack in the ceiling.

"He's gone!" Ree said. "He's left us."

Alex motioned her to silence, indicating that she should follow him toward an outcrop of stone that jutted out forming a shallow alcove along one wall. They waited, weapons drawn, muscles tensed, and hearts racing as seconds stretched into minutes.

Abruptly, a group of men charged around the corner. Alex moved to shield Ree with his body. "Stay back!" he warned. "Behind me!"

Ree saw a group of combatants coming at them. One tattooed Lemorian, a woman, separated from the others, circling right, attempting to come at them from the side. The armor-clad warrior Ree had glimpsed in her far-sight surged ahead of his comrades and hurled a three-pronged trident.

"Get down!" Alex shouted. He dodged and she ducked. The razor-sharp points slammed into the wall behind them.

A heartbeat later, Alex had seized the trident. The warrior who'd thrown the weapon backed water, and two green-skinned men swam at Alex. One thrust a spear at his chest, but Alex slashed downward with his sword, slicing the spear in two and leaving the assailant with three feet of stick in his hand. He brought up his sword to block Alex's charge, but it was too late. Alex's sword arc continued in a figure eight pattern, coming up and decapitating the spearman.

The water turned dark around the headless body, but the second man continued his attack. His curved sword hissed through the water barely missing Alex's left arm, just before Alex ran him through with the trident. Another soldier joined the fray, and Ree heard the dull clash of blades, but could spare no more time watching Alex's struggle.

The tattooed Amazon who'd broken off from the pack hurled her spear at Ree. Ree sidestepped the missile and threw her own spear. The woman saw the cast and twisted to avoid it. The spear struck her in the hip. She yanked it free and kept coming, curved sword drawn back to strike. Ree caught a glimpse of Alex out of the corner of her eye as he nearly cut an opponent in half with a blow from his sword. The falling man dropped his sword, and Ree dove for it.

Before she could reach the weapon, something heavy slammed into her chest, knocking the wind out of her and forcing her back against the jagged wall. Sharp stones cut into the back of her head and her right shoulder as she slid down. For an instant, she nearly lost consciousness, but then gained control as she shoved at the spearhead wedged into the crease of her body armor. The spear fell away, and Ree struggled for breath as the Amazon closed in on her.

CHAPTER 13

Ree managed to hold on to her dagger, but the Lemorian coming at her with murder in her eyes had a bigger weapon, and her arms were longer than Ree's by half. Ree knew her chances of fighting off a sword attack with a knife were slim, but the dagger was all she had. Worse, the bitch wore bulky armor that protected her from neck to knee, a barrier that would be too tough for Ree's blade to pierce.

Instinct told her that her opponent would expect her to try to escape. Ree launched herself at her attacker, and then instantly realized that she was no longer the target. The woman's deadly sword stroke wasn't meant for her. It was directed at Alex's unprotected back.

"Alex! Behind you!" Ree screamed. Nearly blinded by the murky water, she propelled herself up and thrust her blade under the woman's sword arm, sliding the thin blade through an unprotected crack between the sections of upper-body armor.

The woman cried out and twisted away, attempting to complete her swing, but Alex spun and knocked the sword out of her hand. Wounded and bleeding, the Lemorian rolled into a ball and kicked out at Ree. Scooping up the discarded sword, Ree saw that the injured woman was in full retreat. Instead of chasing her, Ree used the weapon to fight off a net-wielding savage with purple skin and a forked tail who suddenly appeared on her left.

This soldier was male, big and ugly with a flat nose and gills along his neck. He didn't look Lemorian, but what race he was didn't matter to Ree because he was trying to kill her with a two-pronged pitchfork. Gill-man cast his net in an attempt to trap her, but she sidestepped it and blocked his jabbing strikes with her sword.

So far, Ree reasoned she'd gotten lucky, but she wasn't sure how long her luck would hold. The woman's sword was curved and the weight unfamiliar. Given her own weapon, Ree had confidence that she was more than a match for most swordsmen, but here . . . under water . . . Her hopes faded, even as she renewed her attempts at driving her opponent back.

She risked a glance at Alex as he countered another parry and dispatched his opponent with a single blow. Gill-man threw his net again. It tangled around her sword arm and he dove at her, but Alex wheeled and severed the net with his blade, then moved to beat back her attacker.

Struggling for breath, Ree dragged the net off and threw it aside. By the time she was free of the webbing, Alex had wounded the gill-man and driven him back out of the alcove. Ree counted three more Lemorian soldiers—one male and two females—on their feet, plus the leader wearing Atlantean armor.

Maybe we will walk away from this, she thought. *Four to two, that isn't bad odds. Not as bad as how we started.*

Someone threw a spear at her. Ree flung herself sideways and grabbed for the spear as it slid past her through the water. She caught the butt of the shaft and turned to defend herself with it. Her stomach twisted as she saw three more screaming reinforcements pour down the passageway toward her.

"Oh, shit," Ree muttered between clenched teeth.

But as suddenly as the ambush had begun, everything changed. The Lemorian warrior-woman in front—who Ree assumed had come to join the attackers—thrust a trident through the back of the man who'd just attempted to spear her. The others charged the two Lemorians challenging Alex.

In seconds, the enemy leader, the Atlantean that Ree had seen in her warning vision, had turned back down the tunnel, swimming for his life. The other Lemorians, minus the purple-haired woman that Ree now recognized as Anuata, fled after him.

The Amazon raised a bloody trident to hurl after the hindmost, but Alex shouted at her. "No! Let them go. Enough have died here." He rushed at Ree and seized her shoulders. "Are you hurt?" he demanded.

She shook her head. "A few scrapes, nothing serious." Other than the knot on her head, she was in good shape. "I'm fine."

Meanwhile, the two Atlantean men who'd accompanied Anuata had swarmed Alex, pulling him from her and throwing their arms around him. A grinning Anuata joined them, nearly knocking him off his feet with powerful slaps to his back.

"Enough," Alex protested. "You'll drown me. You took your good time getting here."

"I tried to tell them." Anuata grinned at Alex's friends. "Neither have the wits of a dolphin. And the little man is as stubborn as—"

"Hold your tongue!" the smaller of the two warned. "Or I'll cut it out for you."

Alex glanced at Ree. "My team. Bleddyn and Dewi. Anuata, you know."

"You've been too long in the Pacific if you'd trust a Lemorian," the man Alex had identified as Dewi grumbled.

"I trust this one," Alex said. "And so will you when you come to know her."

Ree looked at the two strangers. They were obviously Atlanteans by their garments and the style of armor. Both were big men, hard-bodied and keen of eye, and both were unusually handsome. Bleddyn, the taller of the two, was dark haired and olive-skinned with the hint of a beard on his cheeks, while his companion had fairer skin, light brown hair, and blue eyes. Either one could have written his own ticket in Hollywood without uttering a word.

"I'm Ree O'Connor," she said. "And if any of you know a quick way out of this murky hell, I wish you'd show us."

Anuata nodded. "The horses are outside."

"Horses?" Alex glanced quizzically at Bleddyn.

"Sea horses. She insisted," he answered. "They're mean, but fast."

"We could get only four," Anuata said. "Your human will have to ride double with someone."

"We were hoping that you'd be alone." Dewi grinned. "You know how Bleddyn feels about women interfering in his missions."

Alex shrugged. "If you'd seen Ree fight, you'd have a change of heart."

Sea horses? Nothing would surprise her, but the only sea horses that Ree was familiar with were smaller than her hand and floated around in fish tanks. She couldn't imagine a man riding one.

"Let's move," Alex said. "The longer we waste time here, the easier it will be for them to come back with a larger force."

Ree thrust the curved sword through her belt. She hoped she wouldn't have to use it, but if they were attacked again, she meant to have the means to defend herself.

Alex motioned to her. "Stay close to me."

She didn't need to be told a second time. She wasn't squeamish, but the close quarters with spilled blood and mangled bodies were enough to turn her stomach.

Anuata led the way, taking first one corridor and then another, choosing from a division of tunnels that looked exactly alike to Ree. Soon the water around them became clearer and saltier, and she could smell the sea. No more than half an hour passed before the Lemorian woman led them through a small jagged hole in the wall into the open sea.

It took a few seconds for Ree's eyes to adjust to the expanse of blue-green water and the light streaming down from above. Here were towering forests of kelp and schools of fish of every shape and color. A gray shark that must have been at least eight feet long glided by, but neither Alex nor his team members seemed to notice it.

"Isn't that a tiger shark?" Ree asked.

"It is," Alex answered. "But it's already fed. It won't bother us."

"How can you tell?" she asked.

He threw her an incredulous look. "Trust me. If he was hungry, you'd know it." He pointed to a thick wall of foliage. The leafy fronds shook and bulged, and Ree heard a high-pitched sound that reminded her of a tiger-cub's squeal. "I hate sea horses," Alex confided.

"You don't give them a chance," Dewi said. "For a man who communicates so well with other species, you're oddly prejudiced."

"Is this a joke?" Ree asked. "Are we really going to ride sea horses?"

"I'm going to ride," Alex said. "You're going to hold on to me with every ounce of strength you've got. And you're not going to fall off. If you do, and I'm still in the saddle, the beast will probably savage you before I can prevent it."

"They're bred for war," Anuata explained.

Ree looked from one to another, uncertain if this was a hoax.

"Where did you get them?" Alex asked.

"The royal paddocks," Anuata said. "Where else?"

Bleddyn grimaced. "She lifted them, pretty as you please, right out from under the Lemorian guards' noses. And then broke into the stables for the saddles and bridles."

"This is what I've come to," Dewi said. "A hero of Atlantis. A legend in his time. Nothing but a horse thief." He pulled away a section of greenery that disclosed a small clearing in the kelp jungle.

Ree stared, not certain that she was really seeing what she thought she was seeing. Four huge creatures were tethered by gold rings clamped through their lower jaws . . . tethered being a loose term. These magnificently fierce bucking, plunging entities looked as though they had leaped out of a child's fairy-tale book—the old German fairy tales with frightening ogres and shrieking witches.

"Our transportation," Anuata said.

Ree's eyes widened. "They are sea horses." *Hippocampus.* Great muscular beasts with oversized heads and monstrous curved tails covered in spikes. She couldn't comprehend their size. They must have been twenty hands at the withers, if you could call the scaled protrusion between neck and back withers.

"Are they real?" she whispered, taking in the sight of the strange saddles strapped to the vertical bodies.

"Real enough to rip your arm off with those bony plates that serve as teeth," Dewi said. "Or bash in your head with a blow from that tail."

"They aren't known for their good tempers," Anuata offered. "But they are very useful for making a quick escape from hostile waters."

Ree couldn't stop staring. The sea horses' heads were a shimmering silver-blue in color, with silver manes and red glowing eyes. Their bodies darkened until the last half of their tails were a dark indigo blue. They twisted and lashed out with their thick tails, whipping at those on either side and rearing back in an attempt to tear loose from their bonds.

"You're sure these are broken to saddle?" Alex asked. "They look like wild stock to me."

Anuata laughed. "We rode them here, didn't we?" She climbed hand over hand up a pillar of kelp until she was higher than the nearest sea horse, before dropping into the high-backed saddle. The creature squealed and spun, attempting to throw her, but Anuata leaned forward and severed the rope that held her mount captive.

She pulled hard on the reins, drawing the great head tight against the body and spoke soothingly to the sea horse until its flared nostrils relaxed and the undulating muscles in the neck and tail grew less violent. With a self-satisfied expression, she edged the stallion closer to one of the other beasts and seized the bridle. "I've caught him for you, Prince Alexandros. Now it's up to you to ride him."

Ree looked at Alex. If he was amused, it didn't show on his face.

He took hold of her waist and lifted her high up into the branches of the kelp. "Hold on until I tell you to jump," he ordered. "And if you value your life, do exactly what I say, when I say it."

Ree looked down at the restless sea horses, suddenly thrilled by the idea of riding one. She was an accomplished horsewoman, but these creatures were beyond anything she'd ever attempted. She laughed. Beyond anything she'd ever dreamed of seeing . . .

Alex circled the creature that Anuata held by the bridle and chose another mount, one with a tail nearly indigo. He swam toward the stallion's head, undeterred by the fierce snorts and snapping jaws, put one hand on either side of the horse's head and stared into its eyes. Almost instantly, it ceased attempting to bite him and grew still. Alex ran a hand over the proud neck, seized hold of a spike, and swung himself into the saddle.

Leaning forward, he used his sword to cut the sea grass rope, then backed the horse until it was directly under where Ree perched. "Now," he said. "Jump."

He caught her and helped her to settle behind him. Ree locked her arms around his neck and braced her knees against his legs. There were no stirrups, but she could see that Alex had slipped his feet into a hollow in the frame.

"If you start to feel lightheaded, let me know," he said. "This species prefers to swim closer to the surface. The change in pressure doesn't bother us, but you're still an unknown."

"Understood." A thrill rippled through Ree. The barely controlled power of the sea horse beneath them was unbelievable.

The two men quickly mounted and the five of them were off. The speed of the horses was startling, and it seemed to Ree that they were truly flying under water. Far below, she could see rivers of fire and fish and plants too strange to fully comprehend. They passed over deep crevasses, sheer faces of rock, wide ribbons of roads that stretched for leagues, and forests of kelp and sea grasses. Ree saw pods of whales and schools of fish that numbered in the millions, seabeds white with shellfish, and coral wonderlands.

She did grow dizzy, not from the ever-changing pressure, but from the sights and sounds assaulting her. The single constants were the movement of the stallion beneath her and the overwhelming presence of the man she clung to. Gradually, fatigue crept over her. Twice, she caught herself nodding off and forced herself wide awake, but the weariness returned. How long had she been awake? She wasn't certain. She knew she'd be fine if she leaned her head against Alex's back and closed her eyes for just a few seconds.

She was rudely snatched from her catnap by Alex's hand on her arm as he pulled her up in front of him and cradled her in his arms as though she was a child. "What are you—" she protested.

"I warned you to tell me if you were disoriented. The back of a sea horse is no place to sleep."

"I wasn't—"

"You were!" His arms clamped around her, but his touch was no longer that of a lover. "This is no game, Ree. If we're caught in the open ocean by Lemorian troops, we'll have no chance. All the fancy swordplay in the Atlantic won't protect you from a dozen tridents coming at your throat."

She struggled to get free of his grip. "Let me go. I won't fall asleep."

"You did."

"It won't happen again."

"It better not," he threatened. "Carrying you like this, I can't use a weapon or control this stallion if he decides to try and toss us off."

"It was a mistake."

"A mistake could get us all killed."

His words sliced through Ree's protests. She didn't make mistakes, but she just had. And it wasn't the first.

Once before, with Nick, she'd made the wrong decision, and the man she'd loved had paid for it with his life.

With Alex's assistance, she regained her seat behind him. She was wide awake now, but some of the magic had vanished from the ride. How had she forgotten what was important?

Sex with this man had been great, fantastic even, but it was only that, a pleasurable experience. Her life, her purpose for being, had nothing to do with him. Whatever had happened to her, whatever she had seen and been part of under the ocean was real or it was an illusion. If it was a product of brain damage or a deliberate chemical assault, she might be powerless to recover. But if it was real—if Alexandros of Atlantis and all his minions were real—and she was inclined to believe that this was all true, then her near-death experience and physical reconstruction could only make her stronger.

If she was some sort of bionic woman, if she could survive under water and still breathe once she returned to land, she'd be unmatched in her career field. She would be able to do what no graduate of the institute ever had. And it could only make her taking down Varenkov easier, especially if she could use Alex and his team to find him. She couldn't locate him on her own without contacting management, and she didn't want to do that. They might order her back to headquarters.

Which would mean another failure—her last. That wasn't an option. If she completed her mission and eliminated the Russian, explaining where she'd been since she'd vanished off the *Anastasiya* wouldn't be a problem. She sat up a little straighter and tightened her grip on Alex. What was important was to convince him that he needed her, that she would be an asset to achieving his goal.

This time Grigori Varenkov would meet his match.

CHAPTER 14

Orion nodded to his sister-in-law as he entered her private sitting area. He'd always loved this room. It had been his mother's favorite. He could remember her teaching him his first letters by pointing out the ancient symbols carved between the starfish, sea grass, and conch shells into the marble columns. His father had closed up the room after his mother's death, claiming that it was too much a woman's room. It pleased Orion that the new queen had adopted it as her own, and he was sure his mother would approve.

Poseidon stood by one of the floor-to-ceiling doorways, staring out at the city, and the two royal children played on the floor under the watchful eye of a dolphin attendant. Danu had hidden a red-puffer under one of three tiny conch shells, and the little prince was trying to find it. When he lifted the right shell, the scarlet fish would swell to three times its size and spin like a top, much to the delight of the toddler.

"Fish! Fish!" Perseus crowed.

"Yes, it is a fish," Orion agreed. He was a doting uncle, deeply fond of both the boy and girl. He and his wife Elena hadn't started a family yet, but he looked forward to the day when he would be a father. But today, he had disturbing news to report concerning the man his brother

Alex had been ordered to kill, none of which was suitable for children to hear.

He glanced at Queen Rhiannon and then back to the children. She nodded and motioned to the nurse. "Danu, why don't you and Perseus go down and see if cook has anything special for you this afternoon?"

The princess sighed and gathered her shells. The fish, freed from the game, swam up and out the window, while Perseus waved at it. "Bye-bye, bye-bye, fish."

When the children had left the room, Orion delivered his report to the king. "Varenkov is in Pago Pago. American Samoa. One of our operatives confirmed a sighting. He's in contact with at least two of his factory fish-processing ships, one of whom is captained by the man who led the mass dolphin slaughter in Tonga last season."

Poseidon frowned. "Who do we have in the area?"

"Alex, Dewi, and Bleddyn, provided that Alex is still among the living. I haven't heard anything since the word that he'd escaped and the other two were trying to bring him out of Lemoria in one piece."

"American Samoa." His brother went to the mural that covered a large section of one wall. Islands of the Pacific were represented with inlaid pearls, some as large as a woman's fist, the ocean with blue and green tiles. The outlines of larger land masses such as Australia and New Guinea had been crafted of ivory. "Merfolk, of course," he said, answering Orion's question. A few scouts, but they're scattered around the sea. Friendly dolphins, some whales we can count on."

Orion grimaced. "Not enough numbers to prevent another massacre if Varenkov acts quickly."

"He was connected to the genocide at Taiji in Japan, wasn't he?" Rhiannon asked. "When so many dolphins, pilot whales, and porpoises were slain for sport?"

The king nodded. "He was. Dolphin isn't a favored

food in Japan, but in Asia, meat is meat. And wherever Varenkov can profit, he'll be there."

"It's a shame that Alex wasn't able to eliminate him before he could do more harm," Rhiannon said.

Orion winced inwardly. Since he was an infant, he'd lived with dolphins, learned their ways and their language. They were not humanoids and their intelligence was of a different kind, but sometimes he thought they were smarter than the two-legged species. He knew their courage and their dedication to their mates, their children, and their extended families. Among his people, slaughtering dolphins was as heinous a crime as murdering a man or woman. And those who killed the young of dolphins deserved a royal roasting in Hades.

He swallowed. Twice he'd been present at a massacre of dolphins and once of pilot whales. Both times, he'd attempted to save as many of the doomed creatures as possible from the nets and stabbing spikes and sharp blades of the air-breathing humans. He had been born and bred a warrior, yet the sight of so much innocent bloodshed had brought tears to his eyes. And, if he lingered on the memories, it might do so even today.

"We can't stand by and allow this atrocity," he said, thinking back, remembering the smell of blood when the sea had run red and the frantic cries of the mothers as they saw their children hacked and disemboweled, some skinned while still living.

"I agree," Poseidon said. "The question is, what can we do that will make a difference? We'd need to muster dozens, and we don't have the numbers in the Pacific."

The queen laid her hand on her husband's arm. "We don't"—she said— "but the Lemorians do. What if we warn them of our suspicions?"

"Send word to 'Enakai?" Orion considered her suggestion. "Would she heed anything we say? Rumor is that

Caddoc and his mother have sought refuge in her kingdom. If so, they'll only stir up more bad blood between us."

"We have to try," the queen urged.

Poseidon nodded. "Rhiannon's right. 'Enakai may be
our enemy, but the Pacific is her domain. And whatever
we think of her, she's an able ruler. The dolphins and other
sea life in peril there must be of even greater concern to
the Lemorians than to us." He slipped an arm around Rhiannon. "Sometimes I think you should be king, wife," he
murmured affectionately. "You're the wisest of us all."

"You can say that? Knowing that I was born human and
share a heritage with a monster like Varenkov?"

"You were never like him," he assured her. "His crimes
against his own kind are as bad or worse than what he does
to our kinsmen. He deals in weapons and addictive drugs,
buying and selling wherever a profit can be made."

"He's deeply involved in the international sex trade,"
Orion added. "A ship of his that sunk in the Celebes Sea
last year carried thirty-two young girls to their deaths.
Some as young as nine or ten."

"Such evil," Rhiannon said. "And no court has brought
him to answer for his crimes?"

Poseidon leaned and kissed her forehead. "In the world
above the oceans, justice can be slow for those who possess riches."

"I'll see that messages are sent at once," Orion said. He'd
go to Lady Athena and ask her to intervene with the temple mystics. Ordinary means of communication would be
too slow, but if the psychic priestesses here could send an
alert to their counterparts in the high temples of Lemoria . . . He saluted, as he would have to his late father.

Morgan shook his head, moved forward and hugged
him. "Pray that Rhiannon's idea works, but alert the merfolk. Primitive they may be, but they have their own mysterious ways of sending messages across time and space."

Orion grinned. "I'd already planned on it." He started for the door, and then turned back as his sister-in-law called his name.

"And ask the holy ones to say a prayer for Alex," she said. "That he comes home safe to us."

"So he can finish his mission," the king added grimly. "And rid us of this foul Russian once and for all."

Ree opened her eyes, blinked, and then closed them again against the glare of the midday sun. Sun? The thought registered, and she sat upright and stared wide-eyed around her.

"Finally awake?" Anuata asked. "I thought you were going to sleep all day."

The earth was solid under her. Not solid, Ree realized. Sandy. White sand. Palm trees. Coconuts. She could hear the gentle roll of surf and wind through the trees. Not far away, she heard a *plop* as a coconut fell and rolled. Something tickled her ankle and she glanced down to see a small crab. "Get away!" She shook the tiny, black crustacean off her sandaled foot and it scurried off to join an army of companions that darted in and about the trees.

"He likes you," the warrior-woman said.

"The only way I like crabs is on my plate." She brushed sand off her legs, legs that she noticed were quickly becoming sunburned. *How long have I been lying here?* "Is this really land or another illusion?"

Anuata scowled and used her sword to hack the top off of a coconut. "It's real enough. I don't know how you stand the heat of the sun."

She passed her the coconut, and Ree cradled it between her hands. She could hear the swish of liquid inside and realized that she was parched.

"Drink it," the gold-skinned woman urged. "It tastes good."

Ree took a sip of the coconut milk. It was delicious. "Where are we?" She couldn't remember leaving the ocean. The last thing she did remember was riding behind Alex. "The sea horses . . ." she began.

"The little man is looking after them. Alex and Bleddyn are scouting the sea around this island, to make certain we weren't followed."

Ree tried to make sense of it all. Here on solid ground Anuata looked bigger and stranger than ever, but she also appeared as solid as the palm trees. Whatever she was, Ree didn't think she was a figment of her imagination. The blue-black tattoos that covered much of her face and muscular body reminded Ree of those she'd once seen in a display of early artifacts from the Maori culture in New Zealand. "So we're on an island? Is it inhabited?"

"By humans, no. Crabs, birds. There is no fresh water. I believe your kind no longer drink salt water."

"Not if we want to live long."

"Fortunately, it seems to do you no harm," Anuata observed. "You are not quite human anymore, are you?"

"That's what Alex says." Ree took a deep breath, inhaled the salt air. That tasted as wonderful as the coconut milk. She inspected her hands and her body. Nothing seemed changed, other than the sunburn and a few scrapes and bruises.

She'd reached the point where she had to either accept everything that had happened to her since Varenkov shot her as fact, or accept the fact that she'd lost her mind. She didn't feel crazy, so that left only the alternative. She must proceed as if Anuata was as actual . . . Ree searched for the right word and then borrowed one that Alex had used. *Humanoid.* Ree couldn't continue doubting herself or she was doomed to failure. So be it. Anuata and her coconut had made a believer of her.

"He said something else," the Amazon said. "Prince

Alexandros. He said that just before the ambush in the catacombs, you knew the Lemorians were there. You couldn't see them or hear them, but you knew. He thinks you have the powers of a priestess or a witch. Is that true?"

"It all happened fast," she answered, not wanting to admit what she'd kept hidden from outsiders all her life. "He's mistaken."

Anuata shook her head. "No. He isn't." Her harsh features became as hard as flint. "I don't know if you mean him good or evil, but if you betray him, I will kill you myself."

Ree met her gaze without flinching. "I'll keep that in mind." She got to her feet and brushed the remaining sand off her legs. The boy's tunic she wore came midway up her thigh and gave little protection from the direct sun. The last time she remembered, she'd had armor and weapons. "Where is my gear?" she asked. "My sword."

Still scowling, Anuata motioned to a breadfruit tree about thirty feet away. "There. The cuirass must be kept damp. The air and sun will deteriorate it. It isn't metal, at least not any metal you're familiar with. It's an older material, a gift from the star people."

Star people? Ree studied the Lemorian woman closely. *Is she joking?* What Anuata was saying seemed impossible to believe, but Ree had never seen any metal like the sword blade or armor, light but incredibly strong. How could she tell what was truth and what was fantasy? And how could she rationalize someone or something like Anuata? "You don't like me very much, do you?" Ree said as she moved into the shade of a spreading palm tree.

"I don't trust you."

"No more than I trust you."

"Good." Anuata grinned. "It's a place to start. Trust must be earned." She turned away, then paused and glanced back. "Alex said that I was to stay with you until you were

yourself. He said that I must give you food and drink."
She indicated a net bag on the sand. "There are crabs and
a fish. I have obeyed my prince's orders. Now I go to see
what the little man has done to my horses."

"Do you know when Alex will come back?"

The big woman shrugged. "Today or tomorrow, or
when it pleases him."

"He told me that he intended to hunt down the Russian and kill him. The longer we remain here, the farther
Varenkov will be away."

"It's not your affair, is it? If it were not for you, the
Russian might already be dead."

"How am I supposed to cook the crabs?"

Anuata smiled. "My prince said nothing about cooking." She stooped and snatched up one of the scurrying
black crabs, raised it to her mouth and bit down on it. "In
the field, we don't bother," she explained as she chewed a
mouthful of shell and still wiggling crab. "We eat them like
this."

"In that case, don't let me keep you from your meal,"
Ree said, forcing an equally false smile. "There are plenty
more where that came from." Not giving the warrior-
woman time to think of a comeback, she walked off toward the sound of the breakers. She intended to explore
the island. If Anuata had lied, if there were people here,
she would find a way off.

Less than an hour later, Ree had completed her survey
of the island. It was, as Anuata had said, uninhabited, and
Ree found no indication that humans had set foot on this
sand for years. She was marooned, completely at Alex's
mercy. There was nothing to do but wait for him to return.

Of course, if he didn't return, she'd have to resort to
more drastic solutions . . . building a raft or lighting signal

fires. For now, she would have something to eat, drink the milk from another coconut, and try to perfect her patience.

Her sword and armor lay under the breadfruit tree where she'd last seen it. There was no sign of Anuata or of Dewi, let alone Alex and Bleddyn. She felt sufficiently alone to gather dry wood and tinder to cook her afternoon meal. And cook it she would. She'd have to be a lot hungrier than she was before she'd resort to Anuata's style of dining.

She dug a hollow in the sand, added the shredded coconut husk, and stacked her sticks in a teepee. Glancing around to be certain no one was watching, she did what once would have earned her a spanking from her father. She took a deep breath, gathered her energy, and threw live sparks from the tips of her fingers. The tinder smoked and then burst into flame, and in half an hour she was enjoying fire-roasted fish and crabs. She was just licking the last of the crab juice off her fingers when she heard Alex call her name. She got to her feet as he stepped out of the trees, and in spite of herself, her pulse began to race and she felt her cheeks grow warm.

He was just as beautiful on land as under the sea. As incredible as it seemed, the Greek god striding across the sand toward her was as real as taxes. Just looking at him made her imagination start working overtime. *If I was going to be stranded on a desert island with someone, I can't think of anyone better,* she thought. *Damn but he's a fine piece of prime—*

Her welcoming smile faded. Something was wrong. Alex wasn't smiling. He looked mad enough to take a bite out of the nearest coconut, shell and all. "Alex?"

"I want the truth out of you."

"What truth?"

The green eyes flashed lightning. "In the tunnel. You knew they were coming. How did you know?"

"A hunch. Woman's intuition." She took a step back.

He grabbed her wrists. "Not this time, Ree. I want to know who and what you are. And this time, there'll be no more lies between us."

CHAPTER 15

'Enakai lay stretched on a raised couch in her bed-chamber while Caddoc massaged her naked body with sweet-scented oil. "Ahh, that feels good," she said. "Lower . . . around the base of my tail. Yesss." She moaned. "Lovely. You do have your uses, Atlantean."

They had spent the better part of the evening engaged in rather imaginative sexual games, games that often involved her very talented rudimentary tail and the amazing things that 'Enakai could do with her tongue. Despite the vigorous encounter, Caddoc was still as eager for more. When she'd first summoned him, he'd been afraid that she would be angry with him because they'd allowed Alexandros and the woman to escape . . . and because of the men he'd lost under his command.

Not that the setback was his fault. He'd proved time and time again in Atlantis that he was worthy of command. He simply hadn't been assigned enough adequate fighting men. Battle in the confines of the tunnel had been difficult, because Alexandros was able to defend his back with a wall. The struggle had been fierce, but he would have been successful if his brother's reinforcements hadn't attacked the Lemorian troops from the rear.

The fairy informer had failed to tell them that the human was a trained swordsman. No one regretted missing the opportunity to end his half brother's life more than he did, and Caddoc would not accept the blame for an aborted mission.

Nevertheless, Alexandros must still be in Lemorian waters. He and the human female wouldn't get off so easily when the next patrol came upon them. The queen hadn't mentioned the incident since she'd summoned him to her apartments. She might not even know what had happened, and Caddoc had no intentions of mentioning it to her. Losing her favor was the last thing he wanted.

'Enakai turned her head to look up at him through a thick curtain of unbound hair. She was very beautiful, this purple-skinned woman, even if she was someone older than he preferred. Her body was lithe and sinuous, and her knowledge of how to please a man was admirable. He felt himself growing hard as he stroked and squeezed her ripe flesh.

"Harder."

"Your wish is my command, lovely 'Enakai." He ran an exploring hand roughly between her thighs, thrusting first his fingers and then a fist into her. "I do have my uses, don't I?"

She cried out and he shuddered with anticipation. 'Enakai was one of the few females that he'd ever met who shared his pleasure in the darker aspects of sexual play. "Is this what you want?" he shouted. He spread her legs and rammed his erect member deep into her cleft.

'Enakai howled and bucked against him as he seized her by the hair and yanked it, and the pain in her voice lent as much spice to his lust as the feel of her long fingernails cutting furrows in his leg.

"And I would have more . . ." He squeezed her breast and hammered at her, leaning close and catching the skin on her neck between his teeth and biting down until he tasted her blood. ". . . If—"

"If?" she teased.

He withdrew and drove deep again, repeating his assault with even greater vigor. Pleasure-pain boiled in his veins. "If you would . . ."

She shrieked as he squeezed her breast hard, pinched the taut nipple between his fingers. His breath came in hard gasps. He could feel release, feel the enormous wave of ecstasy coming, and he drove into her cleft with every inch of his male pride. She fit him like a glove, her tight muscles contracting around him, her inner ridges scraping and squeezing, adding to his excitement. *Lemorian physiology,* he thought. *So imaginative.*

Abruptly, 'Enakai's body stiffened and went into spasm. With another howl, she arched against him, straining and wiggling, milking his last essence before finally collapsing face down on the couch.

Frantic to reach his own climax, Caddoc made two more vigorous thrusts and felt the dam within him burst. Carnal exhilaration rocked his body, and he groaned as fiery waves of gratification transported him, sending his mind reeling and causing his tongue to protrude and his eyes to roll back in his head. He slumped forward, crushing 'Enakai with his greater weight, finding still more enjoyment from her obvious distress, and he trapped her under him.

After a time, when his brain cooled, he pulled out of her, wincing as the ridges that had given him so much joy when he was fully erect now scraped against his tender flesh. He glanced down, pleased to see the remaining tumescence and the dripping proof of his virility. He took hold of his member and guided it so that he could watch his seed drip over her buttocks and her now-swollen and pulsing, primal tail.

"Enough." She panted, attempting to squirm out from under him, but he pinned her down, glorying in his dominance of the high priestess and queen of all of Lemoria.

"I could do so much more for you"—he whispered hoarsely—"give you so much more if you would lend your support to my cause. If I were high king of Atlantis—"

Something sharp pierced his thigh and he gasped at the pain. Leaping up off 'Enakai, he saw that she had driven a six-inch-long needle of bone into his flesh. Blood welled up to stain the water. "Are you mad?" he screamed. "Look what you've done!" He jerked out the needle and threw it away before clamping his hand over the injury and staring down as blood continued to seep through his fingers.

"Do you never cease?" she demanded, sliding off the couch and away from him. Her mouth was swollen from his earlier love-taps, and her eyes heavy-lidded with sated passion. Yet, the expression in her eyes was oddly reptilian.

"You stabbed me!" he accused.

"Yes, and I will do worse before I'm done."

"'Enakai," he began, unsure of her sudden change of mood. "What—"

"Enough!" she snapped. "You bore me with that tired refrain." She fixed him with her dark, penetrating stare and pointed a finger accusingly. "You are a small man, Prince Caddoc, small in courage, in imagination, and in intelligence. How much of a fool do you believe I am— that I would risk my soldiers to help you claim a throne you're incapable of keeping if I handed it to you on an oyster shell?"

Caddoc stiffened and drew himself up to his full height. "How dare you insult me, you Lemorian bitch? Who was your mother? Your father? You may have been chosen as high priestess, but the blood of Poseidon runs in my veins. My house—"

'Enakai flew at him and ended his tirade with a slap across his face. "Stupid man! You are here at my sufferance! You live by my sufferance! You claim to be a prince—a great Atlantean warrior! And yet, you cannot kill one man and woman in a cave. It should have been like spearing fish trapped in a tidal pool. You had them outnumbered six to one at least. You had the benefit of surprise."

"It wasn't my fault!" Caddoc protested. "Alexandros is—"

"Is one man weighed down by a human female."

"You don't understand. I—"

She slapped him again. "Stop talking. Don't speak unless I ask you a direct question." Her eyes narrowed to mere slits as his whole body tensed. "Raise a hand to me in anger," she hissed. "I dare you. Touch me and my archers will fill you so full of arrows that you'll look like a blowfish."

At that instant, he hated her, found her repulsive, but he knew how to hide his feelings. "My queen . . ." he soothed with oily affection. "I would never—"

"You are a weakling, Caddoc. Your pitiful hag of a mother possesses more strength in one finger than you have in your whole body."

"Please, my precious, for what we have meant to each other . . ."

She spat. "Sharing *shenji?*"

Caddoc winced. His Lemorian wasn't the best, but the word she'd used for their sexual liaisons was the crudest of slang, usually referring to intercourse with a male prostitute. "You liked it well enough," he replied, stung by her insult of his prowess.

"You were a novelty, but one I tire of. And now, when you were given an opportunity to be of use, you allowed Prince Alexandros to slip through your fingers. He killed one of my greatest healers and your Samoan bodyguard as well. But you didn't stop him. You failed me, and killed nine of my best warriors doing it."

A bad feeling came over him as anger gave way to apprehension. Caddoc's heart thudded against his ribs as bile bubbled up in his throat. He could taste the pickled eels that he'd eaten at his last meal. "I told you," he hedged. "It wasn't my fault."

"No? Doubtless you were wounded in hand-to-hand battle with this brother of yours. Where are your wounds? Why are you the only one who escaped without a single injury?"

"My skills kept me safe. Someone had to give orders. What general—"

"I am no warrior, but I command armies, and I know a sniveling coward when I see one." She turned her back on him, picked up her robe from the floor, and wrapped it around her. "Any Lemorian commander who failed as utterly as you have would pay for his poor judgment with his life."

Caddoc's bowels clenched and he felt the urgent need to empty them. "'Enakai, you can't mean . . ."

She pushed the hair out of her face and stared at him as if he was a piece of offal that had stuck to the bottom of her sandal. "Guards!" She clapped her hands together once, and four female soldiers appeared. They arrived so quickly that he realized they must have been standing behind the screen, listening and perhaps watching all that had transpired between the two of them. Shame filled him. He searched for words to defend himself, came up empty, and looked at her gape-mouthed.

"What? You are silent, at last, little man?"

"This is all a misunderstanding. It could have happened to any commander. If you'd give me another chance . . ."

"You must be punished, Caddoc," she said. "And since you have begged my protection, you fall under the laws of Lemoria. Why should you not die in the lava flow as one of my own would do?"

"You cannot! My father was the high king of Atlantis, and my brother Morgan is now Poseidon. If you murder me, you'll start a war between the kingdoms."

'Enakai looked thoughtful. "You're outlawed. Why should Poseidon care if your life is ended? And sacrifice to our goddess is not murder. It's a great honor. You would be assured a place in paradise."

Caddoc's mouth tasted of salt, and sweat seeped through the small scales on his neck. "Consider what you do. A family feud is one thing, but to have Lemoria execute a royal prince of Atlantis would be another altogether. The last war between our nations lasted for eleven hundred years."

She waited, listening.

"Nine common soldiers may have died fighting Alexandros, but how many more Lemorians will die against the might of Atlantis?" he rambled on. "There are many more of us than of your people." He saw doubt flicker in her eyes, and hope swelled in his chest. "Give me another chance to capture Alexandros. Give me more men, and this time I'll bring you his foreskin on the end of my trident."

'Enakai shook her head. "How can I have one law for an Atlantean turncoat and another for my own men? You failed. You caused the death of good men, and you returned without a scratch. The sacrifice must be made."

"Does it have to be me?" Caddoc begged.

"A prince, even an Atlantean, is a noble offering to our goddess. It will end your shame and bring great rewards to Lemoria. Think of it as a blessing." She smiled at him. "All men must die, but to die in a great cause . . ."

"But what if I found someone to take my place?" he asked.

"Your brother Alexandros? That might be satisfactory, if we had him here. But we don't, and even now, he may be beyond our reach. It's too bad you let him get away. I could have considered substituting his life for yours, but . . ."

"I'll find him. I promise you, I'll bring him to you. Alive, if you wish. Surely, your goddess would take one prince for another."

'Enakai pursed her lips. "You bargain like a conch trader, but your hands are empty. You would exchange promises for living flesh. Sadly, you must die, Caddoc." She lifted a hand and two of the big warrior-women seized his arms. "On the next turning of the tide, you will carry our prayers to the Great One."

"No," he argued. His stomach churned. In a moment, he would vomit all over the queen's exquisite inlaid floor. "No. This is a mistake. It will bring war. My brother Poseidon loves me dearly."

"But . . ." 'Enakai raised a ringed finger to her lips. "Your mother is a guest here, is she not?"

"Yes, yes," he agreed.

"And your mother was wife to Poseidon?"

He nodded, not certain where this was leading.

"So, she may rightly bear the name of queen, can she not?"

"Yes!" Caddoc agreed, choking back the remains of his last meal that rose in his throat. "Queen Halimeda, favored wife of Poseidon. Her blood is royal."

"And she is female."

Slowly, Caddoc understood. "My mother would be acceptable to you? She could take my place as sacrifice?" Fear warred with denial. But the idea, once planted in his mind, leaped from spark to full flame. His mother was old, a shadow of her former self, twisted and feeble. Useless. What better thing could he do for her than provide her a glorious death? "Yes," he said eagerly. "A queen must be more pleasing to a goddess than a mere prince."

"And your brother the king would overlook the passing of a stepmother?"

"There has never been love between my mother and my brother," he assured her. "Poseidon would not mourn her passing."

'Enakai's expression became inscrutable. "You would trade your mother's life for your own?"

Caddoc spread his hands, palm up. "For such an honor, that my aging mother might have the honor of carrying your prayers to a supreme being? What loving son could deny his parent such a future?"

The queen chuckled. "You make me remember why I find you so amusing, Atlantean. We think alike in many things. As you say, she is aging, and the best days of her life are behind her."

"Will she feel pain at the moment of sacrifice?" he asked, as the reality of what he'd agreed to hit home.

"I'm told that the pain is brief. Lava is, by nature." She grimaced. "It will be quick. Flesh and bones become ash as the spirit rises."

Caddoc nodded. "She will surely die soon anyway. She's not been herself since Melqart cursed her."

"Very well," 'Enakai agreed. "I'll give the orders." She glanced at one of the Amazons, a huge, ugly woman covered with tattoos. "Carry word to the temple to make ready for the sacrifice of an Atlantean queen."

The guard slammed a meaty fist against her bare breast and hurried off to obey the queen's command.

Caddoc sighed with relief. "Is it necessary that I be present?"

"Unfortunately," 'Enakai replied. "Usually, only the initiated, the priesthood, and the sacrificial offering may venture into the holy site, but since Queen Halimeda is taking your place, it's only fitting . . ."

His gut knotted. "I understand. Mother loves me so,

and parting will be difficult. She would want me there to see her off."

"I'm sure." 'Enakai smiled.

"It is a difficult decision for me."

"Hopefully, you'll have a son someday who would do as much for you."

Caddoc glanced toward the doorway, wanting to get as far away as quickly as he could. "By your leave, Queen 'Enakai," he said. "I'll go—"

"We are not finished here," she said sternly.

"No?" Did she expect him to willingly lie with her again after just threatening to burn him alive in a river of lava? He looked toward the bed. "I thought . . ."

"Your mother's body will substitute for yours and pay for the lives of my soldiers, but I'm still not satisfied. And I find that my evenings' entertainment is not complete."

"You need to be serviced again?" he asked, taking his manhood between his hands and beginning to stroke it. "You need more of my—"

"Not that type of entertainment," she said. "This time, I prefer something more erotic. It shall please me to watch you perform."

"With who?" he asked.

She smiled, and a frizzen of ice slid down the nape of his neck. "Why, with my guards, of course." She waved toward the green-skinned women standing on either side of him, and retreated to recline against the cushions on her couch.

"All three of them?" Caddoc asked, staring up at them with distaste.

'Enakai laughed. "Unless you would prefer more."

Caddoc closed his eyes and began to stroke his phallus harder. He would vomit. He knew he would vomit. "I have one question," he managed.

"Yes?" The queen was obviously amused.

"One at a time, or all four of us at once?"

★ ★ ★

Alex didn't know what had just happened. One second, he was on his feet, facing Ree, and shaking her, demanding that she tell him the truth about who she really was. And the next thing he knew, he was lying flat on his back, staring up into her face.

"Don't ever do that again," Ree admonished before stepping away.

Momentarily speechless, he got to his feet, glancing around to see that Dewi, Anuata, and Bleddyn weren't standing in the trees laughing at him. He couldn't believe it. This woman—this little girl—this human had thrown him. "How did you do that?" he demanded, more incredulous than embarrassed. "Is it magic?"

She kept her distance. "No, not magic or illusion. Just skill. I hold an advanced degree black belt in three martial arts. That was *krav maga*. Much simpler than Bando thaing or Aikido."

Alex eased the kinks out of his spine. He was never as strong on land as in the water, but against a human there should have been no contest. It was impossible that she could have turned the tables on him so completely. "And this is what they teach in culinary arts? This *krav maga?*"

She shook her head. "No, that I learned elsewhere. Take me with you, Alex. If you're going to kill Varenkov, I can help."

"How do I know I can trust you?"

She threw his words back at him. "How do I know I can trust you?"

"You can't. But we're in this too deeply. I have to know who you are."

"I'm your counterpart. Your people want the Russian dead. So do mine. I was there to do the same job you were. We simply ended up getting in each other's way."

He took a step toward her, and she took a step back. "No,"

he said. "There's no need for you to fear me. I was wrong. I wouldn't have hurt you. I shouldn't have tried to—"

"No, you shouldn't have." She nodded. "I've had to accept a lot of things as real in the last few weeks . . . weeks or however long it's been since you appeared on the deck of Varenkov's yacht. I suppose you'll have to do some of the same."

"You're telling me that you're an assassin?"

"If you put it that way. I consider myself more of an enforcer. I carry out the sentence that a court delivers. Men like Varenkov, evil men who kill without remorse, war criminals, and drug lords, those who escape justice. The organization I work for puts an end to men and occasionally women who fit that category."

"So you were not simply in the wrong place at the wrong time."

She shook her head. "No more than you were."

"So you were trained as a warrior."

"Yes. In weapons and hand-to-hand fighting."

"And in other ways?" he suggested. "You haven't explained how you knew the Lemorians were lying in wait for us."

"Question for question," Ree answered.

He reached out his hand to her, but she retreated warily. "Why did you bring me on land? Why don't I remember what happened? I was riding behind you . . . and then I was lying here in the sand."

"Apparently, your transformation isn't complete. You began to have trouble. Breathing. You passed out."

"Maybe I feel asleep."

"No, you were unconscious for . . ." He searched for a unit of time that she would understand. "For half the time it takes for the sun to travel from first light to high overhead. Anuata said that it is a sickness that hybrids suffer. Too long under water, and they can no longer function."

"So I can't breathe under water anymore? I'm completely human again."

He shook his head. "Not that simple. Anuata believes that a short time on land, breathing air, and the sickness passes for the time being. But soon, the times you remain under will become less."

"So, I'm turning back to the way I was before."

She was so beautiful, standing there with the sun shining on her hair, that he wanted to take her in his arms and kiss her mouth, her throat and shoulders . . . that he wanted to taste her skin and inhale the scent that was hers alone. He wanted her again. He wanted to possess her completely. He caught himself, remembering that he had no right to make love to her unless she was willing.

"There is more," he said. "Soon, perhaps in a day or two, maybe more. You will not be able to breathe on land. You will need to return to the sea. You aren't human anymore, but you aren't Atlantean either."

He saw her throat constrict. "I'm sorry, Ree, but there's no going back. You can't be human again, and without help, without treatment in our . . . our medical facilities, you'll die."

"And, if I get this treatment? What then?"

"If you are transformed fully, if you become Atlantean, you will live longer than you could imagine."

"But I'll grow scales and webbed feet?"

He smiled at her. "Do you see scales and webbed feet on me?"

She covered her face with her hands. "I don't know what's real and what's illusion."

"I'm real." He reached for her again, and this time she let him draw her into his arms. "This is real," he said, before lowering his head and kissing her.

CHAPTER 16

Alex tasted as good as she remembered. His mouth was sweet and clean, tasting faintly of the sea, and the caress of his tongue against hers made her tremble with excitement. So simple . . . a kiss between a man and a woman, yet not simple at all, but complex and mysterious. The firm warmth of his lips, the smooth, cool texture of his teeth, and the virile scent of him filling her head combined with the sensual assault of the tropical island around her.

She pressed against him, her thin boy's tunic no barrier between them, but he was wearing that damned armor when she wanted to feel his warm skin against hers. He caught her lower lip between his teeth and nipped gently, sending explosions of sweet sensation through her body.

"We haven't settled anything," she murmured as she wrapped her arms around his neck and pulled him down to her. "I want you to take me with you and let me help you kill Varenkov." She was aware of the heat of the sun dappling through the shade of the palms, and she could hear sea birds above the rhythmic crash of surf, but most of all the man in her arms. She needed him to make love to her, couldn't wait to pick up where they'd last left off . . . but she had to have his word that she was part of his team.

He kissed her again.

Alex was a good kisser, intense and sensual without being greedy. "Can't you take this off?" she murmured between kisses. She tugged at his cuirass, and together managed it, followed by his tunic and hers. The sand was warm under her knees and she smelled the charring bits of shell from the discarded crabs.

If I can hold this moment . . . I'll treasure it and keep it safe always.

He cupped her breast in his warm hand. "Beautiful," he whispered.

How could a man's touch make her feel as if her skin was too tight for her body? As if his fingers left a trail of warm honey over her body . . . and she was bathed in liquid heat?

"Promise me," she said. "I have to go with you."

"We'll talk later." His hands were moving over her, touching, brushing, stroking, sending sweet spirals of vibrating light coursing through her body. She felt her skin soften, felt the flush of warm blood flow up to tint her cheeks, felt her nipples tighten and ache to be licked and suckled.

"Not later." She put her palms on his broad chest and pushed away. "Now."

Their gazes met, and she read boyish surprise and hurt in the green depths of his hauntingly beautiful eyes. He reached for her and she darted away, dashing through the trees toward the sound of the breakers. She could hear him behind her, hear the snap of brush and the heavy tread of his feet, but she prided herself on her speed. She leaped over a fallen tree and around a clump of shrubbery, barely missing stepping on a startled sea turtle as she ran toward the beach.

He caught her at the high tide mark where bits of driftwood and empty shells littered the damp sand, swept her up in his arms, and kept running into the surf. She laughed as the waves crashed over their heads and instinctively held her breath as blue-green water filled her vision.

Still holding her, Alex kicked hard, driving them both back to the surface. The water felt wonderful against her skin, and she wanted more. She wanted to dive deep and feel the tug of the current on her body. She needed to go down to the bottom and view the sun through a changing prism of light and shadow.

"I'm all right," she said. "I can breathe. I'm fine."

He released her from his arms but held a tight grip on her hand. "Are you sure?"

Strange how the minute she was under water his voice came inside her head, clear and perfect. She inhaled deeply, marveling at the strength she felt flow through her muscles and veins. It was true. In the ocean she was a bionic woman, something different from what she had been before, something superior. She laughed, staring around her like a child on Christmas morning. She'd spent years in search of physical and mental fitness, and now she possessed far more of both than she'd ever imagined.

The colors! Oh, the colors were beyond description: greens, blue, brown, gold, orange, and lavender. Sunlight shimmered, turning fish and grass and shells to precious jewels, and turning the water to a dozen hues of blue. "Look!" she cried to Alex. "Look at it all!" It seemed that she'd been blind before, and that now she saw with brilliant clarity. Sound cascaded around her, soothing and invigorating: the roar and boom of the surf, the lyrical rhythm of the tide, and a hundred sounds she couldn't identify, all combining to form a symphony of sky and ocean.

He laughed and swam with her out to deeper water

where a coral reef rose from the bottom, creating a fanciful and ever-changing kingdom of fish and reptiles, plants and invertebrates. Orange and black clown fish darted recklessly among the tentacles of sea anemones, sponges dotted the floor and towering towers of multicolored coral; and where crabs and scallops thrived in the midst of four-foot giant clams, and eels, and sea snakes, and mantas made their homes.

Ree had scuba-dived the Great Barrier Reef off the coast of Australia, as well as smaller coral reefs off the Florida Keys and in the Caribbean. She'd been struck by the majesty of the silent world of turtles, sea urchins, and exotic fish, but she hadn't really *seen,* not as she did today. It was as if she'd been watching an early twentieth-century black and white film, and suddenly the movie had become 3D and high resolution with surround-sound. For the reef was no more silent than the sea. And far from being frightened by this abrupt change of perception in sight and sound, Ree was delighted with it, embraced it, and stared around her in utter wonder.

Alex swam up beside her and pointed as a giant manta ray glided gracefully over the top of the reef, looking like some great exotic bird. "When I was a boy, my brothers and I used to ride them all the time," he said. "If you like, I'll take you some time."

Ree nodded, too overwhelmed to speak. She couldn't stop staring at the immense reef. She'd never realized that there were so many coral species or that they grew in such shapes and colors. Each square foot seemed to be the home of dozens, perhaps hundreds, of living things. There were sea cucumbers, worms, octopuses, squid, and snakes— one of which she recognized by its distinct black and white pattern as a harlequin snake. And everywhere were fish, some swimming in schools, others darting in and out of the coral in search of food, and still others sitting motionless waiting for dinner to wander in to their immediate vicinity.

"I never knew that it could be like this," Ree said, turning to Alex. "So beautiful. So tranquil. This reef is so different from the crowded streets of Tokyo or New York City that it could be on another planet."

"Beautiful, but fragile," Alex replied. "The reef has grown over three thousand years, but one of Varenkov's trawlers could destroy it in hours. Bottom trawling rapes the ocean bottom, wiping out whole species and turning rich feeding grounds to empty desert. Much of the world's coral reefs are already gone, dead or dying from ocean acidification, overfishing, and pollution."

"This seems so pristine," she said. "As if we're the first to ever lay eyes on it."

He grimaced. "Even here, you will find the discarded waste of air-breathers' carelessness. The Atlanteans and the Lemorians do what they can, but I'm afraid we're losing the battle. And if the oceans die, so does the land."

"That's so sad."

He pulled her into his arms. "But today, I don't want you to be sad." He leaned closer still and his lips brushed hers. "This day, let it just be about pleasure."

Ree laughed and wrapped her legs around his waist. It was an offer that was hard to resist, but she wasn't about to let him forget that she intended to be in on the finish when he went for the Russian. Kissing . . . lovemaking under water had its definite advantages. Not only were they freed from the limitations of gravity, for the most part, but, her senses of touch and smell and sight felt heightened. The delicious sensations flowing through her body were more powerful than she'd ever experienced before.

"Promise me," she murmured when they'd kissed yet again.

"You never give up, do you?" he teased.

Again, she thought that she saw a faint pattern of bluish scales on his body, but they didn't repulse her. If anything, they made him all the more beautiful. He seemed as much a part of this reef as the small blacktipped shark that passed overhead.

Ree leaned back in his arms, her long hair floating loose around her, and cupped his face between her hands. "If only life were this simple," she said. "If we could have a day without thinking of anything else . . . of just being."

A guarded expression flickered through the swirling depths of Alex's emerald eyes before quickly being replaced by a seductive charm.

"You don't have to worry," she assured him. "As you said, we're very much alike. There's no room in my life for ties, not to you and not to any man."

"You understand. I'm not cut from the same mold as my brothers. The career I've chosen is—"

"Shhh." She silenced him with a kiss that blossomed from tender to searing as the heat flowed under her skin and made her hungry for even greater intimacies. Alex didn't need her to twist his arm, and within minutes, they had discovered a new and delightful variation on familiar but rewarding practices.

And this time the intense waves of release broke over the two of them simultaneously, freeing Ree for long moments of the weight, the tension, and the stress that she'd carried within her for so many years. Tears of joy filled her eyes and mingled with the salt water, and she was aware of a lightness of spirit she hadn't known since she'd left her parents' home for the last time. Again, she was content to lay back in Alex's arms and let the magical world flow around her.

She lost track of time and hovered in that gray space between waking and sleeping, wrapped in the music of the coral reef and absolutely certain that she was safe in this man's embrace.

. . . Until she opened her eyes and saw two black and white sharks almost within arm's length. "Alex!" Another circled overhead, more than six feet long with eyes as black as obsidian. Ree stiffened and thought of her weapon. *Where did I leave my sword?*

"It's all right," Alex said. "They hunt in packs, but they rarely attack humanoids."

A school of fish, blue with yellow spots panicked and scattered, some darting into crevices in the coral, others rushed in tight formation toward the surface. The blacktip attack was precise and deadly. The sharks herded the remains of the school into a tight ball and tore into them, ripping and tearing, turning the clear water red with blood.

Then, as swiftly as they had appeared, the sharks vanished, and other fish and reptiles ventured out of the reef to partake of the largesse. "Watch," Alex whispered and pointed.

A rust-colored moray eel with black and white dots on his body, jagged teeth, and orange bands on his head materialized from the swaying ferns, and gorged on the bits of debris before slithering back into his hole. Even the smallest fragment of shredded fish was consumed by other smaller creatures before the current washed the area free of blood so that the water was once again a brilliant blue-green.

"Gross," Ree said. "I'm glad we weren't on the menu."

"Not gross," Alex said. "Life. Even dragon moray eels must eat to survive. And all the fish didn't die, just the slower ones, or the stupid."

"Survival of the fittest."

Alex nodded. "Unfortunately, Grigori Varenkov has been one of those survivors. But not for long. Not if I can help it."

"Or me," Ree said. "But I'm serious, Alex. You have to let me come."

"You haven't told me how you saw that ambush. You were never completely human, were you? I suspect you carry the blood of the star race."

She shook her head. "I told you what I was. I hunt bad guys. And both my parents were Irish, pure Irish, going back as far as anyone knows."

"Which is what? Five generations? Ten?"

"And you . . ." She smiled at him. "I suppose you know more of your genealogy than that."

"I'm descended from the first high king of Atlantis, father to son, in an unbroken line."

"How many reigning monarchs?"

He chuckled. "You wouldn't believe me if I told you." He caught a lock of her hair and wrapped it around his finger. "You have the most unusual hair. I've rarely seen this color, and never on a woman so beautiful."

She wrinkled her nose. "Thank you, but yours isn't so bad either. A little long for fashion."

"Not my fashion." He kissed the tip of her nose. "You aren't going to answer my question, are you? You won't tell me why you know things before they happen, will you?"

"If I did, you wouldn't know if I was lying or telling the truth, would you?"

"I don't know. How good of a liar are you?"

He was very close, and she looked directly into his eyes. The intensity of his gaze made it feel as though it was difficult to breathe, as though if she wasn't careful, she would fall into a bottomless pool of . . . *Of what,* she wondered. *And where would I land?* "Take me, Alex. You owe it to me."

He let her go. "You're tough. I'll give you that."

"I've been called worse."

"You didn't listen to a thing I told you, did you? You're sick. You need medical attention. Your body is caught somewhere between human, Atlantean, and Lemorian. Soon . . . I don't know when. It could be an hour, a day, or a month. But soon you won't be able to survive in the ocean or out of it. You have to have help to make that leap between our species. If you don't, you'll die."

"So you're going to what? Check me into the nearest hospital? Explain to the staff that I'm undergoing hybrid sickness? That should give me a fast ambulance ride to the nearest mental facility."

"I'm going to take you home, to Atlantis. It's the only place that can treat you. And . . ." A muscle twitched under the skin of his jawline and regret shone in his eyes. "It may not work, Ree. You may die anyway."

She shrugged. "We all die. My parents . . . Nick—" She broke off as her pulse quickened. How had she let Nick's name slip out? And how could it still hurt so bad after all this time? They were lovers, not sweethearts, not husband and wife . . . just partners in a job that didn't offer a pension plan or a 401K.

"Who was Nick?"

"Just someone I used to know. Nobody, really," she lied, and the pain cut as sharp as a straight razor.

"Right."

"About this disease you say I have, this sickness. You're only guessing. Only taking Anuata's word for it. How do you know she isn't wrong or lying to get rid of me? She's made it clear that she doesn't want me here."

"She wouldn't lie about that."

"How do you know that? People lie all the time. How many times have you lied?"

"Never without reason."

"Exactly. And Anuata's reason is to pack me off to At-lantis. I could breathe on land, and I seem to be doing just fine under the water. If I fell asleep—"

"It was more than sleep. We couldn't wake you."

"Whatever it was, it's gone now. Isn't that what the healer was doing in Lemoria? Changing me from human to whatever? How do you know that it didn't work—that what happened wasn't a tiny aftershock or aftereffect. You aren't a physician, and neither is Anuata."

"I should take you to our healing temple. Think of it as one of your world-class hospitals. They can help you."

"I'll check into your first-aid station as soon as we've finished our mission. And you have a better chance of killing Varenkov with my help."

"If you come, you have to accept my authority. You do what I say, when I say it. No exceptions. Is that under-stood?"

She smiled. "Understood."

"I'm dead serious, Ree. Varenkov tried to kill you once, and he nearly succeeded. My bag of tricks doesn't work twice. Die on me again, and you'll be truly dead."

CHAPTER 17

"I want to come!" Danu cried, leaving the small loom where she'd been painstakingly weaving a tapestry in greens and blues and brilliant purples. The bunched threads and knots and the lopsided pattern gave evidence that this was one skill that she had yet to perfect. "Please, Daddy, let me come. I'll be good."

Poseidon looked at his wife. "It's up to your mother. Rhiannon?"

"Archery? Is the archery range any place for a small girl?" She glanced at the loom and shook her head. "For a girl who's first in her dance class, your weaving attempts are atrocious."

Danu grimaced. "I hate weaving, Mommy. My starfish looks like an octopus." She took a deep breath. "I've finished my homework, and I practiced the harp for two clicks of the water clock. Please let me go with Daddy. Pretty please."

"But Lady Dorkas is coming with Damalis this afternoon. You three children had so much fun last time they visited."

Danu shook her head so hard that her blond curls bounced, and folded her arms over her chest. "Damalis is too little for me to play with. She's only three. Uncle

Orion promised to teach me to shoot a bow. I'll be so good they won't even know I'm there."

Poseidon chuckled. "That I'd have to see to believe. I'll take her. You'll have no peace this afternoon if I don't."

"Yay!" Danu hugged her father's legs and ran to fetch her new red sandals with the gold tassels.

The queen sighed. "You spoil her. She'll be impossible by the time she's a teenager."

Rhiannon was probably right. He did spoil Danu, but the child had secured a place in his heart, in both their hearts, that made it almost impossible to deny her anything within reason. And Danu was an amazing child, far older than her years in so many ways, not to mention her rare psychic gifts. "She only gets to be young once," he murmured, brushing his lips against his baby son's fuzzy head. "And a princess doesn't need to learn the art of weaving to attract a rich husband."

"I suppose you're right. The Lady Athena believes she's born for the priesthood, anyway."

"Or a seat on the high council. And archery would be an asset for either choice. We won't be late."

"See that you're not. We have that dinner with the ambassador from the Scottish Lochs, the strange-looking man."

The high king groaned. "I like state banquets no more than Danu likes her weaving." His mouth tightened. "Don't you wish sometimes that I was only a prince among princes again? Life was a lot simpler before my father died."

"Every day," Rhiannon replied. "And every night. Our time was more our own before you became Poseidon. When you were Morgan, no one cared if we took time away to be with your family."

"If wishes were horses," he answered. "But it is what it is. I'm Poseidon and Perseus will wear the crown after me."

"He may not want it any more than you."

"Perhaps. You should have thought of that when you gave me a son instead of another gorgeous daughter."

Taking his bow and quiver from a servant, Poseidon left by a private exit to the gardens. Echo, Danu's dolphin, swam close behind as they passed two household guards at their station beyond the queen's courtyard.

"Uncle Orion said he was bringing a bow just my size," Danu said. "What color do you think it will be? I like pink. Do you think it will be pink? Morwena says that if I practice, I'll be as good as she is. Do you think I will?"

Poseidon lifted her and placed her on Echo's broad back. "If you practice every day, I'm sure you'll soon be better than me."

Danu tucked the toes of her sandals into the dolphin's green harness and wrapped one small hand around the guide strap. Going with her father to the archery field was much better than staying with her mother. She felt that her daddy was the bestest daddy in the world, and she loved him more than the moon. "I'm being good, aren't I?" she asked.

Echo wiggled her tail, and Danu laughed.

Poseidon ducked his head to pass though an old stone doorway.

"Look at all the barnacles," Danu said.

"The inscriptions were carved by craftsmen long, long ago, when the world was young. Some think the language is that of the starmen."

"Can you read it, Daddy?"

"No, no one can now. Keep your hands in. The shells are sharp."

The passageway was narrow, almost too narrow for such a large and majestic dolphin like Echo, but she was brave and didn't fuss at following him.

The corridor widened as they approached a small prayer garden with a marble statue of a water-horse and another of a boy riding a manta ray. Danu liked this garden. In the tall swaying grass were blue starfish and schools of tiny green sea horses no larger than her thumb. Here the floor was made up of translucent panels, so clear that they could see fish and crabs, and young dolphins swimming in the open sea below.

Two archways led off in different directions. Poseidon was about to take the left hallway when a boy came around a corner.

"Your majesty!"

The king didn't recognize the lad, but his blue tunic with silver trim and silver winged sandals identified him as a court page. The boy held out a scroll. Poseidon took it, and the page bowed and swam back the way he'd come.

"What is it, Daddy?" Danu asked.

"Lord Pelagias wishes to see me. He says it's a most urgent matter."

"But we're going to the archery range," Danu reminded him. "We're meeting Uncle Orion, and—"

"You and Echo go ahead. It's just down this passageway. Echo knows the way. You'll be fine with her. Find your uncle and tell him that I'll be along as soon as I see what Lord Pelagias wants." He unslung the quiver from his back and handed bow and quiver over to his daughter. "Take these for me."

Danu stared at him, and her tummy squeezed tight. Something was wrong. She knew something was wrong because she could hear a funny ringing in her head, like a bell, but quick and sharp. Suddenly, she felt sick. "No, Daddy," she begged. "Don't go. I don't like Lord Pelagias. He has a mean face. Come with me."

"Do as I say, child. You know that I have responsibilities for—"

"No!" Danu cried. "No. Lord Pelagias is a bad man."

Poseidon frowned. "That's enough. Lord Pelagias is a

member of the high council, and he's served the kingdom well for many years. You've no reason—"

"He's a bad man. He'll hurt you."

"Enough, I say. Echo, take the princess to my brother."

Danu knew she shouldn't cry. Only babies cried, but she couldn't stop the tears. "Daddy, you have to listen to—"

"I'm ashamed of you, to carry on so," her father scolded. "Maybe your mother's right. Maybe I have spoiled you rotten. We'll talk about this later. Echo, look after her." And before she could say another word, he turned and moved away down the right passage.

Echo moved toward the left.

"No," Danu said. "We have to follow Daddy."

The dolphin uttered a series of sharp clicks.

"I don't care. He needs us." She kicked Echo's sides. "Hurry!"

'Enakai stood stiffly erect behind her driver in a golden chariot pulled by a team of dolphins with Caddoc beside her. They were in the vanguard of a procession of priests, and nobles streaming from the lower archway of the third level of the grand temple of Lemoria toward the towering volcano and lava fields in the distance.

Soldiers, household guards, and body servants made up the rest of the company, all following close behind a covered conveyance carved from a single, giant, black shell, drawn by manta rays and surrounded by an honor guard of veiled priestesses astride gilded sea horse mares.

Suddenly, without warning, 'Enakai raised a hand and called out to her driver. "Halt!"

He reined in the dolphins and those behind them stopped abruptly, causing confusion and greatly altering the precise formation all down the line as some were forced out of the procession to the left or right, and others collided with those directly in front. The mantas wheeled right and rose so quickly that they nearly overturned the shell, causing the single occupant to scream in alarm.

"What is it?" Caddoc demanded, steadying himself on the side of the chariot. "What's wrong?" His nerves were on edge as it was.

So far, he hadn't had to confront his mother, and he suspected that she was still unaware as to the exact nature of this excursion. Her screams would quickly turn to curses if she suspected that she was the cause of celebration, and he didn't want to be anywhere in her line of vision when she did. His mother's powers seemed to be greatly diminished, but he'd been on the wrong end of one of her spells before. He had no wish to repeat the experience.

"Why have we stopped?" he demanded of 'Enakai.

"My heart is troubled," she said. "There is something . . ." She beckoned to one of the elderly priests behind the chariot, calling him by name.

"Yes, Light of the World," he answered.

"We've come to offer sacrifice, yet this Atlantean is a foreigner who has never sworn his allegiance to me. I ask you, holy father. Is this a breach of custom? Must he be Lemorian to be worthy?"

"Not specifically," the priest replied. 'Enakai frowned, and the elderly man quickly changed his tune. "But it is custom."

"I can see that Prince Caddoc could be the sacrifice," 'Enakai said. "We have offered foreigners before. But it seems to me, if he offers another in his place, it would be more fitting if he had at least given his allegiance to Lemoria and to the throne."

Caddoc's bowels constricted. "You told me that I didn't have to die," he whispered to 'Enakai. "You promised me. You said that Queen Halimeda would make a fitting substitute."

"Shh," she admonished. "This is a serious matter, one

we must get right." She smiled at the priest. "So, what you are saying is that you believe that Prince Caddoc's swearing allegiance to me would make the offering without blemish. . . . If he, in fact, became a Lemorian."

The priest hemmed and hawed. "If . . . if that's what seems right to you, majesty. You, of course, must be the final—"

"Yes." 'Enakai smiled and raised a hand. "On the advice of our holy father, we will offer Prince Caddoc the opportunity to become one of our subjects, so that his offering will be pleasing to the goddess." She looked at him. "You have no objection, do you?"

"No." Caddoc shook his head. "None at all, if that's what's required."

"Good. I feel much better."

She seemed to be waiting for something, but Caddoc wasn't sure what.

"Kneel," she said impatiently. "The tide will turn and it will be too late. Hurry."

He dropped to his knees.

"Prince Caddoc, do you swear allegiance to the Kingdom of Lemoria, rejecting all other sovereigns and claiming Lemoria as your own?"

Sweat rolled down his back, creating a slick film between his tunic and scales. "I do," he cried loudly.

"Do you reject the laws of Atlantis and her Poseidon?"

"This won't keep me from claiming his throne, will it?" Caddoc whispered.

"Not so long as you recognize me as your queen."

"I do so," he stated. "I reject Poseidon and Atlantis."

"Good." Enakai smiled. She tapped the driver's shoulder. "Move on." She glanced at him with a mischievous look in her eye. "If this doesn't drag on too long, we may have time to retire to my apartments for a romp before the evening court banquet."

Caddoc tightened his grip on the chariot bar. Not to reply seemed the safest. All women were difficult, but 'Enakai was impossible. There was no telling what she would demand next. Her latest request was a minor annoyance, nothing more. Once he was crowned Poseidon in his own right, she'd be lucky if he didn't send Atlantean troops against her. Prince Kaleo's attack would be reason enough—that and the Lemorian ordered assassination of his brothers.

A pity his mother wouldn't be here to witness the culmination of her greatest plot. Together, she and her brother, his Uncle Pelagias, had planned the simultaneous execution of Poseidon, Orion, and Alexandros. So far as Caddoc knew, Alex wasn't in Atlantis, so his death would not be accomplished as efficiently. Perhaps, with a little creativity, Pelagias could make it appear that Alexandros was responsible for his brothers' murders and the palace coup. Once the three were accounted for, he'd not need 'Enakai or her soldiers to take what was rightfully his.

Caddoc smiled. Finally. He was sorry that he couldn't be there to witness it and to tidy up. The children would have to die, the new prince, the Princess Danu, and Caddoc's younger half brothers Paris, Marcos, Lucas, and the other striplings. He could never keep their names straight.

His brothers' wives and his sister Morwena need not meet the same fate, so long as they agreed to become part of his household. They would serve well as concubines. He'd long lusted after Morwena and Rhiannon was a tasty morsel ready to be devoured. As for Elena . . . She was attractive enough, but whether she could satisfy him in bed would be the question.

It was all he could do to keep a straight face. 'Enakai thought she was in control. She believed that she held him in her power. Actually, she was doing him a favor, ridding him of his troublesome mother and providing entertainment while he waited for the call. Once his brothers were dead, the high council would summon him. Who else? He was the firstborn son of Poseidon. Becoming high king was his destiny.

The driver reined in the dolphins.

"This is as far as we can safely go," 'Enakai explained. "Already the heat becomes troublesome for the dolphins. The priests can escort Queen Halimeda to the edge of the flow."

Caddoc swallowed and stared at the river of fire that spread across the ocean floor. Great fountains of molten lava gushed and leaped over the glittering stream. "At least it will be quick," he muttered, more to himself than to 'Enakai.

"It's not too late to change your mind and accept the honor yourself," she reminded him.

Caddoc shook his head. "She's old and suffering. And, as you say, this will provide great luxury for her in the afterlife." It sounded good, but for himself he had no belief in gods or goddesses, neither these of the Lemorians, the old earth spirits that the fairy folk worshiped, or the one supreme god of the Atlanteans. When you were dead, you were dead, as far as he was concerned. It was the pleasures that a man could appreciate in this life that counted.

"There's time for you to bid her farewell, if you like," the queen suggested.

Again, Caddoc shook his head. "No. No need to make her suffer. Parting from me . . ." He sighed. "I am her only child, and we were always close."

"So be it," 'Enakai pronounced. She waved and two priests opened the door to the shell conveyance.

Caddoc turned his back. Better not to watch. The sight might give him nightmares. He wished he had covered his ears when his mother began to scream. "I warned you," he said to 'Enakai. "She won't take this well."

The shrieking continued, grew louder, and became foul curses joined by the filthiest and most original swearing he'd ever heard his mother utter—which was amazing, considering the oaths he'd heard from his dear mother through the past several thousand years.

At the last minute, he couldn't stand it. He turned and peeked from the corner of his eyes as the priests dragged her to the top of a high platform. He looked away as they pushed her over, and her last word drifted through the water.

"Ca . . . ddoc!"

Caddoc shuddered and glanced back. She was no longer part of the party at the edge of the lava flow. The remaining priest, a short one, who must have been dragged over with his mother, delivered a short ritual, then hurried back to the procession.

"It's done," 'Enakai said. "Not as tidily as I might have hoped, but finished with some dignity." She arched a brow. "Any regrets, my prince?"

"No." He straightened his shoulders, realizing that it was true. He felt nothing at all. His mother was dead, and she would never trouble him again in this world. "I'm sure she'll thank me for it in her prayers," he added piously.

"I'm sure," 'Enakai replied.

She was unnaturally quiet all the way back to the temple. Once they arrived in the grand courtyard, she left the dolphin chariot and took a seat in a jeweled chair. Eight female soldiers lifted the poles and carried her swiftly down the wide avenue to the palace. Caddoc was forced to follow on foot.

The soldiers conveyed 'Enakai, not to her private apartments as Caddoc had supposed they would, but to one of the smaller reception rooms where she often settled minor disputes among her subjects and meted out justice to criminals.

As they lowered the open chair to the marble floor, 'Enakai clapped. Immediately, two of the guardswomen moved to take hold of Caddoc's arms, one on either side.

"What is this?" he shouted. "How dare—"

"Be still," 'Enakai ordered. "There is a final matter to be cleared up."

"What matter?" Caddoc demanded.

She placed her hands, palms together in a position of prayer. "You have sworn to me, haven't you?"

"Yes. Yes. But what does that signify?"

"Which makes you a Lemorian, subject to our laws."

"What laws?" Urine trickled down the inside of his leg. "What law have I broken? I've done all you asked. I let you sacrifice my own mother to your lava pit, didn't I?"

'Enakai sighed. "Unfortunately, that's the sad point, Prince Caddoc. Causing the death of one's parent is a great crime among my people."

"No!" he shrieked. "I've committed no crime. It was your idea. I only did—"

Another soldier thrust a length of shark tail into his mouth, muffling his cries, and his bowels betrayed him, sending a flood of offal over his sandals. Someone snickered, but Caddoc could hardly hear for the pounding of blood in his ears.

"The punishment is blinding," 'Enakai said with cool disdain. "Take him to the prison and carry out the sentence." She patted his cheek. "It won't be so bad, my precious. I'm leaving you your sacks and rod. You'll still be able to pleasure me."

Caddoc's eyes bulged as terror drained him of his last measure of courage and strength. *Noooo!*

"And cut out his tongue as well," the queen added. "Otherwise, we'll never hear the end of this. He'll drive me mad with his whining."

CHAPTER 18

Alex insisted that Ree return to the surface after they had made love for a second time. "I tell you, I've never felt better," she insisted. "Whatever sickness Anuata is referring to, I can assure you that I don't have it. I'm having no trouble breathing under water."

"To the beach, woman," he ordered. "If I can put up with another day or two on this island, so can you."

Reluctantly, Ree followed him into shallower water. When they reached the breakers, Alex raised his head and shoulders above the crashing surf. "Watch your feet," he warned. "This is a good feeding spot for rays and smaller sharks. You don't want to drive a spike through the bottom of your foot."

After the reef, the small spit of land and palm trees that she'd found so enchanting seemed a barren second choice. She hadn't wanted to leave the coral paradise. "Why do we have to stay here?" Ree persisted as Alex waded ashore. "Every day we waste, Varenkov is getting farther away."

He turned to look at her, and flashed a roguish grin that would have melted a granite sphinx, his wet hair clinging to impossibly broad shoulders, his muscular chest beaded with drops of water. Ree's throat tightened as her gaze naturally swept lower over the hard, taut belly, to linger on his large and well-formed sex. Alex's gaze met hers, and she felt heat flash beneath her skin as desire reared in the shadow of her thoughts.

Maybe he's right, she thought. *Maybe I am part Atlantean now.* She'd always enjoyed sex, but now she found her appetite for lovemaking ravenous and her enjoyment magnified many times over.

"Didn't you just agree to do what I say, when I say it?" Alex reminded her.

Ree nodded, noting with satisfaction that if she was hot and bothered just looking at Alex's naked body, he was just as aroused in seeing hers. "Just don't push your orders beyond the bounds of the mission."

He held out his hand, and she was thrilled by his touch as his strong fingers closed around hers. "What if the mission required tending to the needs of your commander?"

"I suppose it might depend on what those needs were."

Alex laughed. "You have to know that sexual pleasure is the weakness of Atlanteans. We require a great deal of it and in infinite forms."

"I'm beginning to appreciate that." She released his hand and settled onto the warm sand, letting her feet rest in the incoming waves. She'd always been comfortable with her body, and she'd worked hard to keep it in the best shape, but she'd never been as aware of being female as she was here on this solitary beach in the twilight as the red-orange sun sank into the sea. Again, it seemed to her that she'd spent her entire life asleep, and now she'd awakened. Scents were stronger, her vision was clearer, and she was utterly aware of every sensation, from the feel of the sand under her to the caress of the waves and the smell of flowers blooming somewhere on the island.

Alex was all male, as sexual a man as she'd ever laid eyes on, and yet . . . She had to be honest. Her attraction to him wasn't simply physical. He was funny, intellectually challenging, and courageous with a strong sense of honor.

Easy, she warned herself. She was wading into dangerous waters. This was supposed to be business. . . . and sex. She had no time for a man in her life. She'd had one, and that had ended badly. Alone, she could be strong, but she didn't think she could stand the pain of losing someone she loved again.

Alex dropped onto the sand beside her. "Did you ever make sandcastles when you were a child?"

She looked away, focusing on a bleached white piece of driftwood. Playing on the beach with her mother had been a cherished memory, but so old and softened by time that she wasn't certain what was real and what she'd fashioned of wishful thinking and longing for what she knew she could never have again. "No." It was easier to lie than to answer questions that would probe and resurrect images best forgotten.

"It was a treat for Orion and me, to go above the water and race back and forth on a stretch of beach. The sand there was black, and there were high cliffs. My mother was vigilant. She and a company of guards would keep watch while we played. Sometimes we could spot fishing boats in the distance, and when we did, my mother would clap her hands for us to return to the sea. I remember the sounds of wind through the rocks and the sight of flocks of sea birds wheeling overhead."

"Why did she bring you out of the water if it was dangerous?"

Alex dug a hole, heaping the damp sand to form a wall. But each foaming wave that rushed in would cut through the barrier and wash away the sand. "We had to learn to breathe as humans do. There are times when we need to use our powers of illusion to disguise ourselves as one of your kind."

"My kind?" She chuckled. "And what is my kind?" She

raised her hand and pressed it, her palm flat against his wet and sandy one, then leaned close and kissed his mouth. "Make up your mind, Alex. Am I Atlantean or human?"

"I think you're Ree O'Connor, an unknown and fascinating creature." He pushed her back against the sand, and kissed her passionately.

Fire leaped between them as his hands and mouth moved over her. Soon, they were making love again, oblivious to anything but each other while the foam and waves washed around them. And this time, when they could wait no longer and Alex entered her, Ree realized that intercourse with this man was more than physical body parts and familiar motions. His touch, his nearness, the magic that they shared went beyond anything that she'd ever imagined.

It's too late, she thought. *I'm already lost.*

Later, after the world had come undone and shattered into a thousand stars, and Ree had drifted back to earth, she was yanked back into the present by a familiar voice.

"Mother of Vassu! Are you two at that again?"

Ree pushed herself out of Alex's embrace and sat up abruptly to find Anuata and Dewi standing a few yards away and laughing. "What are you?" she asked. "Voyeurs?"

Dewi laughed louder. "It was quite entertaining."

"Most entertaining," Anuata added.

Alex got to his feet and offered Ree his hand. He studied first Dewi and then Anuata. Both wore full battle gear and seemed the worse for wear. Dewi's right eye was black and swollen as was Anuata's single remaining eye. Dewi's chin and shoulder bore dark purple bruises and there was a scrape down one thigh and leg that ended in a gashed knee. Anuata's knuckles on one hand were torn and bloody and her nose and lower lip were swollen. "Have you two been fighting or . . ."

Dewi grinned. "Some of each." He handed Ree her boy's tunic, her armor, and sword, and she began to put them on.

The big Amazon smiled. "The little man and I have come to an understanding. Some things he is very good at."

Ree glanced from one to the other and shook her head. "Crazy, both of you."

Anuata tossed Alex his armor and weapons. "There's someone you should talk with. Out there." She motioned toward the reef.

"An envoy from 'Enakai?" Alex asked.

"No," Dewi said. "Aphrodite. One of your father's . . ." He shrugged. "She says you know her from the palace."

"Aphrodite here?" Alex frowned. "I know she left after my father died, but I didn't realize she was in the Pacific."

Dewi grimaced. "I'd heard she followed Caddoc and his scum when he fled the kingdom. You could ask her, but whether you'd get an honest answer is anyone's guess." He rolled his eyes. "You know mermaids."

"What?" Ree glanced at Alex. "Could you fill me in here?"

"Mermaids are not known for honesty," Anuata said.

"Mermaids?" Ree asked, not certain she could wrap her head around the concept.

"Later," Alex said. "Now, I need to talk to Aphrodite. Come with me if you like, but watch, don't comment. It's better if you don't say anything at all. She's a mermaid, and they have no love for humans, least of all human females. They're jealous of them."

"Of all women," Anuata said. "Of course, they're greatly attracted to human males, but not always to the humans' benefit."

"A mermaid?" Ree looked doubtful. "This I have to see." She looked back at Alex. "I suppose she has a fish tail?"

"Yes," he admitted. "But it's best if you don't mention it. It's bad manners."

Aphrodite proved to be exactly what Alex had said, a mermaid, complete with a scaly fish tail. Ree had to blink to be certain she was seeing what she thought she was seeing.

The mermaid reclined indolently on a bed of sand along the edge of the coral reef. Beside her lay a pile of discarded fish bones, leading Ree to assume the lady had just finished her evening meal. Or breakfast. Who knew what schedule a living, breathing mermaid might keep?

She was very beautiful, this exotic, fairy-tale creature, with her long, black hair and skin the color of sea foam. Her features were delicate; her eyes sea blue and her bare, voluptuous breasts shapely enough to bring a sailor to tears. From the waist up, she was every bit the alluring woman. Her arms were in perfect proportion, her lips were coral pink, her lashes dark and long and curling, and her voice high and sweet. But from the waist down, she had the appearance of a great green and glistening fish.

If this was a practical joke Alex, Anuata, and Dewi were playing on her, Ree thought, this was a good one. And if mermaids were as real as fairies and Atlanteans, what else existed under heaven? The possibilities were endless.

Alex called out to her in a language that Ree had never heard him or anyone use, and the mermaid answered in a burst of emotion. After a few exchanges, they switched to a language that Ree could understand.

"My half brother, is he well?" Alex asked. "Prince Caddoc."

Aphrodite scowled. "I wouldn't know. We parted company soon after we arrived. He had the audacity to suggest that I join him and his . . . his pet, the ugly Samoan in a rather dull game. You know that I enjoy my pleasures, but

I am no common whore. When I refused, Prince Caddoc became difficult. To Hades with him!"

"Fair enough." Alex nodded. "Do you know where he is?"

"When last I heard, in 'Enakai's bed."

"My friends say you have information for me."

"Perhaps," Aphrodite answered. She dug in the pile of fish bones, came up with a skeleton that had meat still clinging to it and nibbled daintily.

Alex waited.

The mermaid sighed and raked long, slim fingers through her hair. "I do. And for the love your brother bore my friend Sjshsglee, I will pass a message. The human you hunt is on the island of Rorakleesan, the land that the air breathers call Pago Pago. Poseidon directs you to proceed there at once and kill him."

"He's still here? Varenkov? In American Samoa?"

Ree's heartbeat quickened. If the Russian was nearby, it might be possible to finish him before he could slip through her fingers again.

Aphrodite nodded. Then she yawned and fluttered her long, thick lashes. "And you must do as the king commands, yes?"

A blinding pain shot through Ree's head, and she doubled over as cramps in her stomach made her clench her teeth against the pain. A gray cloud gathered behind her eyes and suddenly the reef had vanished and she was looking down from a great height at a cove in a rocky coast. Dark shapes bobbed in the water, not swimming shapes, but something unnatural. Bile rose in her throat as she saw the color of the sea, not blue but crimson.

"Ask her about the cove," Ree cried. "Ask her what she knows about the cove."

Aphrodite's head snapped around, and she stared at Ree

in astonishment. "Your woman has the sight," she said. "I had heard much about her, but not that."

"Do you know something you're not telling me?" Alex demanded.

"You didn't ask."

Ree pressed her hands against her head. She forced herself to fight the pain and to look again. This time, her view of the water was more distant, and she could see small boats, and farther out to sea a large ocean-going ship. Blackness closed over her. She thought she was dying. "Blood," she whispered. "I see death and blood."

"She does see the future," the mermaid said. "A true seer. There is a thing your brother the king does not want you to know. The Russian's vessels will drive the dolphins and massacre them by the hundreds at Aunu'u Island. The humans will butcher them and sell the meat. Poseidon knows of the coming atrocity and has sent word to Lemoria asking Queen 'Enakai to send her soldiers to save as many as she can. But 'Enakai is suspicious of messages from Atlantis. Who knows what she will do?"

"When will this drive happen? Do you know?"

Aphrodite smiled. "What does it matter? Your brother the king sends you to kill the Russian while some of my kinsmen try to turn back the dolphins." She stretched and yawned again. "I'm sleepy. I had hoped to sing for you, but—"

"When?" Alex repeated. "When will the killing take place?"

The mermaid's gaze became hard. "When the sun rises over Aunu'u. At dawn, prince of Atlantis, many of your dolphin brothers and sisters will cease to exist. But you will not be there to help, for you will be obeying Poseidon and hunting the Russian."

★ ★ ★

As Danu raced after her father on Echo, she nearly collided with her Aunt Morwena. "Help me!" Danu cried. "Daddy is in danger."

"How?" Morwena asked. "And why are you unescorted? This is not a section of the palace that is safe for—"

"There's no time," Danu argued. She thrust her father's bow and quiver into her aunt's hands. "Lord Pelagias means him harm!"

"How do you know this?" Morwena, a novice priestess, was already late for prayer. She'd already missed too many sessions, and if she went with Danu, she might be dismissed from her class and have to repeat an entire level.

The child drew herself up as tall as it was possible for a six-year-old and placed her hand over her stomach. "I feel it. Here. You must come. They will hurt my daddy."

"If there's danger, it's no place for a child," she scolded the dolphin. "Go and find palace guards. Take Danu to safety."

"No." Danu dug her heels into Echo's sides and the dolphin shot ahead down the hallway. Morwena hesitated only a fraction of a second before going after them.

Danu heard the angry shouts before she reached the enclosed courtyard.

"Usurper!"

"You have no right to the crown!"

Danu knew the second voice. That was Lord Pelagias. "Go!" she urged Echo.

Girl and dolphin shot from the corridor into the walled courtyard. "Daddy!" she screamed. Her father leaned against a painted column clutching his side. There was something sticking out of it, and blood ran down his body in thick streams. "Don't hurt him! He's the king!"

A mean-looking man that she didn't know pulled a knife from his sheath and moved toward her father. "Prince

Caddoc is the rightful king!" the man said. "For Caddoc and Jason!"

"No!" Danu shouted, giving Echo the signal for ramming.

The great mammal surged through the water, catching the man just below his midsection with her beak and bowling him backward. So great was the force of the blow that Danu was nearly hurled off the dolphin's back. Lord Pelagias hurled a spear. It struck Echo and she squealed in pain but turned toward her tormentor. Danu threw herself out of the harness and swam to her father. She caught his face between her hands and gazed into his eyes.

"Run," Poseidon whispered. "Run, Danu!" His eyes widened in fear and Danu looked in the direction he was staring. The bad man was struggling to his feet and coming toward them with a naked blade.

Danu wanted to run, but she couldn't. If she took her hands off Daddy he would slip away. She could feel his life force weakening. There was so much blood. The thing sticking out of his side was a short sword, and that was draining his life away. She wanted to yank the thing out, but something told her that was not the right thing to do. Instead, she concentrated on holding his attention.

"Listen to me, Daddy," she said. "Close your eyes, and listen to me. Feel the cool water. Feel the power of the star. Feel the blood slowing. Soon it will stop, and you'll be fine. You can't die, Daddy. I need you. Perseus needs you."

Danu could feel the scales rising on the back of her neck. She could feel the bad man growing closer. She knew he would hurt her—kill her, and then he would kill her daddy. But she could only do what the light told her. She was a royal princess and she had to remain brave.

"Hold on. Hold on," the voice in her head said. *"Believe in the power of healing."*

Danu's fingers were trembling. Her heart pounded. She was only a little girl. She didn't want to die.

And then she heard the hiss of a missile moving through the water. She waited for the pain of the knife slicing through her body, but it didn't come. Instead, she heard the man behind her grunt. She glanced over her shoulder and saw him pierced through by an arrow. As she watched, the bad man's eyes opened wide and he sank to the tile floor and lay still.

"Back, Echo," her Aunt Morwena ordered. "Back." Morwena stepped in front of Danu, blocking her view of Lord Pelagias. "Don't look," she said. "He won't hurt anyone again. Neither of them will."

"Did Echo kill Lord Pelagias?" Danu asked.

"Yes." Morwena dropped her brother's big bow and knelt beside them. "Is he alive?" she asked.

Danu sighed. "Yes, but he's lost so much blood."

"Take Echo and go for the guard! Tell them to send healers from the temple."

Danu shook her head. "I can't. If I let him go, he'll slip away. Send Echo, or you go. I have to stay with Daddy."

Morwena looked at the child, realizing what she'd just witnessed, realizing that she was in the presence of a powerful priestess, one who had never studied and was too short to reach the shelves of scrolls in the great library, knowing that this small girl commanded knowledge that she might never possess.

"I'll bring help. Echo, you stay with Poseidon and Danu!" Morwena picked up the bow again. "I'll warn the queen and Princess Elena. There may be more traitors in the palace."

CHAPTER 19

Three of Lord Pelagias' armed hirelings, led by his youngest son Creon, charged into the queen's apartments where they found not a helpless woman surrounded by serving maids, but Lady Athena and a troop of her archer-priestesses waiting for them. The would-be assassins fell in the courtyard, all but Creon who, although wounded in the right arm and left side, dodged a hail of arrows to invade the baby prince's room.

"Death to the false heir!" Creon cried. "Long live King Caddoc!"

Perseus' gilded oyster-shell crib hung suspended from the ceiling with braided ropes of sea grass. A blanket-wrapped form lay sprawled across the mattress, and Creon drove his trident into what he believed was a sleeping toddler. When he ripped away the covering, he found only a stuffed dolphin toy. Cursing, he turned away to find the door blocked by Lady Athena.

"Traitor," she accused. "How much courage does it take to slay an infant?"

"Out of my way, high priestess!" he bellowed.

"As you wish." Lady Athena stepped aside and two of Poseidon's fighting dolphins dove past her into the baby's room. "Kill!" she ordered, and the armored mammals made short work of the task, knocking Creon's body back and forth between them as if it was a misshapen ball.

Lady Athena swept from Perseus' room to the court where two dozen of the king's guard shouldered into the open space. "You took your time about it," the priestess admonished.

"Lady." The captain saluted. "We came as soon as we were called. You may be at ease. No rebels will pass this gate again."

She motioned to the now-floating and lifeless bodies of Creon's followers. "Take them away, identify them, and dispose of them. Has Poseidon been found?"

The captain shook his head. "No, lady. No one has seen him. He was not struck down with the others on the archery range." The man hesitated, clearly wanting to speak, but reluctant.

"What else?" Lady Athena asked.

"Two of the royal princes are dead."

"Who?" Queen Rhiannon jerked back as if she had received a physical blow. Then she straightened and came to stand behind her mother, Lady Athena, with Orion's Elena beside her. The queen clasped her son Perseus in her arms, holding him so tightly that the baby squealed in protest. "Which princes are lost? And is it fact or only rumor?"

Tears sprang from the captain's eyes. "Prince Orion and Prince Paris. A merman brought the message. The assassins were struck down within a heartbeat of the treachery, but the princes had no chance. They were shot from behind by men they trusted. One of the traitors was Kiril, oldest son to Lord Pelagias."

"And cousin to Prince Caddoc," Lady Athena said softly. "Creon, too. Lord Pelagias' only children. He will take it hard."

"What of the king?" Queen Rhiannon demanded.

"Our daughter was with him." She looked at Lady Athena with desperation in her eyes. "No one would harm a little girl, would they? She's only six."

Lady Athena averted her gaze. "If the worst had happened, we would have had word. Queen Mother Korinna is safe, and Princess Morwena should have been at the temple. "

"Orion?" Elena's voice came as thin and cracked as an old woman's. "There must be a mistake. Orion can't be dead. We just shared a meal together."

The queen gripped her sister-in-law's hand. "Are they all lost? All my husband's brothers?"

"The whereabouts of young Prince Lucas is a mystery, your highness. And there is Prince Alexandros remaining."

"He's far from here, in the Pacific. How do we know that he wasn't slain as our dear ones here were?" The queen took a deep breath and kissed the baby's head. "Protect my son," she said. "If anything has happened to his father, he is now Poseidon, high king of all Atlantis."

"With our lives," the captain answered.

"And bring me word as soon as you hear," she added. "Good or evil. We must know what's happening."

Elena reached out for Perseus. "Let me take him," she said. Her face was a mask of grief. "It may not be an error," she said. "In emergencies, first reports are often garbled. Orion may be only injured. I can't know that he's . . . that anything has happened to him until I see him." Her mouth quivered. "I won't believe it. Not Orion . . . not my Orion."

"How far are we from American Samoa?" Ree asked Alex when the mermaid had tired of their company and swam away. "Varenkov may be gone before we can reach Pago Pago." She had some knowledge of the geography of the South Pacific, but the distance between Tahiti, which was her last identifiable point, and Samoa were vast. It wasn't as if they could hop an inter-island jet.

Dewi flashed her a scornful look. "We aren't going after the Russian."

"What do you mean?" Ree asked. "Alex promised me—"

"Mother of Vassu!" Anuata swore. "Have you humans no heart? How can you think of hunting him when our brothers and sisters are about to be massacred?"

Bleddyn scowled. "We go to Aunu'u to try and prevent a wholesale slaughter."

Ree appealed to Alex. "Are you the one who decides? You promised me that we were going after—"

"Aphrodite's message changed everything," Alex said. "Try and understand. To us, a dolphin is . . ."

"An equal," Anuata supplied. "Smarter and more caring than a human."

"I know they are intelligent mammals," Ree said, "but—"

"They have a superior intelligence, but different from that of humanoids," Alex explained. "Dolphins are courageous and loyal, but in some ways, they are innocent. They don't lie, and they don't understand treachery. Family is everything to them. If a mate, an offspring, a sibling, or parent, any relative or friend in their complex society is injured or sick, they remain at their side to protect and comfort them, even if it means their own deaths."

"They fight beside us"—Dewi said— "and care for our children. Those who have cast their fate with Atlanteans accept us as part of that family, and we give them the same regard. You consider yourself an American, do you not?"

"Irish-American," Ree answered.

Dewi nodded. "Do you have any Swedish blood?"

"No, not that I know of."

"So, would you stand by and watch Swedish families

massacred, if you could prevent it? Could you turn your back on Swedish children who were going to be gutted alive and skinned for meat?"

Ree's stomach churned. "Of course not, but Swedes are humans."

"Who speak another language and have different customs," Alex said. "For us, it is the same. Dolphins, even wild dolphins who have never had contact with an Atlantean or a Lemorian"—He glanced at Anuata—"are still deserving of our compassion."

Ree nodded. "So we give up our chance at Varenkov and try to stop the dolphin kill?"

"I missed him in Tahiti," Alex said. "If I miss him again at Pago Pago, it matters little. I will get him, and after the Russian, the council will give me a new assignment."

Ree understood that. She'd lost track of the number of undesirables that she'd eliminated. *No, that's a lie,* her inner voice cried. *You know exactly how many there have been. You see their faces in your dreams.*

But none she regretted. The world was better for them being gone. What did trouble her were the occasional mercenaries who got caught in the crossfire or the possibility that some innocent might be killed by mistake. . . . Like Nick.

Not that Nick was innocent; he'd been in the game for a decade longer than she had. But losing him was a wound that had never healed. She'd gone over and over the sequence of what had happened that day, searching for where she'd gone wrong. It always came down to a bad decision that she had made, and nothing she could do would ever change it.

Who would have guessed Varenkov's people would have identified the rental car they'd been using that day? She'd been driving since they'd crossed into Germany, and she should have been the one to leave their surveillance point to get the car. But, she was the better shot, and she hadn't wanted to move off the rooftop until she was certain the Russian wouldn't come out of the apartment building and cross the parking lot. The area was well lighted, the weather was foul, and at that hour of the night, no civilians had ventured out for more than an hour.

So she'd sent Nick to his death. And when she'd heard the explosion, she'd known that Varenkov's agents had spotted them, and that he wasn't coming out. The chances were that he'd been gone long before Nick had unlocked the car door and inserted the key into the ignition. The bomb had been professional and effective. There hadn't been enough left of the vehicle or Nick's body to identify the make or model.

It should have been her . . .

"Ree. Ree. Are you all right?" Alex's strong hand on her shoulder pulled her back into the present.

Anuata's tattooed face loomed over hers. "Has the sickness returned?"

"No. I'm fine. I was just . . . just thinking." She moved away from Alex. "So we're chasing . . . what? Bottom trawlers? Polynesian fishermen?"

"Greedy and misguided humans," Alex replied. "Not necessarily evil, but ignorant. We'll do what we can not to harm any of them, but if it comes to self-defense, or if you have to protect the dolphins, then . . ." He shrugged. "And above all, if you're seen, be certain that you throw an illusion." He looked at Anuata. "You'll have to stay beneath the surface. No one would believe you're human."

Dewi grinned. "I'm not sure if that was a compliment."

"Lemorians are not so . . . so . . ."

"Sneaky?" Dewi suggested. "Deceitful?"

"Illusion is a useful tool we've developed through the ages," Alex said. "It helps us remain hidden from humans when we come in contact with them."

Ree frowned. "I don't understand. What do you mean by illusion?"

Alex gestured to Bleddyn. "Show her an example."

She stared as the soldier transformed before her eyes, changing himself from an Atlantean warrior to the likeness of an elderly Greek woman, complete with a market basket containing a loaf of bread, two fish, and a bottle of wine. Ree blinked and reached out to grab not the arm of a senior citizen but that of a sinewy warrior. "You can all do that?"

"Most of us," Alex assured her. "I suspect you might be able to as well, in time. The physical appearance of Atlanteans and humans aren't that different."

"We're taller, stronger, smarter, and handsomer," Bleddyn said.

Dewi settled an arm around Anuata. "Not to mention sexier."

With an incredulous look, the Amazon shoved him away and raised a threatening fist.

"You know it's true," Dewi said with a grin. And then to Ree, he confided, "She adores me."

Anuata's quick reply didn't translate but came across to Ree as a slurred growl.

"It's simple. Fix a human in your mind," Alex said. "Then imagine yourself in that likeness."

"It's so easy that even a child can do it," Dewi said and proceeded to make himself a perfect mirror image of Anuata, down to her scowl and the fierce expression in her eyes. "See how beautiful I am?" he proclaimed in his own voice.

Anuata laughed. "More handsome than you are in your own form."

Ree concentrated, but nothing happened. "Maybe it's a talent I wasn't born with."

"It doesn't matter," Alex said. "I'd rather not leave you

alone here, but I'm not convinced that you're in the physical or mental condition to take part in this mission. If you
were to pass out again or have trouble breathing, you'd
put us all in danger."

"I told you, I'm fine. If you won't let me help you, then
get me ashore. I'll go after Varenkov myself."

Alex shook his head. "You'll come, and you'll stay
where I put you. My conditions, remember. I give the orders, you obey them."

"And if I don't agree?"

"Then you stay here on the island. Until we come back,
or until you can find your own way home."

Danu remained at her father's side with Echo beside her.
She knew that he was still alive, but barely, and she was
more afraid than she'd ever been in her life. "I love you,"
she told him, over and over. "I'm here. You have to stay
with me. Aunt Morwena will bring the healers but you
have to fight the darkness."

She could see that Daddy wasn't bleeding as badly as he
had been, but she didn't know if that was because he was
better, or if all his blood had already run out. He had to
live. How could she tell Mommy that she'd let him slip
away from her when they needed him so badly? Daddy
was Poseidon, high king of all Atlantis, but most important, he belonged to her and Mommy and little Perseus.

Tears rolled down Danu's cheeks and she rubbed them
away with the backs of her hands. She wouldn't cry! She
wasn't a baby! She wasn't afraid of the bad men who'd tried
to kill her father, but the tears wouldn't stop. They just
kept coming out of her eyes and running down her face.

If only Uncle Orion would come. He had a big sword
and he might bring Uncle Paris and Uncle Alex. They
would chase away all the bad people and take care of her
father. Uncle Alex was her favorite. He had lots of impor-

tant stuff to do, but when he was home, he always came to see her. He would take her riding on giant sea horses and ask the cooks to make honey cakes, even if it was too early in the day for little girls to want special treats. And then Uncle Alex would share her cakes, and he'd tell her funny stories about when he and Daddy and Uncle Orion were small and got into trouble.

If her uncles came, they would take her and Daddy home. Mommy would squeeze her tight and kiss her eyelids and her nose. Danu sniffed and rubbed her nose. There wasn't any reason to cry. Someone would come and take Daddy to the temple and make him better. Aunt Morwena had promised.

Meanwhile, Danu would do her best. She would keep talking to Daddy and pray for him. Lady Athena, her secret grandmother, had told her that the best prayers were those offered by children, and those that were made up naturally were stronger than any recited in the temple. So, she prayed to the Supreme Being to save her father, and she kept talking.

Twice, she heard people in the hallways nearby, shouting and crying. She tried to get Echo to go and see if they were good or bad, but the dolphin swam restlessly back and forth guarding the entrance and angrily jaw-clapping and spewing bubbles from her blowhole. And nothing Danu could say could get the dolphin to go a stroke farther from her and Daddy.

Danu was tired. Her head hurt, and she knew that soon she wouldn't be able to summon the light anymore. "Please," she murmured, squeezing her eyes tight. "Please send help. Send it soon."

"Don't be afraid. I'm here to help you."

Danu gasped and her heart flopped in her chest like a baby dolphin wanting to be born from its mother. She knew that voice. She'd heard it when the bad witch had locked her in the cage when she was little. Something soft and fuzzy rubbed against Danu's hand. Trembling, she bit her bottom lip and opened her eyes.

Light made her blink. Not a bright light, but a soft glow, like the light-fish over her bed at home. Only this light was blue with silver snowflakes sparkling in it. Danu closed her eyes again. "Cymry? Is that you?" she whispered.

"What do you think?"

Danu opened her eyes, just a crack, hoping. And then, just like before, right in front of her hovered a blue sea horse. It wasn't a big one like the ones Uncle Alex took her riding on, and it wasn't a tiny one like those that lived in Uncle Orion's garden. This sea horse was exactly the right size. It had big blue eyes, a long silver mane, and a long, silver-colored tail. Even its hooves were silver, but its hide was a shimmering sea-blue.

"Cymry! It is you!" She hadn't seen her friend since Aunt Morwena and Elena had rescued her from the witch, but the sea horse had promised she'd come back when Danu was bigger. She was bigger now, and she needed Cymry as much as she had then. Maybe more. "Oooh." Danu threw her arms around the sea horse and hugged her. Cymry's fur was as silky as a baby seal's.

The sea horse gave a high whinny sound. "I've missed you, Danu," she said.

"And I've missed you. Why didn't you come back?"

"I have, haven't I?"

"I need your magic. A bad man stabbed my daddy with a sword. Aunt Morwena went to get help, but I don't know how to fix him. I think he might die."

"You're very brave, Danu. And you have your own magic. Powerful magic. You know what to do. You just have to remember and believe in yourself. Make a blue wall of light all around him and fill it with love."

"That sounds easy."

"It is, for you, precious one. You were born with a great gift of healing. Use it now to keep your daddy alive."

"Will you stay with me?"

"Always, but you can't tell anyone, because no one can see me but you."

"Not even Echo?"

"No, not even dolphins can see me."

"Why?"

"Because I come from a different place, far away in the stars. I came to your ocean a long, long, long time ago."

"But why can I see you?"

Cymry gave a whinny that sounded just like a little laugh. "Because you carry the blood of the star people, and they were very wise."

"Oh. My friend Obi told me that his mother said I used to be a human."

"Humans and Atlanteans don't just live one life. They have many. And they are really the same race, did you know that? But the people who live on land and breathe air forgot how to live in the sea, and the Atlanteans don't always remember when they both were the same."

"Oh." Danu rubbed her cheek against Cymry's soft fur. "So I was a human?"

"Sometimes. And sometimes you were Atlantean, and sometimes . . . We'll talk about that another time. Just know that even though you may not remember, we've been friends for a long time."

"Really?"

"What's important is that there's no one like you. When you're grown, you'll remember a lot more and you'll help humans and Atlanteans more than anyone knows. But today, you're going to use your special powers to keep your father from dying until help can come."

"Are you sure I can do that?" Danu asked.

"Positive."

Even though Danu didn't understand everything Cymry had said, she did exactly as the sea horse told her. She concentrated on surrounding Daddy with the blue light and kept talking to him. She didn't know how long they waited for Aunt Morwena, but suddenly, she was back. Two healers were with her, and they quickly took Danu's place on either side of Daddy. None of them noticed the magic sea horse, and Danu didn't say a word about her.

"He's alive," the oldest woman said. "It's all right, your highness. We're taking you back to the temple for care. Everything is all right."

Danu knew that her Aunt Morwena had been crying because her eyes were red, but when she threw her arms around her and hugged her tightly she didn't feel sad. Aunt Morwena felt happy. "Is Daddy going to be okay now?" Danu asked. "Will the priestesses make him better?"

"I don't know," her aunt answered softly. "I hope so."

"They will," Cymry whispered in Danu's ear. "Believe it."

Four of the palace guards hurried in to carry him. Danu saw that the priestesses didn't try to pull the sword out of her father's side, so she knew that it had been the right thing to leave it alone. Her head still hurt, and her tummy felt funny. Cymry was still hovering beside her, but when Danu looked away and then looked back, the sea horse had vanished, and all she saw was another shower of glittering blue and gold flakes. "I want my mother," Danu whispered to her Aunt Morwena. "Can you take me to Mommy?"

CHAPTER 20

O rion opened his eyes to see Elena sitting beside his bed. He felt weak, and his thoughts were jumbled. *What happened at the archery range?* He'd been passing the time until Poseidon arrived by showing Paris the bow he'd commissioned a craftsman to fashion for Danu. The two of them had been standing near the far end of the field. Suddenly, men were shouting, and he saw his younger half brother Marcos take an arrow through the throat.

Orion remembered diving for his own bow, and the shock of the first arrow striking him. It hit him hard, striking him in the chest, and driving him to his knees. He called out to Paris, and then blackness had closed around him. He'd known nothing more until a short time ago when he'd awakened here in the temple. Not awakened so much as drifted in and out of consciousness, hearing scraps of conversations between the healers and muffled words cut off when someone neared his bed.

". . . Attempted coup . . ."

". . . Prince Caddoc . . . topple the throne . . ."

". . . small group of traitors . . ."

"Elena?" he managed. Her beautiful image wavered, and he wondered if she was here beside him or he was dreaming. "Elena, is that you?" If she was here, she was safe. A sense of shame flooded him. But as much as he loved his family, this woman came first in his heart.

"It's me," she assured him. "Shhh. Try not to talk."

"Someone shot me." It was difficult to speak. His mouth tasted of blood and his throat felt dry and raw. Paris? *What happened to my brother?*

"Three times."

Orion groaned. "I only remember the first one. Paris? Where is he? Is he all right?"

Elena shook her head. "I'm so sorry. He was gone by the time the healers got to him."

Pain lanced through him. He remembered the expression on his brother's face, the laughter in his eyes just before all Hades broke out. It wasn't possible that a life so vibrant could be snuffed out so quickly. But in his gut, he knew.

Orion swore softly. Elena wouldn't lie. Paris, laughing, brave Paris, was gone. He didn't have to ask about Marcos. He'd seen the damage the arrow had done, and he'd known that the boy's life was forfeit. "I . . ." He was so weary. He tried to raise his head, but it was too heavy.

Elena gripped his hand. "We thought we'd lost you, too. Heron's lieutenant reported that both you and Paris had been killed by the rebels, but it was Marcos who was the second murdered prince. A dolphin who witnessed the attack said that after you were hit, Paris threw himself over your body to protect you."

"And he died in my place." Orion shuddered and his eyes burned with unshed tears. "He was always too bold."

"And you wouldn't have done the same for him?" she asked softly. Elena raised his bloodstained hand and kissed it. "If it's any consolation, none of the killers left the archery range alive. It must have been a suicide attack. There were only five of them, two noble born and three mercenaries. They must have known that they'd be taken out."

"Paris and Marcos were my younger brothers. I was supposed to protect them." Orion gritted his teeth against the tidal wave of hurt. And then a rush of dread came over him. *Morgan. What of Morgan?* "The king? Is he—"

"Alive. Bad. Worse than you, but still alive. I'll never understand Atlantean resilience and rate of healing. It seems almost miraculous. But I won't lie to you. Poseidon lost so much blood that the healers fear he may never recover. He's still unconscious."

"Where? He wasn't at the archery field."

"Lord Pelagias waylaid him and lured him into an ambush. It was our little Danu who found him. Danu and Echo, with Morwena's help, prevented the bastards from finishing what they started."

"What of the others? Perseus and Rhiannon?"

"Both safe, thanks to Lady Athena, although the traitors tried to get to them. And young Lucas is unharmed. He had skipped archery practice to meet with a young lady."

"And those responsible?" Orion asked. "Caddoc, I'm sure. Was Pelagias the ringleader here in the palace?"

"After questioning Lord Pelagias' servants and one man who lived long enough to give some information, Lady Athena and the council believe that Lord Pelagias conspired with his sons to murder you, the king, and your brothers. They intended to put Caddoc on the throne."

"Did he know about it?"

"Yes. But Caddoc wanted his name free of the taint of treason. His uncle, Lord Pelagias, was going to do all the dirty work for him."

"Halimeda has to be at the core of this. Pelagias is her brother, and Caddoc isn't smart enough to plan it alone."

Elena sighed. "Lady Athena believes that Pelagias wanted to be vizier. He knew that if the coup succeeded, Caddoc would be a weak king. If Pelagias got rid of Lord Zale and became vizier in his place, he would be the real ruler of the kingdom."

Orion tried to take it all in. It was almost a joke that so few men would attempt to assassinate Poseidon, his brothers, and his only son, but they'd almost gotten away with it. "Did they kill Lord Zale, too?"

"They tried, but our vizier outwitted them. He hid in a food cupboard until they went away."

Orion closed his eyes. "I don't suppose anyone has heard from Alex?"

"Nor expected to. There's no way he could know."

He thought he was going to vomit and wished the bed—the whole chamber—would stop swaying. He forced himself to open his eyes again and focus on Elena. "Who's in command? Lady Athena or Lord Zale?"

She sighed heavily. "Now that you're awake, I think it's you. I heard her say that if the king died, they'd crown you in his place."

"Prince Perseus is next in line, not me."

"He's only a baby. Rhiannon refuses to consider him being crowned. She's afraid for his life, and the council agrees that it would be too dangerous to have a child ruler. If Poseidon dies, they all mean for you to assume the throne."

"You didn't tell me how we were going to get from wherever we are to American Samoa in time to prevent the dolphin drive," Ree reminded Alex. "We'll never do it by swimming. You haven't neglected to tell me that Atlanteans can fly, too, have you?"

"*Xchymtrzcy,*" Anuata said. "There's a wormhole no more than five leagues from here."

"Don't confuse her." Dewi motioned to a tiger shark passing over their heads. "Keep your eye on him. That's a big one," he said.

Ree looked up at the dark shadow and suppressed a shiver. She definitely wasn't fond of sharks or the idea of swimming with them. At the moment, she wasn't particularly fond of Alex either. How could he think that he could keep her out of the action? She would have been willing to help him drive off the dolphin killers, but he'd turned down her offer. If she got close enough to Pago Pago, she'd show him how much his authority meant to her.

The four had been swimming not far below the surface of the ocean for what Ree guessed was close to an hour. The island was little more than a speck of green on the horizon the last time they'd surfaced. The seas were relatively calm, no more than two to three foot waves with a ten knot breeze. Clouds hung low overhead, and only the occasional lonely seabirds flew overhead, bound, no doubt, for the spit of sand and trees she, Anuata, and the Atlanteans had just left.

"*Xchymtrzcy* is what the Lemorians call the seraphim," Alex explained. "Think of it as fast transit, Atlantean style."

"Now I understand perfectly," Ree said sweetly. "Seraphim. We're going to be carried to Samoa by Old Testament angels."

"Not exactly," Alex said. "It's difficult to explain but you'll soon see. No angels involved, I promise."

"Now my curiosity is aroused."

"Think of it as a powerful wind tunnel. Seraphim predate humanoids on this planet, and their size is enormous, larger than you could imagine. They didn't exactly die out so much as evolve. Technically, they're still alive, but they no longer move. We travel through their digestive system."

"Fast," Bleddyn added. "Very fast."

Ree stopped swimming and stared at him. "You're joking. Right?" *It would make a good story at McCarthy's Pub in Cork.* She'd seen some pretty unbelievable things since

Alex had come into her life, but traveling through a giant worm's stomach topped them all.

"He's not joking," Anuata said.

"You'll go with me," Alex said. "It's dark, and it's noisy, and if you don't take the right exit, it can be hairy."

"What he means is that it can get you killed," Dewi said.

Anuata grimaced. "If you end up as *xchymtrzcy* dinner."

Alex touched Ree's shoulder. "That won't happen. Anuata is familiar with the route, and she's going first. All we have to do is take the same chutes and hatches that she does. We'll come out close enough to see the coast of Aunu'u."

"Is there a station with turnstiles?" Ree asked wryly. "Do we have to use seraphim tokens, or will they take a credit card?"

"No, we just take advantage of the system," Anuata replied with a grin that showed her pointed teeth. "You'll love it."

Grigori Varenkov stepped out of his shower, mopped the excess water from his naked body, and wrapped a silk lava-lava around his hirsute middle. He thrust his broad feet into a pair of Italian sandals and walked to the sideboard where a steward had laid out a buffet of roast pork, slabs of Kobe beef, smoked salmon, raw oysters, steamed shrimp, Beluga caviar, dark rye bread, and a few island favorites such as yams, taro, and breadfruit.

Varenkov poured himself a water glass of vodka and proceeded to heap a plate. He considered himself a simple man with simple tastes, and he liked plain food, well prepared without fancy sauces and French names. Varenkov prided himself on his legendary appetite. As a boy, he'd known too many days and nights of near starvation to deny himself anything now. And a man with an unlimited ticket could have a great deal of whatever he wanted, be it the pleasures of eating and drinking or those of a sexual nature.

He carried his oversized plate to the table, pulled out his chair and sat down. "Nigel, vill you join me?" Varenkov lifted his glass. "Come. There is plenty."

His new bodyguard shook his head. "I've eaten," he lied. Watching Varenkov eat always took away his appetite.

The Russian bit off huge mouthfuls and gobbled his food with such abandon that he invariably sprinkled his hairy chest and protruding belly with dribbles of grease and gristle, crumbs of bread and cheese, and smears of caviar. Varenkov would continue to stuff himself until he was gorged and his digestive system groaned under the weight. Neither loud belches nor prodigious farts deterred him until the platters and bowls were empty.

Only when there seemed no fresh fuel in sight and the vodka bottle had been drained would Varenkov push away from the table and call for dessert, usually a busty Nordic type female with a fondness for his crude jokes and rough sex. Sometimes, there would be two or three women instead of one, but these would invariably be olive-skinned or swarthy girls with black hair top and bottom.

At least once a week, Varenkov would vary his entertainment with a young male, tall and muscular, crude in appearance, and always Asian. With mundane routine, this latter performance would involve mild S & M, including handcuffs, a leather bit, and a bread paddle with holes drilled in it. At some point, the Asian would cuff Varenkov and threaten him with bit and paddle; the Russian would utter a ferocious growl, break free of his bonds, and dominate his willing partner. After several repetitions, the show would end in the draining of another bottle of expensive vodka.

Nigel wasn't disturbed by his employer's personal habits,

and it didn't bother him that Varenkov wanted him to remain in the cabin during the games as an observer. Since the incident off Tahiti and the Russian's insistence that he'd nearly been ambushed by an intruder, Varenkov rarely entered any room, other than his private bathroom here aboard the *Anastasiya* without an armed guard present.

Three hours later, Nigel ushered the two Samoan girls out of the stateroom and up to the deck where a small boat from the *Anastasiya*'s companion yacht waited to take them back to the dock. He welcomed the fresh salt air and was undeterred by the slight drizzle of rain and the stiff breeze off the ocean. They were anchored in the Pago Pago harbor and even in the darkness he could make out the looming shapes of the surrounding mountains and the outlines of other boats around them.

Varenkov wouldn't remain here long, but business had delayed him, business that would take them ashore in a few hours to meet a Mr. Smith, an accomplice in the trade. Pago Pago was a small town, little more than a village, with a population of less than 15,000, hardly a welcoming shelter for the likes of Varenkov. But American Samoa thrived on entertainment; there were high stakes gambling games and those who could satisfy all sorts of pleasures, if an interested party knew the right people and had the means to pay.

Nigel removed a Fonseca from his shirt pocket, carefully cut off the cap, and lit it. Expensive Cuban cigars were his weakness, and one he permitted himself to indulge in only occasionally. Smoking was a nasty habit and bad for his health. In another three years, perhaps two, Nigel would have enough money in his Swiss account to retire. He would stage his own demise and vanish from the world that he'd made his own, reappearing somewhere in the Outback of Australia or Alaska with a new name, a new identity, and the means to live as he chose for the next sixty-plus years. Until then, he would bide his time and provide excellent service for compensation for Grigori Varenkov.

Anuata was wrong. Decidedly wrong. Ree didn't like traveling by seraphim or whatever outlandish name Alex and the others chose to call it. It was uncomfortable, frightening, and barbaric. Even being crushed in Alex's strong arms as they hurtled along at breakneck speed didn't make up for the stench, the stygian darkness, or the sense of utter vulnerability that she felt. It was a lot like the sensations she'd felt when she was ten and her instructors had blindfolded her and shut her in a high-tech capsule that duplicated both a lack of gravity and being in the center of a tornado.

She didn't want to depend on Alex. She didn't want to depend on anyone but herself, but in the bowels of seraphim, all dignity was lost. She didn't scream, because she clenched her teeth together, but she couldn't stop the tears. Fortunately, they were swept along at such a high rate of speed that any sign of weeping was blown away as fast as it appeared.

They bounced and slammed from side to side in what seemed to be a fun-house tunnel with hard rubbery walls. Weird creaks and moans echoed down the corridors as they tumbled and struggled, sometimes swimming, sometimes bobbing like submerged corks until at last they were spewed violently out into the open sea. Alex released Ree and she slid across the sand bottom, landing on her back, staring up at thrashing forms above.

She rolled off, pushing up onto her knees, and tried to regain her balance. She felt drunk and disoriented, but even the night sea was lighter than the inside of the seraphim's intestinal tract, and the awful smell had ceased to fill her head. A faint odor clung to her clothes, making her swallow hard. An unnerving, persistent clanging vibrated through the water.

"What's that ungodly noise?" she asked him.

"Are you unhurt?" Alex was at her side, slipping an arm around her. He pointed up. "See that dolphin swimming erratically? They must have started the drive early. The noise is made by long metal poles that the humans thrust into the water. They bang on the poles with hammers to disorient the dolphins. Whales and dolphins are primarily auditory learners. The noise terrifies them and makes it difficult for them to communicate."

"It disorients me," she said, shaking her head.

"I've no time to take you to safety. Stay close, and don't get in my way."

"The same to you," she said, rubbing a hand over her eyes. The sick feeling was quickly fading, but the awful sounds still resonated through her body. "How do they get so many dolphins in one area?" she asked.

"This is a migration route. The wild dolphins have traveled the same areas for thousands of years." Alex motioned to Dewi and Anuata. They separated and swam toward the surface. Bleddyn headed off, swimming at top speed, keeping close to the seafloor.

"The dolphins will panic when they start to close in with the boats and nets," Alex said. "Take care that you aren't run down by either. If you see a net, and you think you can cut it without putting yourself in danger, do it. Whatever you do, don't let any of the humans see you, and don't kill any of them."

"Gotten soft in your old age?" she asked. "I thought they were your enemies."

"They are," he agreed. "But we don't kill humans without extreme provocation. The last thing we want are news cameras scanning the oceans searching for extraterrestrials."

"Alex." She gripped his arm. "You be careful."

He nodded. "I'll do my best. It wouldn't do for me to end up in a net on the beach, destined to be someone's sushi, would it?"

Another group of bodies passed overhead. Ree could just make out the silhouette of several large dolphins with smaller calves pressing close to their mothers' sides. And then, she heard the distinct rumble of an outboard motor. Alex swam for the surface, and Ree followed a few yards behind.

She broke the surface to find black water crisscrossed by spotlights mounted on small boats, breaching dolphins, and the occasional gunshot. The sound of so many motors almost deafened her, and that racket was compounded by the blare of air horns and loudspeakers. A dozen, perhaps twenty, vessels had formed a closing circle and were herding groups of panicked animals through the water toward a cove.

Ree could make out a narrow sand beach illuminated by lights. Several larger boats were anchored just beyond the point where the waves broke. And to her right, behind the circle of boats, loomed a freighter. No lights shone on deck or from portholes. It waited, ominously, almost in total darkness.

Vision was poor, and a light rain was falling. The water was choppy, adding to the confusion. Abruptly, to her left, Ree heard the crack of a high-powered rifle, firing once, twice, and then a third time. She looked at Alex to see if he'd heard. Did he even understand what such a weapon could do? For the first time, she felt a rush of apprehension, not for her own safety, but for his. An Atlantean made as ready a target in the water as a dolphin, and as he'd reminded her, he wasn't immortal.

"Go to shore!" he called to her as he drew his sword. "That rocky outcrop!" He gestured toward a finger of stone that rose out of the sea about a hundred yards off the south end of the cove. "Wait there until I come for you. Don't let anyone see you!"

Something heavy struck her foot and knocked it aside. She dove under and swam away, looking back to see a small dolphin, obviously a juvenile, eyes wide and frightened, blood streaming from a gash in its rubbery dorsal fin. Ree wanted to help, but she was at a loss. The dolphin outweighed her by a hundred pounds. How could she communicate with it, or stop its flight toward the beach and certain death?

Feeling helpless, she dove down toward the bottom. Nets. Alex had said that the drivers used nets to entrap the dolphins. Cutting a net should be simple, provided she could find one. She recoiled as she saw the tiny body of a dead dolphin calf, lifeless and floating just above the sandy floor. Another dolphin, larger, clicked and whined, pushing at the baby, but the calf was past heeding its mother's call.

The churning blades of a propeller ground by overhead. Seething with frustration, Ree considered following the boat and attempting to take it out of action, but she didn't know where to start. She'd never felt so useless in her life. She was trained for hand-to-hand combat, but—armed with a sword—how was she to stop men with guns?

Suddenly, an explosion knocked her back, nearly stunning her and causing her ears to ring. And, as she tried to recover, she was nearly run down by a huge bull dolphin with bared teeth. Ree twisted aside as the terrified mammal plunged past, not toward the beach, but back toward the safety of the open sea.

Depth charges? The bastards were dropping depth charges?

She surfaced again, determined to leap into the next

open boat that passed. To hell with Alex and his do no harm to humans mantra. If she could get within grasping range of some of these dolphin killers, she'd make them wish they'd stayed home in bed tonight.

An idling vessel about forty yards away seemed a likely target. She dropped to a depth of twenty feet and swam toward it, but when she reached the boat, she saw something unexpected. Two muscular women rose from the bottom of the sea carrying a length of cable between them. As she watched, they wrapped the cable around the propeller, bringing the motor to a screeching and grinding stop. At the same time, another tattooed and armored shape pressed something against the hull of the boat.

Ree swam closer and realized that these weren't members of her team, and the masked female drilling a hole through the wood planking wasn't Anuata. *Lemorians.* The Lemorians had answered the Atlanteans' call. As she watched, one of the two who'd disabled the motor caught sight of her and raised a hand in salute. Ree waved back and then made herself scarce.

By the time she'd surfaced again, she saw that half a dozen other boats were having engine trouble, and on one twenty-foot-long vessel, figures were swarming over the sides. A man on deck shouted and fired point blank. One of the boarders fell back into the water, but the others climbed over the gunnel, seized the shooter, and pitched him after his victim.

A fin cut the water near Ree. At first, she thought it was a dolphin, but then the creature slid closer and she recognized the outline of a great white shark. If there was one shark, there would be more, and where there was blood . . . She'd started to swim toward the fingers of rock that Alex had pointed out, when she became entangled in a section of net. As she tried to cut herself free with her knife, she saw two dolphins, also caught, attacked by a shark. She wanted to help, but knew the thrashing bodies and flashing teeth were more than she could handle.

Reluctantly, she abandoned the dolphins and turned away from the shore. Those in charge of the drive might be on the freighter, and if it was deserted, she could at least find out why it was here. Who knew? She might get lucky and find Varenkov aboard.

Minutes later, she inched her way up the anchor chain and dropped onto the deck. She didn't know much about freighters, but it was obvious to her that someone had deliberately ordered the deck to be shrouded in darkness. So much the better for her. Keeping in the shadows, she moved from cover to cover. Two men stood at the rail, pointing toward the smaller boats and speaking excitedly in an African tongue, but Ree couldn't understand what they were saying. She moved around them and cautiously entered the first hatchway she came to.

The heavy door led to a metal staircase. Ree took it and soon discovered that she was aboard a factory ship, designed for processing, packaging, and freezing fish and seafood. Moving from level to level, she saw crews' quarters, a galley, and refrigerated cargo holds. Deep in the bowels of the ship lay the engine room. A few men were awake, most she supposed were engineers, cooks, and watchmen. Once, an officer passed close enough for her to touch him, but she pressed herself deep into the shadows and he never suspected she was there. Most of the crew seemed to be sleeping, likewise the captain. The door to his quarters was locked, and she had no tools to open it without arousing the alarm.

She'd about decided that her attempts at discovering something worthwhile aboard the freighter were as futile as her efforts to help the dolphins when she heard an odd noise from the interior of one of the smaller cabins. Curious, Ree pressed her ear to the door. It was definitely the sound of crying, and surprisingly, she was certain that it was a child's voice she heard.

When she examined the door more closely, she found it held shut by a simple bar. Sliding the bar aside, Ree pushed the door open. Her breath caught in her throat as she stared into the dimly lit room. Huddled on the floor, arms around one another, were four—no five—filthy and nearly naked children.

CHAPTER 21

The nape of Ree's neck prickled. A warning, but a warning for what? What harm could these small unfortunates do to her? Ree stood in the doorway, uncertain of what to do. She wasn't a motherly person. She'd always felt uncertain around children . . . at a loss as to how to communicate with them. She'd had no brothers or sisters, and after she'd arrived at the institute, she'd never been in contact with children younger than her own age group.

Still, the sight of this huddled group stunned her, waking some primeval and—until now—dormant urge. She trembled as a powerful need to protect these children swept over her. She had no idea who they were or why they were here. She'd come looking for the Russian, not for mistreated children, but it was all she could do to keep herself from rushing into the cabin and gathering them all into her arms.

The only boy, a white-blond cherub with fair skin and violet-colored eyes, was the smallest. She tried to guess his age. Six? Seven? Tiny for seven, but the expression in his eyes couldn't possibly belong to a five-year-old. The eyes belonged to someone infinitely older, someone who had known loss and pain . . . someone who had lost his innocence centuries ago.

The boy's huge, soulful eyes held Ree's for long seconds, and then he hid his face in an older girl's torn shirt and his shoulders began to quiver. The girls continued to stare, but none uttered a sound. One, a girl of about nine with long black hair, almond eyes, and a delicate beauty, raised a dirt-streaked face as great tears rolled down her hollow cheeks. She hugged herself with thin and bruised arms, but her sobs were as silent as the gray walls around her.

"Who are you?" Ree asked, first in English and then in Spanish. When she got no response, she tried again in French and Mandarin. *When did I learn Mandarin?* she wondered. "Where is your mother?" This time, she spoke in Tagalog, and a flash of comprehension flashed across the almond-eyed girl's face. "Is your mother here on the boat?"

The child's expression shuttered and went blank.

Ree took one step into the room, and the children shrank back. "I won't hurt you," she soothed, using the Tagalog again. "Do you need—"

She broke off as the shrill wail of a siren echoed through the ship. Obviously an alarm, the ear-piercing sound was followed almost immediately by the creaking of steel doors and the clatter of running feet. "I'll send help for you. I promise. Someone will come to help you!" Ree ducked back into the hallway and pulled the hatch shut behind her. *Had opening the cabin door triggered the alarm? Were they searching for an intruder?*

As Ree started back toward the ladders that would lead her up to the top deck, she felt the ship tilt and sway under her feet. She nearly lost her balance, recovered, and began to run, nearly colliding with a small, Asian sailor in blue work twills and a navy ball-cap.

What had Alex told her about using the power of illusion to deceive humans into seeing something other than what was actually in front of them? There was no time to think. If she was to keep from being discovered, she had to work the trick perfectly the first time. Without hesitation, she imagined herself clad in the same uniform as the little man facing her.

"Watch where you're going!" he snarled before ducking around her and continuing on down the corridor at a run.

Ree laughed and shouted an appropriately rude insult after him. She wasn't certain of the Indonesian dialect, but she knew she had the pronunciation correct. Apparently, she decided, being Atlantean, or even partially Atlantean, had its perks.

The ship was a maze of stairs and passageways, but by the time she opened the final hatch and felt rain on her face, she'd figured out that the ship had broken loose from its anchor or anchors and was drifting helplessly on the storm tide. Wind gusts of at least forty knots tore across the open deck, buffeting her and making it difficult to reach the stern.

In the dark, it was impossible to make out the surface of the water, but she had no difficulty seeing the Lemorian warriors scrambling over the sides of the ship. Those of the crew who were on deck had seen them as well. Screaming, they ran for their lives. And when a six-foot tattooed Amazon came at Ree with a raised sword, she took the nearest exit and dove over the side.

It seemed as though she plunged downward forever until at last she sliced into the water and the angry waves closed over her head. The force of her dive carried her deep, and once her momentum slowed, she swam with all her strength for the sea bottom. Above her, Ree could sense rather than see the drifting freighter.

She clamped her hands to her ears, trying to drown out the vibration of the great engines whining and sputtering, and the shriek of twisted steel as the disabled screws ground to a halt. The familiar pain flashed through Ree's head and with absolute clarity she saw an image of the factory ship washed ashore, tilted crazily onto one side, and beached by the receding tide.

For an instant, Ree thought of the children, trapped and helpless in that cabin, and wondered if they had remained silent or finally given voice to their fear. But the vessel wasn't going to sink. She was certain of that. They would be safe from drowning, but she could do nothing to help them now. She didn't know how, but she would alert someone to their plight.

Around her, the ocean boiled with panicked dolphins, hungry sharks, and sunken boats. Bodies—human, Lemorian, and dolphin—rolled on the tide. The salt water was stained dark with blood. Ree could taste it.

She couldn't remain here. She had no idea where Alex was or where his team members were, and she didn't know if they had died with so many others. Wearily, she remembered Alex's instructions. He'd told her to go to the fingers of rock and wait for him there. She didn't know what else to do. If she could reach the spot, she would do as he'd instructed. Hopefully, he would find her there, and if he didn't . . . If he didn't, she would have to make her way to shore and then to Pago Pago. If Alex was lost, she still had a goal—kill Varenkov. And once he was dead, she could rescue the children, or at least send the authorities to investigate. Something was terribly wrong, and she couldn't just walk away from them.

Deciding to swim to the rendezvous point and actually getting there were two different things. The bottom of the sea, here in this bloody cove, was a bad place, but the surface was worse. The storm had worsened; gale winds howled down over the mountain peaks and whipped the waves into a fury.

Boats with disabled motors crashed into one another and capsized. Men swam for their lives, fighting water, tangling in their own nets, and being pulled under by angry Lemorians. And everywhere were the sharks: tigers and great whites, blacktip reef sharks, and smaller species that Ree couldn't identify.

Twice, she had to fight off attacks by tiger sharks, and once, she was nearly seized by a maddened bull dolphin with huge wounds on his head and side. If she kept to the sea bottom, it was easy to become disoriented, but on the surface, tide and wind made it almost impossible for Ree to fight the current. Finally, nearly exhausted, she pulled herself up onto an outcrop of rock. Here, the wind continued to buffet her and the waves washed over her with ever increasing fury.

"Alex!" she cried. "Where the hell are you?"

As the first purple rays of dawn broke over the horizon, the rain had become a torrent and the winds continued to howl and churn the white caps into a frenzy. The roar of the surf was thunderous, but the cries of the injured and dying had stilled. As Ree had expected, the factory ship lay on one side, hopelessly grounded off the beach. Of the small boats that had darted and raced the night before, there was no sign but a beach littered with wreckage.

Ree's hands were raw and scraped from hanging onto the rocks. Every inch of her body ached, and somewhere in the hour before the passing of night, she'd given up hope that Alex would come for her. She could imagine him, washing across the seafloor, cold and stiff, his beautiful green eyes devoid of life. Or ripped and shredded by a high-powered rifle or a great white shark. She wanted to believe that it wasn't possible that he could die, but she knew better. Nick had died. She'd loved him, and she'd believed that he was invincible, and then he was gone.

Was it the same with Alex? Had her loving him killed him? She'd tried so hard to keep her emotions from interfering with her life. She hadn't wanted to ever risk her heart again. But she'd failed. Somehow, Alex had gotten past her defenses and made her care again . . . made her love again. And now, she'd lost him, too.

Ree felt as broken as the shattered hulls on the beach. Her entire life had changed from the moment she'd laid eyes on Alex. She'd changed. And she had the feeling that there was no going back . . . that without Alex to guide her, what future she had would be short and empty.

If she could end Varenkov's reign of terror, her life might have some meaning. At this moment, she doubted her ability to do that as well. What use had she been to anyone in last night's slaughter? She was caught, impossibly, between two worlds, and without Alex she didn't have a place in either.

She lowered herself into the water, letting the current catch her and drag her under. She half expected to choke, but she didn't. Beneath the surface, she felt stronger, more alive. She'd taken the first few strokes toward the beach when Alex loomed up in front of her.

He was grinning.

"You took your sweet time about getting here," she said, then flung herself into his arms. "Are you hurt?" She covered his face with kisses. "Are you all right?"

"If you don't drown me, I'll be all right." He laughed, kissed her back, and then broke free of her embrace. "Let's get out of here. This water is unclean."

"Where?"

"Pago Pago, eventually. The others are on their way there now."

"They're okay? All of them?"

"Dewi nearly lost a leg to a great white, but Anuata came to his rescue. If he didn't have a soft spot in his heart for her before, he does now."

"Will he be—"

"He'll heal fast enough, but he won't be of much use to me for a few days. Anuata will take care of him. Bleddyn has gone ahead to scout out Varenkov."

"We're going for him?"

Alex nodded. "But if he's on the island, on Samoa, he can't go anywhere in the next day or two. The weather's only getting worse. Planes are grounded, and no captain would put out to sea under these conditions. We have a few hours to unwind . . . to be alone. That is, if you want to be with me."

"I do," she answered without hesitation. "But what happened here . . . what the Lemorians did. Won't that cause trouble for your people? Someone must have seen something. They killed humans. I saw them. And the boats—they sank the small boats."

Alex shrugged. "It's true. Men died, but innocent dolphins died as well. I won't lose sleep over those butchers who got caught in their own trap. Without the Lemorians, Dewy, Bleddyn, Anuata, and I wouldn't have made much difference. But they came, and they put an end to the drive. Most of the dolphins escaped, thanks to them."

"But if they were seen. What will happen when the men tell what they saw?"

"Most of the men in the boats died. And if any survived, they may not say a word. In a storm like that, boats overturn. Men drown. Sharks feast on the bodies."

"And on the living," she said.

"And on the living," he agreed. "It's what sharks do. And any man who's lived through this will be thought a liar if he starts spouting tall tales about fish men coming out of the water to attack the boats. Sensible men will hold their tongues, and the fools will probably be laughed at."

"But you told us no killing," she insisted.

"I did. And I held by my order. I didn't kill anyone. If the Lemorians got a little over enthusiastic, that's not my fault. I didn't ask for their help. It was my brother the king and the high council. It had to be. So the blame, if there is any, falls on them."

"I was on that factory ship, before the Lemorians cut the anchor lines and destroyed the screws and bow thruster."

"Why? I told you to go to the rocks and wait for me."

"I wanted to make sure Varenkov wasn't on board."

"Did you find him?"

"No. He could have been aboard. Hell, half the U.S. Navy could have been aboard. I didn't realize how big it was inside. But I did find something disturbing, five children. They looked starved."

"Probably children of the factory workers. There are a lot of women workers. They cut up and process the fish and dolphins. They aren't supposed to bring their children on board, but you know mothers. They probably sneaked them on."

"But they seemed so frightened . . . They were terrified."

"Probably thought they'd be put ashore. Separated from their families."

"No." She shook her head. "I think it was something worse than that."

"But you don't know for certain."

"No, I don't."

"Then, let it go. If there are children on that ship—"

"There are, I tell you. I saw them."

"The ship went aground. Most of those on board were shaken up, but not killed. The Lemorians aren't wholesale murderers. They wanted to make certain that the ship was out of action, that it would process no fish or dolphins anytime in the near future."

"So we just leave them."

"They're humans, Ree. Atlanteans don't interfere in human activity and hope the humans don't interfere in ours." He swam to her, cupped her face in his hands, and kissed her tenderly. "We can't risk becoming involved with those aboard that vessel. We have a mission to fulfill."

"I know that." She nodded, but she had no intention of letting this go, no matter what Alex said. She tried again. "But, if you'd seen them . . . how frightened they were."

"I'm tired, woman. I've had a hell of a night. And I can't wait to get you alone. Is that so terrible?"

"No, but . . ."

"No buts, Ree." He hugged her against him. "You've gotten under my scales, and I don't know what to do about it."

She laid her head against his chest, listening to the strong beating of his heart, feeling the warmth of his body next to hers. "I think we need to rest and eat," she said finally. "And then, maybe, we can figure this out. If you're certain we have time." *And I need to work out how I can return to find those frightened kids.*

"We'll make time. There's a place I think you'll like."

"Anything like the seraphim?"

"Wait and see."

The next time Ree surfaced, it was to find herself in another cove, sheltered this time from the wind, lashed by rain, but devoid of death in any form. Tired and aching, she followed Alex up onto the deserted beach. "Where are we?" she asked.

"American Samoa. This is a preserve, a protected area. This section is almost impossible to reach by land, and as you can see, no sailboats, no motorboats. My lady, I give you your own beach."

She chuckled. "Nice, very nice, but a wet beach." Somehow, being out of the water and wet was different from being wet in the ocean. She was cold and hungry, and she wanted to curl up someplace warm and sleep for twenty-four hours. "You're certain Varenkov isn't getting away while you're playing Boy Scout."

"What is *boy scout*? I don't know the game."

"A long story, best told over toasted marshmallows, graham crackers, and Hershey bars."

His hand closed over hers. "Come with me."

"Do I have a choice?"

Alex laughed. "You always have a choice, Ree. But this time, I think you'll like what I have to show you."

He gathered her up in his arms, lifting her as if she weighed no more than a small child, and carried her up through the swaying palms. There, blending in so completely with the vegetation that it was hard to see through the driving rain, Ree saw a silhouette of a traditional Samoan hut. The oval-shaped structure stood on a raised foundation of coral and had a pitched roof covered in thatch. The normally open sides were sheathed in mats woven loosely of coconut palm fronds.

"This is where you're bringing me? It looks like something out of a movie set," she cried, delighted.

"It's an authentic Samoan *faleo'o*, a beach *fale* or house, with a few modern touches," Alex said. "My guess would be that it was built for the upscale honeymooning tourists, but since no one is using it . . ."

"I love it!" she shouted above the rain and kissed his wet cheek.

"A tropical paradise at your command, my lady. All you need is a grass skirt and two coconut shells." He ducked his head as he entered the single room and lowered her to the pebbled floor. There, on an intricately patterned, hand-woven mat, a meal of steamed shrimp and crab, baked sweet potato, bananas, breadfruit, clams, and pineapple juice waited.

"How did you manage this?" Ree demanded. "It's wonderful." She traced the braided lashing that covered one of the center support posts. "You didn't swim over and prepare this and swim back for me? Is it real or an illusion?"

Alex laughed, "You're the illusion, Ree. If there's any trickery, you've done it to me. The hut was already standing here, and Bleddyn lowered the *pola,* the side coverings, and arranged the meal. He thought you deserved pampering after all you've been through."

Ree sat cross-legged on the edge of a mat and plucked a fat shrimp from the bowl. "You really are a prince of a man," she teased before peeling the shrimp and popping it into her mouth. "Mmm, delicious."

Alex removed his sword and armor and settled on the mat beside her. "Woman," he said. "You've caused me more trouble than I can ever tell you, and you're probably going to cause me more, but you're worth it."

Ree laughed and arched an eyebrow. "Really?"

His tone grew serious. "It's not just sex between us," he said.

"It's good sex," she teased. "Maybe the best."

"But it's not enough," he said, "not enough for me."

She broke off a crab leg and cracked the shell. "Well, between the sharks and the Lemorians, we haven't had much quality time. With a little practice, I'm sure I could do better."

"There's something I should tell you."

She used a shell to dip up some of the sweet potato. "Before I eat?"

He leaned close and she offered him a bite. Alex shook his head. "I'd rather watch you enjoy it."

She reached for a banana. "Seriously, I'm starving. The shrimp is really good. Don't you want some?" She peeled the banana, took a bite, and then asked, "What did you want to tell me?" She chuckled. "Wait. You aren't an Atlantean. You sell insurance in Toledo, but—"

He took the banana out of her hand, tossed it aside and kissed her. "I think I'm in love with you, Ree."

Her heartbeat quickened, and the urge to run washed over her. It wasn't possible. It was better to keep this light, to tease and laugh, to make love and walk away. "I'll bet you say that to all the women you rescue from mad Russians," she murmured when the kiss finally broke and she came up for air.

"Only to you, Ree O'Connor. Only to you."

CHAPTER 22

He wiped a bit of shrimp off her lower lip and kissed her again, slowly, tenderly. Ree's insides turned to mush as desire rose and she felt the heat of his body envelop her.

"It's true," he whispered, kissing her throat and the soft place beneath her ear. "I've shared sex with many women, but I've never felt about any of them as I do about you. You've bewitched me."

She drew in a deep, ragged breath and closed her eyes. She could still feel his gaze on her, and the warmth of his lips tugged at her heartstrings. "Don't say what you don't mean," she begged him. She knew the ground was crumbling under her, knew how close she was to falling head over heels for him, and knew—most of all—how it would end. How it always ended . . . badly. "I can't," she uttered softly. "I can't do it again."

He pulled her against him, holding her, stroking her back, rocking her. "Can't what, Ree? Can't love me?"

She turned her face away, and clenched her teeth. If she tried to speak, she didn't know what would come out. Her throat tightened. Fear shot through her. She couldn't. She couldn't risk loving someone else. Everyone she'd ever loved had died.

"Ree, look at me."

She opened her eyes and turned her face up to his. "Save the sweet talk," she said, her voice harder than she meant it to be. "It's better if we keep things physical. Better for me, better for you."

"It's not enough."

"It has to be." She shook her head and lied. "I don't feel that way about you." She drew in another breath, finding strength from the lie. "As you keep telling me, I'm human, and you're . . . whatever you are. It's a lot simpler if we stick to business, killing Varenkov. It's what we came here to do, isn't it?"

He let her go and got to his feet. "Enjoy the food," he said. "The sleeping mats are there along the wall. Get some rest. When the storm eases, we'll go after him."

He was only an arm's length away, but the distance between them seemed like an eternity. "No reason we can't take advantage of this place," she said. "I've no objection to sharing your bed. To the contrary." She shrugged. "Didn't you just say that I'd cause a lot of trouble for you in the future? It doesn't have to be that way if we go back to the way it was supposed to be, just fun between adults."

"I'll come for you when it's time." He turned toward the entrance and picked up his armor and weapons.

"Don't go," she said. "There's no need for you to go."

He glanced back at her and she winced at the hurt in his gaze. "There's every need," he said and ducked low as he exited the hut.

"Alex?" She followed him to the doorway, but when she looked out into the rain, he was already gone. "Alex!"

No answer.

Wind tugged at the mat that hung across the door. Rain beat against Ree's face. "It's better this way. You'll see." She looked back at the food and realized that she was no longer hungry. "We never stood a chance in hell," she whispered, only half aloud. Alex would realize that. He'd come back and things would be as they had been.

She shivered, suddenly chilled. She might have lost her appetite because she was cold and wet. There was a small stone fireplace set into the far wall of the *faleo'o,* definitely not authentic Samoan décor, but welcome. A basket of logs, kindling, and coconut-husk tinder stood beside the hearth. She looked around for matches, but finding none, resorted to her gift.

Quite a comedown, she thought. *Using twenty years of psychic higher education to start a campfire in a grass hut.* But it worked. A few sparks and the coconut-husk burst into flame. Slowly, she fed small twigs and then larger ones, arranging four logs over the growing fire. The fire took the dampness out of the room, and she unrolled the sleeping mats and the padded egg-crate bedding.

If Alex wants to sit outside in the rain, so be it, she decided. He'd probably gone back to the ocean where he belonged. "But where do I belong?" she murmured into the empty room. "Where have I ever belonged?"

When she was small, her parents had kept her away from other children, away from all but a few close friends of theirs. They'd warned her not to talk to strangers, and never to start fires unless they were with her and could assure that it was safe.

She'd always known that she was different. Different even from the other students in her age class at the institute. She couldn't remember having a single friend there . . . no one she could trust . . . no one that she could be certain would be there the next morning.

"You were born for this," one of her teachers used to say. "We understand you. We can help you find your purpose in life. Without the institute you'd be freaks. In earlier centuries, your kind was hunted down and put to death. Don't think that because the world has become more sophisticated that you'd ever be accepted. You aren't like other people, and that frightens them."

Maybe it was true, what he'd said. Her mother hadn't been afraid of her, but she'd suspected that her father had been. He'd shared her gift of commanding fire, but not her ability to see into the future. And if he hadn't feared her, he'd feared what the world around them would think and do. Or maybe he'd always known what they'd do . . . maybe her father's worst fears had come to pass when an unknown assailant had burned the house around them. Sometimes, Ree had wished that she'd been at home with them that night. If she had, she suspected that she would have died, too . . . but then she wouldn't have been alone.

The exchange with Alex had shaken her. She'd ventured so close to the edge, but she had control again. It would hurt to let him go out of her life, but not as it had hurt when she'd lost Nick. And she'd never admitted to Nick how she had really felt about him. At least, she thought that she hadn't. If he'd had the sense God gave an onion, he must have guessed. But it wasn't meant to be. She was different. She had no one but herself to depend on and when her time came, she'd leave no one behind to suffer heartbreak as she had suffered.

Ree pulled the mats over in front of the fireplace, lay down, and pulled a thin cotton blanket over her. And when she slept for twelve hours straight, she dreamed not of her lost Nick, but of the coral reef in its myriad of colors and shapes and its abundance of life. She saw again—with the clarity and brilliance that her superhuman, Atlantean vision gave her—the stunning shades of green and orange and blue, and she savored each new sight with wonder and tears of joy.

★ ★ ★

"Vere are zay?" Varenkov demanded. "I pay for prime stock, not alley trash." In frustration, he hurled his glass across the stateroom and it smashed against the far wall. "Do you know vat zis vill cost me? Grigori make promises. Important men expect him keep vord. Powerful men make bad enemy."

Nigel sat his glass, still half full, on the bar. His stomach was uneasy, and the constant roll of the yacht wasn't helping. He'd never been that fond of boats, but being shut up here during the storm listening to Varenkov whine and shout for the last thirty hours in badly accented English made him wish that he'd stayed in Hong Kong.

"Vat? Vat he say? Ven I see merchandise?" The Russian sank into an easy chair and ran a hand over his head. "Is bad my ulcer, zis. Ship out of commission. *Nyeht* dolphin. *Nyeht* fish. Bad. If Varenkov not do himself, not get done right."

"Phirun said that they were in bad shape, but not beyond recovery. He promises to find out who abused them."

"I say treat zem like royalty. Feed zem until zey plump like roast chickens. Scarecrows vorthless at auction!"

"Phirun understands. He'll make sure that those responsible will be severely dealt with."

Varenkov poured himself another glass of vodka. "Deal vith? Ha! Is only one vay to deal vith fools." He made a slashing motion across his throat. "Bad business to disappoint important client. Hmmp."

"Phirun hired a skiff and brought them to Quon's place, here in Pago Pago. He can bring them here to the yacht or—"

"*Nyeht! Nyeht!* Never on *Anastasiya.* No business on *Anastasiya.* How many times I tell you? No business here. You go see cargo. If Phirun try cheat Varenkov, you kill him."

"You're not coming with me?" Nigel asked.

"Vat you zink? Varenkov go strange house, not know zis Phirun? Maybe he American CIA. Maybe vork for Chinese mafia. Maybe enemy of Varenkov. You go. Vat I pay you for? Take chances. Earn your money."

"You're the boss." At least it would give him the opportunity to get off the yacht for a few hours. "I'll leave right away, if you'll have one of the Zodiac's lowered."

The Russian shook his head. "Not yet. Ve vait for new shift guards come other yacht. Zen you go. Plenty time. If Phirun honest, it not matter make him vait. Make him sveat. Next time, he not screw up."

"You follow that Zodiac," Alex ordered. "Bleddyn and I will continue surveillance on the *Anastasiya*."

Ree nodded. She would have rather kept watch on Varenkov, but she wasn't going to be unreasonable. Alex was in charge of this operation, at least at the present. He'd been cool toward her since he'd returned to the hut this morning, but they hadn't argued, and she thought that was good.

The weather remained foul, but the wind had lessened in force, and the seas weren't as rough as they had been. The rain no longer came down in torrents, but only as a hazy mist.

She slipped through the water, easily keeping pace with the Zodiac as it left Varenkov's yacht and crossed the Pago Pago Harbor before heading out into the open sea. The Zodiac zipped along, riding the waves, hugging the coast for half an hour before cutting into a small inlet.

Ree surfaced and watched as the craft nosed against a cement dock and one man climbed out. He started up toward the shore while the other two remained in the inflatable and snugged it tightly to a mooring post. *Wherever he is going, he expects to return,* Ree thought. It was too dark to be concerned about being seen as she left the water, but she was cautious by habit. By the time she reached the line of palm trees, her target was just disappearing in the distance, and she hurried to catch up.

There were few houses here, and even fewer lights. Ree thought these must be vacation homes or rentals, and this was the rainy season, probably not the best time for tourists, even adventurous ones. She moved from tree to tree, always keeping aware of her surroundings but not letting the man get too far ahead.

She wished it were Varenkov she was trailing. It would have been easy to slip up on him and finish it here in this dark rain forest. She would have had him before he realized that he'd been followed. But he rarely left his yacht unless he was at home in Russia or entering one of the larger cities such as New York or Hong Kong. Suspicion was what had kept him alive so long.

After perhaps ten minutes, the man she'd trailed from the Zodiac approached a house with a high wall around it. He stood at the gate until someone from inside opened it, and then he went in. Ree waited. Not more than twenty minutes later, he came out again and started back toward the beach. She followed, careful to keep from being seen.

The headache struck as she was leaving the shelter of a coconut palm. A scene flashed behind her eyelids, but one so impossible that she froze, unable to draw breath. She saw, or thought she saw, Nick's face illuminated in the darkness. So stunned was she by the vision that she lost track of time. A second? Two? More.

The feel of cold metal against her throat yanked her out of her trance.

"One move and you're dead," the voice said. "Who are you, and why are you following me?"

For the space of a single heartbeat, Ree hesitated, caught between action and the impossible. Action won.

Flame flew from her fingertips, scorching her assailant's face and hands. Shocked by the burn, he released pressure on the knife at her throat for a split second. Ree seized the advantage, driving an elbow into his midsection and spinning out of his grasp. In the same motion, she drew her own weapon and blocked the blow from his incoming blade.

The edge of her sword met his slashing knife, and to her surprise, his blade shattered. He leaped back out of range of her return swing. She recovered and took a defensive stance as what had just happened played over in her mind.

What *had* just happened? Had her senses betrayed her? Her mind scrambled to solve the unsolvable . . . until he spoke again.

"Ree? Is it you?"

"Nick?" She sucked in a gulp of air. Her mind reeled. "Nick?"

He laughed, and goose bumps rose on the back of her neck. She'd heard Nick laugh like that before, usually just after he'd squeezed off a killing shot. She could barely make him out in the black night, but the height was right, and he appeared to be wearing a suit and tie.

Always the best for Nick, a designer suit, black or charcoal gray, a black dress shirt—French, and black, hand-sewn Italian shoes. It was his uniform, even when he was engaged in wet work. He was bareheaded in the rain, his brown hair stylishly cut short. That was pure Nick, as well.

"Who did you think it was?" he quipped. "The Christmas elf?"

"But . . ." She couldn't find the words. Her tongue cleaved to the roof of her mouth. "You died in that car—"

"You were supposed to *believe* I died in that car bomb, or at least everyone else was. I'd hoped you would figure it out over time."

Pain lanced through her chest. "It can't be."

"I assumed that you were dead. You're overdue, you know. Your trainers have put a price on your head."

"I haven't done anything wrong. I was badly injured. I couldn't report in."

He made a sound of disbelief. "That's not the way it goes, Ree. You don't break contact with your handler. They think you've jumped the fence."

"How do you know that?"

"I have connections. I may not be part of the system anymore, but it pays to know what's happening." He stared at her for a long minute. "I thought we'd meet up some day . . . or night, if you were still alive. I just didn't expect it would be here."

She sucked in another breath, and the air scalded her lungs. Oddly, she found herself longing for the sea where it was easier to tell friend from enemy. Nick was alive. Nick had just come within a hair's breadth of killing her. "Why?" she managed. "Why did you do it?"

"I wanted out. I was tired of doing all the work and getting none of the rewards." He shrugged. "You know the organization. There's only one way out, feet first."

"I thought you were dead," she repeated dumbly. "You let me believe you died in my place."

"Ease up, honey. It's all a game. You didn't take it serious, what we had between us. Did you?"

She didn't answer, couldn't answer. "All these years . . ." And then pieces of the puzzle started to come together. She didn't like the picture they were forming, but she was powerless to stop it. "We were closing in on Varenkov that night."

"*You* were closing in on Varenkov. I knew where he was. I'd just come from a very profitable meeting with him."

"But the body. They found . . . pieces of . . ." She swallowed. "Who died in that car?"

"If it's any consolation, the man was already dead before the Russians put him into the car. A homeless guy who happened to fit my suit."

She didn't buy it. Not now. Not anymore. The coincidence was too easy. A homeless guy happened to drop dead just when Varenkov needed someone to fill in for Nick. They'd killed him. Maybe Nick had killed him. She'd never know the truth.

Ree felt sick. She was glad she hadn't eaten since those few bites when she'd first arrived at the hut with Alex. If she'd had anything in her stomach, she would have lost it. "I loved you," she said. "I thought you loved me."

He laughed again, a hard, brittle sound. She'd heard that tone before, but Nick had never used it with her. "You thought wrong, baby. I graduated from the same school you did. And if you'd learned your lessons, you'd know that love is for losers. Love will get you nothing but trouble."

"I guess I didn't learn that part."

"You should have."

"I suppose you're right. I should have. So, you're working for Varenkov."

"Finally, she gets it."

"How could you work for him of all people? You know what he is."

"Listen to yourself. Do you think Varenkov is any worse than the bastards who trained us? The high and mighty organization who sits back and decides who deserves to live and who should die?"

"They keep the world safe from scum like Varenkov."

"They are scum like Varenkov," he said.

"They rid the human race of mass murderers, child molesters, and war criminals when no one else can touch them. Have you forgotten that?"

"Most of our targets deserved what they got. I'll give

you that much. But did you ever think what price we paid to be part of their little experiment?"

She took another step back, trying to sort this all out in her head, struggling to know what was real and what was illusion. She felt disconnected, weak, and it seemed as if every breath was harder to take in. Her head was hurting, but not as it did when she was about to have far-sight and not the same as when she made fire. This was different and it frightened her. She was never sick. Her legs seemed to fold under her, as if the earth was pulling her down, and she fought to remain on her feet.

"You were a commodity, Ree," Nick was saying. His voice was distorted, sounding as though it was coming from far off instead of only a few feet away. "I was a commodity. The gifts we were born with made us valuable to the institute. And they'd do anything to acquire us. Anything."

"I don't know what you're talking about."

"You know. You've always known. You just don't have the guts to admit it. Who do you think burned your mother and father into charcoal?"

She stared at him, unable to reply, unable to believe what Nick was saying. Her mother and her father? The organization had ordered their murders?

"You're dumber than I thought," Nick said. "Maybe too dumb to live."

She saw a flash of light and heard the muffled thud of a silencer. The bullet smashed into her chest, and she tumbled backward into a dark and smothering nothingness.

CHAPTER 23

"How is my brother?" Orion asked Lady Athena at the doorway to the inner sanctum. Orion held minor priestly orders; all members of the royal house did. But his ranking wasn't high enough to pass through into the central healing chamber here in the great temple of Atlantis. His own wounds were healing quickly, but so far the news of Poseidon had not been heartening. An exception had been made for the queen, and she remained by his side, but that left Orion without trustworthy information on the king's true condition. Orion felt that his only honest reports had come from his young niece Danu.

"Daddy is sick," she'd told him. "Very sick. Grandmother says he has to stay asleep until he's stronger. She put a powerful spell on him to help him get better." Her small mouth had quivered and tears spilled from her beautiful eyes. "But he might not get better. He might die. I don't want him to die."

"Neither do I, darling," Orion said. "None of us do."

"Why did the bad men want to hurt him?"

Orion shook his head. "Because he was king. Because Caddoc wants to be king."

"He won't be," Danu flung back. "He won't! He's far far away where it's dark all the time. And he's never coming back to Atlantis, so he can't be king."

Orion had assumed the reins of command, but he refused to conduct business from his brother's throne, and he would accept no greater title, not even regent for the infant Prince Perseus. "He has a living mother and a father," Orion had insisted. "I'll not usurp their power."

"As you will, Prince Orion," Lord Zale, the vizier, answered, following Orion from the Hall of Justice and hurrying to keep up as Orion moved down the gilded corridor of mirrors. "But if the worst happens, you must take the crown. Prince Perseus is too young, and infant kings have a high mortality in Atlantis."

"Is that a threat?" Orion whirled on the older man and glared at him.

"Don't insult me," Lord Zale answered. "You know that I'm loyal to your house and the monarchy. But I'm a student of history, and I could relate tales of the suspicious deaths of infant kings in the past. I only speak of such evil so that you will realize how serious this matter is. Perseus can't be Poseidon for many years, if ever. You are a seasoned warrior. The people know and trust you."

"But someone still tried to kill me."

"And paid with their lives for the attempt."

"And how many rebels haven't we caught?" Orion asked. "When do I stop looking over my shoulder whenever I enter a dark hallway?"

Lord Zale shook his head sadly. "Perhaps never, but that is the price of being born to the royal house."

"Unless I rid us of Caddoc's opposition forever." Orion left unspoken what they both knew. If his half brother should die, there would be no challenge to the throne and Poseidon, Alex, Lucas, Perseus, and Morwena would be safe. *I could give that order,* Orion thought. *I could send assassins to murder Caddoc and put an end to his scheming forever . . . if I wanted to pass a death sentence on my own father's son.*

For a moment, Orion considered the unthinkable. Would Alex give such an order if he were king? Orion was certain he knew the answer. Of the three brothers, Alex was most like their father, and maybe more of a king than either he or Morgan would ever be.

Orion could almost hear Alex's voice. "Consider the lesser of the evils," his twin would say, his eyes narrowing and darkening to a dangerous shade of green. "If someone has to die to prevent more rebellions, why not Prince Caddoc? Better our father executed him and his mother when they conspired to seize the throne the first time. He showed them mercy and now two of his other sons are dead because of it."

But Alex wasn't here, the weight of responsibility rested on his shoulders, and Lord Zale was clearly waiting for him to say something. "Morgan never wanted to become Poseidon."

"Yet he has been an able king, wise beyond his years, wiser even in some matters than your late father, if I may be so bold as to say so. Not all accept the crown by choice."

"My brother is still king. He's alive, and he's going to remain alive!"

"May the Supreme Being will it so." The vizier sighed. "I hope and pray you are right, Prince Orion. But if it is not to be, you must be prepared to act decisively, before the kingdom is thrown into chaos and before Prince Caddoc returns to challenge you for the throne."

Ree gasped and fought her way up out of darkness. She couldn't breathe. Her ribs felt as if they were crushed. Each attempt to draw in air was agony. She forced her eyes open and had the vague impression that Nick was standing over her, a pistol in his hand.

He'd shot her. Nick, her Nick had shot her. She pressed her hand against her breast expecting to feel the gush of her life's blood, but instead of a gaping wound, her seeking fingers brushed loose a metal slug that had been partially trapped in the creases of her cuirass.

"Wearing body armor?" Nick said. "Clever girl. But not clever enough." He stepped closer, lowering the muzzle to within inches of her forehead. "No armor here."

She concentrated on the pistol, threw every ounce of willpower into sending a lightning bolt of flame up the barrel. Steel wouldn't burn, but flesh would. And steel could melt.

A vision flashed across her mind. She saw Nick squeeze the trigger, saw the results of that deadly missile penetrating her temple, saw what remained of her skull once the bullet penetrated flesh and bone and brain matter.

And released her single arrow of fire . . .

For an instant, time seemed to stop, and then she heard Nick scream as the pistol glowed red with heat. She rolled away, trying desperately to avoid the falling weapon, but she needn't have worried. The fiery walnut pistol grip adhered to the skin of Nick's hand. He screamed again, flinging the misshapen blob of metal and charred wood away, ripping skin and flesh from his hand, exposing quivering tendons.

Headlights turned the corner, and Nick bolted into the shadows, clutching his injured hand. Ree crawled on hands and knees into the darkness in the opposite direction Nick had taken. He would need immediate medical attention, and she doubted he would come back to try and finish her off, but she couldn't be sure.

The vehicle, an aging SUV full of passengers, drove by and turned into a private driveway a block away. Ree gritted her teeth and got to her feet. She could feel the grate of bone on bone and knew that at least one of her ribs was broken. Still, she felt as though she'd gotten off lucky.

How could she have been so wrong about Nick? Had

he been lying to her when they'd been an item, or was he lying now? She couldn't accept that he'd never cared for her. It would be more in his character to make his choice and try and defend it later. Making her think that he'd never loved her might be easier than admitting he'd betrayed her. Either option was a lose-lose, as far as she was concerned. All these years she'd mourned him, and he wasn't worth one tenth of the tears she'd shed for him.

He'd tried to kill her, not once, but twice. Any doubts she had about how he felt about her now were moot. Whatever he'd once felt, that was gone. The man she'd thought she loved was dead. If he'd ever existed, she'd never know.

He'd called her a fool. Maybe she was, but she wasn't stupid enough to give him an opportunity to kill her a third time. Nick had chosen his side, and it wasn't the one she was standing on. *Swimming on,* she thought with black Irish humor. How had she been so blind? The pain in her chest was nothing compared to the ache in her heart, not for Nick, but for all she could have had and had thrown away.

Alex . . . Whatever he was, Atlantean, visitor from space, or a figment of her imagination, he was a better man than Nick had ever or would ever be.

But she wasn't sorry that she'd followed Nick and been confronted by him. He'd given her information that she'd searched for all her life. Click, click, click. The puzzle pieces that had eluded her since she was a small, frightened child had all dropped into place. And the truth was, she'd always suspected that the organization had been to blame for her parents' deaths, suspected and pushed it away, burying it in the far corners of her mind because it was too terrible to accept.

She hadn't fit in anywhere but the organization. She had no family, no friends, no clan or community who could accept her for what and who she was. And now, her only refuge had turned hollow. She couldn't go back if she wanted to, and she didn't want to. The hatred she carried inside her for her parents' murderers, all her plans for revenge dissolved into despair and confusion. Some anonymous and radical political group hadn't killed her mother and father. She had to face the fact that if she hadn't been born, they'd probably still be alive.

It was too much to take in. Her head pounded and her stomach knotted. The weak feeling, the sensation that she was walking through knee-deep mud returned, and she suspected that her trouble breathing wasn't simply the result of a broken rib or two. Instinct told her that Anuata was right. She was suffering from some strange sickness that had her longing for the feel of salt water on her skin and the cool and shadowy depths of the ocean.

But old habits die hard. She'd followed Nick here to see what he was up to. If he was working for Varenkov, everything he did was at the Russian's bidding. And she'd been trained to be thorough. The way to a target was to know everything about him. Varenkov had sent Nick here for a reason. She was in no physical condition to go after Nick and try to take him out, but she could attempt to learn why he'd gone to that particular residence.

Drugs, prostitution, weapons dealing, pornography, Varenkov had his dirty hands in all of the mortal sins. It would be logical to investigate the house rather than to report back to Alex with nothing other than the name of Varenkov's associate. The problem was that high wall around the house. Normally, walls and fences were easy. She'd learned to disable state-of-the-art security systems and pick locks when she was twelve. She hadn't tried scaling a ten-foot-high cement wall with a broken rib and no equipment. Still, she reasoned, it wouldn't hurt to take a look.

She choked back a bitter laugh. That was incorrect; it would hurt. It would hurt like hell, but the need to see inside tugged at her. And once she'd fixed on an idea, it was hard to shake. Intuition had rarely steered her wrong, and physical pain would be a small price to pay if she learned something worthwhile by being persistent.

Ree had gone half a block when she heard footsteps on the wet ground behind her. Her hearing wasn't as acute on land as it was in the water, but she was no slouch. She moved into the foliage and waited. Nothing. No sound but the wind through the palms and the patter of falling rain. Had she been unnerved by Nick's ambush and imagined that she'd heard someone coming? She doubted that Nick was anywhere in the vicinity now. Unless he wanted to apply for permanent disability, he'd be at the nearest hospital having his burned hand tended to by a specialist. So who else—

She heard a twig snap to her left. As she watched, a tall, muscular figure flowed out of the shadows, a silhouette with a long scalp-lock dangling down her back. "Anuata?" she called softly.

The big warrior-woman materialized out of the wet night. "Why are you here?" she asked. "This is not a place for us. It stinks of humans."

"Alex sent me to follow a man from Varenkov's boat."

"I know that, but Alex was worried about you. He sent me to back you up."

"How did you know where to look?"

"A seagull told me."

"A seagull?"

Anuata chuckled. "You fell for that one easily enough. Seagulls don't talk. Or if they do, I don't speak their language." She stifled another laugh. "Have you seen many seagulls flying around tonight?"

"Then how—"

"The Zodiac. It's moored at the dock. Alex told me you followed it." Anuata moved closer. "Why are you holding your side? Have you an injury?"

"The man I was trailing shot me. My armor protected me, but the force of the blow may have broken a rib."

"Shot you with what? A spear-gun?"

"A pistol."

Anuata nodded. "I have heard of the humans' pistols that shoot bits of metal. They are like the rifles that the dolphin killers use."

"That's right. My injury isn't severe, but I need to get into that house, and there's a high wall around it. I'm not certain if I can climb it." Somehow, the big Amazon with her childish sense of humor had grown on her, and she found herself glad of Anuata's company. "Do you think you can help me over the wall?"

"Is the man you follow inside?"

"No." Ree shook her head. "He came out of the house. That's when he shot me, but I hurt him worse. He's gone, probably seeking medical care."

"You want to see inside the wall?"

"Yes. I think it's important. Whoever lives there probably works for the Russian as well. I need to know what they're doing. I'm sure they're involved in some criminal activity, but I don't want to go back to Alex and say what I think. I have to be able to tell him what is."

Anuata nodded. "Then I will help you. But why go over the wall when there is a gate?" She pointed. "A gate on land is much like a gate under water, isn't it?"

"That's true, but the people inside probably have guns. It could be dangerous."

"More dangerous than the Lemorian warriors we faced in the catacombs?"

"They could be."

"Anuata is not afraid. Is Ree afraid?" The Amazon

laughed. "You look more like a human than me. Knock on the gate and see what happens when it opens."

"Just like that? Walk up to the door and knock?"

"Sometimes the straight way is better than the roundabout." She looked Ree up and down. "Can you do illusion? So that you don't look like a woman in armor?"

"I can try," Ree answered. She'd done it on the factory ship, hadn't she? What they'd do once they got inside, she didn't know, but the way her ribs hurt, Anuata's suggestion sounded better and better.

The two crossed the street and approached the compound. Ree watched for cameras, but saw none. When they reached the gate, Anuata flattened herself against the wall, keeping out of sight. Ree pushed a button and a loud buzzer rang.

Nothing.

"Try again," Anuata urged.

Ree hit the button a second and then a third time.

"Who's there?" shouted an angry male voice. "Go away!"

Ree rang the bell again. This time she heard a door bang open and quick, heavy footsteps.

A man cursed and threw open the gate. "What do you—" he began, but got no further before Anuata seized him by the throat, dragged him through the doorway, and slammed him back against the block wall. His head hit the hard surface and he slumped forward. The gun in his hand slipped into a puddle of water, and Anuata snatched it up. It had happened so fast that Ree could hardly believe what she'd seen.

"You take it," Anuata said, shoving the Glock into Ree's hand. "You want I should break his neck?"

Sweat broke out on Ree's forehead as she tucked the gun into her belt. She felt lightheaded from the pain, but she wasn't about to wimp out now. "No, drag him inside.

We don't want any good Samaritans driving past, seeing him, and calling the police. See if you can find something to tie him up with."

"Easier to kill him."

"You heard what Alex said. No killing unless we have to."

"You could tell him that we had to. He likes you. He wouldn't be angry if you told him—"

"Just tie him up, and gag him as well. We don't want him yelling for help."

As they entered the inner courtyard, a dog charged around the corner of the house and ran at them barking. Anuata threw the man to the ground, drew her sword, crouched and growled back at the animal. So fierce and frightening was the Lemorian's war-cry that the big mongrel stopped short, cowered down, and began to whine pitifully. "Like sharks," Anuata confided. "You must show them who is master."

A twenty-year-old convertible stood outside the garage, top down. "Wait," Ree said. She opened the driver's door, found the release, and popped the trunk. "Put him in there," she ordered Anuata.

"Dog or human?"

Ree stared at Anuata, and then the woman laughed, threw the still unconscious man over her shoulder and carried him to the car. She dumped him into the trunk and slammed it shut. "Better than tying," she said. "In the box, no one will hear him."

Ree pushed open the front door.

From somewhere inside, a woman's high voice called, "Phirun?"

Ree and Anuata rushed inside just as the Polynesian woman came from the hall. "Phirun?" She caught sight of Anuata, screamed, and fled into a back room and slammed the door. They could hear the sound of a lock click and then the woman shrieking.

"Am I so ugly?" Anuata asked.

Ree glanced over her shoulder at her. "Not ugly, just different."

Anuata smiled and then broke into a grin. "Good. Different is good."

Systematically, Ree began searching the house. In the kitchen, they found a bag of marijuana and what appeared to be cocaine on the counter. Two open bottles of beer stood on the table. Anuata eyed them suspiciously. "Is to drink?" she asked.

"Yes, but you wouldn't like it," Ree lied. She didn't know what effect alcohol or drugs would have on her associate and didn't care to find out. They passed through what was evidently a living room with a big screen TV blaring an eighties comedy and continued to inspect each room. The woman didn't come out or stop shrieking for them to go away.

As Ree pushed open the door to the second bedroom and switched on the light, she knew what had driven her to check out the house. Crouched in the center of the bed, holding on to one another and sobbing, were four of the children she'd discovered on the factory ship.

CHAPTER 24

Four children. Ree leaned against the doorframe and pressed her hand to her midsection. There had been five kids before. Where was the boy with the face of a frightened angel? She couldn't be wrong about that. She'd never forget his face. "Where is the little boy?" she demanded, using Tagalog, the language that had gotten her a response from the girl with the almond-shaped eyes before.

"Don't take Remi. Please!" the girl cried. "Take me instead. I'll be good."

Two of the other girls began to weep, but the fourth only stared past Ree at Anuata. When Ree had last seen them in the ship's cabin, they'd been filthy with dirty hair and faces. They'd obviously bathed since then. The rags had been replaced with identical white men's undershirts, but the children were just as thin and bruised, and the hollows in their cheeks and dark circles under their eyes remained. And now she noticed marks on their wrists, making her certain that someone had tied them up.

"I saw you before, on the boat," Ree said in a softer voice. "There was a boy. Did something happen to him?"

A muffled whimper came from under the bed. Ree started to kneel down to look under it, but the grinding pain in her ribs brought tears to her eyes. Her breath caught in her throat, and she motioned to Anuata.

She dragged a dresser in front of the door to block it, before advancing on the bed and crouching. She slipped a hand under, then snatched it back, and looked at the small teeth marks on one tattooed finger. "It bit me," she said, more surprised than annoyed. "The little human bit me." A grin split her face. "He shows courage this small man child."

"We aren't going to hurt you," Ree said to the almond-eyed girl, clearly the spokeswoman for the group. "Tell . . . What is his name? Remi?"

The girl nodded solemnly.

"Tell Remi that it's safe for him to come out," Ree said. "We only want to help you."

The child shook her head. "The man said to get rid of us. He said we were worthless. If Remi comes out from under the bed, you'll kill him."

"No," Ree insisted. "We came here to find you, to help you get away from these bad people. Is that your mother in the other room?"

The almond eyes grew as lifeless as glass. "She's Phiron's whore. She's mean. She put Mayuni's bowl of rice on the floor and made her eat it like a dog because she wouldn't speak. Mayuni never talks, not even to us."

"Where's your mother? Your family?"

The girl shrugged. "She sold me when I was little."

"Do you have a father? A grandmother? Anyone?"

"I have Pilar." She glanced at a blue-eyed waif beside her with short brown hair. "We take care of Remi. Sometimes."

Pilar raised a tear-stained face and looked at Ree through impossibly long lashes. "If you buy Julita, buy me, too. Please," she whispered. "I'm a good girl. I cause no trouble."

Ree choked back the sickness that rose in her throat. These children had been sexually abused, bought and sold like crates of pineapples or boxes of bananas. "Where did you come from? Are you Filipino?"

Almond-eyed Julita shrugged again. "Nowhere. Everywhere. It doesn't matter. If you buy us, we will make a lot of money for you. If you kill us like the man said, you will have nothing."

Anuata pulled the little boy from his hiding place and cradled him in her arms. "Mother of Vassu!" she swore. "He is all skin and bones. What monsters would do this to a child?" Remi had no shirt, but wore worn man's boxers, tied at the waist, so that they fell below his knees like a skirt.

Ree felt the floor tilting under her feet. The urge to get back to the sea was overwhelming, but she didn't know if she had the strength to walk so far. "Anuata . . ." she murmured. Her voice had that far-away, tinny quality again. "I think I'm sick."

The Lemorian glanced at her. "I can see you are. What do you want to do?"

"We can't leave them here," Ree said. "The woman will let Phirun out of the trunk, and then he'll either sell them again or do worse. We have to get them to safety."

"Arra, arra," Anuata crooned as she rocked the terrified boy. "Anuata will not hurt you." She brushed a lock of white-blond hair from Remi's face. "Only tell me, Ree, where is safe? Where for these little ones has your world ever been safe?"

"I won't abandon them."

"Then we must take them with us."

"Where?"

"To Atlantis."

"But they're human. How could they . . ." Ree blinked back the waves of nausea. Black spots danced before her eyes. *How can I exist beneath the ocean? But I can. Anything is possible.* "Are we putting them in worse danger?" she tried to ask, but the words drifted away and the floor came up and hit her.

Caddoc stumbled along, trying to keep up with the guard who led him by a cord linked to the collar buckled around his neck. His eyes no longer pained him and the place where his tongue had been had healed into a ragged stump. Sightless and dumb, he had to depend on his sense of hearing for everything. Like a dolphin, he was learning to avoid swimming into solid objects by humming and feeling the sound vibrations against his scales.

He had not been beaten or tortured or locked in a cell. The clothing he wore was as fine as ever, and the food he was served was the best the palace had to offer. He sometimes wondered if he could have only one of his ravished senses back if he would choose his sight or his voice. He spent long hours considering what his best option might have been, if he'd had one. Without his eyes, he was helpless, but without his tongue, he could make no protest.

But, as 'Enakai reminded him, she had left him intact, still potent and virile, still able to enjoy the pleasures of the flesh. True, he could feel, but he could not see, and he didn't receive quite the same satisfaction when he couldn't appreciate the gleam of her oiled skin or the way her hips swayed when she walked.

"It is time I gave my people an heir," 'Enakai said. "It matters not who sires the babe. Perhaps you will be the lucky one. Would it please you to know that your daughter would ascend to the throne of Lemoria? How amusing that the prince who expected to be king of Atlantis would father a Lemorian queen. But, alas, you are only one of many. And those who frequent my bed know the benefits of impregnating the royal womb."

He made no answer. To grunt or moan was beneath his dignity. And with luck, he might still be Poseidon. A man could rule without eyes, couldn't he? And a king could write his commands and have others read them. His spies had brought him no word of his uncle's move against the royal house of Poseidon. Perhaps the time hadn't been right, or a messenger simply hadn't arrived yet. He could already be the sole surviving son of his father, already be king and not know it.

And when he was king, he would send his armies against Lemoria. He would show no pity to the military and the nobility, but he would have the head of any man who laid a harsh finger on 'Enakai. He would have her brought to him in golden chains, clad in pearls and her dark curtain of hair. Then he would summon the lowest scum of his kingdom; the crosses, the mermen, and the naiads. One by one, he would command them to have their will of 'Enakai, and when they were done, if a single spark of life remained in her broken body, he would have her chopped into chum and fed to moray eels.

Let 'Enakai laugh and mock him. When he was Poseidon, when he clasped the golden trident of Atlantis in his hand, she would know who was king and who was a common whore to be used and discarded like the garbage she was. Nothing could restore his sight; his eyes had been burned away with red-hot coals, but the healers of the temple were skilled. It was more than possible that they could construct him a new tongue, so that he might speak again.

"Caddoc!" 'Enakai's voice cut like the lash of a whip. "Between my knees. I am in need of stimulation. I hope your staff is stiffer tonight than it was the last time you came to my bed. If you fail to please me, I will send you to serve the stable boys and the waste carriers. And smile. I hate a gloomy face. You must at least pretend to be enjoying yourself." She laughed. "What did you say, Prince Caddoc? I didn't quite hear you?"

A guardswoman twittered.

They are here again, Caddoc thought with a sinking heart, *gathered around the royal bed, making suggestions, making me feel like a worm on the end of a hook.*

Coarse hands began to stroke his naked body, running callused fingers over his face and tugging at locks of his hair. Someone pushed him roughly to his knees and he was forced to crawl to the foot of 'Enakai's couch.

"Hurry up," she said. "I have the ambassadors from the Japans waiting. I would not have summoned you if this wasn't my most fertile day. You may get lucky, Prince Caddoc, providing you still have the means to provide what I need most."

Someone unsnapped the lead that had connected to his collar, and he found the bed covering with his right hand. *I may not feed her to the eels,* he thought. *When I am crowned high king of Atlantis, I may have her cooked and served in a pie for my coronation feast. Or better yet,* he mused, *I'll have her stuffed, and roasted, and served with a starfish in her mouth.*

When Ree opened her eyes, the first thing she felt was the lack of pain in her chest, and the second was the ease of which she was able to draw breath. The relief was enough to bring tears to her eyes . . . that saw only vague shapes and muted colors. But it didn't seem to matter. She sighed with pleasure. She was in the water again, safe in the sea, cradled in the warm caress of an endless tide. Nothing else mattered.

"Ree? Can you hear me?"

She sighed.

"Ree!"

Alex. It was Alex's voice. She smiled and asked lazily, "Where am I?"

"With me. An island off the coast of Chile. Rapa Nui."

She blinked. Chile? Hadn't she been in Samoa? She

tried to remember, but her thoughts kept slipping away. Her vision was becoming clearer. She could make out a pair of dolphins moving as gracefully as ballet dancers in the clear blue water. "How . . ." It was hard to keep her thoughts and her words connected when she just wanted to experience the freedom and beauty of the schools of bright colored fish and the swaying columns of kelp. "We're in the sea, aren't we?"

"Yes. It's been two weeks of your time since I carried you from American Samoa. We've gone from island to island, because I needed to have you on land part of the time. You can only breathe under water for a day or two at a time. We were on Rapa Nui for almost two days."

"But this feels right to me . . . to be in the ocean . . . to feel the salt water against my skin." She couldn't organize her thoughts. It was as if her mind was packed with cotton batting. Thick clouds of haze blocked out her reasoning, parting here and there and allowing her brief glimpses of memories.

"Shh, don't worry. I'll take care of you. We're going home. If anyone can cure this sickness, it is the healers of the great temple. My sister Morwena serves there. She'll look after you."

She wanted to touch Alex, needed to feel that he was real. She was thinking only of Alex, but another man's name rang out. "Nick."

"It's Alex."

Was that hurt she heard in his voice? "I know who you are," she answered. "Nick's eyes are brown."

"I'm not him, Ree."

She shook her head. "No, I know that, but I just remembered. The man I followed from Varenkov's yacht. I knew him a long time ago. His name is Nick."

"He calls himself Nigel now," Alex said. "Are you sure it's the same man?"

"He was my partner."

"More than a partner, I think." He paused and then said, "You kept repeating his name."

"Because the bastard tried to kill me." She tried to sit up but weakness prevented her from raising more than her head. "What's wrong with me?"

"You're seriously ill. Don't try to talk. Save your strength until you're stronger."

"No," she protested. "You have to understand what happened. Nick shot me point blank. His bullet struck my cuirass, but it didn't penetrate the armor. It knocked the wind out of me, and I think I cracked a rib, but my chest feels fine now."

Her vision was still squirrely but she didn't want to mention that. It was more important that Alex realize that whatever she had felt for Nick—whatever twisted loyalty and guilt she'd felt for all those years—it was gone. He'd blown it away with the squeeze of a trigger. Everything she'd felt for Nick had been based on a lie, and the only solid thing remaining in her life was the man beside her. Whether he could ever forgive her for rejecting him, he had to understand what he meant to her.

"Once you returned to the sea"—Alex explained— "your ribs healed quickly. Two were broken, another cracked. But that isn't the problem. It's the sickness that nearly took you from me. I should have carried you back to Atlantis long ago." He leaned down and kissed her forehead. "I thought you were going to die, Ree. If I lost you . . ."

She saw the muscles of his throat tighten. "You took care of me all this time? Two weeks?"

He nodded.

"But what about Varenkov?" She remembered now. Alex had been watching the Russian's yacht while she trailed Nick. "Did you kill Varenkov?"

Alex's gaze hardened. "He slipped away again. By helicopter. I believe Nigel Kent—the man you know as Nick—must have warned him. I followed the helicopter to the airport, but Varenkov boarded right on the tarmac. He never entered the terminal. The two of them flew out in a private jet bound for Paris."

"And Nick was with him . . . when he got on the plane?"

"Yes. I caught up with him at the gate. That's how I heard his name—*Nigel Kent*. The attendant welcomed him aboard. One of his hands was wrapped in a thick bandage, and he said something about seeking a prominent French surgeon."

Ree had another flash of memory. The image of a flaming pistol and Nick's cry of pain. "I did that. He was going to put a bullet in my head." She closed her eyes and let the water current comfort her. "You say I have to be on land for periods of time?"

"Anuata told me it would be so. When you can no longer breathe in the water, I must take you to solid ground, and when you begin to struggle there, you must return to the sea. The periods grow shorter with each episode and your reaction grows stronger each time."

"You're right," she murmured. "About Nick and I being more than partners. It doesn't matter now. I was wrong about him. He was one of us, trained as I . . . was trained."

"He serves the Russian now."

"Yes. Apparently, Nick has secretly worked for Varenkov for years."

"A traitor."

She nodded. "I thought he was dead . . . but it was a ruse. He pretended to die to get away from . . . from the people I work for." She coughed. "Correction. The people I *worked* for. Nick says they think I've gone rogue. If they find me, they'll kill me."

"Then I'd better make certain they never find you."

Something troubled her. She couldn't remember what was so important, but she knew that . . . "The children!" she cried. "The children. What happened to the children?"

CHAPTER 25

The memory of that house with the wall around it came flooding back. Like snapshots in an old photo album, she saw an image of the open gate, saw Anuata frozen in the act of throwing an unconscious man over her shoulder, and saw terrified children huddled in a bedroom. "Two weeks? It was two weeks ago?"

"Yes." Alex tried to take her in his arms, but she pushed him away.

"No, that can't be. It's impossible." Arms clasped tightly over her chest, Ree rocked back and forth, sickened by the pain of her failure . . . her betrayal. "I promised to help them," she said. "I promised."

"So Anuata told me." He grimaced. "Ree O'Connor, you are a great trouble to me. Will you never cease making bad situations worse?"

"How could I make it worse? I abandoned those helpless children. They could all be dead by now. Probably all murdered by that awful man and woman. Or sold to perverts."

"As dead as those baby dolphins in the cove?" His voice grated. "The ones who heard their mothers being slaughtered first?" He checked himself. "Forgive me, Ree. That was cruel. What happened in the drive wasn't your fault. It's wrong for me to take out my anger on you. Your human children are all alive, or they were when we left Samoa. Whether they're safe or not remains to be seen."

"Where are they? What happened to them? Did Anuata summon the authorities?" As soon as the words were out of her mouth, she realized how ridiculous the idea was. How could a Lemorian warrior-woman dial 911 or whatever passed for an emergency call in Samoa? "Did someone call child welfare?"

Alex chuckled at the thought. "An interesting concept, but no, that's not what happened." He stroked his chin. "Lemorians don't have the talent for illusion. Can you imagine what the police chief would think if he saw Anuata? At the least, he would have believed her a star traveler."

"So?" Ree stared at him expectantly. "Don't keep me in suspense. Tell me what happened. I blacked out. I have no idea how I got out of that house, let alone the children."

"Anuata carried you, and the boy, I think. The girls followed. I believe she convinced them that you were some sort of angel come to rescue them. Or maybe she threatened them with beheading, but apparently, they trailed after her like ducklings."

"But she did leave them in a safe place?"

Alex exhaled slowly. "That would have been the rational option . . . what I would have done. Human children, human problem. But no. Anuata isn't always rational. She took them."

"How? Where?"

"I believe she tossed Varenkov's two men out of the Zodiac, loaded you and the children into it, and motored you all back to the *faleo'o* on the beach where she'd left Dewi."

"She drove the Zodiac?"

"Anuata's resourceful. Or maybe one of the children knew how to operate the engine. Anyway, they got to the hut; she left the kids there and submerged you in the sea to keep you from going into shock and suffocating."

Ree tried to follow what he was saying, but it didn't seem possible that Anuata could have gotten her and the children out of the house and away without been seen or caught.

"Dewi came for me," Alex continued. "By that time, I was on my way to the airport, but eventually we met up."

"I don't understand. Why would Anuata take the kids to the hut? There wasn't another soul within miles." She yawned. She was exhausted and desperately wanted sleep, but she had to know what had happened to the children.

"I told you. Anuata took them all."

Alex wasn't making any sense. "Took them where?"

"First to the hut where we stayed, and then into the sea. She convinced Dewi and Bleddyn that the young ones had no chance of surviving in the human world. Somehow she got the two of them to help her."

"But how? The children aren't Atlantean. They'd drown."

"You didn't drown, did you? Because you were with me, you had the ability to breathe under water, even before your transformation."

"So why can't I now? I'm still . . ." She took another deep breath. "With you. Can't you . . . do whatever it was you did then?"

"You weren't sick before. You were shot, maybe dead from Varenkov's bullets when I carried you from the yacht, but you didn't have the illness that you have now."

"So where are they now?" She looked around, seeing the two dolphins but nothing else larger than a yellow starfish. "Are they here? With us?"

"Hardly. It takes a great deal of effort to keep humans alive under water. Usually, the transfer is done one to one, one Atlantean, one human. But there are five children.

Anuata and Dewi are each helping two to adapt. Dewi is smitten with her, so I can understand that he could be persuaded, but Bleddyn is the one I count on to be sensible."

Ree tried to imagine the three warriors caring for Julita, Remi, and the others beneath the surface of the sea. It was impossible to imagine. "But there were five children."

"Bleddyn, who should have known better, is caring for the fifth. Their progress will be slow. They have to get out of Lemorian territory without being caught, and if they reach a portal to travel by seraphim, they'll have to take the children through one at a time. It will be far less efficient than normal. We'll reach Atlantis long before they do, if they make it at all with their small humans still alive."

"But why? Why would Anuata take the risk?"

"Who the Hades knows?" Alex rolled his eyes. "Suppressed motherly emotions, a kind heart. Lemorian insanity?"

"My guess would be the kind heart. If she hadn't helped me . . ."

"I give her that. But you have to realize my position. I'll have a great deal of explaining to do. First, I must tell my brother the king that I've failed to take down Varenkov again. Next I present him with a human hybrid who needs urgent medical care."

"I'm sorry," Ree mumbled.

"Wait, there's more," Alex continued. "And then, if he hasn't ordered me banished from the kingdom for breaking more laws than I could relate to you in the turning of a water clock, there's my turncoat captain of the royal Lemorian guard that I have to vouch for. Not to mention five human children that she's bringing with her and insisting they be transformed into Atlanteans."

"They can do that? Transform human children?"

"It wouldn't be the first time. Actually, my niece, Poseidon's daughter, was born human. But don't mention it. She doesn't remember any of it, and it would be an extreme lapse in manners to cause her distress."

"If his own daughter was human once, your brother should understand."

"Understanding is one thing. Ignoring the laws of Atlantis because his younger brother is the perpetrator is another. Poseidon may be sympathetic, but that doesn't mean I may not face banishment or worse."

"What could be worse?"

"Being sealed in an ice floe for five hundred years." His tone grew husky. "Being separated from you, Ree. Being trapped in utter silence, unable to move a muscle and wondering if you'd survived. And if you still lived, if you'd forgotten me and taken another to your heart."

"All along, I thought what we had was just . . ." She wasn't ready for this. She cared for him, cared more than she wanted to tell him, but commitment was such a frightening thought that she wanted to run.

"That it was just sex?" He chuckled. "That's what I told myself. It was what it had always been with women, pleasure between two consenting adults. But right from the beginning, I knew that you were different."

"Because I was human."

"No." He brushed her lips with his. "That was the hard part for me. I've spent my whole life resenting air breathers, hating them."

"Because of your mother's death?"

He nodded. "I couldn't understand when my brothers fell in love with human women . . . I thought they were forgetting our mother . . . forgetting what happened to her. What is that human expression? Now I'll have to eat gull?"

Ree smiled at him. "I think it's *crow* not gull. You'll have to eat crow."

"And after I stopped caring that you were human, when you were just Ree, I reminded myself that it wasn't fair to become involved with you, that someone in my line of work shouldn't have a wife."

Ree's heart skipped a beat. "You're right. It's a big leap, from not hating me for being human to using that word. I can't make a decision like that . . . not yet . . . maybe not ever."

"Because we're of different species?"

"No, hell, no. Because . . ." How could she tell him that the people she loved died? Or betrayed her. Alex wasn't Nick, but she'd thought she'd known Nick and she wouldn't have married him. "I'm not the kind of woman who needs a husband," she said.

"But if you were?" he persisted.

She sighed. "If I was, you'd be the first man I'd consider."

"You'll come with me to Atlantis, then? You aren't angry that I brought you this far when you were incapable of deciding for yourself?"

"Is it far, your Atlantis? You never told me where it was."

"We don't. The location of our city is a secret, but you'll know soon enough. Atlantis lies in the deepest trench of the Atlantic, between the British Isles and America."

"I'd always heard that it was in the Mediterranean. Or in the Caribbean."

"Outposts, colonies. Our kingdom stretches back to the dawn of time. We have fortresses and palaces scattered across the Atlantic. One of the oldest is off the coast of Wales."

"But they've never been discovered in all this time?"

"Some have, but your scholars believe what they wish. They attribute the ruins to various civilizations—Mayans along the shores of Mexico and Central America, Mycenaeans near Crete. Atlantis is a myth. No serious archaeologist would consider that they've found one of our sites."

Ree stretched. "I think I'm feeling better. I know I am."

"At daybreak, when I carried you from the island, you were burning up with fever. It's been almost impossible to get you to eat or drink. And when you do wake, you don't remember being sick."

"If I receive this miracle cure, what will I be? Human or Atlantean?"

"It's complicated. The Lemorian treatments you received make you different from anyone I've ever heard of. You may be the first to carry the genes of all three species."

She forced a smile. "That's me, always different." He still didn't know the extent of her psychic abilities. "You don't have to do this," she said. "If you leave nature to take its course, you can avoid a lot of trouble."

"Leave you?" His eyes narrowed. "You think I could do that? After what the two of us have been through together?" He shook his head. "You really don't know me, do you, Ree?"

"You're always talking about being rational. It would be the rational thing to do. You could go directly to France, after Varenkov."

"He won't get away. Eventually, he'll make a mistake, and I'll be there to finish him. But not until you're safe, and now, not until Anuata, Dewi, and Bleddyn are cleared of charges. Without me, they might suspect her of being a spy and them of helping her."

"And the kids? What will happen to them? If they're transformed, as you put it?"

"With human children my people are understanding. They will take these small ones to their hearts. Every child is cherished in Atlantis."

"But these kids are different. How can they forget what they've been forced to do? If anyone learns why Anuata stole them, they couldn't possibly be accepted."

"Atlanteans live many times longer than humans. We have time to learn from our mistakes. No person could blame an innocent child for the evil done to them. And the young ones' minds will be wiped clear of the bad memories. They will forget, be reborn in body and mind, and there will be loving families eager to adopt them."

"Is that how your brother got his daughter? He stole her?"

"No. In Danu's case, my brother found her dying in the ocean. She'd been attacked by predators. He brought her back to life, much as I did you. Thus, he became responsible for her. Their lives will be always linked."

"Are you responsible for me?"

"Yes." Alex nodded. "But the bond that ties me to you is more than honor. I love you, Ree. As a man loves a woman, now and forever."

She turned her face away. She wanted so badly to accept that love, to tell him that she loved him in return, but the words wouldn't come. How could she trust her judgment? She'd been so wrong about Nick. How could she ever know what was the right choice again? And how could she pledge her love to Alex, when loving her might mean his death?

In his apartment in the Lemorian palace, Caddoc threw back his head, ripped out great handfuls of his hair, and howled in anguish.

Iorgos, the young nobleman who'd carried the news of the failed attempt on the throne of Atlantis, stared at his prince in horror. "What have I done?" he cried. "My brother Zotikos died for you. Have I lost my home, my

wife, my family, and fortune to crown you Poseidon? Did
I throw away a life of ease and splendor for some maimed
madman who couldn't govern an oyster bed?"

Caddoc continued to howl as the distraught messenger
fled the apartments, obviously eager to distance himself
from his rightful sovereign. Caddoc didn't need to see Iorgos' face to read the contempt there . . . the pity.

Caddoc dropped onto a settee, stunned by the realization that his last chance to become Poseidon had died with
his uncle and his cousins. All but two of the rebels had
been slain, and they had run for their lives. Iorgos' older
brother Zotikos had escaped with him, only to be attacked, stung to death, and eaten by jellyfish a few leagues
from Lemoria.

How had it gone wrong? Why had the fates turned
against him? Iorgos' words burned into Caddoc's brain.
They had been foiled at every turn. Poseidon had been
shot and was badly wounded but still lived, as did his infant son, Perseus. Orion had survived the ambush at the
archery range and had assumed control of the throne. So
far as Caddoc knew, his most hated enemy Alexandros was
still very much alive and well.

They'd come so close to victory to lose all in a single afternoon.

There would be no crown, no throne, no accolades for
Caddoc. He would never hold the reins of power, never
command the armies or the bevies of nubile and beautiful
women who waited to serve the king. He would never go
home again, never walk the halls of the palace or drink in
the majesty of the city. So long as he lived, he would be
an outcast, a supplicant, a whore for 'Enakai and any man
or woman she wished to lend him to.

All his life, his mother had promised that he would be
high king. If he would only do as she said, she would see
that he had his reward, the prize that should have been his

from the day of his birth. He, not Morgan or Orion or Alexandros, he was Poseidon's firstborn son. But his mother had lied to him. None of what was promised had ever come.

His father and his brothers had never loved or respected him. And despite her many pleas to the contrary, his mother had never loved him either. All he had ever been to Halimeda was a willing tool, the means to the throne that she could never gain on her own.

Caddoc buried his face in his hands. Empty eye sockets could weep only blood, and a tongue-less mouth could not utter a shattering scream. Anger and regret boiled in his brain. He wished that 'Enakai had taken his ears, as well. If he had lost the sense of hearing he wouldn't have known that all was lost, that his entire life had been for nothing . . . that for him there was no hope, only endless days and nights of ridicule and degradation.

He sunk to the floor and curled into a fetal position, utterly alone and desolate, without reason to live. Soon, if she hadn't already heard, 'Enakai would learn of the failure of the plot to put him on the throne of Atlantis. Iorgos would eagerly spread the word, anxious to win patronage from the high queen.

'Enakai had no mercy. Caddoc knew all too well. She would taunt him, stripping him of whatever pride remained in his ruined body. He, Prince Caddoc, would become the laughingstock of the Lemorian court. Servants would scorn to wait on him, and the guards would whisper behind his back and make crude gestures that he could no longer see.

Had he the nerve, he would fall on his own sword, but he knew he was made of weaker stuff. Killing others was easier, but to pierce his own body impossible. Suicide wasn't an option. All he could do was commit some act so terrible that 'Enakai would order his execution. Even being thrown into the lava flow would be a gentler passage than living for thousands of years as a joke.

But if he was to die, why not die in a manner that would cause his name to go down in history? 'Enakai had insulted and abused him. She had dared to treat a prince of Atlantis as she might the meanest slave. And that contempt would be her undoing. If his life was over, why not bring down the throne of Lemoria as his final act?

'Enakai would summon him to her bed tonight. She would not miss the opportunity to belittle him. She would demand his service, and he would give it in a manner that she least expected. The thought heartened him and put steel in his spine. He rose from the floor, arranged his garments, and rang for his body slaves and his barber.

Tonight, he would go to 'Enakai's chambers garbed as a prince, his body oiled and scraped, his scales shining. He would charm her and whip her lust to an aching hunger. The high queen liked it rough. He would give her rough. Caddoc smiled, feeling better than he'd felt in weeks, perhaps months. Tomorrow the bards would write songs of him, of the last bold deed of Prince Caddoc, and for eons his name would be remembered.

It was small vengeance for all he had suffered, but it would be better than letting the bitch live to enjoy his misery.

CHAPTER 26

Anuata jumped through the portal with Remi in her arms and Zita strapped to her back. The passage through the seraphim had been relatively easy, considering that she carried two children with her and had to assist each with breathing. Dewi was just behind her with Julita and Pilar.

Bleddyn had been the first to enter, but she saw no sign of him. She hoped that he hadn't taken a wrong passage. The chutes were tricky, and the corridors winding and narrow. This Pacific seraphim was one of the oldest surviving, and coming this way was risky. But she and Dewi had talked it over with Bleddyn and decided that it was the wisest course. The longer the children were under water without transformation, the more dangerous it was for them. She wouldn't think of what would happen if the Atlanteans refused to accept the children. They must.

"Are you all right?" she asked Zita. In answer, the tiny girl patted Anuata's neck, and the sensation caused a wave of tremendous emotion. Above anything, Anuata had to protect these little ones. They could never return to the world of land-walkers. The very idea was repugnant.

Remi smiled up at her, and Anuata leaned over and brushed her cheek against the top of his head. It plagued her that she hadn't broken the neck of the man with the gun when she'd thrown him into the land-travel machine. She could have done it easily, without Ree's knowledge. Anuata knew many ways to cause death to her enemies, some lingering and painful. Leaving the cowardly woman alive to work more wickedness troubled Anuata as well. Both Ree and her prince Alexandros were too soft.

Those who would mistreat an innocent child deserved no mercy. It gave Anuata some consolation that all must be judged by Vassu when they passed from this life to the next. She, Anuata, had been a soldier for centuries, and she had committed many acts of which she could not boast, but she had never harmed a humanoid child, a whale calf, or a dolphin.

She had no fear that in the weighing of her many sins against her acts of kindness and courage, the Supreme Being would see fit to pardon her weakness. Surely, He, in his infinite wisdom, would smile at her imperfections, and give her another opportunity to be reborn rather than casting her into dark oblivion.

From the first, Anuata had found herself drawn to these two smallest and weakest children. The knowledge that they had been bought and sold as sexual slaves for the pleasure and profit of evil men like Varenkov ignited a raging fire in her breast to protect and care for them.

Zita's large hazel eyes and round little face reminded Anuata of her own baby sister, and as for Remi . . . Anuata felt her single eye grow teary. Precious Remi . . . She'd begun to think of him as her Remi. *And why shouldn't they be mine, both of them?* Too long had she swam the oceans alone. Was a Lemorian any less worthy than an Atlantean to parent Remi and Zita?

At first the children had been frightened of her size, her scars, and missing eye. Now they ran to her, climbed into her lap, and traced her tattoos with curious fingers. Remi shyly referred to her as *'Ama,* and both kids insisted on sleeping curled against her, one on either side.

That hadn't pleased Dewi, who preferred more adult sleeping arrangements, but Anuata had soon straightened him out. These little ones had seen enough. As much as she enjoyed sharing pleasures of the flesh with Dewi, there would be no sex between them until the children were safe in Atlantis. And if Dewi wanted to remain on her good side, he would concentrate on taking care of his charges, Julita and Pilar.

For all his protests that caring for children was a woman's job, Dewi was kind and gentle to Julita and Pilar, though not fatherly so much as acting the part of a protective older brother. She watched him laughing with them, calming their fears, and insuring their breathing, even as they slept. With each passing rise of the moon, Anuata's respect for Dewi grew, and she found herself watching him and wondering if there might be something more than sex between them. He might be boastful and an Atlantean, but his strength of character and bravery more than made up for his flamboyant ways and his lack of tattoos.

Anuata waited, watching the portal, and conscious of the time that had passed since she, Remi, and Zita had exited. Where were the others? Then, to her relief, Bleddyn and Mayuni burst through the opening, safe and sound. Mayuni was smiling, so the passage must not have been too rough for her. But where was Dewi?

Anuata glanced at Bleddyn. "Did you see them? He just behind me at the last major intersection. He should have come out before you." She'd been the one who'd insisted that they take this seraphim rather than swim the great distance. If anything happened to Dewi and the girls, she would never forgive herself.

Bleddyn shook his head, and Anuata, although he answered with bravado, read worry in his eyes. "He'll be all right," Bleddyn assured her. "Dewi is smart and tough, none bolder. He—"

With a pop, the portal opened and Dewi flew through the entrance. He stumbled, fell to one knee, but recovered his balance. His head bore a nasty scrape from left eyebrow to chin and his arm bled from a deep gash. Normally calm Julita clung to his back, her eyes huge and frightened. Pilar, clutched tightly in his arms, was bruised and weeping.

"What happened?" Anuata cried, taking the sobbing girl from him. "Are you hurt, child?"

Dewi grinned. "We got caught in the current and struck a wall. The rope that held Pilar broke and she was swept away. I nearly lost her, but Julita caught sight of her shirt. We had to fight our way upstream until we reached her. She'd had the sense to grab an underwater ledge and hold on. If she'd let go, she would have ended in the worm's stomach chamber. She may be a little battered, but she'll be fine."

Dewi unstrapped the rope that bound Julita to his back and lowered her to the sand bottom. She lunged through the water to Pilar and hugged her tightly. Both girls were laughing and weeping at the same time.

"You lost Pilar in that madness and went back for her? Against the current?" Anuata shook her head. She doubted that she would have had the strength or the audacity to attempt such a feat—let alone survive it.

Dewi grinned wider. "I may be a small man but I'm a stubborn one."

"No. I was wrong. You are not a small man," Anuata declared. "You are a hero, the greatest warrior I have ever had the pride to know." And she flung her arms around him, pounded his back, and kissed him so thoroughly that Bleddyn and the children shrieked with laughter.

★   ★   ★

Nigel crushed the cheap cell phone under his boot heel and threw the broken pieces into the darkened Arno River. A cold rain lashed his bare head, beat against his face, and soaked his suit jacket. He should have worn a raincoat or at least brought an umbrella on such a foul night, but he hated unnecessary layers of clothing, and the wind had the damndest habit of turning his umbrellas inside out.

The pain in his burned hand nagged at him. He dug in his pants' pocket for the bottle of painkillers, popped two in his mouth, and swallowed. The bandaged hand was stiff, and the physicians had warned that a great number of nerves and several tendons had been destroyed, and he might never regain full motion. Regardless of the gloomy prediction, Nigel knew his hand, despite the agony he suffered, would eventually heal.

It was no wonder they were ignorant. His was a special ability, one that even the best surgeons were unaware existed. Nigel had never met another or read of another human who shared his capacity for regeneration of destroyed skin, muscle, and bone, not even among his gifted classmates at the institute.

He'd been born with a physical makeup that enhanced healing in his own body. That had become apparent when, as a seven-year-old, he'd fallen from a third-story window and shattered his left hip, wrist, and elbow. The doctors hadn't expected his bones to knit properly, but within three months, he had completely recovered. His story had been a news sensation around the world for a few weeks, and had brought him to the attention of the organization. That advantage, the super-human ability to heal himself, thankfully, he'd retained.

His second talent, the ability to move inanimate objects from a distance—using only the power of his mind—had surfaced soon after he'd been enrolled in the institute. He'd quickly become a star pupil, singled out for advanced training and special recognition by his instructors. At his peak, if conditions were right, he'd been able to manipulate the actions of humans and animals.

No more. That skill had vanished with his innocence, he supposed. In the last few years, the most he could manage were mere parlor tricks: the turn of a card or a doorknob, sliding a knife off a table, or rattling cupboard doors. Fortunately, he'd continued to hone his skills in his career field, so that he had no need for psychic ability. It was one talent he'd excelled at, outshining even Ree O'Connor with all her special abilities.

But that knowledge gave him small satisfaction. He'd screwed up on Samoa, let Ree get the best of him in a situation where he had every advantage. She should have been dead within seconds of their meeting, but he'd hesitated. He'd been surprised to find that Ree, of all people, was the one tailing him, and even more astounded to see her armed with a sword and dressed like an actor from the Hollywood flick *Achilles.*

He supposed that somewhere, buried deep inside his brain, he still held some measure of affection for her. And that weakness had shifted the advantage from him to her and nearly gotten him killed.

He'd underestimated her. Ree had changed since they'd known each other so well. Her powers had increased tenfold, while his gift, sadly, had become almost dormant. When he'd graduated from the institute, some years before Ree, he'd been one of most promising candidates that the organization had trained in years. No one expected her to ever match his legendary knack for killing.

As for his temporary setback with the burned hand, other than the constant pain and annoyance, it wouldn't prove too much of a difficulty. As he'd explained to

Varenkov, he was ambidextrous, as deft with his left hand as his right. He was still a deadly marksman with firearm, crossbow, or throwing knife. He was as capable of wielding a garrote or planting a car bomb as he had been before the accident.

From Paris, immediately after he'd been discharged from the hospital, he'd put in a call to a Chinese associate of Varenkov's in Hong Kong, informing him of a problem in Samoa. Valuable merchandise destined for Wong's international auction had been waylaid by an undercover agent, working for the American CIA, who went by the name of Ree O'Connor.

Ree, of all people, would enjoy the humor in that. CIA? Ludicrous, but Wong couldn't know that, and blaming the CIA for any frig-up was one of Varenkov's favorite ploys.

In addition, Nigel had informed Wong that this same CIA operative was responsible for the execution of Phirun, the independent transporter. He hadn't bothered to mention Phirun's Polynesian woman who'd died with him. The fact that two of Varenkov's employees had actually done the deed after he and the Russian had flown out to Paris wasn't relevant. What was important was that the Chinese mafia would mark Ree for extermination.

Tonight, here in Italy, Nigel had hedged his bets by contacting an informant in Dublin, Dermot Brady, who sometimes provided assistance to the organization. Nigel introduced himself as a mutual friend, and told him that one of the organization's rogue operatives had surfaced in Pago Pago working for Grigori Varenkov. Brady was aware of the price on O'Connor's head and seemed delighted to get the tip.

"Three's the charm," Nigel murmured under his breath as he started back to his hotel. If Varenkov's men didn't get her, either the Chinese mafia or the organization would make certain that Ree never got in his way again. If his hand didn't hurt so much, he might be a little regretful. He and Ree had had some good times. But all things must end, he thought. And the sooner Ree O'Connor was dead, the easier he'd sleep at night.

The storms at Cape Horn were worse than Alex had ever experienced. Normally, beneath the waves, in the depths of the sea, surface weather mattered little, but this was different. If he couldn't get Ree to the healers in Atlantis soon, he feared for her survival. He'd had to take her ashore again yesterday, and the length of time that she could breathe on land was growing shorter. Any delay could be fatal, and he wasn't strong enough to swim and carry her in these tides.

Another seraphim stretched across the seabed just east of the Falklands. If he could reach it, it would carry them north to Ascension in the middle of the South Atlantic. There was an Atlantean colony there with a small temple and healing priestesses. Home lay almost four thousand miles beyond that. There were other smaller seraphim in the South and North Atlantic, but if Ree's energy wasn't reinforced, he was afraid that she couldn't take the pressure and power of the current inside the seraphim passageways.

Caring for Ree, finding food that she could eat, holding her while she slept, and standing watch over her when they were forced to take refuge on land had only intensified his feelings for her. She was utterly dependent on him for life, and the responsibility weighed heavy on his soul. He tried to think what he could have done differently, but each option led to a dead end.

If he hadn't rescued Ree from Varenkov's yacht, her death would have been certain. At first, he'd protected her out of a sense of duty, but gradually his feelings had changed. He'd come to love this beautiful human, so different from him. More than that, she'd become the center of his world.

And now, when he'd accepted that he wanted her with him always, wanted to take her home to his family and claim her as his wife, he might lose her forever. He had to think of some way to keep that from happening, and he had to do it soon.

Alex considered leaving the water and trying to cross Tierra Del Fuego on foot, but he knew that was folly. The terrain was too rugged; the winds were too fierce, and the distance too great for him to travel. He could breathe air for short periods, but not more than a day or two, and each time he climbed out of the sea, he grew weaker. "If only I did have the power to fly," he muttered. "I'd fly with you in my arms and carry you home to the great city."

Slowly, he swam to the surface, risking the fury of the waves and the driving rain and sleet so that Ree could take a few breaths of air. As they rode the top of a whitecap, Alex noticed a series of blows, far to the south, away from the boiling current, and knew instantly what they were. Blue Whales. Dozens—perhaps a hundred—or more, come up from the cold waters of the Antarctic to calve.

"What is it?" Ree asked weakly. "What do you see?"

"*Mysticeti.*" He waited for her to take a dozen breaths and then swam with her down into the calmer depths where she wouldn't take such a beating.

"I don't understand," Ree said. "What are *mysticeti*?"

"The largest whales that ever lived on this planet in the time of men."

Alex inspected her closely. She appeared cold and exhausted. Ree's face was deathly pale, with dark circles under her eyes, and her cheeks were sunken so that her prominent cheekbones were even more evident. She'd clearly lost weight since they'd left American Samoa. "I need to make contact with them," he added. "I might be able to persuade them to help us."

"How do you make contact with a whale?"

"It's a long story. Trust me."

"That's what you keep telling me, and look where it's gotten me."

He forced a smile. "I've kept us alive, haven't I?"

"So far."

"Then trust me a little longer." He motioned to his back. "Put your arms around my neck."

"I can swim."

"Save your strength." She did as he told her, and he headed in the direction of the blows. The *mysticeti* were elusive creatures, only rarely encountered, even by Atlanteans. But they were gentle and kindhearted; how kindhearted, he was about to test.

"Why are we trying to find whales?" Ree asked.

"You humans have a legend about a man. Jonah?"

"From the Bible. He was swallowed by a whale and saved by the mercy of God."

"If we're lucky, the same thing will happen to us."

chapter 27

'Enakai settled back onto her cushioned throne on the dais and smiled at the Atlantean ambassador who'd surprised her by bringing warning of the impending dolphin slaughter. She was garbed in her finest gown, crowned with a garland of rubies, and surrounded by a bevy of beautiful ladies in waiting.

On either side of the ambassador stood soldiers, and behind them, Lord Mikhail's attendants. She had chosen to receive him in a secluded pavilion, one known for the splendor of its terrazzo floor, featuring scenes from early Lemorian folklore, its domed ceiling set with gems, and its walls of living kelp. Luminous jellyfish, chosen for their variety of colors and lack of poison, floated around the vast chamber.

The ambassador bowed his head, and she returned the courtesy with a regal nod. "Please." 'Enakai waved and four servants carried in a bench for Lord Mikhail. "Be seated. I'm in your debt. We need not adhere to formalities among friends."

He took his seat with a swirl of robes and a serene expression. This is a proud man, 'Enakai thought, not easily awed by her might and majesty. She hoped he had wit and intelligence to go with his refined manners, because the weighty matters she had to discuss with him were delicate.

"It pleases us to see this change in your kingdom's attitude toward Lemoria, Lord Mikhail," she said graciously.

A steward offered her a tiny crystal goblet of *blue fayzon* and a tray of sushi, pickled sea horse, and caviar on a rare species of seaweed. She snapped her fingers and waited as her taster stepped forward to sample the precious liquor and nibble at the delicacies. When he had pronounced all safe, 'Enakai took a small swallow of the *blue fayzon,* savoring the bite on her tongue, and handed it back to the steward, who offered it to their guest along with the food.

Lord Mikhail politely declined the *hors d'oeurves* and accepted the goblet. "Many thanks, your highness," he said. "I confess that I hoped to have the opportunity to sample your legendary drink while I was your guest."

"It is a rare treat, even for me," 'Enakai answered. "Only a single liter is distilled in three years."

"And it is my understanding that the process requires the labor of several hundred of your subjects."

"It's true," she admitted. "Not to mention the demise of so many shellfish, but all that is valuable requires sacrifice. Don't you find that true?" She smiled at him. "But you did not travel so far to discuss the distilling of *blue fayzon.* You come to bring a message of peace from Poseidon. My heart is gladdened. Too long have we quarreled like foolish children. The oceans are vast, large enough for both of us."

"Atlantis agrees," the ambassador replied in perfect formal Lemorian. He took a tiny sip and handed the goblet back to the steward who offered it again to her. "I'm sure that your soldiers gave you a full report. It is my understanding that Prince Alexandros himself led the Atlantean forces."

Her ladies leaned forward, eager to hear news of the handsome Atlantean rogue. 'Enakai motioned them away.

"Leave us," she ordered. "And the soldiers, too. All of you! Away! We have no fear that Lord Mikhail means our royal person harm."

"The Creator forbid," he said.

"You were saying that Prince Alexandros led the Atlantean forces." She smiled. "I would hardly call them forces," she murmured, once the audience chamber was empty and they were alone. "As I understand, there were no more than three of your people involved."

"Four"—Lord Mikhail corrected—"plus two North Atlantic mermen. And as you know, mermen are prodigious fighters."

"But, nevertheless, far too few to make a difference without my Lemorians."

"We agree wholeheartedly, your highness, which is why Poseidon sent word as soon as we learned of the planned atrocity."

'Enakai's lips tightened. "You must know that your Prince Alexandros is unwelcome in our kingdom. He has committed crimes and is suspected of murder and kidnapping."

Lord Mikhail made no answer.

"He brought a human female to my palace. Are you aware of that? We do not involve ourselves with those from the land, and it displeases us that he would do so. It puts our kingdom in danger."

"Has his guilt in this murder and kidnapping been proved beyond doubt?"

'Enakai made an impatient gesture. "He is unwelcome here. So long as he absents himself from Lemoria and the territory that we command, we are prepared to forgive his offenses." She sniffed. "Although the healer that he killed was a highly respected one."

"Is suspected of killing . . ." Lord Mikhail corrected. "I

find it hard to believe that Prince Alexandros would harm a healer-physician. That would be a mortal sin among our people."

"Just so," she said, draining the goblet of the last delicious drops. "I wondered the same, myself." She met his shrewd gaze with her own. "And, you doubtless have heard that Prince Alexandros is not the only Atlantean royal prince who has paid us the honor of his presence."

The ambassador's face remained expressionless. "You refer to Prince Caddoc. Not a royal prince, a half-blood prince at best, one who never was in line to inherit the throne. Are you aware that Prince Caddoc is charged with high treason in Atlantis? That he and his mother, Lady Halimeda, conspired to murder our late king?"

'Enakai clapped and a servant ran from a small doorway. He dropped to his knees in front of her, lowered his head, and offered a thick scroll. 'Enakai took the scroll and dismissed the lowly creature.

"You may not be aware that since you left Atlantis, there has been another attempt on the throne," she said as she passed him the scroll. "You may take this translation and read it at your leisure. A small number of rebels thought to crown Prince Caddoc by killing Poseidon and all his brothers. The king barely escaped murder as did Prince Orion. Unfortunately, two of the younger princes died, victims of base treachery, shot down at an archery range by men they believe loyal friends. But fortunately, the coup was utterly crushed and most of the traitors executed."

Lord Mikhail half rose in his seat and his mouth gaped. "An attempted coup?"

That information cracked the polite mask, 'Enakai thought. "I'm sorry to have to give you such distressing news, but I can tell you that Poseidon may still be alive, and his brother Prince Orion definitely is."

"I did not know," he said breathlessly. "When I left Atlantis, all was well."

She sighed and fingered the thick strings of pearls that cascaded from her throat, nearly covering her breasts. "I fear the source is Prince Caddoc. A pity that two of your royal house had to die needlessly. It was Prince Caddoc's misfortune to suffer an accident resulting in terrible injuries." She looked meaningfully at the ambassador. "Only a brief time before the attempted coup. But of course, his supporters could not know that their attempt was doomed from the first."

"Injuries?"

"Maiming injuries," 'Enakai said. "He lost his tongue and both eyes."

"How?"

"Attacked by sharks while escorting his mother, *Queen* Halimeda, home from the temple where she had been worshiping," she lied smoothly. "Such a devout woman. She will be greatly missed. Prince Caddoc fought bravely, but was unable to save her. She was eaten, and he was left a cripple."

"Prince Caddoc is blind?"

"Yes."

"Unable to speak?"

She nodded. "Tragic, isn't it? Sharks ripped out his tongue. Such a promising young man, such a great orator, to come to such an end."

"You must realize that no maimed prince can ascend the throne of Atlantis," Lord Mikhail said, attempting to recover his composure. "Poseidon must be perfect in mind and body."

"Naturally." She crossed her legs and shifted to one side, allowing him a glimpse of her tail. "We follow the same custom in Lemoria," she purred. "My own body is without flaw."

"It goes without saying that your beauty has no equal."
He appeared to be considering what best to say next, and
she decided to be merciful.

"Our sympathies lie with your king. Rebellion threat-
ens the natural order, and regardless of birth order, it is our
understanding that his mother was always a minor queen."

"That is true, your highness."

"I would be rid of this troublesome prince, but I doubt
that Poseidon would welcome him back with open arms."

"Hardly. More likely, he would be put to death."

She nodded. "But he has already suffered greatly. It
could be that he was innocent of the last attempt to seize
the crown."

Lord Mikhail looked unconvinced. "Possibly."

"He has been my guest and under my protection. I have
decided to send him into exile in some distant palace. Assure your king that his brother will not be without the ne-
cessities of life." She laid a hand over her womb. "I am with
child, Lord Mikhail. I fear it makes me tenderhearted. You
have my word that Prince Caddoc will trouble your king
no more. He will live out his life in quiet contemplation
and comfort. And perhaps, in the centuries to come, he
will find redemption in prayer and meditation."

"I bow to your wisdom, Queen 'Enakai."

"Will your king be satisfied?"

"I believe he will."

"Then we are pleased." She nodded. "This audience is
at an end. You have our leave to depart at once for your
homeland. Please tell Poseidon that I have commanded a
thousand prayers to be offered daily for his recovery."

She clapped again, and her honor guard returned to escort her from the chamber. She was eager to return to her
own rooms and summon Caddoc. He would be doubtlessly
thrilled to hear that his seed had proved fertile and she carried his daughter in her womb.

'Enakai was relieved that she'd quickened with a princess. It had saddened her to have to do away with the last two fetuses, but she would have no more mettlesome princes to contend with. A royal daughter would be welcomed, and Caddoc's reward would be his life and an honorable existence far from Lemoria.

Ree watched in awe as the blue whales approached. She had known that they were enormous in size, but photographs in books or film footage didn't do them justice. They were not, as she had supposed, entirely blue in color, rather a muted blue-gray with lighter patterns on their bellies. Each whale's markings were different, making them not just a pod of nameless creatures but individuals of grace and beauty.

The leviathans' heads were long and flattened, and their shining bodies were slimmer than the other great whales. The lead whale must have been nearly a hundred feet long with dark eyes and a great tail tipped with white. As it swam past, it gazed directly at her, and Ree was struck by the intelligence in the huge orbs.

"They're baleen whales," Alex said. "Instead of teeth, they have smooth plates in their jaws. They feed entirely on a diet of tiny krill."

Ree nodded, her imagination caught by the sight of so many, moving through the water like ghosts. Not like ghosts, she corrected. The ocean vibrated with their haunting calls, a singing that brought a catch to her throat and tears to her eyes.

"Their mouths are huge," she whispered. Her thoughts reached out to him. Under water, communication was so much easier. Mind touching mind, rather than voices struggling to be heard.

"They are. Your Jonah, of Bible fame, could have been swept boat and all into that gaping mouth."

"You know the Bible?" She was constantly astounded by the man.

"The Old Testament, I believe," he answered. "Yes, it was my mother's wish that we study the great faiths of those who walk the land."

"What did you think of them?"

He smiled at her. "That there is truth to be found in most, and that for all your differences and quarrels, they are more alike than different."

"Different from your own religion?" What was it about being near these magnificent mammals that made her remember the sensation of walking into the great cathedrals of Europe or the tiny, country church she'd once come upon hiking through Vermont? She should have felt dwarfed by the presence of so many giants, but she didn't. *Am I dying?* she wondered.

For years death hadn't concerned her. But now, she realized how much she wanted to live . . . how much she wanted to experience life with Alex.

"If you ask what I believe"—he said—"it's that there's but one Creator, the Supreme Being who reveals himself to us according to our understanding."

The thought was comforting. "So I won't be compelled to reject my own beliefs?"

"No. Never."

Her fingertips and toes began to tingle, a signal that she needed to surface, but they were deep, and she wasn't certain if she had the strength to manage the swim to the top.

"Be brave," Alex said to her. "Fill your mind with images of blue water and warm currents. Blue whales are shy. They frighten easily, and they will defend themselves if they feel threatened."

"Threatened? What could possibly threaten them?"

"Humans. In my lifetime, I've seen their numbers dwindle from hundreds of thousands to . . ." He shook his head. "Barely enough to keep the species alive. Your people have no idea what they've done, how much wisdom they've slaughtered. Blue whales have so much to teach us." He choked up. "Wait here, while I go and see if any will talk to me."

She blinked. "You . . . you can talk to them? You're kidding me, right?" She wasn't certain that she'd heard him correctly. She felt giddy, as though she'd had too much to drink. Not sick, but weary . . . so weary.

"It's a gift I was born with. Not whales alone, but other species who share our oceans." He hugged her, kissed her cheek, and released her. "Be strong a little longer," he urged.

She drew in a long breath. "I'm trying."

If she'd had some idea that she would hear or understand what Alex said to whales, she was disappointed. The prickling sensations moved up her arms and legs, and her head began to pound, as the great animals moved around and over and under her. She drank in the sight, marveling at their beauty and majesty. She'd seen whales before, but from above, one seemed much like another.

Here, she was acutely aware of individuals with different personalities and degrees of intelligence, and she wondered how men who could go to the moon in search of knowledge could fail to value how much was here, alive and thinking, sharing their planet.

She began to shiver. Losing the ability to control her temperature wasn't new, but the sensation that the water around her was crushing her was. Alex had warned her that she might begin to feel the effects of pressure. Her thoughts flickered, skipping wildly, and she began to laugh. *Was this what divers felt when they went too deep?*

She needed Alex. Fear crept around the corners of her thoughts, raised the scales at the back of her neck, and made her shiver even more. "Alex!" she called. She drew her knees up and clutched her middle. She was sinking. She knew she should swim, but it seemed to take too much effort. She could still see Alex, but he was getting farther and farther away. She closed her eyes, just for a second, and waves of blackness washed over her.

Suddenly, his arms were around her. "Ree. Ree. Listen to me. You have to stay awake."

"I'm sleepy." She sighed, dropping her head onto his shoulder. "I'm cold, and I'm sleepy, and . . ."

He kissed her mouth. No, not a kiss; he was breathing into her mouth, sharing his life force with her. "I love you," she murmured sleepily. "I love you."

"And I love you," he said. "I love you more than life."

Ree opened her eyes to see a whale looming over them, the great jaws opening, and she felt the first twinges of fear. "No," she said.

"Yes," Alex said soothingly. "Don't be afraid. This is Oysmulgmi. She's near her time to deliver her baby, but she has a heart as large as the ocean. She's agreed to carry us around the Horn and as far as she can before she calves."

"Carry us?" The whale's back was a mountain. "How could we hold on? The current would . . ."

Oysmulgmi opened her mouth wider.

"It's all right," Alex said.

"We're going to travel in the belly of a whale?"

He laughed. "Not quite. Her mouth is large, but her throat is far too small. You have a wonderful imagination, Ree."

"Then how . . ."

"You'll see," he promised. "Trust me."

CHAPTER 28

Caddoc's heart hammered in his chest. He'd almost given up hope that 'Enakai would summon him to her apartments again, and if she didn't send for him, how would he ever carry out his plan?

But she wanted him, couldn't bear to be without him. She'd sent serving women to rub him with precious oil, to dress him in new garments, and to curl his hair. They'd come with platters of oysters and other shellfish reputed to add to a man's vigor and prolong his sexual strength.

"The queen asks that you come to her," the effete messenger said. "She longs for your touch and cannot wait for you to share pleasures of the flesh. May I tell her that you are willing?"

Willing? He would have waded the fiery river of lava to reach her. "Tell her majesty that I long for the sound of her voice," Caddoc scribbled on a message block. "Tell her that I swear that this will be a night unlike any she has ever experienced."

He was ready early, waiting for his escort and praying to every god that he had ever heard named or cursed that 'Enakai would not change her mind. His palms sweated, his bowels betrayed him so that he was forced to run three times to the bodily easement room. His stomach twisted and knotted, regurgitating the shellfish and the bottle of wine that he had consumed to steady his nerves.

He had expected to be led to the queen's chambers, but this time, she'd sent a chair and an escort of royal guard. So much the better. The more witnesses, the greater would be his triumph. One thing troubled him. Should he end her life before he shared pleasures or after? They would undoubtedly be the last chance either of them had to experience the rapture in this life, and he hated to think that his best performance was already behind him. If he swived her first, he would please himself, but that meant satisfying 'Enakai's lust as well. Why should he do anything for her when she had destroyed his life?

If she'd supported him, given him the army he'd asked for, this all would have ended so differently. He would have been crowned high king of Atlantis. She would have the comfort of knowing that her former guest was now a mighty ruler in his own right. But 'Enakai had been short-sighted and foolish, worse than foolish, too stupid to see her own advantage. The lack of a few thousand—even hundred—hardened Lemorian soldiers had brought his plans to naught.

Caddoc slipped his hand under his tunic to make certain that he could reach the dagger he'd strapped to his thigh. It was extremely sharp, obsidian, the blade so thin that he could have shaved with it—if he'd been human. Such a blade was delicate, but it sliced through scales and skin and flesh with the ease of a shark's tooth cutting through a man's belly.

His empty eye sockets burned, still irritated by the salt water. They should have healed, but they remained tender, scarred holes. Until now, he had mourned his sight, but no longer. The lack of eyes kept others from looking into them and reading his intentions. He smiled. Likewise his missing tongue. He had no fear that he would say the wrong thing in anger or warn 'Enakai or any of her protectors. Having no powers of speech could be a blessing, too. He managed a deep, rolling chuckle.

He could imagine the splendor of the passageways, the curious onlookers, the whispered comments of the courtiers. "She calls for him," one might say. "The Atlantean prince."

And another might reply, "And why not? I hear he's hung like a walrus." The noblewomen and serving maids would twitter, but they too would long for him, would wish that just for one night, they could be the object of his desire.

He had pleasured many females in his lifetime . . . and just as many males. He'd had his way with mermaids and naiads and uncounted humans. He hoped that the songs the bards would sing of him would do him justice.

Ah, the porters had stopped at the first guard post; there were three. None but the most trusted were ever admitted to the queen's inner apartments, and today, he was 'Enakai's most welcome guest. A short delay, an exchange of passwords, and the chair moved on. Caddoc leaned back, enjoying the ease of being carried. In his father's palace, he'd never had the honor after he'd passed the age of traveling in his mother's lap. She had favored the luxury of a chair, and hers had been much richer and heavier than the Lemorian style. It took six men to carry an Atlantean *klismos.*

Thinking of his mother soured his mood. She was dead. She would never nag or threaten him again. Wherever her spirit had gone after the lava flow had claimed her body, he hoped it was far away. Whether she'd been whisked to the Lemorian version of Olympus or had dissolved into nothingness, he didn't care—so long as he never had to look into her hateful face again.

When he was reborn, and he was certain he merited rebirth, if anyone did, he would study prospective parents more carefully. He would avoid choosing a mother with ambition, brains, or beauty, and above all, he would pick one without the slightest degree of psychic powers. He needed a plain woman whose hopes would be fulfilled by the birth of a son, a female who would never gainsay or belittle him. Naturally, she must be the first wife of a monarch and queen in her own right, so that he would have none of the troublesome annoyances of dealing with other claimants to his throne. Next time, he would be far wiser.

The porters climbed a staircase and stopped a second time. Here the exchange with the guards took a little longer. Caddoc didn't care. He ran his finger over the knife blade and winced as he felt it slice through his skin. It was a pity that 'Enakai would die so quickly. If he lived long enough, he would bathe in her blood—dance in it. But no matter how brief a time he lived after the deed was done, he would have the satisfaction of hearing her screams of pain and the death rattle in her throat.

The chair was moving again. Not far now. Caddoc's bowels growled and he passed gas. Luckily, his stomach was empty. He would not shame himself in his finest hour. Moment, he corrected himself. Ridding the Pacific of the bitch 'Enakai would take no more than seconds. So incensed would her royal guard be that they would fall on him and dispatch him instantly.

The final checkpoint seemed to take forever. At last, Caddoc heard the groan of the great stone double doors swing open and the hum of voices from 'Enakai's suite. Musicians played a soft background for one of the queen's tiresome poets as he recited his latest tribute to 'Enakai's beauty or wisdom or piety. The chair rocked back and forth and settled onto the floor.

"Prince Caddoc," the queen said. "You are welcome to our eyes."

Eyes. She was taunting him already, showing him up before her women and guards as being sightless. His pulse raced and sweat beaded on his palms. How dare she!

"Come, my prince," 'Enakai called. "I have been waiting for you. I have much to tell you."

A servant took his hand and helped him down from the chair. He reached out to keep from swimming into one of the double rows of columns. Someone stifled a giggle, and Caddoc saw red. *Where are you, majesty?* he wondered.

"Here, on the couch."

He went to her, barely containing his trembling anger as she embraced him. "Darling," she whispered into his ear. "I have a surprise for you."

And I for you, he thought. In one fluid movement, he drew the knife from the hidden sheath and raised it to plunge the point into 'Enakai's throat. A woman cried out, and he put every ounce of strength into his thrust.

Something cold touched his upper arm, followed by a gush of hot liquid. Caddoc froze, stunned, unable to fathom what had just happened. He could no longer feel the knife in his hand. He couldn't feel his hand or his arm.

'Enakai screamed, not in pain but in rage. "What are you waiting for?" she shrieked. "Off with his head!"

Caddoc grabbed for the knife with his left hand, grabbed and found nothing but water. *His right hand? Where was his right hand?* He heard the swish of a sword and for an instant, he felt the same icy touch on his neck that he'd felt against his arm. There was a sharp pain, and then he felt nothing at all.

Caddoc looked around, confused. His eyes worked perfectly. How was it possible that he'd been blind and now could see? Had he undergone surgery? Was he still drugged from the operation?

He had no memory of where he was or how he'd gotten here. It was an odd place, devoid of water. Hot sand grated under his feet, and a harsh wind lashed at his head and body. Above him stretched a pewter sky without a cloud. The sun blazed down, an unforgiving ball of fiery heat. He could feel his scales withering, his mouth drying out.

Outcroppings of rock littered a barren landscape that stretched to the horizon. Caddoc could see no sign of life, no plants, no fish, no habitation, nothing but sand and stone and emptiness. He opened his mouth and shouted. "Where am I? Is there anyone here?"

This was bad . . . bad. No water, not a lake or bay, not even a pond in sight. So far, he was having no trouble breathing, but how long could he last on dry land? He yearned for the feel of salt water on his body, thirsted for it. "Someone!" he cried. Was it a nightmare? Would he wake and find himself safe in his own bed?

"Caddoc, my son."

He whirled at the sound of the taunting voice to find his mother standing not an arm's length away. It was Halimeda. There could be no doubt, but it wasn't the hag that the Lemorians had thrown into the lava. This was the beautiful queen that he'd known for most of his life. Her face and body were flawless; her complexion as smooth and lovely as any goddess.

"Mother?" No. It couldn't be. This had to be a nightmare. He dug his fingers into his arm and then stared down. Two arms. Two hands. He had eyes and a tongue once more. He blinked, hoping she would vanish, but when he opened his eyes, she was still there, garbed in a spotless white tunic, still looking at him in that way she had of letting him know that he'd disappointed her. Again.

"You failed me. Didn't you?" she accused.

"No, I—"

"You couldn't manage a simple revolution. All you had to do was eliminate your half-brothers." Her features twisted. "You should be king of Atlantis, and what are you? What are you, Caddoc?"

His throat constricted and he felt the urge to urinate. "I'm sorry, Mother."

"Sorry? Sorry? You're sorry, all right, the sorriest excuse for a son that I've ever seen. You have the nerve to call yourself a prince?"

"I did my best." He took a step back. The sand crumbled under his feet, and he stumbled and fell to his knees.

"Failure!"

"Don't say that," he pleaded.

"Stupid, cowardly, whining failure." She advanced on him. From somewhere, she'd acquired a whip such as she'd used on him when he was a child. She brought the whip down hard across his face. "Pitiful excuse for a son!"

Caddoc covered his head with his hands and crouched down. "Where are we?" he cried. "What place is this?"

"Don't you know?" she howled, standing over him and lashing him around the head and shoulders with the whip. "Are you so ignorant that you don't know?"

"No, Mother. Please, don't hit me anymore. Don't hurt me. I'll be good. I promise. I'll do whatever you want me to."

"It's too late for that," she said. "Too late, you fool. This is Hades, and we're trapped here."

"Trapped? Here?" He stared up at her in disbelief. "For how long?"

"Not forever," she hissed. "Not more than a few thousand years."

"No." He pressed his face into the sand and heaped

handfuls of it over his head. "That can't be," he wailed. "It can't be."

"But there's one good thing about it."

"What's that? What could possibly be good about it?"

"You're not alone, Caddoc. You have me to share your misery."

Ree lay with her head against Alex's chest. His arms were around her, and she felt safe, despite their precarious position between Oysmulgmi's jaws. The blue whale's thick tongue made a comfortable cushion for them to recline upon, and the arched roof of her mouth rose over them like a strange arbor. Through Oysmulgmi's open mouth Ree occasionally glimpsed the monstrous waves and heard the howling winds. No wonder she and Alex had been able to swim this passage, she thought as she snuggled next to him.

As frightening as the idea of letting a whale carry them in her jaws had been, Ree had to admit that it appeared to be working. And despite the rough water and bumpy ride, Ree felt better than she had in days. Oysmulgmi's sleek body cut through the powerful currents and dove deep beneath the waves to find the calmest water. The storms and heavy seas had little effect on the whale's progress, and her regular return to the surface to breathe gave Ree a chance to do the same.

"If she can get us near the colony, we can get you the medical help you need," Alex said. "I don't know if they have the crystals they need to complete your transformation, but they should be able to do enough for me to get you home to Atlantis."

Best of all, she'd had time with Alex. They'd laughed together, and Alex had told her tales of his childhood. Never having had a family, hearing about his close ties with his twin, Orion, and with his brother Morgan and sister Morwena touched her and made her a little envious. *What would it be like to have siblings whom you could trust?* It was difficult for her to imagine.

The few casual friends that she'd had at the institute had always vied to best her. You were expected to develop your gifts, to excel in academics and physical prowess. Twice a year, students were eliminated from the program, and the rumors were that those who were dismissed didn't simply return home. Ree and most of the others suspected something more sinister. No, it didn't make for close friendships because the person you told your secrets to might be gone the next day, or they might be doing everything in their power to get rid of you.

"You'd lost your mother," Ree reminded him. "That must have been terrible for you." *As it was for me,* she thought.

He'd flashed a bittersweet smile. "It was, but my father chose a new queen almost immediately. He had many wives, but the number one wife was the most important. He picked Korinna, and it was one of the best things he ever did for Morgan, Orion, and me. Morwena is Korinna's daughter. She could have ignored us, favored her own children, but from the start Korinna was everything you could ask for in a mother. You'll love her, I promise. And she'll like you."

"That's what you said about Morwena."

"Morwena's a lot like Queen Korinna."

"Your stepmother sounds like a wonderful person."

"She was. She is. We remain close, even though my father is gone. And Morwena's brothers—my half brothers—Paris, Marcos, and Lucas are more like their mother than our father. I'm close to all of them, especially Paris."

Ree shook her head. "It sounds like something out of a

children's fairy tale, although in the fairy tales, the wicked stepmother and her kids always plot against the stepchildren."

Alex chuckled. "I have one of those kinds of stepmothers, too. Lady Halimeda, Caddoc's mother. She's a witch, a schemer, and probably a murderess. She tried to poison my father to make Caddoc king."

"Ahead of you and Morgan and Orion?"

He arched a golden brow. "Her intention was to assassinate all of us, as well, including Korinna and her brood. Luckily, she didn't succeed." He leaned close and kissed the top of her head. "You seem to be breathing easier."

"I am," she agreed. "I know I am. I think I'm recovering from whatever was wrong." The tingling feeling had disappeared from her extremities, and although she was tired, she no longer had memory loss. "I think we should take the seraphim near the Falklands that you mentioned. If we have to go to Atlantis, we need to get there quickly. The longer we delay, the more time Varenkov has to get away."

"I won't take the chance of losing you," Alex replied, stroking her hair. "Once I know you're in good hands and receiving treatment, then I can decide what to do about Varenkov. Plus, I need to wait for Bleddyn, Dewi, and Anuata to get there."

"With the children," Ree reminded him. "They will bring the children, won't they? They won't let anything happen to them?"

"Not if they can help it. I'd trust any of my team with my life."

"You should have had them with you in Tahiti. Why did you try for Varenkov alone?"

"Poor judgment." Alex grimaced. "I'll be more careful next time."

"*We'll* be more careful. I mean to go with you, one way or another."

"And afterward?" He looked into her eyes and brushed a stray lock of hair off her forehead. "What then, Ree? You know I want you to stay with me, be my wife." He tightened his arms around her. "Do you love me?"

She looked away, as fear skittered down her spine. She wasn't ready to commit herself, no matter how much he meant to her. And the thought of tying herself to someone in marriage was terrifying. "You know I do," she answered lightly. "But let's get the Russian first." Once Varenkov was dead, things might look different to her. "We should finish the assignment," she said. "We owe it to the kids."

Oysmulgmi carried them as far as the Falkland Islands and deposited them in shallow water not far from the mouth of the seraphim. "I'll never forget you," Ree said to the great whale.

Alex translated, and Oysmulgmi blew a great gout of water through her vent hole before gliding away to the north.

"I can't believe I let you talk me into this," Alex said. "We should have gone to the temple at Ascension to have the healers check you out."

"Look at me," she insisted. "I'm breathing fine. I'm starving." They'd had no opportunity to eat while they traveled with the Blue Whale, and now she felt as though she could devour a six-foot tiger shark, fin and all. "Just feed me, and I'll be ready for your crazy wind-tunnel passage through the worm's intestinal track."

"It's water, not wind that we move through" he corrected.

"Fast enough for a wind tunnel." She caught his arm. "There really is an Atlantis, isn't there? You're taking me there?"

"I told you so, didn't I?"

"You did," she answered.

Alex caught her in his arms and kissed her. "You'll love it, believe me. There's no city in the world to match it."

"So long as they don't imprison you in an iceberg."

"If they do, you'll just have to figure a way to break me out."

"I mean it, Alex," she said. "You've gotten under my skin. And people I care about have a habit of dying on me. I couldn't stand it if anything bad happened to you."

"Or me to you. We'll just have to make certain it doesn't."

She shrugged. "Easier said than done, considering our line of work."

CHAPTER 29

By the time Ree and Alex reached the outskirts of Atlantis, she realized that the sickness had returned full-blown. Each breath was a struggle, and only Alex's strong arm kept her upright in the chariot. Thankfully, she was no longer in pain, and the headache had given way to a sense of euphoria. Rational attempts at thought had vanished somewhere in the last turbulent rush through the final seraphim. She was content to go where Alex told her, and accept whatever he said.

The tradeoff was a marvelous sensation of lightness and freedom. She had no worries, no regrets, and no guilt. Whatever happened, happened, and she was content to ride the wave to the end. Even the realization that she was losing the ability to breathe held no fear for her. She was aware that she could die, but death's door opened before her as a great new adventure. The only thing that remained real and solid was the man who cradled her in his arms, whispered encouragement and love words in her ear, and repeatedly shared his life force with her.

"Fight," Alex urged. "You must stay awake."

She heard his voice, as if from afar, and she wanted to make him happy, but found her will slipping away with each league the dolphins carried them. *How could Alex be concerned?* she wondered. *Surely, death, if it comes for me, would be a gentle deliverance. How could anything bad happen to me in this glorious wonderland?*

Atlantean soldiers stationed at the exit port had recognized Alex at once and summoned an escort that included a chariot shaped like a silver conch shell pulled by four dolphins, and twenty of the royal palace guard, all fully armed for war and mounted on giant sea horses.

The water here, deep in the mid-North Atlantic, was the vivid blue of the Mediterranean, not devoid of light as she would have supposed, but lit by a radiant blue-green light that illuminated the wide stone road, the marble columns, the statues of stone sphinxes that lined it, and the country estates, small roadside temples, and military stations. The sea around them teemed with vast schools of fish, turtles, dolphins, squid, rays, and octopi. Fields of seaweed and grasses lined the highway, interspersed by what appeared to be crops planted in endless rows.

The road was busy; they passed dozens of conveyances, some carrying families or groups of passengers, others heavily loaded with shellfish or produce. Alex pointed out one beautiful building carved out of pink coral, so exquisite that it looked like a jewel box. "It's a primary school," he said. Dolphins swam around the entrances, rolling and playing, diving and hovering. "Those are the children's companions," he said. "Come to carry them home when studies are over for the day."

"Dolphin nurses?"

"Think of them as a combination of bodyguards, best friends, and a big brother or sister. Insurance against an attack by sharks or other predators. You haven't seen fierce until you've seen a nurse-dolphin protecting her Atlantean foster child."

Images of the children whom she'd left in the care of Anuata, Dewi, and Bleddyn surfaced in her mind's eye.

"They should have had a dolphin," she murmured. "They would have been better than the mothers they were born to."

As they left the country and entered the suburbs, houses stood closer together, many two and three story rambling affairs with walled courtyards and outbuildings. They were built of stone, glittering white, resembling the domed and graceful architecture Ree had seen in the Greek Islands. Everywhere were gardens and statuary, outcrops of kelp groves, and more public buildings. Ree saw miniature pyramids no taller than four stories, and open air corridors lined with columns and statuary. Uncounted Atlanteans went about their daily business, visiting, shopping, playing, working, all too perfect and too beautiful in physical appearance to be real.

"It's like a dream," she murmured to Alex.

"Wait until you see the city proper," he answered. "Palaces, libraries, temples, theatres, and parks. You'll love it."

"Will I?" she asked. If she was hallucinating, it didn't matter. Her field of vision was growing narrower, but the colors brighter, and her surroundings more fantastic. But, *"Will they love me?"* went unspoken. This was Alex's home, his paradise, and there had never been a place where she belonged.

She gazed up into his face, and tears clouded her eyes. Had there ever been a man so magnificent, so strong and virile as Alex? *Maybe I am dying,* she thought. *What else would make me forget the code I've lived by and let myself fall for this man?*

"Hang on just a little longer," Alex said. "We'll be at the temple soon, and the healers will know what to do."

In Ree's perception, the colors around her began to smear and run together. A blot of nothingness crept from the corners of her line of vision, slowly enveloping Alex's face and hair until all she could see were his liquid-green eyes staring into hers.

"Don't leave me," he begged her.

But there was no fight left in her, and she let the nothingness carry her into the absolute silence.

Alex sent riders ahead to warn the temple healers that he was coming with a critically ill patient. By the time he turned onto the Grand Avenue and reached the temple steps, Alex couldn't tell if Ree was dead or alive. Her face was the color of ash, and as far as he could tell, she wasn't breathing. He gathered her in his arms, lifted her out of the chariot, and started up the marble staircase to the main entrance.

Abruptly, the doors swung open, and Lady Athena and a bevy of priestesses appeared, followed by his sister Morwena clad in the formal tunic and veil of a novice healer. "Thank the Creator you're safe," Lady Athena said when the attendants placed Ree on a stretcher. "We'll do what we can for her, but you must go to Poseidon at once. This is a dangerous time for Atlantis."

He clung to Ree's limp hand. "I saw that the military was on full alert," Alex said absently.

"Yes," Lady Athena agreed. "We'll see to her. But you're needed at the palace. The king and Prince Orion have been frantic over your absence."

He hadn't wanted to go, had tried to follow them through the great doors into the sanctuary, but Morwena had first embraced him, and then barred his way. "We didn't know if you were dead or alive," she said. "There was another attempt on the throne. Poseidon was nearly killed." She hesitated and then went on in a rush, breaking into tears as she told him of Paris and Marcos' deaths at the hands of traitors. "Paris gave his life protecting Orion."

"I heard," Alex replied. "The soldiers told me." He gripped her arms. "I loved them both." He moved toward the doors again, but she tugged at his hand.

"You can't go with her. You know you can't enter the inner courts," she said. "You're not initiated. Royal prince or not, you won't be allowed past the public sanctuary."

"Ree needs me."

"She needs the healers. I'll stay with her, but Lady Athena's right. You have to find the king. Go, now. If I'm going to accompany your woman, I have to hurry. Once they start the ceremony, they won't let anyone in."

"I love her," he said.

"I thought you were immune to love, Alexandros." A hint of a smile lit her blue eyes.

"So did I."

Morwena sighed. "She's human, isn't she? You're as bad as Morgan and Orion. None of you can stay away from them."

"She was human. I'm not sure what Ree is now, but it doesn't matter. If she'll have me, I'm going to marry her."

"That's easier said than done." She grimaced. "In any case, you can't help her now. If you try to force your way in, you'll cause a fuss. It could delay her treatment, make things worse for her."

"I can't lose her."

"Lady Athena will do everything possible to save her. You know how she loves Rhiannon. Go on. I'll find you as soon as there's news. I promise."

"Keep her alive for me, Morwena."

"I'll do my best."

A platoon accompanied him to the king's inner chamber where he found, not Poseidon, but his twin Orion seated on the throne. "Where's Morgan?" Alex demanded.

Orion waved a hand and the two generals he'd been conferring with, their staff members, and the guardsmen left the hall. Orion descended the dais and threw his arms around Alex. "Welcome home, twin. There's no one I'd rather see."

"Where's Morgan? He's not—"

"He's alive," Orion said. "It was a close thing. He lost most of the blood from his body. Danu kept him from dying. She's blessed when it comes to the healing gift. If I were you, I'd ask Rhiannon to send her to help with your—what's her name?"

"Ree. And how did you know about—"

"Palace telegraph." He chuckled. "You should know that nothing remains a secret long here. But I'm serious about little Danu. I think her mother and father are a little awed by her gift . . . and frightened. Can you imagine what a healer she'll make when she's older?"

"Morgan," Alex reminded him. "The king. Why are you in his place?"

"He's recovering. I'll take you to him. Rhiannon's orders. She's fierce, I can tell you. She hasn't left his side."

"And he's weak enough to let her make the decisions?"

"She's with child again, this time with twins. You know Rhiannon's our big brother's weak spot. He can't bear to cause her grief." He looked at Alex meaningfully. "She wants him to step down. Perseus was nearly killed as well. One of the rebels broke into his bedroom and tried to run a sword through him."

"But he's all right?"

"Safe and sound. But the attempted coup terrified Rhiannon. She's afraid it will happen again, and next time . . ."

"Is Morgan considering it? Giving up the crown?"

Orion nodded. "First the council and then Morgan—Poseidon—asked me to assume the throne. But I'm no more suited for it than he is. He was happiest when he could spend time with his wife and kids, when he spent his days checking lobster traps and fighting pollution. He and Rhiannon have plans for setting up an ocean sanctuary. The queen left a fortune back on land, and it's growing every day. They want to buy a chain of islands in the Caribbean and protect them from fishing and from the onslaught of tourists."

"Has it ever happened before? Has Poseidon ever abdicated?"

"Hades if I know," Orion replied. "Let me fill you in on what happened during the rebellion."

"Do you expect a second attack?"

"Not now." Orion grinned and slapped him on the back. "Poseidon doesn't even know yet. You're the first to hear. I just received a message through Lord Mikhail's merfolk network. Both Caddoc and his mother are dead."

"Dead? Is it definite?"

"You know mermen. Never wordy. But I'd trust the information. It seems our late stepmother was tossed into the lava flow as some sort of offering to the Lemorian gods, and our half brother tried to assassinate Queen 'Enakai and lost his head in the attempt."

"They cut off his head?"

"Pretty messy, I'm sure. I could almost feel sorry for Caddoc. He never could stand pain or blood, if it was his own."

"So it's over." Alex turned to a window and looked out at the endless sea. "Caddoc's ambition died with him. He never fathered a son, did he?"

"No, none acknowledged. And to be royal, you remember, a male child has to be entered in the book of kings."

Alex watched two rays swim past, rising and diving like seabirds in the air. It was hard to concentrate on what Orion was telling him about the attempted coup, when

Ree's pale face kept filling his mind. *What if she wakes and finds herself among strangers?* He had the feeling he should have insisted the healers let him stay with her.

". . . Seriously, brother. You have to choose."

Alex whirled on him. "If she lives, I'm not going to give her up! If I face trial and sentence for loving her, I—"

"By Aphrodite's sweet ass, Alex! Morgan and I both fell in love with human women. Do you think we're such hypocrites that we'd allow you to be charged for the same crime?"

"It's the law, and I broke it." His mouth twisted into a shadow of a smile. "Shattered it, more like."

"It's a bad law. One you'll have to change."

"Me?" Alex stared at Orion in confusion. "How me?"

"I've discussed this with Morgan . . . with Poseidon. We're in agreement. We want you to take the crown."

"Why?"

Orion rose up off the throne and motioned to it. "It doesn't fit. Not Morgan, and not me. Rhiannon has begged him to step down for the sake of her and the children. He's considering it. I think it's what he wants in his heart."

"So, you take it. You're the soldier. You have the loyalty of the army. You worked your way up through the ranks to general. You'd make a far better king than I would." Alex shrugged. "I'm an assassin. I'd look ridiculous on that throne."

Orion shook his head. "You're the one most like our father. You have the right instincts." He looked at Alex shrewdly. "If you suspected that Caddoc was planning rebellion, could you have sent someone to kill him?"

"I'd have killed him myself. Better one man die, even my half brother, than Rhiannon have to live in fear that someone would murder her baby son. I was in Lemoria. If I'd known what he was up to, I'd have rung his worthless neck then and there."

"Exactly my point. You'd have acted for the greater good, and you wouldn't have worried about feeling guilty later."

Alex's brow furrowed. "I'm not immune to guilt, but my family and my kingdom come first."

"Father's philosophy." Orion grinned. "He had his failings, mostly female, but he was a great king. You'll make a better one. Men respect you, and most of them fear you."

"And the women?"

"They adore you. Nothing like a bad boy to make a lady hot and bothered."

"I don't know. I'll think about it. I never wanted to be Poseidon."

"All the more reason you should accept the responsibility."

"Limitless power. I'm not certain I'm the one you should hand that to."

"Morgan and I are. We've spoken to a few council members: Lady Jalini and Lady Athena. The vizier. They would accept either of us in Morgan's place."

Alex folded his arms over his chest. "Have you asked Elena? She should have a say. She might want to be queen."

"Are you kidding? She wants me to take enough leave to help her excavate Alexander's tomb. Not yours." Orion grinned. "The Macedonian boy wonder. Elena's obsessed with that site." He grew serious. "We're going to have a child, too. She just found out."

"Congratulations."

"It changes everything, knowing I'm going to be a father." Orion's chest puffed out and he stood a little straighter. "I'll admit, I don't want to have to worry if she and our child are safe when I'm in the field with the army. You said it; I'm a soldier, not a statesman."

"I'll think about it, if you're sure that's what Morgan wants."

"It is."

"I have to talk to him, but I'll give it some thought."

"You realize that it would mean giving up your . . . your career. Being Poseidon is a full-time job, no running off to the Pacific with some mermaid."

"Or human?" Alex began to pace. "It might be time I found another profession. I'm making too many mistakes. I missed Varenkov again."

"I heard. He's in Greece, at a villa on one of his private islands. He's entertaining some influential people."

"Drug or gun runners?"

"Politicians. But then, they're pretty much the same."

"My team will be coming in soon. With a few additions." Orion listened while Alex related the tale of Anuata and her kidnapping.

"So what you're telling me is that you're bringing a former captain of 'Enakai's Lemorian guard, who could be a spy, and five more humans. Wonderful. I can't wait to try and explain this to the High Council."

"They're my problem, twin. I'll handle it."

"You could handle it fine if you accept the throne. Poseidon's above the law. You'd get to keep your woman . . . or should I say women? And you avoid a trial for capital crimes and stay out of an iceberg." He slapped Alex on the back. "Come on. We've got to tell Morgan the sad news about brother Caddoc's demise, and we can ease Rhiannon's fears about a repeat rebellion."

"How long does it take?" Alex looked out the window again. "At the temple? How long before I know something about Ree?"

"I don't know. With Elena, it was relatively simple."

"She means everything to me, Orion. I've never felt this way about a woman before. If she dies . . ."

"Trust Lady Athena and the healers. This won't be the

first time they've attempted to transform a human female. I don't think they've lost one yet." He threw an arm around Alex's shoulders. "But why don't we find Danu and see if her mother will let her go help? It can't hurt, and our niece is a very special little girl."

"And Ree's a special woman." Pain twisted in his chest. His brother's suggestion that he become king in place of Morgan was disturbing, but nothing like not knowing what was happening to the woman he loved. Without her, he didn't have a future.

Orion nodded and started toward the private archway that led to the king's apartments. "Seeing you will raise Morgan's spirits more than hearing that Caddoc's no longer a threat. He was worried about you."

"You go ahead," Alex said. "I'll be along directly. There's something I need to do."

"Don't be long. Morgan will want to see you and hear all about your Lemorian henchman and Ree."

"I won't be." He left the chamber and moved down a narrow corridor to enter a small sanctuary. There, he did something he hadn't done in a long time. He dropped onto his knees and prayed.

CHAPTER 30

A lex stood in Ree's chamber staring down at her. A few hours before, Lady Athena had ordered her transferred to his apartments in the main palace. He'd been with Ree since they'd carried her in and placed her in the giant conch shell bed, but she hadn't awakened yet. "Are you certain she's all right?" he asked Morwena.

His sister smiled at him. "Look at her. Does she look like she's dying? She gorgeous, isn't she? I don't know what she was as a human, but as an Atlantean, she's a knockout."

Alex had to agree. With her curling, red-gold hair spread out around her face, her rosy complexion, classical features, perfectly-shaped lips and the faint dusting of gold freckles across her cheeks, Ree was more beautiful than he'd ever seen her. "If the transformation went well, why isn't she awake?"

"Be patient, brother. It's a complicated process. The Lemorian restoration was well done, and she may even have advantages over us in some areas. The human, Lemorian, and Atlantean gene mix makes for a super intelligent and uniquely talented individual. Her physical condition, other than the breathing problems from being stuck between species, was already superb. When she's fully recovered, Ree O'Connor may even out-swim you."

"How are the kids? Any change?" Anuata, Dewi, and

Bleddyn had arrived the night before, and the five children had immediately been admitted to the pediatric healing unit. According to Morwena, three of the girls were adapting well, but the boy and Pilar were struggling, and their conditions were considered critical. Anuata remained at the temple steps, unable to enter, as he had been, but unwilling to be any farther from the children than she had to be.

"I believe that the girl is holding her own, but the little boy is getting worse. Your Lemorian recruit is greatly distressed. She's refused food and fresh clothing, and she won't retire to our guest quarters. I believe Dewi is remaining with her."

"He would be," Alex said. "The two of them have become close."

"A strange combination," his sister replied. "Half the unmarried girls in the city are mad for Dewi. Your Anuata seems a little rough for him."

"I'll admit she isn't your typical Atlantean beauty, but she has other qualities to recommend her."

Morwena bent over the bed and placed a crystal in the center of Ree's forehead. Immediately, it began to produce a hum and radiate a green light. "Good," she said. "I expect her to wake soon. Her vital signs are excellent."

"You like this, don't you?" he asked. "The healing studies."

"Yes." Morwena beamed. "I know the value of prayer and of working together to produce vast screens of illusion to protect Atlantis from the human world, but this feels right to me. It's the longest course of study. It may take lifetimes. Lady Athena says she's constantly learning something new."

Alex nodded. He loved his sister dearly, but she never used one word when thirty would do. She didn't disappoint him.

"Lady Athena believes that Danu is an old soul, that she brought her gift of healing with her. She's with Remi, the little boy. She won't let go of his hand. Rhiannon thought it might be too much for her, remaining at the temple for so many hours, but Danu wouldn't budge. And you know how stubborn she can be." She took a small shell from her medical pouch and poured the contents into her hand. It looked to Alex like fine black sand.

"What's that?" he asked.

She rubbed her hands together, and the substance created a pale yellow lather. Morwena brushed her hands lightly over Ree's head, throat, and shoulders. Then she stroked her arms and rubbed the last of the mixture onto Ree's palms. "That's it," she pronounced. "I'm out of here. I promised to stop and check Lady Jalini's sister. She's pregnant with her first child and she's—"

"Spare me the lady's medical condition," Alex said. "Are you sure that Ree's safe to be left alone?"

Morwena chuckled. "She's not alone, is she? You're here, and I'm sure you're the one she wants to see most. She'll be hungry when she wakes up. Order her anything she wants from the kitchen. There aren't any medical restrictions on her meals. Just make certain she gets plenty of rest for the next few weeks." Her smile widened. "And yes, brother, she's free to engage in pleasures of the flesh. She won't break and she won't melt. She's one of us, now."

"Morwena?" When she nodded, he went on. "She never asked me to become Atlantean. I always believed that a human had to ask of their own free will before the procedure could be implemented."

His sister shook her head. "Ree's a special case. You started the process when you carried her from the boat and brought her back from the brink of death. And then the Lemorians did whatever they did. By the time we got her, she was more Atlantean than human. It was either complete what you started or lose her. Lady Athena healed her rather than letting her die."

"But Ree can't exist on land anymore."

"No, no longer than I could or you. The door to the human world has closed for Ree. Let's hope she finds her future a better place. It will certainly be longer. Lady Athena tells me that humans rarely live past a hundred years."

"So I've heard."

"Poor things. No wonder they procreate in such numbers. They die of old age when they're barely out of adolescence. They haven't lived long enough to gain wisdom."

She came over to him, stood on tiptoe and kissed his cheek. "I hope the two of you find happiness together," she said. "But if you don't, you know you're still responsible for her as long as she lives. You gave her life, Alex. It's a tremendous responsibility, and it could get sticky if either of you found a new partner."

"That won't happen," he said. "She's the only one I want."

"Then, I hope—for your sake—that Ree feels the same way." She started for the door, and then stopped and glanced back at him. "Are you going to do it?" she asked. "Accept the crown if Morgan steps down? Become Poseidon in his place?"

"I don't know. I haven't made up my mind yet."

"Fair enough." She smiled at him again. "You'd make a good king. You know I love all three of you. Morgan and I have always been especially close, but you'd make a better ruler. Morgan is courageous and kind and wise, but he isn't tough enough. Not like Father was. And Atlantis needs a strong king. We need you, Alexandros."

"So speaks my little sister," he said lightly.

"So speaks a future healer and council member." With a nod, she left the chamber.

Alex turned back to Ree, removed his sandals and lay

down on the bed beside her. He put his arm around her, kissed the crown of her head, and then he waited.

Ree dreamed that she was in Alex's arms. It was so real that she could smell his special scent and feel his silky hair against her cheek. She turned over and touched his bare chest, running her fingers lightly over the ridged muscles and smooth scars.

"Mmm," she murmured. *Have we just been making love?* They must have. She could feel none of the normal tension in his body. He was completely relaxed. She thought he must be sleeping. She sighed and snuggled closer to him.

She had been dreaming, but it was a good dream. They were on the beach in Samoa. She could hear the surf, and the air was filled with the odors of growing plants, salt water, and flowers. She had a warm feeling between her thighs, not desire . . . not exactly . . . but a sensual stirring. "I love you," she whispered.

Alex's big hand moved to cover her breast, and he began to gently stroke her nipple with one callused fingertip. She savored the sweet sensations, keeping her eyes closed and concentrating on the pleasure of being held and touched. "Have I told you that I love you?" she whispered.

"Ree?"

"Shh," she said. "That feels good. Don't stop."

"Are you strong enough?" he asked. "Are you certain, you—"

She caught his head and pulled it down so that his mouth brushed her nipple. "Make love to me," she murmured.

"If you're sure . . ."

"I'm sure." She pressed her body against his, welcoming the rush of heat that kindled in her loins. "I need you."

He lowered his head, found her nipple with his mouth,

and drew it tenderly between his lips. He suckled at her aching flesh until she squirmed with pleasure and lifted her other breast for his attention.

He groaned. "Woman, you'll be the undoing of me."

Memories flashed across the screen of her mind. She remembered parts of the trek from the Pacific, the interlude in the mouth of the whale, and the frantic journey to reach Atlantis. She could recall gentle hands and women's voices. She opened her eyes wide, looking past Alex to the filmy hangings, the wall frescos, and the luxurious furnishings. "This isn't the temple, is it?"

"You're with me"—he said—"in my apartments."

"I'm not sick anymore, am I?" She sighed. "I don't feel sick. I feel wonderful."

"Are you sure?"

She laughed and wrapped her legs around him. "Make love to me, Alex. I'll show you how well I am."

He rolled onto his back, pulling her on top of him. "You do the work, this time," he teased.

She could feel his excitement, hard and swelling between her thighs. She leaned forward, kissed his mouth and throat, and drew her tongue across his right nipple until he gasped and squirmed beneath her. She was already growing moist between her thighs, and the thought of having him inside her was exciting. She rubbed herself against him and cried out when he caught her hips and lifted her so that she could take him in.

She settled down, gasping with pleasure as he filled her with his throbbing length. He was big, so big, but she arched her back and spread her legs wider, wanting all of him, wanting him deeper and harder. "Love me," she urged him. "Love me, Alex."

They moved together, instinctively giving and taking joy from each other, reaching together for a shared rapture, and letting the flood tide of their unleashed passion carry them over the edge. And when they washed up together on an emotional shore, he was holding her and whispering love words to her in a language that now was familiar as the light in Alex's eyes.

Later, when the fervor had passed and they kissed and whispered and laughed in the warmth of a newfound togetherness, Ree realized that she was content as she had never been before.

"Are you hungry?" he asked.

"Starving."

"I'll call for food. You can have anything you want."

"Angus beef?"

He chuckled. "Maybe not anything, but . . ."

"Just teasing. I don't want anything now. Just you. Just us, together."

"You really are all right?" he asked, raising on one elbow and looking full into her face. "You understand what's happened? You're an Atlantean now. There's no going back."

"I don't want to go back."

She traced the line of his jaw and brushed his eyebrows with her lips. "You do have scales," she said. "Tiny ones, but definitely scales, blue."

"Do you find them repugnant?"

She chuckled. "I find them very sexy. I find you sexy."

"Better yet."

She had the feeling that she'd never seen him before as he truly was, as he was now in all his glory. "I like what I see," she said.

"You're changed, inside and out," he explained. "You'll live longer, swim faster, hear and see a hundred times better than you did before."

"The bionic woman."

"Something like that." He kissed her again. "I still want

you to marry me, Ree. But there's something you have to know."

"You already have a wife, and I'll be number two? If I accept?"

He chuckled. "My brother wants to abdicate. They've asked me—he's asked me to accept the crown."

"So now you're telling me that they want to make you king?"

"Poseidon," he said. "Our high king is always titled Poseidon."

"Don't you have a twin brother? Orion?"

"He turned the job down."

"Are you going to accept?"

Alex shook his head. "I don't know. I wanted to see what you thought of the idea. If I take the position, it's for life, and it's a package deal. It comes with an open slot for queen."

"Queen? How could I be queen? I don't even know how to be an Atlantean. I just got off the boat, so to speak."

"It's a great responsibility. My people, what's best for Atlantis would always come first. Ahead of everything else."

"Ahead of me?"

"Sometimes. I wouldn't want it to, but the monarchy requires everything a man can give."

"And if we did marry, if I accepted the assignment, what would be expected of me?"

He ran his fingers through her hair, bringing a lock to his lips and rubbing the length against them. "As much or as little as you like. My mother—my stepmother—Queen Korinna, was an active ruler. She sat on councils when she wanted to, heard petitions, and made judgments. But not all of our queens have chosen that path. My brother's wife, Rhiannon, the current queen, has dedicated her life so far to her family, her home, and her children. She does some charity work, but she's never involved herself in the daily business of the kingdom."

Ree considered what Alex had just told her. She was certain that she loved this man, but she wasn't sure she was ready for marriage. And becoming queen was so far out of what she'd planned for the rest of her life that it was almost ludicrous. Almost . . .

"And how would your . . . " She searched for the right word. "Your kingdom like having a queen who used to assassinate people for a living?"

"Many of our queens have led armies," he said. "We have a tradition of warrior women. It's why Anuata will fit in here."

"But for me, if I take this gig . . . no more hunting bad guys."

"For me either. And, I thought you'd given up on that occupation, at least with—what did you call them—the organization?"

"I've got unfinished business with Varenkov."

"He's in Greece. On an island."

Ree sat up. "I'm going after him."

He shook his head again. "*I'm* going after him. You're staying here until you're fully recovered."

Anger flared in her chest. "You're not king yet, Alex. I have as much right to settle with him as you do."

"It isn't personal for me," he said. "You've let it become personal. That's when it gets dangerous. The council has declared Varenkov guilty of murder and other crimes against the people of the sea."

"He profited off those innocent children." She clapped a hand over her mouth. "The children! How could I . . . Is there any sign of Anuata and—"

"They're here, all of them. They all made it this far. Morwena told me that the kids are all being treated in our medical facilities. Don't worry. Atlanteans cherish every child. They'll be well cared for."

"I want to know what happens to them. And I'll want to see them."

"As soon as it's permitted," he promised.

"All right." She let out a long breath. "It's important to me that we save them, Alex, not just physically, but really save them."

"I can see that." He nodded. "They'll have a future, one without pain."

"Good." She brushed the hair away from her eyes. "And I have to make certain Varenkov never harms another child. And if that's personal, so be it."

"Let me take care of Varenkov."

"I owe him. He tried to kill me. I do take it personal."

"When you do that, it becomes vengeance. You stop acting as an agent delivering a sentence and become a predator."

She sat up and pushed away from him. "You've asked me to become your wife. You've told me all this crap about Atlantean women being equals, and then you expect me to sit here counting seashells while you go off to hunt down Varenkov. He has Nick working for him. And Nick is very good. I know Nick. I know how he operates."

"I can't risk your life."

"But I can, and I will. And if you expect me to consider your offer, then you'll give me the respect you'd give a man, the respect you offer Dewi or Bleddyn, or even Anuata. You're taking me with you, Alex. I'm going to be part of this mission or the two of us don't have a chance in hell of making a life together."

Dewi found Alex several hours later as he left the king's apartments where he'd been closeted with Morgan and

Orion. "They've offered me the throne," Alex explained to Dewi as they took refuge from the crowded palace corridors in a walled garden. "I told them I'd think about it, but I had to finish my last assignment first."

"Varenkov?" Dewi asked.

"He's at one of his villas in Greece."

Dewi nodded. "I'm in, but I've got to ask a favor."

"Anything. Just name it?" He looked at Dewi with open curiosity. "Does this have to do with the kids? I should have asked. How are they?"

"Pilar seems to be improving. Remi is just hanging on. They've promised Anuata she can see them in a little while."

"They'll pull through. Kids are resilient." His thoughts were still on Ree. How could he take her with him? Risk her life when they had so many possibilities ahead of them?

"If they don't let Anuata in soon, I think she may tear the doors down." He laid a hand on Alex's shoulder. "You know I've never asked you to use your position for me before, but this is . . ."

"Since when have you ever been at a loss for words?"

"It's Anuata. She wants the kids."

"Wants them how? If they're getting medical treatment, how—"

"No, you don't understand. She wants to adopt them, all five of them."

Alex grimaced. "That's not going to happen. She's not Atlantean. There won't be any problem with her being allowed to remain here. I already spoke to my brothers, told them what she did for me, that she's sworn her loyalty. But adopting? The kids will be Atlantean. They can't go to a Lemorian, no matter how much she cares for them."

"Try and tell her that."

"You know I'd do anything for you, but I doubt that the bureau of children's rights would—"

"You just said it. An Atlantean could adopt them. The favor I asked for? I want you to ask that we dispense with the bans and allow Anuata and me to marry immediately. Tonight. There's nothing to prevent me from petitioning the bureau for the kids. And, as my wife—"

"She'll have automatic citizenship." Alex dropped onto a bench. "Are you sure this is what you want? I knew you two were—"

"I want her to be my wife, with or without the kids," Dewi said. "You know I have an estate and the means to support them. Anuata can never have children. When she was young and chosen for the military, they sterilized her. She didn't have a choice. This may be the only chance she ever has to be a mother, and she wants it. I want it for her."

"Neither of you has to go with me tomorrow."

"I'll go. I can tell you now, if any of those kids are in the slightest danger, she won't leave the temple steps. I can't get her to eat. Not a bite."

"And this is what you want? Marriage and a ready-made family?" Alex asked him.

"It is. A man's luck only lasts so long. I have an idea I've used mine up. I promised Anuata, that after this one, I'll find another occupation. Maybe breed and train giant sea horses. I asked Bleddyn if he was interested in going partners in the venture."

Alex chuckled. "And?"

"He told me where I could put my bright idea."

"Sounds like Bleddyn."

"So you knew I was planning another mission. Bleddyn?"

Dewi nodded. "He and this sexy merman . . ." Dewi grinned. "I think the gentleman has a friend who works for Lord Mikhail. Bleddyn knew Varenkov was in Greece. I knew you wouldn't pass up the chance to get him in your own backyard."

"So you want to get married? Tonight? I suppose Bleddyn is going to stand up with you."

Dewi shook his head. "He said I was crazy. He'd have no part of linking me to a barbarian Lemorian warrior-woman."

"So you're in need of a priestess, a special permit to marry, and a companion?"

"Looks like it."

"I can't perform the ceremony, but Morwena can. I'm certain Poseidon would sign a dispensation to allow the two of you to circumvent the law and marry tonight."

"I still need a couple to stand up with us."

Alex offered Dewi his hand, and they gripped forearms in the custom of blood brothers. "I'll be glad to stand with you," Alex said. "And even though Ree isn't speaking to me, I think you can persuade her to act as Anuata's companion."

"She's not speaking to you?"

"We had an argument. She wanted to go with us after Varenkov, and I won't let her."

"Why not?" Dewi asked.

"Why not? I love her. She's my woman, and I want to protect her."

"You can't forbid her," Dewi said. "You've never gone back on your word. You accepted her as part of your team. And if she wants in, you have to allow it."

"You're as crazy as she is."

"Maybe, but if you're going to be king, you need to think of the good of your people. You can't change laws to please yourself."

"How can I let my future wife put herself in danger?"

"She's a professional, she's tough, and she's as stubborn as Anuata. The only way to hold a woman like that is to let her make her own decisions."

"Since when are you giving your prince unasked for advice?"

"When it comes to women, I'm the expert. Believe me; a man has to know when to pick fights he can win."

CHAPTER 31

Ree pulled herself hand over hand up the sea-grass rope to the ledge of volcanic rock where Alex and Dewi waited. Alex caught her hand and helped her to scramble up the last few feet. "Careful," he warned, and Dewi reeled up the dangling rope and coiled it over one shoulder. "It's a long way down."

There was no moon and not a single star cast light on the island below. Ree glanced back over the edge. The ocean more than two hundred meters below was only an inky void. Caught between thick, low-hanging clouds and the algae-covered stone, the normal sounds of the sea were muffled and distorted. Humid air and an earlier rainfall made each step slippery and precarious.

Anethikos, Varenkov's private island, lay to the east of Ikaria in the Aegean, not far off the coast of Turkey. Travel here from Atlantis had taken the better part of two days, during which time, Lord Mikhail's mermen had scouted the property and assured Alex that Varenkov was still in residence.

As Dewi had predicted, his bride Anuata had elected not to accompany them on the mission. While all of the children had survived the transformation from human to Atlantean and were on the road to full recovery, she had been unwilling to leave them, even for a few days. Having lost all memory of their former lives, but still emotionally fragile, the children were all too glad to be fussed over and coddled. And Anuata, as stalwart in motherhood as she'd been in battle, was determined to be foremost in her son and daughters' future from day one.

"What if we both were killed?" she'd asked Ree. "What would happen to the children? They might be split up, and if any kids deserved to be a family, it's the five of them. I'm staying, and if Dewi knows what's good for him, he'll come home in one piece and become a responsible father."

A rock shifted noisily under her right foot, and Alex grabbed her shoulder to steady her. "Shh," he admonished. Quickly, she regained her balance, and he removed his hand. Although they were out of the water and could have spoken to one another by voice, they continued to communicate silently, using only the power of their minds. Any sound might alert the guards or be picked up by the ultra high-tech sound and motion security system.

Most islands had more than one beach, but Anethikos had only one, a small pebble and rock cove on the south side of the island. Sheer rock rose from the sea on the other three sides. There had been two boats anchored at the concrete dock, a high speed bullet-shaped vessel and a squat pontoon craft. Varenkov hadn't reached the island by either one. According to Lord Mikhail's contacts, two men had flown in by helicopter. A crack unit of sixteen security guards maintained the roughly eleven-acre island at all times. There were no paved roads and no motor vehicles on Anethikos, other than a single golf cart and a half-dozen four-wheel-drive ATVs. All other travel on the island was done on foot.

The helicopter pad and guard compound was located on the north side of the island; the villa stood alone on the highest point, flanked by an infinity swimming pool, and a stone terrace, featuring a sunken hot tub. The security force worked in twelve-hour shifts with all cooking, cleaning, and serving done by guards. Three would always be on duty in the house, five maintaining watch at stations and vantage points around the island.

Tonight, there were only fifteen guards and five ATVs remaining on the island. According to one of the mermen Alex had spoken to, one member of the security force had gotten drunk several nights ago, missed a steep turn, and ridden his machine off the mountain into forty meters of ocean. Neither ATV nor human had surfaced or been retrieved, and apparently no replacement had yet arrived.

Landing in the cove would have been simple, but Ree worried that the beach might be rigged with explosives. Varenkov's Ukrainian country estate was surrounded by a mine field he had planted, a rumor which had proved true when an undercover agent from the Polish Secret Service had accidently activated one and blown himself into small unidentifiable shreds. Thus warned, Alex elected to climb the rock face, directly below the villa.

The plan was simple. Bleddyn had gone ahead to disable the helicopter to prevent Varenkov from escaping by air. The rest of them would find the Russian and kill him before the security force realized the Atlanteans were on the island. "The odds aren't bad," Dewi had remarked. "If it comes to a fight, the odds are just over four to one. The day I can't best four humans is the day I'd be better farming oysters."

"Sixteen including Nick," Ree reminded them. "And don't forget Varenkov. He's not going to lie down and roll over for us."

"You worry too much," Dewi said, sketching a map of the villa and adjoining grounds.

The traditional whitewashed stone house with domed ceilings was modest for a man with such a lavish lifestyle. The villa consisted of a tiny kitchen, a dining-lounge area, two bedrooms, two bathrooms, and a wine cellar. The bedrooms and wine cellar were on a lower level, dug partially into the bedrock.

There was an exterior door leading into the lounge, and another opening to the kitchen. The windows throughout the villa were quaint, narrow and deep-set, too small for an adult to fit through; and the archway on the far end of the lounge led to the bedroom wing, which had no windows, only skylights set high in the ceilings. Ree surmised that the house, an odd choice for Varenkov who'd spent a lifetime evading his enemies, was a trap. She'd voiced her concern to Alex, but he shrugged off her suspicions. "He thinks he's safer on Anethikos than on his yacht. He has state-of-the-art electronic security and his own private army. If trouble did come, he'd expect it to be by helicopter or boat. And if the dock is rigged with explosives, as you think, then the helicopter landing pad may be as well."

It was the most that Alex had spoken to her since their argument other than to give general orders to her as part of the team. She knew that he was still furious with her for insisting that she be part of the hit. Still, she'd hadn't expected him to relent and agree for her to come. If they survived this, there would be time to mend fences. The question of marriage still hung over her like a guillotine. She couldn't begin to make a decision until Varenkov was dead.

As for Alex's becoming king and her a queen . . . that was beyond belief, let alone consideration. She'd face that obstacle if and when she decided to marry him. "One crisis at a time," as her favorite instructor had once said. If she died here on Anethikos, worrying about becoming queen would be a waste of energy, and if she didn't . . . She refused to think about it anymore tonight.

Regardless of Alex's disapproval, she was glad she'd come. Remaining behind, wondering what was happening would have been worse than anything Varenkov could throw at her. She reconciled to fully accepting Alex's underwater world, but she knew that she'd never find peace until this chapter of her life was fully closed.

The Russian had to die, and there was no way she'd allow Alex, Bleddyn, and Dewi to come after him alone. He was too dangerous. Nick was too dangerous. As for Nick, she knew that she was as likely to have to kill him or be killed by him as she was Varenkov. Strange that as much as she'd once loved him—or believed that she'd loved him—Nick meant nothing at all to her now. He was Varenkov's man, and it would be too bad for Nick if he got in her way. Alex motioned to Dewi, and Dewi braced himself against the mountain and made a cup with his hands. Alex stepped up into the handhold, onto Dewi's shoulders, and then leaped for the edge of the concrete terrace. Alex pulled himself up and swung over the side.

For long minutes, there was absolute silence, and then Ree heard Alex's voice in her head. "One guard down, fifteen to go." His head and shoulders appeared over the rim, and Dewi tossed the coil of rope up to him. In less than a minute, she was standing beside Alex. Dewi quickly followed.

The terrace was as dark as the surface of the ocean had been. Ree could make out a faint mechanical click and a hum. She instinctively turned toward the sound, and she heard Alex say, "Invisible fence. You want to bend, step high, and duck your head. You have three feet of clearance." He gave exact measurements, and took the lead, successfully crossing the force field. Again, she went next, while Dewi came last.

She nearly stumbled on the body of a man sprawled between a table and chairs and the hot tub. The dead guard's face was dimly illuminated by a string of twinkling Christmas lights that ringed the hot tub. "I wouldn't step too close," Alex warned. "Some of the flagstones have a different consistency than the surrounding ones. I'd venture they have a nasty surprise for anyone who steps on them."

Ree nodded. She didn't know how Alex had arrived at that conclusion, but she didn't doubt that he was right. Her respect for him as a professional jumped a notch. His many talents continually surprised her.

What did concern her was that Varenkov's security force was armed with the latest firepower, including grenades, mines, and who knew what else. Alex's force, in direct contrast, carried bows, javelins, knives, and tridents. Being a traditionalist, Ree knelt beside the dead guard and slipped his Glock from his belt holster. She took the time to find additional ammunition, much to Dewi and Alex's amusement.

"Ree, you circle the house," Alex ordered tersely. "Watch for a second guard. I'll take the right door. Dewi, you go in by the kitchen. Varenkov should be in the larger of the two bedrooms, the one at the end of the hall. I'll go for him." He winked at Ree and grinned. His face, darkened by camouflage, flashed green in the Christmas lights. "Don't shoot one of us by mistake," he teased.

Ree gritted her teeth. She'd wanted to go into the house, but she knew better than to question Alex's orders. First rule—never argue with your team leader during a mission. Curse him out later if you want, but knuckle under and obey. Alex and Dewi moved toward their respective doors while she started around the house, keeping to the shadows.

She was halfway around when a violent explosion and the sound of automatic rifle fire split the night. Another burst of gunfire and then alarms blared warnings from a dozen places on the island. Searchlights flared, followed by more shots and a second explosion.

The house, which had been dark, lit up like Times

Square on New Year's Eve. Two shots rang out from inside the house. Ree hit the ground and rolled out of the light, barely missing a rain of bullets that originated somewhere to her left. She slid down a slight embankment, took shelter behind a stone flower urn and returned the favor. She fired off three shots and was rewarded by a cry of pain. Something heavy clattered against rock, and she heard a distinct thud.

She kept her head down, counting to one hundred. When she reached ninety-nine, she started to move to a new position, then checked herself and started silently counting again.

A stocky figure dashed away from the house, automatic weapon spraying fire and shot. Stone chips flew from the planter and she ducked again, rising up seconds later to shoot back.

"Get out of the house!" she screamed silently to Alex and Dewi. The sound of ATV engines roared in the distance. "Alex? Alex, answer me!" Why wasn't he answering? No one but Atlanteans could hear their communication.

Icy fear gripped her. Pistol shots in the house. Not Alex or Dewi. They didn't have firearms. "Dewi!" she called. "Speak to me! Get Alex out of the house. Reinforcements coming fast!"

Abruptly, Alex appeared around the corner of the house, pistol in hand, and dashed directly into the path of the searchlight. "No!" she screamed. "Go back!"

Behind her, the automatic rifle chattered. Bullets sliced into Alex's head and unprotected throat, knocking him off his feet. Blood gushed from the gaps in flesh and bone.

Time slowed to a crawl for Ree. Stunned, she still reacted as she'd been trained. She rose to her feet, turned, and took aim at the source of the shots, emptying the Glock into Alex's killer.

"Get down!" Alex yelled.

Ree dropped to the ground, frantically reloading. The thought that she could still hear Alex barely registered. He was dead. Not even an Atlantean with the luck of a Vegas blackjack winner could survive the force of those high powered bullets tearing into his body.

Another volley of shots came from inside the house. Someone was shooting through the windows. Bits of dirt stung Ree's face and arms. She whirled and started to fire back, but the other gun went silent.

"Move it, Ree!" Alex shouted. "Back to the terrace!"

She lowered her weapon. She heard the command, but was incapable of obeying. She had to go to him, had to look into his ruined face, had to touch him one last time.

"Run for it!" the haunting voice came again.

Tears filled Ree's eyes as she walked to Alex and dropped to her knees beside him. She could hear him still, not understanding how, but knowing it was his ghost she heard, knowing that the man she loved was lying dead, and still calling out to her to save herself.

"Alex," she said. He was lying face down, thrown back by the force of the bullets. "Oh, Alex," she murmured. "I would have married you. I would have done anything for you."

"Even be my queen?"

She rolled his body over and stared into what was left of Nick's face.

"Have you lost your mind, woman?" Strong arms seized her and threw her over a familiar shoulder. "Didn't you hear me? I said to get out! The mission's over!"

He ran around the house with her dangling over his shoulder like a sack of grain. "Alex!" she screamed. "Alex?"

"Catch her!" he roared.

The next thing she knew, she was flying through the air.

Dewi groaned as he caught her, rocked back, and caught his balance. "What's wrong with you?" he demanded. "The mission's over."

"But Alex—"

Alex grabbed her hand. "Are you going to stand here and get us all killed? Over the rim! Dive! Dive!"

The scream of ATV engines blasted just before the first bullets pinged around them. Dewi went over the edge first.

"Do as I say, woman!" Alex ordered. "Dive deep!"

This time, Ree acted. She leaped off the terrace, vaguely aware of Alex beside her. It seemed as if she fell for hours, but eventually cool salt water closed over her. Bullets sprayed the surface of the ocean but deflected harmlessly as the three of them continued down and down until they finally reached the white sand floor.

Alex caught her and pulled her hard against him. "Did you mean it?" he asked. "Will you marry me and be my queen?"

She stared hard at him and touched his face, then burst into tears again. "I thought you were dead," she said. "I saw you . . . I saw . . . How . . ."

Dewi's laughter pierced her confusion. "Illusion, Ree. He threw his image over that man you called Nick. Varenkov thought it was Alex and shot his own body-guard."

Alex kissed her so long and passionately that she nearly forgot to breathe. She put her arms around his neck and hugged him as hard as she could. "I thought I'd lost you," she cried. "I thought you were dead." Then she remembered Varenkov. "We missed him again, didn't we," she said. "It was all for nothing."

"You didn't miss him." Bleddyn's deep voice came out of the shadows. "You killed him right after he killed Nick."

"I shot Varenkov?"

"Didn't Bleddyn just say so?"

"But how did he get out of the house?" Ree asked.

"He wasn't in the house," Alex said. "He must have been taking a walk as he did nightly on the yacht."

"Not a bad mission," Dewi said. "We were on the island, what, Alex? Maybe fifteen human minutes? Bleddyn took out a helicopter, two ATVs and four of Varenkov's men. You killed the Russian, and Alex got Nick."

"Strictly speaking, Varenkov got Nick," Ree corrected. "Alex did get that first guard. What, exactly, did you do, Dewi?"

That brought a round of laughter from all of them, including Dewi, who followed it up by saying, "Don't tell Anuata that. She'll never let me live it down."

Alex motioned to his two companions and nodded.

"I think that means we're to make ourselves scarce," Bleddyn said.

"Maybe we'd better," Dewi agreed. "I can't stand it when Alex gets all soft and mushy with a woman."

Alex threw him a look; they both laughed again and swam off. Alex kissed Ree again. "It's too late to change your mind," he said. "You're in for the whole game now."

"You intend to accept the crown. You've decided to give up all this fun and be king?"

"Only if you'll be beside me."

"As your wife?" she said, her pulse racing faster than it had when she'd been dodging bullets back at Varenkov's villa.

"As my wife and my queen," he answered. "You took out Varenkov. You won."

"And what did I win?"

"Me." He grinned at her, and then he kissed her again. Suddenly, Ree knew in her heart that she'd finally found exactly where she belonged—with this man—now and forever.